THE BONE ROAD

THE BONE ROAD

N. E. SOLOMONS

First published in paperback in
Great Britain in 2022 by Polygon,
an imprint of Birlinn Ltd.

Birlinn Ltd
West Newington House
10 Newington Road
Edinburgh
EH9 1QS

www.polygonbooks.co.uk

9 8 7 6 5 4 3 2 1

ISBN 978 1 84697 614 8
eBook ISBN 978 1 78885 510 5

Typeset in Adobe Garamond by Polygon, Edinburgh
Printed and bound in Great Britain by Clays Ltd, Elcograf S.p.A.

In cycling it is often said that the rider who suffers longest, wins.

PROLOGUE

The second body was washed up out of the River Drina in the dawn light. Two fishermen found it sprawled on some rocks as they dawdled for early morning carp. It was one of Inspektor Simo Subotić's own favourite fishing spots, and it seemed less sacrosanct, tarnished and bloodied by the discovery of the swollen and headless corpse. Simo stepped closer and peered down at the unidentified body, the *Petar Petrović*, what the Americans called a John Doe. The cadaver was naked except for a pair of torn and filthy Y-fronts, and bloated from the water. As Simo stepped closer he saw immediately that the body also lacked hands and feet.

They'd found the first body six weeks ago, two miles downstream, caught in mooring lines. Part of a torso only, and it had been in the water for so long and deteriorated so much that the pathologist was unable to determine cause of death, or whether the damage to the body was ante-mortem or post-mortem and, if it was post-mortem, whether it was a result of being in the river – limbs softening, rotting tissue being hit by boat propellers or rocks, nibbled by fish until they fell away – or whether they'd been removed deliberately. The picturesque Sokolović bridge at Višegrad, only twenty miles upstream, was both a World Heritage Site and a favourite suicide spot. Damaged bodies fished out of the river were both tragic and commonplace. Simo couldn't entirely blame the coroner for leaving his verdict open.

Yet this time Simo had little doubt. Whoever had dumped this man's body in the water didn't want him easily identified when he turned up. He wondered, uneasy, whether these bodies were only the ones that they would find. Two headless, mutilated bodies within weeks was unusual, even along this stretch of river. There wasn't much they could do, however, to test his hunch except wait and see if there was another body. Dredging the Drina or sending divers was an impossible task. The river was fast and wide, hundreds of kilometres long and forceful enough to power several hydroelectric plants.

Several officers were combing the riverbank but Simo held out little hope – the unfortunate soul had merely washed up here. He was certain he had been dumped upstream and that the real crime scene was elsewhere. The officers combing the site had clearly taken the same view, as to his dismay they were sharing a cigarette as they scrabbled among the rocks and mud.

'Put it out!' he ordered, outraged.

Grumbling, they obeyed.

Simo glanced up at the sky. It was light now. Cold and bright. The wide river glittered, startlingly green, twisting amongst the rocks in a mass of foam and spray. An icy breeze blew from the east, carrying with it the stench of death.

Later that afternoon, Simo stood in the autopsy room observing while the eager pathologist re-stitched the Y-incision in the anonymous *Petar Petrović*'s chest and abdomen. Simo was a man used to unspeakable things, but this was a particularly unpleasant autopsy, as the body had been in the river for so long. He watched in silence as the pathologist, a young Serb who couldn't be much over thirty, struggled to fill in the required form. There was no head or brain to weigh, no contusions to assess. No fingers to print. No feet to measure for boot size.

'He's fifty or fifty-five from the bone density. About your age, Inspektor,' said the pathologist, and Simo looked at him dubiously, wondering if he was trying to make a joke.

As Simo peered closely he noticed damage to the upper legs. It looked like . . .

'Is that a dog bite?'

'Yes. I think so,' agreed the pathologist. 'I thought, at first, it might be post-mortem damage, from flotsam in the river, but it isn't. These are definitely teeth marks from a large dog. And on the wrists, see?'

With some reluctance Simo stepped closer.

'Defensive wounds. Likely from the same attack,' continued the pathologist. 'And he's been badly beaten. Several broken ribs.'

Simo nodded, listening as the pathologist listed further injuries. Historic fractures – and new ones from more recent beatings. What had happened to this man? Where had he been? He had fought for his life, over and over. Something uneasy stirred deep inside Simo. He'd seen wounds like this before, but not for nearly twenty-six years. The pathologist was far too young to recognise them. Simo studied the pattern of injuries with a ghastly stirring of recognition. He closed his eyes and took a breath. If he had been religious, he would have muttered a prayer.

'How long ago do you think our *Petar Petrović* died?' he asked.

'Two weeks. A couple of days either side. It's hard to be exact with this level of decomp.'

Simo stared at the body on the table, puzzled and unsettled. He'd hoped never to see such things again.

1

On the flight to Sarajevo, Heather had sipped a gin and tonic and imagined Ryan's reaction when she knocked on his hotel room door, his surprise and delight when he opened it to find her standing there with her suitcase. Before each work trip over the last year, he'd pleaded with her to come out and join him as he covered the Tour de France or the Giro, until she'd finally decided to surprise him, bringing out their bikes so they could explore the Balkans for a few days. Things hadn't been great for the last few months. She had made a remarkable physical recovery, one that any regular person would be thrilled by. But Heather wasn't a regular person, or at least she didn't used to be. It felt to her like she'd been robbed of her superpowers. As well as more ordinary things like her ability to remember which bus to catch. Everything annoyed her. Except Ryan. Even in the bleakest moments he could make her laugh with a filthy joke. And this gesture would show him how much she cared. However, when it came to it, as she stood in the corridor of the Best Western, heart pounding with glee, smile tickling her lips, and he opened the door, he was anything but pleased.

He stood there in his socks, absolutely still, his eyes widening with horror. She searched for another word for it, but no, that was it. Horror. For the briefest moment she wondered if there was another woman inside, and she'd caught him. Everyone told her how he used to be a player before they'd met. But, that had all changed after they'd got together. He hadn't left her side, not for months after it happened. Of course there wasn't anyone there. She peered round into the room. He was alone. He hadn't been drinking either.

Before she could accuse him of ingratitude or worse, a smooth mask of delight slid down across his tanned features and he hugged her and kissed and took her out to dinner and they came back and had sex – good sex. Yet later, as she lay in bed, listening to the rhythmic sound of his breathing as he slept, or pretended to, Heather was haunted by the expression of dismay on his face when he had seen her standing there. A look of fear and dread.

When she woke the next morning, Ryan was up before her. He thrust a cup of coffee at her and kissed her on the nose.

'I'm taking the day off. I've a bit of leave for the end of the tour and it can just start early. Freddie can cover the rest of the tour. Let's go exploring. Let's just get on a train and go to Mostar.'

'Okay, but I want to ride around Bjelašnica for a few days first. This place is beautiful and I've heard the biking is amazing.'

Ryan was bouncing on his toes, his eyes oddly bright. 'Come on, let's go to Mostar.'

'Why? I've brought the bikes all the way out here, and suddenly you want to leave? Well, I'm riding here for a few days with or without you,' said Heather, annoyed. She sighed, a lump building in her throat. She really didn't want to fight. She'd come out here to be with him and to remember the good times.

To her intense relief he threw up his hands.

'I'm sorry. You're right. Of course I'll come with you. I'm being ridiculous. Mostar after?'

'Sounds perfect.' She gazed at him in happiness. Of course he was pleased she was here. She'd caught him off guard, that was all. 'I love you. Let's watch the finish of today's stage together. I like watching you work,' she declared with sudden ebullience.

He stared at her, taken aback. 'Are you sure you're ready?'

In truth, she wasn't, but she nodded anyway, it was too late to take it back. 'Yeah. It'll be good to see the old gang. It's about time.'

She glanced away, so that he couldn't see her face. She clenched her fists behind her back, digging her nails into her flesh.

In the small village at the foothills of Bjelašnica, Heather looked around. It was better than she expected to be in the mêlée before a race again, even if she was on the wrong side of the barrier, amongst the journalists rather than the riders. Several of them were pleased to see her; Freddie hugged her so tightly, she had to ask him to release her. Yet, she sensed a wariness amongst some of Ryan's colleagues. Two or three watched her unsmilingly. She supposed that they were probably supporters of Jessie, or else they'd witnessed one of her outbursts. Heather used to have perfect self-control, but since the accident, when riled by an absurd or intrusive question, she'd been known to really lose her temper. Ryan remained staunchly by her side. Probably worried she was going to freak out. Although, to be fair, so was she. Just a bit.

'I don't want to stay with the press pack. I want to be in the middle of the crowd. It's more fun,' said Heather.

It was partly true. She also wanted to be far from people she knew, just in case she did have one of her episodes. There was a good number of people there for a mountain stage. Heather liked that no barriers had been set up. She understood that lots of the riders didn't like it – uneasy that the fans were literally in touching distance, but she always felt it was good for the sport for the stars and the followers to be as close as possible. It added to the thrill of the race.

They wandered away from the bar where the press pack was gathered to the heart of the crowd and elbowed their way to the front until they found a good vantage point. The narrow mountain road snuck through the village, snow-covered peaks rearing up on either side. It was unseasonably warm and the first spring flowers unfurled in the sunshine, and vendors hawked bottles of water and soft drinks and beer to the crowd. Scarlet banners in English and Cyrillic declared 'WOMEN'S TOUR DE BALKANS', and small children sitting on the broad shoulders of their fathers and uncles and grandfathers waved matching flags, eager for their first glimpse of the race, or simply delighting in the carnival atmosphere.

Heather peered down the road, listening for the sound of the official car, revealing that the riders were on their way. Silence. Only the happy chatter of the crowd and the wind rustling the pine trees lining the road on either side.

'I've always had a penchant for these smaller races,' said Ryan. 'Better than being crammed in a press room with another five hundred sweaty journalists in front of a French television set, before running to climb onto an official bus with another fifty journos, in the vague hope of yelling a question at one of the riders at the finish.'

It was true, thought Heather, that standing here in the mountains on a bright spring morning listening to the burble of a few hundred joyful cycling fans, as well as many bemused but cheerful locals, had a lot of charm. Despite herself, Heather experienced the familiar pre-race tingle in her belly. Ryan reached for her hand and squeezed it.

'How you doing?' he asked, a note of anxiety in his voice.

'Fine. Please stop fussing.'

Yet, as Heather glanced about, she noticed several police vans and a pack of police officers standing at the edge near the finish line. She nudged Ryan.

'That's not normal.'

He looked uneasy. 'The Balkans have quite a past. Sometimes things get nasty. Tempers get testy, even at things like this. I guess they have to be careful.'

'Okay,' said Heather, unconvinced.

But, before she could say anything else, the race car appeared. The voice of the commentator boomed out of the loudspeaker. They were coming. It was a steep incline to this point . . . A good thirty-three percent gradient, and then a three-kilometre sprint on the flat to the end of the stage on the outskirts of the village. They should see the rider win the stage. She strained to hear who was in the lead. The commentator rattled away quickly on the loudspeaker. Jessie Taylor of Great Britain's Team Pure Jooz^{TM} was out in front but only just. *Jessie Taylor*. The name made Heather shudder, like swallowing a shot of lemon juice. She tried to root for her old rival and former domestique. A Serbian rider was attacking Jessie and clinging to her wheel. The two were in a breakaway well ahead of the peloton of other cyclists, and, on hearing this, the crowd exploded. A local Balkan rider had a chance of winning over the British Olympic medal-winning favourite. At once, the contented Sunday afternoon good cheer shifted into something darker and more volatile.

'Did you feel that?' asked Heather.

'Yeah,' said Ryan. 'It's like being in the wrong stands at a local derby.'

Ryan grabbed Heather's hand and he tried to take a step back, away from the edge of the road, and collided with a large man's juddering belly. He apologised. The man said nothing, only grunted, eyeing him unsmiling. They looked around for the rest of the press pack. They were more than two hundred metres away, in a huddle at the other end of the street, chatting and laughing together at a safe distance from the crowd. Heather and Ryan couldn't reach them quickly. There were far too many people now; more seemed to have emerged from the concrete houses and wooden chalets, all cheering, red-faced and staring intently at the road.

'It's fine,' said Ryan, in a voice that didn't sound fine. 'This is the Balkans, not France. Cycling is pretty new here – no one really gives a damn about a road race, honey.' He smiled at her, but the smile didn't reach his eyes. She'd never seen him so edgy.

'Ryan,' she said, 'I'm fine. It really is okay. There's police everywhere. Just relax and watch the race.'

She looked up the road, white and smooth against the taut blue sky. The leaders. Two tiny riders at the edge of the horizon. The spring sunshine spilled cool yellow light and flashed off the molten silver of the leader's helmet as she came at the spectators, faster and faster. Behind her followed the second rider, bent low over the handlebars, attacking, determined to close the gap, chasing the leader down, relentless in her hunt. They hurtled along the road towards the onlookers, the rest of the peloton now appearing over the ridge, following in angry pursuit, the sound of their wheels a furious hornet's buzz.

The first rider was past them in a second, in a spray of pebbles, and Heather felt the spurt of air from her slipstream. Then, the next rider, hardly any air between them as they sprinted on towards the finish line in the distance. The crowd was yelling, the noise frantic, somewhere between desperation and pleasure.

As Heather leaned forward, peering into the sun, trying to make out which rider was ahead and listening to the frenzied tones of the commentator, she was aware of yet more police vans pulling up several hundred yards ahead. It was odd. She'd never experienced anything like it in all her years of racing.

Jessie Taylor of Great Britain, declared the announcer.

There was a buzz of dissatisfaction amongst the locals. Grumbles of discontent. Heather watched, with a pang of envy and regret sharp as a stitch, as Jessie's teammates surged forward to congratulate her the moment they rode across the finish line. She remembered that rocket of adrenalin and bliss. Oh to have that again! Even one last time . . . But then, as the riders huddled around Jessie, police in blue uniforms and baseball caps swarmed amongst the assembled teams gathered beyond the finish line.

There was a racket from the sky, like a small explosion, and glancing up she saw a helicopter circling above. It wasn't a police or news helicopter, but looked military perhaps, and it was in bad shape. It seemed remarkable that the machine could remain airborne. Ryan stared at it. The noise was tremendous. The boom filled the sky like thunder directly overhead. The helicopter landed on the road at a distance from the crowd, spitting up dust, and a few more policeman sauntered out – presumably more senior than those already on the ground. The rotor blades stopped, and the machine thankfully fell silent. The pilot hopped out – not in police uniform but jeans and a Guns N' Roses T-shirt, and lit a cigarette, idly surveying the scene.

As Heather watched, the police were upon the riders themselves, as well as the support teams, roughly pulling them apart and arresting them, yelling. The riders, masseurs, coaches, drivers were all being lined up and handcuffed and shouted at to sit on the ground with their hands in front of them. One or two of the younger riders looked like they might cry.

'What the hell . . . ?' asked Heather.

'I have no idea,' said Ryan. 'Come on. We need to get to the press pack.'

As they hurried back to the press area, police cars raced down the empty road and stopped at the finish line. Heather glanced over her shoulder, staring as team managers remonstrated with the police in a multitude of European languages, gesticulating in fury. It achieved nothing, as the managers and support staff were arrested alongside the riders, handcuffed and herded into waiting police vans.

The crowd lost it. They were pushing and shoving and

shouting in fury. Not only had the local favourite lost, but now this farce. A bottle whizzed past Heather's ear. She ducked and swore. An elbow landed in her ribs, and she gave a whine of pain. Ryan gripped her hand tightly and tugged her through the crowd. There was a stink of beer and sweat and anger. She was being pushed and shoved, but Ryan would not let go of her. Her hand was slick with sweat and she fumbled for his fingers, trying not to lose him. More police sirens. A small child began to cry. Others, clearly, were deciding that they'd had enough, and the families began to drift away.

Taking advantage of a small break in the crush, Heather saw Freddie only fifty metres away. He waved, frantic.

Ryan grabbed her arm.

'Come on.'

They ran, reaching the small cordoned off area outside a bar that had been designated the 'press area'.

'Doping?' demanded Heather, when she saw Freddie.

He frowned. 'Nah. Can't be. That's not a police matter. Must be something else. I'll see if I can find someone local to brief us.'

They watched as a hundred riders and their support teams were made to sit down as searches were conducted. Some people were arrested and driven away. It was a large and coordinated operation.

'There is no way this is doping,' muttered Ryan.

Some of the crowd remained, curious, buying beers, settling in for the remainder of the afternoon, deciding that this was an alternate kind of entertainment, better even than a bike race. The cycling fans were angry, convinced that their race had been hijacked. A couple of men in yellow jerseys wandered over to the press pack and started to fire questions at the journalists.

'No idea, mate,' said Ryan with a shrug. 'Sorry.'

One of the men in yellow noticed Heather. 'Hey, Heather Bishop! Great to see you here. I was such a fan.'

Heather winced. She loathed it when people spoke about her in the past tense. She wasn't actually dead. The man didn't notice and continued to rattle away.

'My brother-in-law had a T.B.I. but he didn't make anything like recovery you have. He still needs a stick to walk. And he really struggles with depression and that now. But you're all good, right?'

'Great,' she mumbled, trying to force a grin and not stare at her feet. She ought to be used to members of the public knowing her medical history. All the lurid details had been printed in the press, after all. The cycling fans were invariably kind and meant well, but she always detected a tug of pity. She felt Ryan watching her, ready to pounce and cut off the conversation, in case she lost it. She pushed down the anger that bubbled in the pit of her stomach like indigestion, and the buzz of resentment and anger in her ears that built and hummed like tinnitus.

She was saved from the awkwardness of the encounter by the arrival of a policeman. He was tall with thick greying hair. He ambled over, hands thrust into his pockets, and nodded amiably at the assembled press.

'Good afternoon. I'm Inspektor Simo Subotić. I've been asked to come and tell you what is going on. This isn't my case, but I speak the best English, so hey, lucky me, and lucky you. We received a tip that this race was being used to smuggle drugs into the Balkans. I can't release any more than that at this stage without jeopardising the ongoing investigation.'

There was a groan from the reporters at the lack of actual information and then a cacophony of questions was instantly fired at Simo. He held up one hand with a peaceable shrug.

'Hey. One at a time.' He pointed at Freddie. 'You.'

'What drugs? Which team? How?'

'Can't say. Don't know. And couldn't tell you, even if it was my case.'

A man joined Simo. He was wearing a Guns N' Roses T-shirt and Heather recognised him as the pilot of the helicopter. He spoke to Simo in a low voice. Simo nodded then looked around the faces in the sunshine. 'Anyone else?'

A classroom of hands shot up and Simo sighed. He pointed to a female journalist in dark sunglasses. 'You there.'

'Were there riders involved?'

'Again. It's not my case. I'm only talking to you because I speak the best English. But even if this was my case, I couldn't say. This is going to be a very unsatisfactory question-and-no-answer session. I'm enjoying this pleasant sunshine, and we can keep at it. But maybe you want to wait until the department releases a full statement about the afternoon's events.'

Ryan's hand was in the air. 'Can you confirm that the drug was cocaine? And that you've found a stash in one of the support vehicles?'

Simo studied Ryan for a moment. 'I can say nothing at this moment. As I said, you need to wait for the afternoon statement.'

Heather tugged on Ryan's arm. 'I've had enough.'

He nodded. 'Okay, let's get outta here.'

As they walked away, Heather looked at him. 'Where did you hear that it was cocaine?'

Ryan shrugged. 'You know me. I asked one of the local reporters. I'm good with languages.' He smiled at her, and put his arm around her shoulders.

2

Heather was relieved to leave the chaos and confusion of the race behind them and ride out into the peace of the open road. By mutual agreement, she and Ryan barely discussed the previous day's events. It cast a pall over breakfast. They were both subdued and saddened. Heather had dedicated her first life to racing, and she'd give anything to have her career back, so the thought that anyone would jeopardise the sport enraged her with numb fury. If she thought about it too much, it was going to spoil everything. She mustn't get too upset. She mustn't. Something was beginning to hum inside her skull.

Ryan had mapped out a full day's riding but declined at first to say where they were heading. The route lay in the shadow of the mountains, creeping skywards, unlit by the morning sun. An old tractor had crashed over the rusted barrier some time ago, and no one had moved the carcass. It sprawled tyre-less, windows smashed, a warning to careless travellers.

'I want to make a detour to see the old Olympic rings from the eihty-four Winter Games. They're at the top of Bjelašnica peak. It's a bit of schlep, but the view is astounding. All abandoned. It's sad and weird – kinda poetic. Nothing else, just the rings and a derelict cable car station, on a mountaintop,' said Ryan, peering into the glare through his Ray-Bans.

'You're kidding? A detour? For Olympic rings,' said Heather, hurt.

Ryan clicked his chinstrap. 'Okay, we won't be able to get right to the top. We'd probably need to hire mountain bikes to get all the way up there, but we'll get a great view even from the end of the road.'

'Ryan, I don't want to see the rings.'

'I know, honey. But I think you should.'

He pedalled off, ending the discussion, and Heather had little choice but to follow. Her legs were tired; they felt soft, like they used to after over-training, and she climbed slowly, already hurting, not attacking the incline with her old fury. Despoiled Olympic rings felt horribly like her own ruined dreams. She wanted to tell him that she understood that she was supposed to fade with dignity and embrace a gradual decline. But the athletes who had managed that had been at least allowed to compete at their peak; and even if they'd lost, never touched gold or even won a single race, they hadn't had their best snatched from them. There had been time to prepare for retirement. The now familiar anger pulsed through her veins like a heartbeat. Yet her irritation began to dissolve with the last of the morning's mist – Ryan was right, the view was remarkable. High puffs of clouds cast shadows on the coarse grass sloping down the valley; a silver river idled between rocky foothills stubbled with dark forests. As they cycled higher, the trees became sparer, only the odd ragged pine until they pierced the treeline entirely. Bleached boulders studded the steep valleys, and the paved road surface became more and more uneven. The white houses below were as small as teeth. They passed shattered buildings.

'Avalanche?' asked Heather.

'War,' said Ryan.

They stopped for a drink and a snack at a viewpoint, and Heather started to disappear behind a bombed-out house to relieve herself. Ryan grabbed her arm.

'Don't. It isn't safe. There were minefields here. Don't go off the road. Just pee here. I won't look.'

'Jesus.'

After pulling up her shorts, Heather looked at Ryan with some hesitation. She knew he hated to talk about his time during the conflict. She understood he'd been here as a U.N. peacekeeper during the war, but whenever she tried to get him to talk about it, he'd change the subject. He'd seen things he didn't want to talk about, but she wished he would.

'Were you here then? In ninety-two? Is that how you know about the minefield?'

He looked at her strangely and then laughed. 'I was here last week with a hundred and fifty of the world's best cyclists. They didn't want one of the women going off the road and getting blown up. That's not really the sort of publicity the Tour de Balkans is after.'

'No. Especially after yesterday.'

There was an eerie stillness biking high up in the mountains. There was little sense of life above the treeline – no birdsong and barely even the skitter of insects. The wind buffeted the bikes and trembled the tiny wildflowers that were sprayed across the grass like dabs of blue and purple paint. The road skittered into rocks and stopped. Ryan climbed off, sweat pouring down his brow.

'Jeezus,' he said, drinking from his bottle. 'Whose stupid idea was this ride? I'm too old for this shit.'

'Hey,' said Heather. 'Go easy, or you'll make yourself sick.'

She looked up and saw the concrete of a ruined building stark against the bold blue of the sky. Behind it were the rings themselves.

Ryan placed a hand on her shoulder. 'You made it. Not the way you wanted to, I know. But you did.'

Heather swallowed, unable to speak for a moment. 'But what do I do now?'

Ryan shrugged. 'You'll figure it out.'

Heather wanted to believe him. 'Can I have a minute?'

He planted a kiss on the top of her head and walked away, flopping down with a groan beside a clump of brilliant blue gentians. Heather pulled down her sunglasses and swallowed the lump in her throat. Ryan was right. She needed to come here, see the rings and grieve for the lost part of herself. The last few months hadn't been her best. She'd been edgy and ill-tempered. Until recently, it had all been about her recovery. That had defined her. In many ways it hadn't been so different from training. She'd understood it. She had an impossible goal, something out of reach to strive for as all the nurses and physiotherapists marvelled at her progress. It was easier to focus on her recovery than to try and consider what she had lost. That was too big. But she was better now, or as better as possible, and she needed to consider who she was going to be next. Now that she was no longer *the* Heather Bishop. The uncertainty was making her tetchy, triggering the mood swings again. The counsellor said that was to be expected. Part of the recovery process. She needed to accept the change and come to terms with this new version of herself. Only, she didn't want to. She preferred the old one. Besides, 'recovery process' was bullshit. It suggested that recovering the previous 'Heather' was possible, like an old corrupted file being restored. This was a total rewrite.

Everyone kept telling her how lucky she was to have survived, but the truth was she hadn't. Not all of her. The time had come to finally accept that and try to let go. She glanced at her palm and saw that she'd plucked one of the tiny papery yellow flowers and was mulching it between her fingers. She blew it away, and it caught on the wind like flakes of gold.

It was dusk by the time they reached Zikoč, a dreary collection of buildings huddled in the shadow of the foothills at the base of Jahorina mountain. One or two of the houses were old or had been repaired but most were clearly new, built after the war. It was a charmless town. A pink neon sign missing the 'H' announced 'otel. The hillside resonated with the sound of barking dogs. A man yelled and the barking paused for a moment and then resumed.

They checked in and Ryan had the first shower then sat with a cold compress on his knee. He was tired and short-tempered after the long ride.

'Why don't these motels ever have a bath? And why is the water pressure always like some dude pissing on you?' he grumbled. His Californian accent always grew stronger when he was annoyed, and, when he emerged, he was rubbing his very blue, now slightly bloodshot eyes.

Heather went into the bathroom, stripped off her clothes and climbed into the grubby shower. The water was barely warm. She shivered.

'It's cold,' she yelled.

'It was hot when I had mine,' he called back. 'Anyway, you like ice baths.'

'That was different,' she muttered.

Heather closed her eyes and counted, willing herself not to feel the burning cold. Felt a creak of discomfort in the bridge of her nose where it had been broken in a crash long ago. In the cold, the old fracture prickled. It had given her small nose a slight bump, which she didn't mind. Without it she thought she looked too much like a china doll, green-eyed and small-boned. She'd always been tougher than she looked. Opponents underestimated her, and her lightness was a godsend on the hill climbs.

Climbing out of the shower, she palmed a couple of pills, then jumped, realising that Ryan was eyeing her from the doorway.

'Which pills are you taking, honey?'

'Just the painkillers. The nerve in my neck is playing up.'

He studied her for a second to see if she was lying, and Heather closed the door on him. She couldn't bear it when he watched her like this. He called it concern. Love. She tried not to find it claustrophobic, but she knew how much he worried about her. She'd put him through hell. In the early days after she'd been allowed back home, he'd been called to the supermarket to pick her up after she'd gone out alone, bloody-minded in her determination to be independent and buy a tub of Ben & Jerry's in mid-December. The doctors all told him that he had to let her – to just go with it. But then she'd forgotten why she was in Tesco. And who she was. She was sitting on the floor panicking amongst the rows of humming freezers, and Ryan sat down beside her and held her as she sobbed, and then he walked her home. It hadn't been the last time he'd received one of those phone calls.

These days she often felt him watching her while he pretended to check his phone or stir the pasta. Every time he went on tour he worried that he should cancel. Now she felt compelled to put on a performance of coping at every moment.

'Are you sure you're okay?' he demanded, the anxious, habitual frown creasing his forehead.

Heather rubbed the familiar fault line of the scar running just above her right eye. 'I'm fine. Absolutely fine. I love you.'

It was exhausting.

They had dinner in the one restaurant the little town had to offer. They were a handsome couple: Ryan older, but not uncomfortably so – enough to intrigue and warrant a second glance. Even after nearly two decades in the U.K., he maintained a permanent Californian tan. She supposed it was the constant travel to sunnier climes.

A few locals had wandered in now and were gathered at the bar, drinking beer and the unnamed local spirits. Ryan snuck a look at them. Heather studied him with concern.

'Are you okay? Do you need to call Freddie?'

'No. Why would you say that?'

'You keep looking round at the bar. Do you want a drink?'

Ryan reached for her hand. 'It's fine, I'm just people watching.'

'Okay.' Heather shrugged, feigning nonchalance.

'Have some faith, Heather. Please.'

'I do. You know I do.'

Ryan's phone began to vibrate and he picked it up, listening intently. He ran his fingers through his hair, a worried tell. He swore softly as he hung up and shook his head, leaning back in his chair. 'It was cocaine. Hidden in support vehicles. They confirmed it.'

'Which team?'

'Zero-Zoom.'

'Shit.' Heather stared at him.

Ryan looked around again at the bar, as though desperate for a drink. 'I feel real bad for the riders. Managers should have known better. Free transport. Free drivers. If a thing seems too good to be true . . .' he concluded with a helpless shrug.

'Are you going to write about it? It's a good story.'

To her surprise, Ryan shook his head. 'No. It's too goddamn depressing. They've cancelled the rest of the tour. Everyone is flying home. They're at the airport. What a goddamn shame.' He gave a sigh. 'Almost makes me long for doping.'

'I know you feel bad for the riders, Ryan, but do you not think that it was their job to ask questions? I know I did.'

'Sure, Heather Bishop. Paragon, on and off the road.'

'That's not fair, Ryan.'

She felt two points of colour rising in her cheeks, twin angry suns. She pushed back her chair and slapped some money on the table to cover her share of the bill. 'I'm going back to the hotel. I'm going to bed.'

'I'm sorry,' he said. 'I'm just sad about the race. I shouldn't take it out on you.'

'Okay.'

'Come here.'

He caught her wrists and then, pulling her closer, kissing her, sliding the cash back into her pocket at the same time.

'I'll get the cheque. Be along in a minute.'

Heather walked back to the little hotel, listening to the idle barking of the dogs and the growl of a motorbike. Lights were on in several windows. She could see the blue flicker from old TV sets. The night was clear and cold, and she shivered. Tangles of stars were strung all around the mountain peaks like Christmas lights, impossibly bright and clear.

She brushed her teeth. Her neck hurt and her mind was buzzing; she felt restless and jumpy. She took another pill – it would help her sleep. Ryan wasn't here to see her take it and fret. She fell asleep the moment she undressed, vaguely aware that Ryan had not come to bed.

She woke to find his side of the bed empty. Reaching out, she grabbed her phone. It was nearly two in the morning. She wondered vaguely whether she ought to go and look for him, but she was so tired. She would wait half an hour and if he hadn't come back, she'd go look for him. Please don't let him be in the bar. Please.

It was light. Early sunshine trickled in beneath the stained net curtains and puddled on the brown carpet, illuminating the cigarette burns. Heather glanced at the empty space beside her. She sat up, heart hammering. She supposed she'd have to go and start checking near the bar. She knew she ought to have made him call Freddie. That's what sponsors were for.

No. This wasn't her fault. This was Ryan's disease; it belonged to him and she couldn't take responsibility for it – it wasn't fair on either of them. She rehearsed the support group's phrases, unsure whether she believed any of them.

There was a crash against the door, it burst open and there was Ryan, holding two cups of coffee, a paper bag between his teeth.

He dropped the bag on the bed and, after setting the coffee on the bedside, gave her a quick kiss. He smelled of coffee and soap. Nothing else. Heather exhaled the breath she didn't know she was holding.

'Thank God. I was worried.'

He shook off her concern, handing her a coffee. 'Here, it's not bad. And I found croissants. They look pretty good.'

'I didn't hear you come in last night, Ryan.'

He sat on the edge of the bed, stirring his coffee. 'No. You were dead to the world.' He leaned over and kissed her, first on the forehead and then on her mouth.

Heather left Zikoč without regret. It was frustrating to be carrying their luggage with them – Heather was obsessed was keeping the weight on her bike low – but she was an expert at packing light. There was little in her panniers except a single change of clothes, a fleece, toothbrush and a phone charger. The village was drearier still in the pinkish glow of morning. They cycled past a few residents on their way out of town. A plump woman swaddled in a lurid pink dressing-gown sat on a doorstep, texting and smoking a cigarette. Two old men huddled together, drinking coffee and arguing companionably. A pair of stray dogs slept and scratched, silent now. As they left the village, the road immediately began to climb steeply up into the mountains. Trees gave way to scrub. There were fewer and fewer dwellings, and here and there as they turned onto smaller roads, roaming higher and higher, they passed the ruins of military towers, remnants of the war. Yet the landscape had a wild and ancient beauty. The distant peak of Jahorina loomed darkly in the distance, bare and ragged above the plateau. Yellow wildflowers were sprinkled like stars across grassy slopes that ran sharply down vast craters scooped out by the glaciers of a distant ice age. Heather understood how myths had been told about this place. The stories felt close to the surface, etched into the hillside in ice and rock. The wind thrummed a song in a high strand of barbed wire. The road fell away steeply where it had been hewn into the mountainside and many of the crash barriers had collapsed. They rode briskly but with caution, Heather dutifully waiting for Ryan every half hour. He struggled and huffed as the road became progressively steeper and more ragged, cut up and cracked by endless winter frosts. After a while, he barely had the energy to steer around the cavernous potholes, and once or twice nearly came off, swerving far too close to the unguarded precipitous edge, so that Heather screamed at him from the switchback above, making him wobble even more.

'Take a break. Push, if you need to,' she yelled.

He shook his head, too tired to speak.

He was sweating so much that it dripped like rain down his brow, and he blinked it away from his eyes. She'd offer to take his panniers on her bike, but she knew he'd only refuse. Ten minutes later, after she watched him nearly collide with a boulder on the edge of the carriageway, she kicked at her chain and gave a yelp.

'My chain's come off. Give me a hand, will you?'

He caught up and, climbing off his bike, flopped beside her on the bank, closing his eyes. 'Do we have to pretend that you need my help? Can't I just take a nap?'

She laughed. 'Yes. But drink some water and have something to eat.' She unwrapped a Mars bar and fed it to him in chunks. 'Who was the leader in this section of the Tour?' she asked.

Ryan propped himself up on his elbows and peered down, shading his eyes, remembering. 'Jessie Taylor.'

Heather winced at the name. If he noticed, he pretended not to.

'Holy shit, this road is brutal. I'm not the first rider to get caught by those potholes.' He pointed to the shattered cliff edge. 'Over there. One of the Americans crashed, taking out two of team Monaco-Red. There was still snow on the top here a few weeks ago. Skidded all over the place. Huge crash.'

Heather closed her eyes, trying to visualise it all, hearing the excitement in Ryan's voice.

'It always amazes me – you seem to love writing about biking as much as actually doing it. No, definitely more sometimes.'

Ryan shrugged and then took a long drink of water. 'Writing about cycling takes imagination. There are as many stories up here on the mountain as there are riders. I like to sift through them, piece them together. Heroes. Attacks. At fifty or sixty kilometres an hour in the sun and ice and snow. Victory and defeat.'

'You make it sound like war.'

'It's nothing like war,' said Ryan, quietly. 'It's a sport. A joyful, thrilling sport.'

In the late morning, they reached the road's summit, which had a glorious view of Jahorina peak, and they took an early lunch. It was cool at this altitude, and as soon as they stopped moving, they shivered in the wind. The woods far below looked as soft and stroke-able as moss. They looked down at the way they had come. The grey road slithered in and out of the mountains, weaving between cliff faces and brown scrubby grass battered by last winter's weather. A few goats and skinny Alpine sheep picked their way among the stones. There were more signs warning of minefields. A lone pick-up truck wound its way up the hairpin bends on the other side of the hill, travelling towards them.

'Race you down?' said Ryan.

Heather only laughed. He wasn't serious. He hated it when they raced. Yet Ryan was on his feet, strapping on his cycle helmet. 'Well, if you're scared of being beaten by an old man . . .'

Heather raised an eyebrow and started to pack away the snacks. 'You're on. But don't be stupid. It's really uneven. I want to spend the afternoon in a spa, not sampling local hospitals.'

'Okay then. Gimme a proper head start. Say, five minutes.'

'Fine.'

Ryan gave her a cheerful wave and pedalled off, whistling. Heather laughed. Ryan liked downhill runs. He was as fearless as a ten-year-old kid. It was oddly charming. The descent wasn't nearly as steep as the ascent; it wound almost leisurely down this side of the mountain. This was the easy, pleasant part of the ride. She gave him a good five minutes and then followed. She could just make him out ahead, zipping above the treeline, then disappearing round a bend. He was going fast, having found his legs. She quickened her pace; it was fun having to catch up. She soared round the corner on an excellent line but he'd already gone. She smiled. Good for Ryan. She was impressed. He really was fearless on the downhill runs. She checked her Garmin – she was chasing him at fifty-five kilometres an hour. Fifty-six. Fifty-seven. Lots of professional riders lost their nerve on high-speed descents. Those were the ones you had to watch out for. They'd wobble and suddenly take a wallowing line. If you weren't careful and you got trapped when they bombed out, they'd take you out with them. But not Ryan, thought Heather with something like pride. The uphill this morning had taken it out of him. It had been wickedly steep, vertiginous, with the altitude high enough to make you gasp, and yet here he was rushing down fast and efficient, so quick that she was having to sweat to catch him. The slope levelled off enough that she started to pedal, and hard. There was still no sign of his silver bike. She had to give it to him – this was more fun than she had expected.

She swept round another corner and regained the treeline. The road ahead was smooth and empty. He'd sprinted on. She changed gear again and gave chase. The breeze tickled her back. A kite soared above, surfing the warm air currents. She found that she was laughing at the sheer joy of it. This sensation was as close as she'd ever come to flying. She imagined the peloton just behind, frantic to catch her as she tore down the peak in pursuit of Ryan in the leader's yellow jersey. A river curled beside the road, bouncing over stones and making the road slippery. This route had it all. Ryan was right. It was a magnificent place to ride and the lack of traffic was a dream compared to Nice or even the French Alps.

She picked up her pace again and sailed around the bend, bent low over her handlebars, feeling the burn in her legs. She realised she was starting to sweat properly, more than she'd sweated before in a race with Ryan. He was really going for it. The road was tightly wooded and she couldn't see beyond fifty metres ahead. He was probably around the next bend, only just in front but hidden. She pedalled faster, conscious that lactic acid was starting to build in her legs. She was going quickly now, much quicker than Ryan could cycle, and she ought to have caught him. A faint unease fluttered birdlike in her chest. He's just around the corner. He must be. Heather remembered the truck that they'd watched heading up towards them. When it reached her, she would flag it down and ask them where they'd seen Ryan. There was only one road up and one road down; it would pass her in a minute.

She turned. Another tight bend. Trees. Nothing else. She was descending velodrome fast and, now she was amongst the trees, she couldn't see the long spread of the road, only the short stretch before the next bend. She checked her watch. She'd been chasing him for nearly half an hour. She ought to have caught him a long time ago. It was odd. The joy of earlier popped like a series of balloons. Anxiety rose in Heather's chest like indigestion. Ryan was always furious with her when she didn't stop and wait. Perhaps he was trying to prank her. Maybe he'd stopped and let her ride past to try and spook her. Confusion as well as fear jostled in the pit of her stomach; it wasn't really like him to tease her. Other people perhaps, but not her.

She slowed down and sitting back on her bike, yelled, 'Okay, Ryan. You've had your fun. Come out now. Don't be a dick.' There was no sound but the whirr and tick of her own tyres on the stones. She yelled again. 'Ryan. Ryan! For fuck's sake.'

The unease built up in her like lactic acid, ripping through her muscles, burning. She took out her phone and dialled his number. It rang out.

She started to pedal again. Perhaps he'd had a problem with his brakes and had just hurtled down very fast. If he'd had an accident, she would have found him on the road. With a prickle of dread, she thought of the steep drop at the side of the carriageway higher up. The broken barrier. She'd not looked over the edge at any point. But surely, if he'd fallen, she would have heard something? The mountains echoed when there was a crash, didn't they?

'Ryan! Ryan!'

Her voice sounded hollow and thin. It certainly didn't echo around the hillside. She kept calling his name until her voice became hoarse and she was too breathless to pedal. She was starting to shake but couldn't tell whether it was fear or exhaustion.

She turned the next corner and all at once the road opened up into a clear route straight through a long, low valley. She could see miles of clear and empty road, nothing but smooth grey tarmac and waving emerald grass. There was no Ryan. No bike. He had simply disappeared.

Heather climbed off her bike and sat for a moment at the side of the road, wondering what to do. She checked her phone. Nothing. No missed calls. Not a text. She dialled

Ryan again, and again it rang out. She left a message. She couldn't phone the police and report an accident. She didn't know that there had even been one. She supposed she ought to start calling hospitals, and the next hotel. Perhaps he'd got a lift? But why hadn't he called? Was his phone broken? She was going to kill him. She had one bar of reception. Just enough to call the place they were staying tonight. Hotel Jelena.

'No. Mr Ryan Mackinnon has not yet checked in. We look forward to welcoming—'

Heather hung up. She didn't have enough of a signal to start looking up hospitals in Bosnia and calling them. In any case, what were the chances of them speaking English? And, she reminded herself, she hadn't seen any sign of an accident and there was only one road.

She took a deep breath. She must turn around and look for him. Make sure he hadn't fallen and slipped near one of the barriers. Or under it. She shuddered. A billowing wave of nausea rose in her throat.

'Stop it,' she told herself. 'Get a hold of yourself.'

Quickly, she climbed on her bike and traced her route back to the foot of the mountain trail. It didn't feel so gentle on the ascent. Her legs were spent and it felt like cycling with elastic bands instead of functioning muscles. It was nearly two o'clock and she'd been cycling since nine, and the adrenaline surging through her body was making her tremble and feel sick. She forced herself to drink some water and eat a chocolate bar. If she let herself get too tired, then she wouldn't be able to get back up the hill and search for Ryan. She pedalled agonisingly slowly, at the very edge of the precipice, so that she could peer over and scan the void for his bike or signs of a rockfall. She stopped every few minutes to listen and call his name.

'Ryan! Ryan?'

Nothing. Only the insect hum of the early spring bees. A thrush watched her mournfully from the spindly arm of a withered pine. The river burbled cheerfully below, while on the path above, the signs announced the minefield. Surely Ryan hadn't stopped near there for a pee and got into some kind of difficulty . . . Heather stopped herself. No, because even if Ryan had done something stupid, his bike would still be there. She squinted, shading her eyes against the afternoon sun, and scrutinised the hillside. There was no sign of either Ryan or his bike.

The descent had taken a little over an hour. It took Heather nearly three to climb it again, and the mountain was bathed in a rich afternoon glow when she reached the peak again at five o'clock. There was the spot where they had stopped to picnic for lunch. The scrubby grass was washed with pinkish light, making it look softly furred, like the huddled back of some massive slumbering beast, and it was eerily quiet. No birds sang. There was no undergrowth, only bleak grass and the white rocks like scattered skulls, the gory remnants of some long-distant battle. Here and there the ground was scooped out into massive craters. It was a barren moonscape, bathed in reddening light. Heather lay back and closed her eyes. The pain in her shoulder was sneaking up her neck into the base of her cranium. She couldn't endure rides like this anymore, or she wasn't supposed to. Her body couldn't manage it, even if her brain willed and cajoled it to. She reached into her pannier for a heat pad and stuck it onto the old scar tissue on the back of her neck. It didn't help. A cricket started to tick in the grass, then another and another, like the winding of a hundred pocket-watches. The sound unnerved her. She felt like they were scratching on the inside of her head. She really needed to be lying down in a dark room with a cold compress. She forced herself to ignore the pain. She needed to just suffer through it. That's what she was trained to do. It's what separated the very best endurance cyclists from the others – not their remarkable oxygen levels, or muscle torque, but their ability to endure mental and physical pain.

She sat up and strained her eyes in the failing light, staring and staring into the valleys and roads below for movement. The sound of a car engine miles away. Another. The twin pincers of far-off headlights. No Ryan. No Ryan. He'd been wearing his grey Lycra cycling shorts and grey T-shirt and his black helmet. He merged perfectly with the darkening landscape. If only he'd been wearing red like her, it would have made him so much easier to spot. Even his stupid bike was silver, apart from its single yellow streak, and blended into the grey rocks of the mountainside.

For the second time she phoned the hotel where they were supposed to be staying. No, Mr Mackinnon had still not checked in. Yes, of course, they would ask him to call if he did. Was there a problem? Yes. No. Heather didn't know. The woman on the other end of the line was too kind, and in the face of her concern Heather worried that she might break down and cry. She couldn't cry, not yet. She had to get down off the mountain first. There's no problem, she found herself saying, a misunderstanding. She hung up, took several deep breaths. The air was thin up here, cold and getting colder.

God, she was so tired. She was shivering and barely had

the energy to rummage for a fleece from her pannier. She hadn't felt like this on a bike for a long time. There had been one time, on a training ride in Scotland, when she'd got lost in the hills far from the camp in Inverness. A sudden *haar* had blown in and she'd been both dog-tired and panicky. She had ridden for miles and miles, up and down hill after hill, trembling with worry and cold, without a signal to call for help. Yet even that hadn't felt like this. She'd known that at some point people would come looking. People in a Land Rover with a blanket and a flask of tea. And, sure enough, she'd found a desolate pub with a landline and it had all become a jolly anecdote. A rare weakness that teammates ribbed her about with vicious delight. Heather Bishop. Not the perfect rider, after all. Pinpoint sense of direction foiled by a dab of fog.

This wasn't the same. She wasn't scared for herself. Where the hell had Ryan gone? It didn't make any sense. He'd been so keen to race and he loathed racing her. It was always her who had to cajole him into it and then force him to take the head start. This time he'd actually asked for a head start. He'd never done that before. Had he? Her injury did mean that she couldn't always remember things as accurately as she used to. Sometimes she felt that was the hardest part – never being absolutely certain of anything. Even of yourself.

She took a gulp of thin air. Either the altitude or panic was making her overthink.

'I need to get off this mountain,' she said aloud.

Zikoč was the closest village, and realistically she didn't have the reserves to reach anywhere else. Besides, she consoled herself, there was always a small chance he had somehow circled back there. Quickly, she downed an energy drink and clambered back on her bike, sliding gels into her gloves to soothe wrists that were aching and jarred.

The descent back to the village was horrifically steep and lined with loose pebbles. The light was starting to go, making her misjudge her line and come off several times, skidding on piles of scree.

'Shit!'

Heart thudding furiously, she started again and again, peering desperately into the gloom for a safe route down. Dust rose about her like mist and she was reluctant to remove her sunglasses, as although she could see better without them, she knew that by the time she reached Zikoč her eyes would be bloodshot, battered from the microscopic pieces of dust and flint kicked up from the road. She kept looking for Ryan at the cliff edge, but it was gathering dark and it was as much as she could do to keep to the carriageway herself. The pain in her neck throbbed, an old unloved friend. She accepted it. Pain was her companion again.

An owl circled above, idling on smooth white wings. She was grateful for the company. One more bend. One more bend. Ryan will be round the next one. Only he wasn't. He never was. She longed for him. That goofy smile. A hug. Then, at last, the lights of Zikoč. The scrubby hamlet looked almost welcoming. Yellow lights blinking.

Heather puffed up to the hotel with its pink neon 'otel sign and, leaning her bike against the wall, stomped into the grimy reception, vaguely aware she was spraying grit and mud with every step. She figured the carpet was so revolting, no one would notice. An older woman in a patterned headscarf sat at the desk.

'Hi. You speak English?' said Heather.

The woman shook her head.

They surveyed one another for a minute.

'Ryan. Ryan Mackinnon? Did he check in?'

Heather took out her phone and turned it to show a picture of him. The woman shrugged and shook her head. Either he wasn't here, or she didn't understand. Heather scowled, a pang of disappointment rising up in her throat and sticking like a fishbone.

The woman held up one finger and said something in Bosnian.

Heather bit her lip in frustration, unable to comprehend. The woman slid a laminated price list of rooms in both English and Bosnian across the desk and pointed to one. 'Single room: forty dollars.'

The woman repeated the phrase slowly in Bosnian, not unkindly, holding up the price list.

Heather understood. Was she alone? She had absolutely no idea. She sighed, defeated, and pointed to the plastic-backed list of tariffs.

'A single room, please.'

The woman nodded.

'Passport.'

That word of English the woman knew. Heather handed it across and watched as the woman laboriously copied her details into the hotel registry. She leaned over the counter and saw, with a growing dread, her own name and Ryan's inscribed from yesterday in his handwriting. There were no new entries. Ryan was not here.

3

Simo sat on the riverbank, not fishing. It was near dark; a yellow bubble of moon floated between the bony ribs of the trees on the other bank. The river sluiced over the granite rocks; the green weed and moss smudged to black in the gloom. The half-submerged slabs took on monstrous forms in the darkness – a writhing backbone here, a tooth and fin there. He held a rod, the hook was even baited, but he wasn't fishing so much as thinking, mostly about death. In Serbian the word for death was *smrt*. It was masculine, which struck him as appropriate, so much death being wrought by men rather than women. Despite his frequent dealings with death, Simo neither feared nor dreaded it. He loathed the fear and destruction and misery left in its wake, but he viewed that as the fault of men, not of death itself. In his years on the job, particularly in this part of the world, he had learned to think of death as a silent companion. Death just appeared: bones unearthed from long ago in the foundations of a new shopping mall, or a body pulled from a river, clothes rotted or torn away. When he listened carefully enough, death would bestow secrets. It had been an excellent teacher and had taught him to be a good listener. When you paid attention, death gave answers.

He came out here to think. Someone had gone to great lengths to disguise the body in the river. They'd relied on the river hiding it and disguising much of the crime. Still, they'd left nothing to chance, taking off the head so the police couldn't use dental records, and hands so they were unable to run fingerprints. Which made Simo also think that it was possible the *Petar Petrović* had a criminal record and was in the system. They were trying to match him with possible missing persons, but the list was long and they had so little to go on that it was hard to know where to start. The beatings and badly healed fractures made him wonder if they were looking for someone who had been living on the street. Simo thought it was possible that the victim frequently had to fight for survival and, like many homeless, didn't trust or bother with hospitals, associating them with the authorities and the police. That would certainly be true if the victim was in the criminal system, which corresponded with the killer's removal of *Petar*'s hands. The homeless disappeared silently and no one looked for them. Simo had asked the lab in Banja Luka to run the DNA but that always took time, and unless they had a family member to try and match to, it wouldn't tell them much.

The recent injuries were macabre and like those he'd seen twenty-six years ago on the victims in prison camps. The dog bites. The positioning of the wounds on the legs. It was as though someone harboured a grudge and all these years later was trying to finish the job.

Simo mused that, whatever the reason, even twenty-odd years after the war, someone wanted this man dead. Not only dead, but to suffer. The wounds and the resentment ran deep, but now the hostilities did not usually stretch to physical violence. The Serbs defaced Bosnian graves and monuments. They scrubbed out Bosnian place names and replaced them with Serbian ones. Even Simo's bosses told him he was supposed to stop actual violence – money only flowed from the EU if there was peace.

He knew several former camp prisoners who had been released during the war and granted asylum in England and Holland. After hospital treatment there, rather than live quietly, they'd mostly come back to Bosnia to fight. They'd rejoined their old brigades, if they still existed, or formed new ones. Some men stayed in England or France or Germany, but it wasn't home and they often came back after the war, determined to reclaim the rags of their former lives. They returned after two years or two dozen.

In the village where Simo had lived as a child, an old woman – eighty years old perhaps – had returned from Paris to her former house to find a notorious Serbian criminal living there. He'd been a particularly vicious thug during the war, but the old woman pretended not to be frightened. Perhaps she wasn't . . . The old woman swore at her unwanted guest in French and Bosnian and refused to move. It was her house. She cooked sausage with lots of garlic and fennel and kept cats. It turned out the war thug was allergic to cats; they made his eyes swell and he sneezed from dawn till dusk. He moved into the shed. The old woman persuaded her cats to use it as their litter tray. He left. She poisoned the cats. Well, all but one – so Simo heard.

Had this man, the *Petar Petrović*, tried to kick the wrong person out of his former home? Had he accused someone's father or grandfather of war crimes? Had it all gone wrong, and had the victim ended up on the streets?

Simo stretched out a cramp in his leg. He was fifty but half a lifetime on the job didn't make it any easier. It just turned his hair a littler greyer. He grunted. Who was he kidding? It couldn't get any greyer. At some point, during the last five years, he had turned into his father. Though he was fitter than his father, he thought, with something like pride. He could run a mile only a little slower than he had at thirty-five.

There was rustle amongst the grass and the clatter of footsteps.

'Simo!'

'Over here.'

David Horvat stumbled out of the gloom, clutching a flask and a fan of papers. Simo rose to his feet and waved.

'I've brought coffee.'

'Then you can stay,' said Simo, only half joking. David was his oldest friend and longest irritant. His table manners were unspeakable, and he loved nothing better than to annoy Simo, but his heart was good and he was a crack shot with a rifle. They had been friends since school, when they'd hurled paper aeroplanes at one another in Geography and learned to recite the heroes of their nation's past. They disagreed on almost everything, but David was one of the few fellows with whom that didn't matter. They could argue without it being life or death. David was also a repository of information. He'd been everywhere during the war – one of the rare souls who managed to glean secrets from both sides and knew how to keep them.

David sat close to Simo and poured a coffee, spilling it all over Simo's shoes. He didn't apologise. Simo said nothing. He knew it was deliberate. Part of the ritual to try and provoke a response. It had been like this since they'd been at school together. If Simo allowed David to know that he'd riled him, then David had won.

Simo felt a frantic tug on the fishing line. He fumbled with the rod in annoyance. He didn't want to catch anything – this might be a prime spot for trophy fishing but he only wanted to sit here peaceably in the dark, listening to the burble of the river. He waited, hoping the perch, or trout, or whatever it was would free itself. To his relief, the line twisted and went still. He didn't rebait the hook. He felt a buzzing against his leg and thought for a moment the fish was having another go, then realised his phone was vibrating. He picked it up.

'Subotić.'

'It's Josif. Did I wake you? I know old men like to go to bed early.'

'Well, this old man likes to fish at night.'

Simo's boss, Josif Borisov, was twenty years younger than him. He was a political animal, the opposite of Simo. A careful and shrewd operator who both understood the game and was willing to play it. And, in Simo's view, a half-decent cop. David leaned in so that he could hear the conversation.

'Where have you got to on the *Petar Petrović* in the river?'

Simo gave him a summary.

'So, basically nowhere?'

Simo snorted. 'It's been a day. We don't have much to go on. Whoever killed him doesn't want us to know who he is. That in itself is informative. Why go to so much trouble?'

'Keep me updated. I want it out of the press. Clear it fast.'

Josif hung up. Simo looked at his phone contemplatively.

'I wonder what's got him so riled up.'

David chuckled and stretched out his legs. 'Rumour has it that Josif Borisov is positioning himself to run for mayor in the election in autumn. He's aiming for a seat at the National Assembly one day, make no mistake.'

'Is that why you leant him your beloved helicopter for the raid on the bike race? You hate Borisov's guts?'

David chuckled. 'The police department are very helpful in securing me my tourist licence. More helpful than you, old friend.'

'That thing is a liability. It has more bullet-holes than body-work.'

'She has character. Come for a ride, you'll see. She's a delight.'

'She? Is this because you've not had an actual girlfriend for so long?'

David looked down at Simo's side, where he had a box of feathers, string and a knife and was making his own fly lures.

'A man who spends his evenings sculpting fly lures for fish doesn't get to tease anyone else about his sex life, or lack of.'

Simo laughed. He was quiet for a moment then asked, 'So, is it true about Borisov? Josif is running for mayor?'

'I think so.'

There were worse mayoral candidates. And, for the most part, he and Josif managed to get along okay. Simo could do with an ally in City Hall.

'You don't seem appalled,' said David, watching him narrowly. 'I always thought he was an operator. Slick as a weasel.'

'He is. But he's not all bad. He actually managed to

increase the police overtime budget in Višegrad. That was a supernatural achievement.'

'And he did it because he's manoeuvring to get elected. None of it is altruism, Simo. He also doesn't give a toss about the appalling repair of the roads, lack of refuse collection or the massive youth unemployment in Višegrad, not unless he can persuade the young to turn out and vote for him in the autumn. Then I'm sure he'll be really passionate.'

'Okay, okay.'

The wind ruffled the trees on the opposite bank. To Simo's disgust, he felt another twitch on the line. Stupid fish. He reeled it in and watched it flap around on the mud by his boots. He bent and grabbed it, feeling it muscular and frantic in his hands as it drowned in air. He unhooked it and chucked it back.

Simo stretched his legs and inhaled the cool, fresh air. He loved this country. The recent past was bloody and foul, but the legends, when one went further back, were magnificent. Although perhaps that was only the effect of time and distance and he was guilty of romanticising history, longing for a misremembered past. Simo was well aware that some of his countrymen were guilty of the worst crimes of human nature, yet he also knew that others were amongst the bravest and best. Men like his old friend David. Irritating as he was.

Simo knew that Josif and his ilk viewed him as pathetic: a once influential cop who had allowed his controversial personal opinions and endless insubordination to trigger a helter-skelter career slide into obscurity in a border town. Simo knew they were wrong. He was something else. Something unusual. He was a Serb who wanted his fellow countrymen to face up to their recent past. He wanted a true reckoning. Only then could they rebuild this part of the world into the great nations they deserved to be. The best in the world. Most of all, Simo knew, he was an optimist.

4

Heather let herself into the dismal single room, the door catching against the chipboard of the bed. The room smelled sharply of cheap rose perfume, sweet and synthetic, mingling with the tang of bleach. The mattress sagged as she sank onto the flowered counterpane. A damp patch bloomed on the ceiling. She closed her eyes for a few seconds then made herself open them. She couldn't risk falling asleep; she must search for Ryan. What if he was hurt? She'd called out to him but if he'd knocked himself out, then he wouldn't have heard her. The thought of Ryan cold and terrified and alone on the mountainside was unbearable. Sitting up, she reached for her water bottle and took a long drink. It tasted metallic – a hint of blood – and she realised there was a cut on her lip where she'd bitten it on the ride down.

Heather suppressed fluttering waves of panic. She was in a foreign country, unable to speak the language and alone. She wanted to call her mother, just for the comfort of her voice. The way Deirdre's voice lit up, turned a lemony yellow and said, 'Darling, it's you!' whenever she rang. But it wouldn't help. Mum was useless in a crisis. Dad had cosseted her mother, adored 'darling' Deirdre, and after he died it was Heather who had to steer her gently through life: reminding her to pay the bills so the gas and electric wouldn't be cut off. Lovely Deirdre, prematurely aged at sixty-three, would offer her no help at all.

Forcing herself to stand, Heather grabbed a dry fleece and hurried out of the room. It was milder than the previous night, with clouds masking the sky, and it started to drizzle – creeping, insidious rain that snuck beneath her collar, making her shudder. She hurried into the restaurant where she and Ryan had been the night before and cast about for him, just in case. It was a little after eight and only a couple of tables were full. Two men sat alone, shovelling food while they read the papers. A few other men lingered at the far end of the bar, drinking with intent. Ryan wasn't there. Dizzy with disappointment, she took a seat up by the bar. It was panelled in orange pine with framed posters of Bosnian beauty spots tacked up around the walls, hanging at odd angles where they had been bashed into by customers and no one had bothered to straighten them. The barman drifted over.

In English, Heather asked for a Coke. The barman poured it for her and then, grabbing a bottle of spirits from the shelf behind him, poured her a shot of something into a glass and placed it next to the Coke, saying something in Bosnian. She couldn't understand the words, but took him to mean: 'You look like you need it.'

She swallowed it down. It was sweet and burned. She took out her phone and scrolled down to a picture of Ryan and held it out to the barman. 'I was here yesterday with this man. American. Have you seen him?'

The barman shrugged and shook his head. He turned and served another customer. Heather sipped her

Coke and examined her phone. She texted Freddie.

Have u heard from Ryan?

Almost immediately the phone buzzed.

No. Everything ok?

She hesitated. It would be good to talk to someone in her own language. To someone who loved Ryan, but there was nothing Freddie could do and she needed to focus on finding him. She texted back . . .

Just let me know if he gets in touch . . .

The phone buzzed again. Freddie was trying to call this time. Heather sent him straight to voicemail. She didn't want to talk. He hadn't heard from Ryan and there was nothing else he could do to help her. She dialled Ryan for the umpteenth time. Still no answer. She left another message. She felt dizzy with fear and worry. Please don't let him be hurt. But if he wasn't injured then where was he?

She sipped her drink, realising that her hand was shaking from lack of food. She needed to eat something. Pointing to the laminated menu, she ordered some chips and then slid off the bar stool and went in search of a quiet spot to make some phone calls. She was suddenly conscious that she was sweating again, and that her skin was giving off a nasty acid smell. It was as though her fear, skittish and animal, was seeping out through each pore. A young woman with bleached blonde hair and a grubby faux fur coat in a lurid shade of petrol blue smoked a cigarette and watched her through heavily mascaraed lids. Heather knew that she needed to be sharp, but tonight she felt like she was pulling down thoughts through a haze.

The blonde continued to watch her with frank curiosity.

Heather made eye contact, but the young woman continued to stare unabashed, reaching into her purse and reapplying lip gloss. Heather supposed that newcomers must be what passed for entertainment in Zikoč. She considered stepping outside for more privacy, but it was starting to rain heavily. She looked up the number: *Policija*: 123. She dialled.

A woman spoke to her in rapid Bosnian.

'Do you speak English?' asked Heather.

There was a pause; another voice came on the line, male this time.

'Yes, what is your emergency?'

'My boyfriend has disappeared.'

'There has been an accident? He is hurt?'

'I don't know. We were cycling near Jahorina and he vanished.'

Heather wished she could make the uncertainty and the tremor disappear from her voice.

'There has been bike accident on Jahorina? Please, which road? He was hit by car?'

'No. I don't think so.'

A pause.

'Madam, what is the nature of the crime?'

'I don't know.'

The operator spoke very slowly, as if to a child. 'Miss, what is it that happened to your boyfriend?'

'I don't know! I don't know!'

Heather realised she was shouting into her handset.

'I am understanding you very upset. Please be calm. I need to understand the emergency or I cannot be assisting you.'

'My boyfriend has disappeared. He's missing. He was there and then he vanished.'

'How many years old?'

'Forty-seven. No. Forty-eight.'

'How many hours he been gone?'

Heather checked her watch. It was after eight. She'd last seen him a bit before one . She rounded up.

'Seven hours.'

'Just seven?'

She could hear the incredulity . . . the concern receding into irritation at the timewaster.

'An adult can be reported missing at the local police station after twenty-four hours. There is nothing more I can do at this time.'

Heather hung up. She looked up the number for the British Consulate in Sarajevo. She found one for a twenty-four-hour helpline and dialled it. After a minute, a British woman answered.

'Hello, British Consulate.'

Heather explained as clearly as she could what had happened, trying to keep her voice calm and level. The woman on the other end of the line said nothing, merely let Heather talk.

'He was there and then he disappeared. Just disappeared,' repeated Heather, still only half believing it.

'It must have been very frightening,' said the woman, in a practised, professional tone.

Heather said nothing, afraid that if she agreed, her voice would crack and her carefully constructed self-control would break.

'Once twenty-four hours have passed, you can report

him missing to the local police. I'm afraid that the British Consulate can't assist in a missing person's case. If that's what this is.'

Instantly Heather's fear kindled into anger.

'What the hell does that mean: "If that's what this is?"'

There was a studied pause on the other end. 'When people go missing on holiday there often hasn't been a crime. Sometimes they go off for a while. Holidays with loved ones can be stressful. They usually reappear. Bit shamefaced. It's not very nice, but it is better than the alternative.'

'Ryan wouldn't do that to me,' snapped Heather.

'Well, you know him best. But, as I said,' said the woman evenly, 'it's better than the alternative. Do call again in office hours, if we can be of any further assistance.'

'You haven't been of any bloody assistance,' muttered Heather, disconnecting.

She leant against the wall, feeling her head swim. There was a cracked and filthy mirror hanging on the wall opposite, and she saw a stranger's face staring back at her, exhausted and wide-eyed, skin horribly pale and freckled with mud. There was another snaking cut from a stone chip all down one cheek with a little smear of dried blood. She looked half wild. No wonder the blonde wouldn't stop staring. Her stomach growled treacherously. She really needed to eat something or she would be useless hunting for Ryan tomorrow.

The peroxide blonde offered her a cigarette.

'No, thanks.'

'Your boyfriend left you,' stated the blonde in a matter-of-fact tone, not unsympathetic.

'He disappeared,' corrected Heather, and then, realising

that she was being addressed in English, showed the woman the photo of Ryan on her phone. 'Have you seen him?'

The woman shook her head.

'Please . . . ?'

'Petra.'

'Please, Petra, can you help me ask around in the bar if anyone has seen him?'

Petra shrugged. 'Sure. We can ask. But is better to drink and forget him. He did this?' she asked, cocking her head to one side like a robin and reaching out to gently brush the cut on Heather's cheek with her fingertips.

'No, he didn't,' snapped Heather in irritation, pushing away her hand. 'It's just a graze. I fell off my bike. And he hasn't left me. We were out on our bikes, I turned a corner and he'd gone.'

Petra chuckled and walked back towards the bar so that Heather was forced to hurry after her as she called, 'Gone on a bike. Gone in a car. Is the same. He gone. Have a look, see someone else you like?'

There was nothing Heather wanted less. She surveyed the array of closed faces, either starting at her or deliberately not looking. The locals made no concession to travellers beyond the plastic-backed menu translated into English. The odd tourist hardy enough to find their way here was supposed to pass through, stick to the track on their way up the mountain paths and not linger. She wondered if anyone had deliberately spent more than a night in the village. She was so tired, she could slump down on the gritty floor and sleep. Only sharp fear was keeping her awake. The bar was lit with a nasty blueish light, and a Bosnian rock band thrummed on the sound system. The bar smelled of unwashed floors, and old beer and stale chip fat, and alcohol sweated through the same pores, night after night.

She pressed her phone into Petra's hand, opening up the photo of Ryan.

'Please. Help me ask. Let me buy you a drink?'

The young woman took Heather's elbow and steered her up to the bar and spoke rapidly in a low melodious voice to the barman. He placed a basket of chips in front of Heather and two more shot glasses on the counter, filling them. Petra gestured to the basket.

'He says you order them. They cold now. Not his fault.'

'It's fine. Can you show him the picture?'

Petra downed the shot, leaned across the bar and shouted to the barman, who turned to her with a frown. He glanced at the phone and then, looking at Heather, spoke quickly.

'What is he saying?' she asked.

'He says of course he remembers him. He remembers you too. You were both here yesterday. You were fighting. He grabbed your wrists—'

'He did not! Ryan would—'

'Hey, lady. You wanna hear what he say or not? I don't care. I am here to drink and avoid my piss-antler stepfather.'

'Okay. I'm sorry. And, it's piss-ant,' said Heather.

'I liked mine better.'

'Me too . . . Please.' Heather gestured for her to continue and Petra relented.

'He says you left. He stay. After you gone, he drank more rakia.'

'Rakia?'

'This.' She pointed to the shot glasses.

Heather reeled. She felt sweat snake its way down her

spine. Ryan did not drink. But if he did, he didn't stop. She remembered that she'd woken in the night and wondered where he was. Several hours were missing. He'd certainly been there in the morning and not in the least worse for wear. If Ryan had been drinking, either he wouldn't have come back at all or he would have stumbled in reeking of booze, and later he'd have been full of furious self-reproach. He would have been much too hungover to go for a bike ride.

Since they'd been together, she'd only known Ryan lapse once. Although, she'd heard rumours of other times on his trips away, but until now she'd always dismissed them as gossip. She recalled the broken window in their flat, as he'd tried to wake her by flinging pebbles at the bedroom window from where he stood on the pavement, singing 'Yesterday' at top volume, having lost his phone and his keys. She wished she could forget the pitying, pious complaints of the downstairs neighbours when their baby had been woken by Ryan's yelling. He'd been so ill afterwards, and she'd felt awful realising how bad he felt, contorted with regret, no matter how much she tried to reassure him. He wept and apologised again and again that he'd let her down.

This morning he hadn't been that Ryan. If anything, he'd been calm and at peace. That wasn't Ryan after a lapse. The barman must be mistaken. She wanted to argue with him, to yell at him that he was wrong. She forced down the urge, and with a huge effort simply asked, 'How long did Ryan stay?'

Petra leaned over the bar and yelled out the question.

The barman answered, irritation growing.

'Dejan doesn't know,' said Petra, grabbing a handful of peanuts. 'He leave early. His wife phone. His kid was sick.'

The barman silently refilled their glasses. Both women drank. It tasted of plums and fire.

'Will you ask him again? Ryan *definitely* was drinking?'

Petra rolled her eyes.

'Please. And some more drinks for us.'

'I'm hungry . . .'

'And food. Whatever you like – just ask him.'

Petra leaned over the bar, yelling and fluttering her thickly painted eyelashes like weighted butterflies as the barman shouted back, openly annoyed.

'We are getting very good local dessert. I think you will like. And soup. This rain, it makes me want soup.'

'And what did he say about Ryan?'

'He says he carried on drinking after you gone. He come back here, he buy lots of rounds of drinks.'

'That's a lie,' Heather snapped, starting to lose her temper. This wasn't good; she needed to gain control of herself. She ran through the exercises in her mind. Her breath came in short bursts, and pearls of sweat formed on her brow.

The barman barked something back at her. Petra translated.

'He barman. He memorises drinks orders until he pours them. Not for a damn lifetime. And he says he answer enough questions. You too rude.'

Heather bit her lip, fuming. It wasn't true, Ryan hadn't been drinking. She refused to believe anything the barman said. All of it was lies. Ryan had grabbed her wrist but only for a second to stop her leaving, and it was apologetic, not aggressive. Surely, anyone could have seen that? Couldn't they?

They sat in silence for a minute, Petra drumming glacé

bejewelled nails on the bar, Heather conscious of her own short and dirty ones. Petra saw the direction of her glance.

'They hideous. Come to my salon in morning. I sort them for you.'

'Thanks, I'll check it out,' said Heather.

'You are lying,' said Petra, with a chuckle.

'Yes,' agreed Heather.

To her relief, she felt her anger subside. She found herself liking Petra. She couldn't understand – *had* Ryan been drinking? She was sure he'd been drinking Coke, but she couldn't be certain that there wasn't vodka in it. He'd certainly snapped at her. Was that a sign he wanted a drink? She remembered how he kept glancing at the bar. She'd even suggested he call Freddie.

Two steaming bowls of bean soup with slabs of black bread were slapped carelessly in front of them, slopping onto the saucers, and Heather found that she was ravenous.

'Will you help me ring the hospitals? Check he's not been hurt? I'll pay you.'

'You don't need to pay. What kind of people you think we are?' asked Petra, between mouthfuls.

'I'm sorry.'

'Your phone.'

Heather meekly handed it over and sat quietly eating her soup while Petra made half a dozen calls, asking rapid questions. Eventually, she passed Heather back her phone.

'No British cyclist brought in. No British man at forty-eight years age in any hospital in area.'

'He's American.'

'Is same thing.'

Heather did not correct her. She glanced around the bar

again and noticed the bosomy waitress from the evening before.

'Please. Ask her.'

With a sigh, Petra stuck two fingers between her lips and whistled. The waitress turned around, saw Petra and scowled. Petra shot her a sugar sweet smile and a Tinker Belle wave.

'Show her a little money. She not like me very much,' said Petra.

'Why?'

'I screwed her boyfriend.'

Wordlessly, Heather reached into her pocket and held up a note. The waitress ambled over, eyes narrow with loathing, nostrils flaring like she'd just smelled cat shit. She refused to glance at Petra.

'Hi,' said Heather.

The waitress said something in Bosnian, which sounded very much like 'Fuck you' to Heather, but she took the money she proffered, sliding it into her jeans pocket.

'Can you ask her if she's seen Ryan?'

Heather waited while Petra translated. The waitress's mouth set into a thin white line. She answered, staring intently at Heather without so much as a glance at Petra.

'She says, of course. She served you both yesterday. She had to come to your table three times. You arguing so much you not notice she there to take order. Your boyfriend an arsehole. He came back to bar later and chatting to some lady.'

'Okay,' said Heather, feeling herself flush and wishing she could stop. She was not the jealous type. Ryan travelled a lot, and their relationship wouldn't work if she didn't trust him, and she did. He wasn't that guy anymore, whatever his friends or anyone else insinuated. Yet, the waitress was the second person who'd said that Ryan had come back to the restaurant alone after they'd left. Something animal gnawed at Heather's guts.

'You mean he was chatting to a girl he met at the bar?' she asked.

Petra translated the question to the waitress, who shook her head.

'No. He came back later and there was lady waiting for him at a table in corner. In booth.'

The waitress pointed to one of the wooden booths at the back of the bar, under a wonky photograph of the mountains dipped in snow, and then carried on speaking rapidly, warming to her account. Petra held up a hand for her to pause, so she could translate.

'They seemed, how you say, good friends?'

'How could she tell? She doesn't speak English,' said Heather, riled. 'Were they kissing?'

Petra quickly translated the question. The waitress continued to stare unblinkingly at Heather as she answered, and Petra did not translate immediately, but gazed at her for a moment, frowning.

'What? What did she say?' demanded Heather.

'No, they were not kissing. They kiss hello. And they hug. They hold hands. And she say that your boyfriend was not talking to the woman in English but in Serbian. Real good Serbian.'

Heather twisted uneasily on her bar stool. A hug. A kiss hello. That was okay. Wasn't it? But why not tell her about it, or invite her along? She was hurt as well as confused. Ryan had said that he knew a few words of Serbian, but he hadn't told her that he was fluent. She thought back to Ryan's question to the police offer about cocaine and his subsequent brush-off when she'd asked him about it. His Serbian was way better than he ever admitted – but why hide that from her? Heather felt unsteady and colours began to pool in the corners of her vision. She clenched her fists, willing herself to keep it together.

'And, he called her *Dušica*,' added Petra, looking at her with concern.

'So?'

'It means sweetheart,' said Petra, almost apologetically. 'I tell you. However they leave it is all the same. Big-Tits here is right. He is arsehole.'

Later, after she'd returned to the hotel, Heather lay back on her bed and studied the coiling tentacles of damp on the ceiling. It was clear that they all thought she was some unfortunate deluded woman who'd been dumped by her boyfriend. He'd been so attentive when she woke up that morning, with his kisses and his bag of croissants. She refused to even consider that it was guilt. Heather gave a short laugh. During the season, Ryan worked away for weeks at a time, only coming home for a weekend here and there – if he wanted to cheat on her, he had plenty of much easier opportunities. There was really no need to sneak off while she slept a few hundred metres away.

And if Ryan wanted to leave her, he would leave. He would tell her, matter-of-factly and honestly. He was the kindest man she knew. Okay, he could also be insensitive, self-righteous and infuriating, but he was never cruel. To abandon her here like this, without a word, was both cruel and odd. It wasn't *Ryan*. She was much more likely to be the one to storm off, or start the fight. Especially recently. It had been hard to adjust to being a no one, and there were days when the voices in her head wouldn't leave her alone. They nagged at her, telling her she was nothing, but it was worse when she could hear them whispering about her from another room. Ryan assuring her that they weren't real didn't help. They were real to her. And what they said was true.

When she'd first met Ryan, four years ago, Heather was a star, surrounded by attentive acolytes. Somehow he was never just another of those, but he still understood he had to pay homage, even with one eyebrow raised. And then everything shifted. The world spun and spun, until Heather realised it wasn't the world spinning but her, and she was terrified that she would never ever stop. Ryan never left. Loved her even though she was a discarded, broken thing. Ruined and despoiled.

She remembered the first time she'd seen him. It was at the end of one of those press junket days. She'd spent the whole day in a five-star Manchester hotel with the rest of the British Cycling team, being interviewed in the run-up to the Olympics. She was the only one the journalists really wanted to talk to. She was the supernova. Ryan was the last journo of the day, and her smile was worn out and crumpled. She was bored of rehearsing her training schedule: 'It's tough, but it's what needs to be done.' . . . Her views on her teammates: 'They're great girls, all working their hardest.' . . . What she was most looking forward to eating when the Olympics were over: 'A roast dinner at my mum's.' Total bollocks. Deirdre couldn't cook anything unless Waitrose cooked it first, and all she had to do was pop it in a microwave, but Heather knew what people wanted to hear. So when Ryan burst into the suite, unshaven, with his crumpled shirt and lopsided grin, declaring in his Californian tones, 'You look bored rigid, let's go to the pub!' she'd followed him with enthusiasm and relief.

Neither of them had actually drunk any alcohol: Ryan because he announced with cheerful frankness that he was an alcoholic, and Heather because she was training. She'd felt buzzed just the same. There was something about Ryan. The smile that crinkled his eyes, and the way he concentrated on you with absolute intensity, so that the rest of the world disappeared. He had never been one of those people half looking over your shoulder to see if someone else – more attractive, funnier, more likely to sleep with him – might appear. When Ryan spoke to a person – an interviewee, a friend, a date – they had all of him. It always made Heather want to confide in him all her secrets – he'd have been an excellent cop. That day, surrounded by gleaming mahogany and tucked up on a Chesterfield as he smiled (again) and offered her a salt 'n' vinegar crisp, she'd felt a static tingle along her skin, and on a whim started giving him real answers to the rote questions. Jessie Taylor was talented but a stone-cold bitch who thought it was unfair that Heather, after winning silver in London, was being given the chance to go for gold in Rio at the geriatric age of twenty-nine. It ought to be her turn. Heather had joked with Ryan – if you hear I've been poisoned or fallen down a well, tell the police it was Jessie. Ryan had laughed. The rest of the team were average. And too nice to win. The real answer to what she was looking forward to most after the Olympics was a Bloody Mary. Or a Dirty Martini. The dirtier the better. She didn't care, she wanted to get filthy, forget-her-name drunk. Shit. She'd apologised – this was a really inappropriate conversation to have with an alcoholic. Ryan had laughed again and waved away her apology. He had a great laugh. Threw his head back and guffawed like he really meant it. Heather was good at lots of things, but she'd never made people laugh, yet Ryan found her funny and charming. When she'd read his article later, she saw that he'd corrected all her answers to ordinary, anodyne ones, presumably filching them off another journalist without needing to call and ask her. As soon as she woke up the next morning, she knew she'd done something really stupid – if he had printed what she'd actually said, it would have caused almighty ructions within the team. Yet, somehow, even then, on the basis of just half an hour, she'd known she could trust him.

After drinks, he'd walked her back to the flat she shared with the rest of the girls and, on the doorstep, he'd leaned in, pinning her slightly while her heart fluttered.

'This is very inappropriate,' he'd said.

And then he'd kissed her. She kissed him back and when finally he pulled away, she was glad that the other too nice, average girls were upstairs, as otherwise she'd have been tempted to invite him up, and that would be a very bad idea. She recalled the hard pang of regret and thwarted desire, fierce and insistent, as he walked away. And she'd noticed that he had a great arse – taut, like a cyclist's.

She'd wondered if he'd call, hoping equally that he would and that he wouldn't. She really didn't want the distraction. He didn't. She was relieved and annoyed. He didn't fancy her as much as she'd thought. Or he was an excellent cycling journalist and knew she wouldn't want a diversion. She tried to forget about him. Mostly she managed. And after the accident, when it all went to hell, Ryan was the first one to call. He never left.

Heather lay back on the bed in the stuffy motel room. The people in this shit-heap of a town didn't know anything. Ryan would *not* do this. He wouldn't do this to her. They'd been together for more than four years. She knew him. She thought of the photo she'd found of him here with the U.N. in the nineties – a bunch of guys jogging in the snow. Most in their U.N. peacekeeper blue berets and others in fleeces. He'd shown her a couple other pictures, but he hadn't wanted to talk about any of it. She kicked off her shoes. Little uncertainties and doubts buzzed around her like tiresome mosquitoes, nipping at her no matter how much she swatted them away. She'd heard him speak Serbian when they'd ordered dinner, but she didn't realise he could speak it fluently. And who the hell was *Dušica*?

5

Simo sat at his desk an hour before his shift was due to start, studying the file on *Petar Petrović*. Josif had promised him whatever resources he needed, which was unusual and at this point unnecessary. 'Whatever the great Subotić needs,' Josif had declared, slapping him soundly on the shoulders. When it was convenient, Simo became the renowned police detective, rather than the notorious and insolent one whom they cursed and threatened and shoved aside to a border town. Simo knew that his name had long been a warning to recruits – a parable of what might happen to even the most promising career if one didn't toe the official line. In this region, politics was power and Simo was a terrible politician. It was how he'd ended up single and using garden furniture in the dining room of his one-bedroom apartment that rattled every time a train passed. His ex-wife had the house with the river view. Yet Simo didn't want it. He'd been away working, and it was she who had made it beautiful. Her house, not his.

He looked back to the file. Many of the criminals now working in drug gangs had been in Serbian paramilitary units during the war. They'd swapped one form of violence for another and now used the same torture techniques on each other as they'd once used when brutalising civilians in the camps. Simo thought grimly that they called this 'transferable skills' in the job market. Had *Petar Petrović* been mixed up in the drugs trade? Was his death somehow linked to the cocaine bust at the cycling race? The timing was right. *Petar* had died shortly before the police raid. Had he been suspected of disloyalty? The drug gangs were brutal enough to torture rivals or those they suspected of betrayal. Simo was bothered by the careful and brutal effort to disguise the identity of the victim – a small-time drug runner wouldn't be worth it. Although, it was possible that it was a calling-card of one of the gangs – a warning to others who crossed them. Simo wasn't familiar with this particular signature, but someone in the narcotics unit in Banja Luka might know. He made a note to call them.

So far, Josif had mostly succeeded in keeping the case out of the news. None of the papers had picked it up – there was only a story on one website. The fishermen hadn't talked, and the brief piece was a vague and dull story about a probable suicide. Damage to the corpse post-mortem.

Simo read the autopsy report again. After a few minutes he became aware of raised voices and furious shouts exploding through the station. He went to the door, expecting to find Josif on the warpath, but as he listened, he realised that for once Josif's outrage had nothing to do with him.

'He's been out for less than three months! *Glup ku kurac!* And he has to do it here. In my district. I'm going to kill him.'

Simo came out of his office, realising after a moment that the shouts had nothing to do with his case, but the cocaine smuggling and women's cycling race instead. 'You've got new evidence Drakulić is involved?' he asked his boss.

Josif turned on him in fury. 'Of course my idiot father is involved, and, no, we don't have evidence. If we did, I'd arrest the piece of shit myself.'

Simo studied him closely. Josif was sweaty with rage. Having a war criminal – or war hero, depending on one's politics – as a father was more of an asset than a liability in a mayoral election. Josif's inability to keep Drakulić from openly running drugs in the district, however, was in danger of making him look weak, and that wouldn't help. Simo was extremely glad he'd not been assigned the case. It was about politics, not crime, and those cases never ended well for him. In the old days Drakulić's men had smuggled cocaine in cases of bananas, or other fruit, from Colombia. The operation went on for years. Probably still did. They were impossible to catch. Like ghosts. They moved all across the Balkans, and whenever one police force closed in, they switched to a different country, taking full advantage of the fact that none of the forces liked to cooperate.

Dragan Drakulić was ruthless enough to cut off the head of any man who betrayed him. Simo thought back to the war. It certainly wouldn't be the first time Dragan had disposed of corpses in the Drina. Josif might have ordered Simo to follow the evidence and quickly clear the case, but Simo wondered whether that still held if the perpetrator turned out to be Josif's own father. The chief's yells echoed through the corridor, but Simo was unsure whether the outrage was genuine or for show. If David's information was correct and Josif was running for mayor, Simo was confident who would be Josif's largest campaign donor. And Simo was equally certain that, for all his bluster, Josif Borisov would not want his father arrested either on drugs charges or for murder. Josif might have changed his surname to his mother's maiden name in a deliberate placing of political distance between himself and his father, but to have his father newly arrested would besmirch that meticulous cleansing of history. The present narrative was supposed to be that Dragan Drakulić, war criminal, was out of prison and going straight, his relationship with his moral, law-abiding, law-enforcing son strained and distant. Simo viewed the entire story with cautious scepticism. He hoped rather than believed it was true. Blood was thicker even than the foaming green waters of the Drina.

He decided this was a good moment to slip out of the station and go speak with an old friend who happened to be in town. As he walked through reception, he could still hear Josif berating everyone within earshot and cursing the recklessness of his father, whether for the crime of using the women's race to run drugs or for the idiocy of getting caught, Simo couldn't tell. He climbed into his car and drove off with relief.

Jenny Fraser was a forensic anthropologist with whom Simo had worked in the years after the war, trying to piece together the narratives of the war crimes for prosecution at the International Court at The Hague. She had stayed with Simo and his family for weeks during the hot and insufferable summers of ninety-five and ninety-six, attempting to identify victims of the massacres in the regions around Višegrad. She was both stoic and meticulous in the face of absolute horror. The work had won her plaudits across Europe, an MBE and a Chair in the Sciences at the University of Glasgow, and it had gained Simo the first of many demotions and pay cuts. He tried to persuade himself that he had gained as many friends as he had lost; the gratitude of the victims' families was worth more than any job title. His then wife remained supportive, if unconvinced, especially when he was no longer able to pay their mortgage on his meagre salary, and she'd pleaded with him for once just to keep quiet and do his day job. Did he have to work for The Hague, too? But Simo was never one for staying quiet. Weren't women meant to love you for your unflinching moral resolve? When he was demoted to the sheriff of the Eastern District, she'd reluctantly accepted his one-man crusade for post-war justice. Until she didn't. Simo sighed.

It was still early and Simo drove straight to Jenny's hotel in Višegrad. She was having breakfast in the gloomy dining room and looked up from her scrambled eggs and scattered papers, delighted to see him. They embraced, old friends, and Jenny fussed, pouring him coffee, offering him toast. They were good enough pals that Simo didn't bother with the pleasantries that interested neither of them. He didn't ask about her journey or whether she had slept well.

She was staring at him, trying not to smile.

'What?' he demanded.

'I brought you a present.'

He eyed her quizzically, oddly touched. 'No one's given me a present for a long time.'

'That's really sad, Simo.'

'Fuck off, Jenny. And give me my present.' He paused. 'Unless it's a tie. I've got one of those. A black one for court and funerals.'

'It's not a tie.'

She reached into her pocket and produced a small box, the size of a jewellery box, beautifully tied up with ribbons.

Simo raised an eyebrow. 'Is this a proposal?'

'No. I'm very happy with Mr Fraser, thank you.'

He unwrapped it and found to his delight a beautiful feathered fly-fishing lure, with a splayed plume.

'Pheasant,' he remarked of the copper-coloured feather.

'Grouse,' she corrected.

He shrugged. 'I love it. Thank you.'

'Handmade – from a shop in Fife. Been there a hundred years.'

She pulled a catalogue from her bag. 'You can peruse this too.'

Simo realised that he was more excited than was reasonable at the prospect of browsing the fly-fishing catalogue. Perhaps David was right, and he did need to go on a date with a person rather than a fish.

'Jenny, did you read through the file I sent?'

She reached into the same bag and brought out the thin file of documents.

'Anything you can help me with?'

'The most recent injuries and torture reminded me of those we used to see from the prison camps.'

Simo nodded. The prison camps that his government now said had never existed.

'See the canine bite-marks,' Jenny continued, indicating a close-up photograph of a wound. 'A few of the camps used dogs to terrorise prisoners.'

Simo was only too aware of the recent history. 'And some of the militia also used them to hunt down Bosniaks hiding out in the woods. It's possible that whoever tortured him was either a camp guard or served in the militia. They're using their tried and tested torture techniques. I'm looking at the drug gangs. Perhaps even Drakulić's. He's out of prison and apparently running again.'

Jenny sighed. 'His son won't be happy.'

'Why do you think I'm here and not in the station?' Simo took a sip of coffee. 'But I can't do anything until I identify the victim. It's all theory and guesswork at the moment. So, who is he?'

Jenny frowned. 'His historic fractures weren't set in a hospital. See . . . This one in his femur healed badly. And there is still shrapnel in his leg. He might not have had access to a hospital at the time of the injury.'

'So, you're thinking he was a fighter during the war? Patched up by a friendly doctor as best he could?'

'It's certainly possible.'

She looked again at the photos. 'His skin is badly damaged by the water. It's crêping and starting to peel away.' She paused. 'But here, on his shoulder, this looks like part of a tattoo. I can't quite make it out. Can you leave the pictures with me?'

'These copies are for you.'

She looked at him sharply. 'You'll do everything you can, Simo. If it gets too much, go fishing.'

He grunted in reply. 'I'm happy to see you, Jenny. But how many is it this time?' he asked softly.

Jenny's presence in the country must mean another war grave had been found. The International Commission for Missing Persons did not request the presence of Professor Jenny Fraser unless they had found something significant.

'You heard about the outbreak of stomach upsets near Lake Peručac after the floods?'

'I remember.'

'They tested the waters. There's evidence of contamination in the nearby streams. Toxins from decaying corpses are leaking into the groundwater. They've traced the source. Several dead horses buried on farmland—'

'Didn't they bury dead animals on top of mass graves?'

Jenny nodded. 'A rotting animal corpse would put off anyone who came digging around. And that's why they called me in. Yesterday, after we dug up the horses, we found the first human bodies.'

Simo shook his head. Putrefying corpses leaching into the groundwater and making children sick was a deeply troubling thought. Yet the living needed to know what had happened to their loved ones. There were gaping holes in families all over the country; thousands were still missing. Still missed. To Simo, it was both grotesque and fitting that the dead corrupted the waters, poisoning the living, indiscriminate of creed. The after-effects of past crimes sickened the present. Even Simo found himself troubled while sharing meals with old Bosniak friends. Trying to ignore the gaps around the table where other members of the family were supposed to be was like staring at a beautiful woman's smile and pretending not to notice that several of her teeth had been punched out.

After he'd said goodbye, Simo went back to the station and pulled out another much thicker file, fanning the contents across his desk. Several dozen older pictures of the missing, pictures of people he'd promised to find. People the state would prefer remained lost forever. They stared at him and he felt their reproach. He wanted to reach for a drink, but didn't. It would anaesthetise the anguish, the self-recrimination, and he didn't want that. He wanted to feel it all. It was a fraction of the agony that their families felt, and he deserved to feel it until he'd found them. Every last one.

6

Heather woke up early. She hadn't meant to close her eyes, but sleep had pulled her under. A grey dawn poked nicotine fingers in beneath the curtains, staining the windowsill with yellowish light. She reached out automatically for Ryan. The bed was cold. Empty.

And she remembered. For a brief, honeyed moment between sleep and waking, she'd allowed herself to forget. She sat up with a start and felt her shoulder crack. There was a stiffness in her muscles and joints that she hadn't felt for years and a bright ache throbbed above her eye, whether the result of the local brandy or the altitude of yesterday's ride, she wasn't sure. Anxiety lay on her skin like cooling sweat, and the damaged nerves in her neck hurt.

She fumbled for the bottle of pills, took one, and then thought sod it and took two, swallowing them without water. Ryan wasn't here to quiz her, after all. She reached out for her phone. Nothing. She tried Ryan one more time. It went straight to answerphone. Either he had turned it off or run out of battery. She left yet another message.

She checked the time. Not yet seven. She couldn't go to the police until one. In a couple of hours she ought to start calling some of his friends and colleagues back in England, on the off-chance one of them had heard from him. There was no point ringing his family. He hardly ever spoke to them. His father was dead (a mutual grief they had bonded over in the early days) and his mother lived in sheltered accommodation in California, disabled after a stroke.

After some time making several fruitless calls to England, Heather left her room. Half an hour later she sat in a cab, peering out at the sharp cliff edge. It was uncannily beautiful. Tightly wooded pines and wild streams edged with the ghostly trunks of silver birch. The car bounced along the steep mountain road. She'd asked the driver to take the same route she and Ryan had taken yesterday, but the rain had turned the road into a muddy paste. The car skidded and the driver cursed loudly. They passed the treeline and she gazed out of the window down towards the barren moonscape, the weird craters covered in wavering brown grass. She longed for a glimpse of a bike, a flash of a yellow helmet stripe. There was nothing, only the misshapen boulders strewn at the side of the road and the spiky grey grass. They reached the peak and she yelled at the driver to stop and wait. She climbed out of the cab and stood in the battering rain. The cloud hovered low and thick as woodsmoke, burying the valley below.

'Ryan!' she yelled into the void. 'Ryan!' And then, in a whisper, 'Where are you?'

There was only the furious pounding of the rain beating against her anorak, mingling with the sound of her own heart. The rain washed her face clean. She clambered back in the cab and slammed the door, realising she was now sitting in a puddle.

The taxi began the descent. Swathes of cloud engulfing them at every turn, the driver hurtled down at speed, rushing round each bend until Heather felt sick and had to wind down the window. She called for him to slow down, but he pretended not to understand. They reached the treeline again. The rain swayed the pines and bedraggled mountain sheep with crusted tails surveyed them miserably from under a haunch of rock. The trees were so close together that the light between them had a greenish cast, and for the first time Heather noticed narrow tracks veering off into the thick of the forest. She pointed to a track.

'What is that?'

'Army tracks in war. Bosniak soldiers hide here. Now for hunting. Good boar. You like?'

He made the motion of firing a rifle, taking both hands off the steering wheel, and then had to put them back as the car hit a large pothole and swerved. Heather scrutinised the too green primordial wood, unsure if she expected to see the faces of Bosniak soldiers, half-feral and full of fury, or the curling tusks of a great wild boar. Or Ryan . . . tempted down one of the untravelled paths, lured into the woods and lost.

They arrived in Višegrad a little after eleven. The town lay in the fertile valley between two hills, nestling in the fold. The wide Drina river rushed along the base of the valley and through the middle of the town, the waters a startling turquoise even on a dull day. A huge stone bridge spanned the river, its massive arches lidded, watching eyes. The rain had stopped, but the clouds hung low, warning of more to come. The cab deposited Heather in the main square, the driver gesturing vaguely in the direction of the police station.

Everything in the town appeared at once old and new.

The style was nineteenth century, but there was something about it that made her think of a sinister theme park. A large brass statue, at once broadly smiling and malevolent, beamed down at her. Cafés with primary-coloured awnings and timber-fronted shops faced the square. It was absolutely empty, bereft of shoppers. If it was a theme park, it was one after all the visitors had gone home. Something about it gave her the creeps. Instead of ancient cobbles, the square had been paved with slick marble slabs, shining wetly with rain. They looked better suited to a hotel bathroom than a town square.

She hurried through the deserted square, arriving with relief in a busier part of town. The street had a grocers and a pharmacy and a few pedestrians, umbrellas thrust out, barricading them against the drizzle that was starting up again. At least this part of the town looked lived in – ordinary red-roofed houses mixed in with the ubiquitous ones hurriedly rebuilt in concrete block. Yet there remained an odd atmosphere about the place. It was too big for the number of people, like a shrunken man buckled into a pair of vast trousers. The town hall was large and ornate; even the churches were decorated and grand. They whispered of a more illustrious, peopled past. Heather looked around for the minarets of the mosque with their bright Ottoman blue and splash of cheerful gold.

She took several wrong turns and was soaked by the time she arrived at the police station. The station itself was relatively quiet. A drunk dozed on a bench, a bored sergeant stood behind a desk. He grunted as he saw Heather. There was no one else waiting as far as she could tell, but he made her stand for another ten minutes before summoning her.

'I want to report a missing person,' she said.

The sergeant turned around and called out, 'Inspektor!' An older man appeared a minute or two later. Heather recognised him as the policeman who'd given the statement after the drugs bust at the race. He looked at Heather and gave a short nod.

'Inspektor Simo Subotić,' he said in crisp, barely accented English. 'May I help?'

'My boyfriend is missing, Inspektor Subotić.'

'Please, call me Simo.'

She realised she'd been handed over to the Inspektor because he was the only one who could speak English. She hoped his talents extended beyond languages.

'This way, please. Follow me.'

There were three policemen on duty, and they surveyed Heather with lazy curiosity as she passed. One sat with his feet up on his desk. Simo hesitated, saying nothing, and the feet were hastily removed with what Heather guessed to be an apology. He held open the door to a cramped office crowded with files and papers and gestured for her to sit.

'When did he disappear?'

'Yesterday.'

'Tell me what happened, from the beginning.'

He listened patiently, without interrupting, as she described the events leading up to the disappearance. He made a few scribbled notes, turning to them once she had finished.

'Why do you think something bad has happened to Ryan?' he asked. 'And that he hasn't, I'm sorry to say . . . ?'

'Left me?'

Simo shrugged. 'Possibly. Or, you say he is a journalist.

I've known in my life quite a few journalists, British and American. They can all drink. Did Ryan drink?'

'Absolutely not. Never.'

'Ah, okay. So he was an alcoholic.'

'Yes,' said Heather with some reluctance. She looked at Simo, grey-haired with a neat, triangular beard and shrewd black eyes like wet stones. She wondered why he was stuck here and not in the capital. It appeared to her, even after only a few minutes, that he was somewhat over-qualified for this uncanny little town.

'And when was Ryan's last . . .' the policeman paused, swirling his hand in the air as he reached for the word, 'his last relapse?'

Heather swallowed, met his eye. 'A long time ago. Before he met me.'

Simo smiled. 'I am not sure you're being absolutely honest with me. I want to help you find Ryan, and I can only use what you tell me. But okay, Ryan has not had a drink for a long time. It's not possible that he met with this attractive lady and had a few too many plum brandies – we like that here – and did something he regretted? Then, feeling guilty, decided to go off for a while?' he pressed, not unkindly.

Heather shook her head. 'No. It's just not him.'

Simo sighed. 'It's boring, it's sad, but I'm sorry to say it's what men do. Even to those we love.'

'No,' said Heather, vehement. 'I know him, he wouldn't. I was injured. He stood by me.'

'Okay,' Simo said, letting the topic go.

He took out a map and asked Heather to mark exactly where he had disappeared. She drew a circle.

'I think it's about here. I was aware that I hadn't seen him for a while – really since the descent from the peak. I can't be exactly sure.'

'Of course.'

'And there was a truck. I saw it at the top. But it never reached me. That's odd. Don't you think that's odd?' she said, hearing the note of desperation.

'Did you see a number plate?'

'It was too far away.'

'What kind of truck?'

'White. I think. No. A van.'

'So, it was a truck or a van? Maybe white.'

'I didn't know it was important at the time,' snapped Heather.

'No, of course not. How could you?'

Simo poured her a glass of water, and Heather drank gratefully. She glanced at his desk and took in the framed photograph on his desk, of a woman and two young women, his daughters presumably.

'Where are you staying?' asked Simo.

'Zikoč.'

'An ugly town on a beautiful mountain,' he said. 'An unusual spot for a romantic trip.' Simo was silent for a moment, considering. 'What sort of journalist is Ryan? Political?'

'No. Cycling.'

'Okay. And you say he was following the Tour de Balkans for the last few weeks?'

'Yes,' said Heather, growing impatient.

'We had a problem with this year's tour. One of the teams was targeted by a drugs gang and used to bring cocaine into the country.'

'I know. We were there. We watched the arrests.'

'You did?' He looked at her sharply.

Heather prickled. 'Yes. Ryan was really torn up about it all.'

'Okay. Then the next day he goes missing.'

'There is no connection,' Heather insisted.

'You seem very sure.'

'I know Ryan.'

'And I don't. So tell me a little more about him. He speaks good Serbian. When did he learn?'

'He was here during the war, from nineteen ninety-two. With the U.N.'

'From nineteen ninety-two?'

'Yes.'

'And you're quite sure?'

'Yeah. He was here for a few years. He doesn't like to talk about it. I know he saw some really awful stuff.'

'That's this place. Terrible and beautiful. Some of our loveliest sites hide our ugliest secrets. You saw our town bridge?'

Heather nodded.

'During the war, every evening at sunset they lined up Bosniaks and shot them off the Sokolović bridge right here in Višegrad. No one knows how many. Maybe one thousand. Maybe three thousand. Men. Women. Little children.'

She felt the colour drain from her face.

'It stopped only because the corpses blocked the hydroelectric dam down river. But it is a very beautiful bridge. A World Heritage Site. You should see Lake Perućac in June. At first light. Ah, that is something. The water here is very mineral. So blue . . . like the Madonna's robes. Of

— 81 —

course, she hides so many bodies. They've found about four hundred so far, but I still have eight hundred missing person cases just from this town.'

Simo's voice was even, as though he was reciting from a tourist brochure, but he watched her steadily with his black eyes.

Heather met his gaze. 'Are you telling me that you won't look for Ryan? That you have too many old cases?'

He shook his head. 'To me they are not old. And no, of course not. Everyone matters. Of course I'll look. But some of these bodies we found in the lake, they were from the Second World War. On top of them were new ones. The people here knew for more than fifty years the good places to hide a body, and how to keep it a secret. These are not people who talk.' He sighed. 'Your Ryan, he is probably gone off for a few days and he will come back, a little embarrassed but nothing worse.'

Heather bit her fingernail. 'You tell me that nothing has happened and I shouldn't worry, and then you tell me how people round here know how to hide a dead body for fifty years.'

Simo had the grace to look sheepish. 'Yes. I am not very used to tourists. Perhaps I should take the refresher course. It has been suggested.' He was silent for a moment, thinking. 'Ryan is an American?'

'Yes.'

'And he was here as a U.N. soldier during the war?'

'Yes,' said Heather, annoyed, sitting back down. She couldn't see what this had to do with anything.

'I don't know of any who learned to speak Serbian. Not more than a few words.'

Heather said nothing, wondering if Simo was trying to trip her up.

'I know these things as I was a translator for one of the American regiments,' said Simo. 'I knew some of them quite well. They liked to learn a few words. It was a good game. But mostly they liked to learn dirty words, or how to order beer. That's all.'

He studied Heather, but she was careful to make no reply.

'Or perhaps the waitress did not hear so well, and his Serbian was not fluent, after all. But I don't think so. I remember him, I think. My friend David said something to me at the press conference and your Ryan overheard, and he asked a question about it. His Serbian is excellent.'

Heather looked at him in surprise that the policeman had remembered such a detail, as well as Ryan himself.

Simo smiled. 'So, your Ryan speaks Serbian. It is interesting, at the moment, nothing more.'

'Okay,' said Heather, tight with worry.

'And perhaps the waitress did not see what she thought, and he did not kiss this lady. I know nothing. After all, I don't know him at all.'

Heather remained silent. They both heard the other question, even though it remained unspoken: how well did *she* know Ryan?

Unable to find a taxi willing to take her on the long drive back to Zikoč for some time, she stayed in Višegrad for the rest of the afternoon, roaming the empty square and keeping away from the bridge. Somehow its beauty made it worse – the perfect symmetry of the stonework stretching between the sculpted green foothills, the elegance of the archways reflected into smooth circles in the aquamarine water. Every time she caught a glimpse of it, she saw the ghosts of the unnumbered dead.

It was dusk by the time Heather returned to Zikoč. Ryan had been gone for more than twenty-four hours. He was officially missing. She suspected Simo would file the report, although she couldn't imagine him pursuing the case with any diligence. Everyone had made their opinion quite clear. There was no evidence of any crime, and this was a country accustomed to the very worst crimes of humanity, so they knew how to recognise the signs. A missing cyclist. No sign of a struggle. No shell casing. No blood. No weapon. It was nothing at all.

She was exhausted by the time she reached the hotel. It really was an ugly town on a beautiful mountain. Though by now the charm of the mountain was wearing thin. The trees were too thick and oppressive. The earlier rain had brought a slide of mud onto the road, thick and visceral. A squat buzzard eyed her from a blasted pine.

She went straight to her room and rifled through her bag. Soon she'd have to find somewhere to do some laundry. She caught herself with a ripple of self-loathing. How could she think about that when Ryan was gone? She wouldn't let everyone else's slow drip-drip of whispers make her doubt him. Not one of them knew him. Even Simo was full of insinuations and he'd never spoken to him.

She hurried into the squalid bathroom and washed her face in the sink, scrubbing at her skin again and again. If she could only get it properly clean, scrape all the dirt and filth from her skin then everything would be all right again. She stood there for some time, the taps running at full pelt. The water was warm, trickling all over her hands but when she looked down at them, she realised that they were bleeding and cut. She rinsed off the blood and saw that the knuckles on her right hand were seeping. She glanced up and saw that the mirror above the sink was smashed. Her reflection was shattered. She stared back at a broken version of herself, splintered into a myriad of tiny pieces. She stared down again at her bleeding hand. She must have punched the mirror but had no recollection of the apparent act of violence. A small cry of horror escaped her lips. She sat on the floor of the bathroom and began to whimper with fear and confusion. What had she done?

It took her several moments to realise her phone was ringing.

She raced back to the bedroom and grabbed it.

'Miss Bishop? Inspektor Simo Subotić.'

Adrenaline coursed through her veins like heat. 'Have you found him?'

'No, no. I looked at the place he went missing, on the map. And I made some calls. They were hunting boar near there yesterday.'

Heather swallowed, feeling sick. 'So, it's possible there was an accident?'

'Hunters rarely shoot near the road. There are penalties. Though it can happen. I would like to organise a search for tomorrow morning, to rule out the possibility. You would like to come?'

'Yes. Please.'

Her voice sounded garbled and strange. The police officer gave her details for the search, but Heather could barely take it in. After he hung up, she lay back on the bed, head swimming. Her thoughts felt distant, like they belonged to someone else. A radio blared in another room and she thought that she'd heard someone say her name. That wasn't a good sign. She listened again. Yes, she could hear them talking about her on the radio. She took a deep breath and told herself that it wasn't real. She realised she'd forgotten to take her medication and quickly swallowed a pill with some water. The skin around her forehead tingled and buzzed like a mild electric shock.

An hour later she sat in Café Bulozi nursing a plum brandy. As she clutched the glass she glanced at the cut to her hand. It wasn't deep and she'd strapped it as best she could with plasters and a bandage from her first aid kit. But her hand was trembling.

'Don't. You spill it. Horrible waste.'

Looking up, Heather saw that Petra had slipped onto the barstool beside her. Petra gestured for the barman to bring them two more.

'What happened to your hand?'

'I fell.'

Petra nodded in sympathy. 'I ask all day about dark-haired *Dušica* with Ryan. No one know anything, no one see anything.' Petra underscored her point by downing her drink.

'Thank you for asking.' Heather glanced around and felt the heat of a dozen pairs of eyes on her skin. 'Maybe I'm paranoid, but I feel like everyone is watching me.'

Petra shrugged. 'You not paranoid. Everyone *is* watching you. They wait to see if you crack. Nothing much happen here. Or nothing much for a while. When things happen, they happen real bad. A family was killed not so far from here in the winter.'

Heather stared at her in horror. 'These things happen often?'

'No, of course not. Mostly nothing ever happens at all. It boring as shit.'

Heather told Petra about the search the following morning in the woods, and Petra took her hand and squeezed it with surprisingly strong fingers.

'I come with you. I bring some people. Not everyone in this village assholes. Most of them. But not all. We help look.'

Heather found herself trying not to cry. She hadn't cried since Ryan had disappeared, worried that if she started she might not be able to stop.

'Please don't be too nice. I can't stand it. It's just, Bosnia isn't what I expected. Bosnians aren't what I expected.'

Petra gave her an odd look.

'Heather, this isn't fucking Bosnia.'

'What? Of course it's . . . Bosnia and Herzegovina.'

Anger began to rise again, quick and just beneath her skin. Heather was tired of people playing on her anxiety and grief. She was going crazy with worry; she wasn't crazy.

'This isn't fucking Bosnia. It's Republika Srpska. The Serb federation. No one in this god-forsaken shithole of a village is Bosniak. Not anymore. Didn't you notice?'

Heather stared at her. 'How am I supposed to tell? Do you look different? I can't speak Serb or Bosnian.'

Petra shrugged. 'I thought travellers supposed to take basic interest in where they going.'

'We were just on a cycling holiday. Passing through,'

said Heather. She knew she ought to feel chastened, but she was too tired, too concerned about Ryan to consider her ignorance as a tourist.

'You should know. It is basic courtesy. And in some places, basic safety. People very sensitive. Me, not so much. My mother is Serb, but my father was Bosniak. Muslim, as you say.'

'And you?' asked Heather.

Petra downed another brandy. 'I think all religion is cowshit.'

'Horseshit or bullshit.'

'Really, the type of shit matters?' said Petra with a raised eyebrow. 'The point is, my father was put into a camp because he was Muslim. Bad things happened to him. Very bad things. He never say. I never ask. He come back looking like a skeleton. And he lucky, he come back. Only, he didn't really. Not all of him. Some of him always stay there in that place.'

'I'm sorry.'

'Don't be sorry. You don't even know where you are. You not sure what country you are in.'

Heather was both shamed and irritated by the rebuke.

'Anyway, Papa always say the ones who make it are the ones who don't remember their dreams. Or say they don't and don't fucking talk about them. And then, after about fifteen years, he woke up one morning and started talking about his goddamn dreams. And he wouldn't shut up about them. We tried to listen. And believe me, I didn't want to hear that shit. You can't unhear it. And . . . then he shot himself.'

Petra pulled a cigarette from her pocket and tried to light

it, taking several attempts and singeing the fur of her coat, so that she swore, loudly and creatively in what Heather now took to be Serbian. Cigarette now lit, she studied Heather through her heavily made-up lashes.

'You say Ryan was here during the war?'

'Yes. For several years.'

'Then he also must have seen stuff. Real bad stuff.'

'He must have. But he never talked about it.'

Petra inhaled deeply. 'That's good.' She paused. 'Did he dream?'

Heather walked slowly back to the hotel. The dogs growled and fought, and mingled with their barking was a distant howling from deep in the woods. She tried to remember whether there were wolves in Bosnia. *Republika Srpska*, she corrected herself. Ryan had never mentioned his dreams to her, good or bad. She wondered whether it was possible that coming back here – to this terrible, beautiful place – had triggered something. She needed to find out where he had actually been stationed, realising with another pang of hurt that she didn't even know the name of his unit. She tried to think of someone who might know, and then, once again, decided upon Freddie, who had left her half a dozen messages. She dialled and he picked up at once.

'Heather! Thank God! Have you found him?'

Swallowing hard, Heather heard herself admit that she had not.

'What do you need? Do you want me to fly out?'

'Not yet. But if he's not back in a few days, then maybe. How long was his longest, you know—'

'Bender? About a week. Ten days, perhaps.'

'And did you hear from him?'

'No. Not once. But Heather, he was doing so well. Even though the two of you were, y'know . . .' His voice tailed off.

'Were what?' demanded Heather. 'What are you trying to say? That because we were squabbling, this is my fault? Every couple fights.'

'*Squabbling*? Is that what you call it?' asked Freddie, his voice sharp and bitter. He instantly backtracked. 'I'm sorry. I didn't mean that. No one can know a relationship from the outside. God knows, Ryan couldn't be easy to live with.'

Despite Freddie's apology, Heather was hurt and furious, and it took all her willpower not to hang up. How dare Freddie put any of this on her? But she needed more information. She took a breath and scratched at a brown stain on the eiderdown. Probably her own blood from earlier. 'Freddie, did Ryan have bad dreams?'

There was another long pause, and for a moment she thought the call had dropped. Then she heard a deep sigh.

'He said they were getting better. Even stopped the medication. Said he didn't need it anymore. He said he was going to tell you.'

'He didn't.'

Heather sat alone on her bed in the sickly yellow glow of the bedside lamp. Ryan seemed to know everything about her, and yet, despite four years together, it appeared that there were holes in her knowledge of him. It was as though part of him had always been missing, even before he disappeared.

7

The drive to the woods was in silence, conversation made difficult by the intrusive clatter of the 4x4's engine and the rattle of the uneven mountain road. Simo glanced at his passenger. Heather's gaze was fixed on the landscape outside, as it had been since they'd left town, straining for a sign of her missing boyfriend. Simo felt a twinge of guilt at how he'd treated her yesterday, but the coincidence of Ryan Mackinnon disappearing the day after the race rankled. Simo had pointed this out to the investigating officers on the cocaine case and they'd promised to look into it. He knew with absolute certainty that they would not. It didn't matter. The Mackinnon case belonged to him and he was permitted to pursue it that way. Usually, the disappearance of a grown man after a fight with his girlfriend was of little concern, but something about this one nagged at Simo. If there was a connection between the cases, he would find it.

Yesterday's rain had given way to a shimmer of spring sunshine, and the hillside was spread with buttery light. Yellow and purple flowers erupted amongst the spiked grass. The alpine streams were fat and full. Heather held onto the strap on the roof, the vehicle bouncing so much over the ruts that her head hit the ceiling.

'This is about where you last saw him, yes?' he asked.

'Yes!' yelled Heather.

Simo leant forward and shouted at the driver to turn, and immediately they swerved off down one of the narrow tracks leading into the forest. Simo banged on the roof, and the vehicle juddered to a halt. Heather climbed out with apparent relief, taking deep breaths of cool morning air. Simo took out his phone and started making some calls, and within a few minutes another couple of ancient 4x4s drew up behind them and out climbed several locals from Zikoč. A young woman bounded up to Heather and gave her a hug, announcing loudly, 'You see, not everyone in Zikoč total bastard. Some okay. We want to help you find useless boyfriend.'

'Petra?' said Simo with a grimace. 'Why are you here?'

They started to row loudly in Serbian. Then, suddenly, they were finished and Simo threw his arm around Petra's shoulders, declaring, 'I surrender. It's pointless arguing with you. Just come.'

'Good. It's why I love you, Uncle Simo.'

She planted a kiss on his cheek.

Heather stared at Petra. 'He's your uncle?'

'Cousin, on my mother's side, but I call him uncle. Everyone is related here.' She gave a shrug.

Simo frowned, a little embarrassed. He gave instructions in Serbian, apologising to Heather. 'It is quicker if I speak Serbian. I'll explain to you after. You stay with me, Miss Bishop. Next of kin.'

They searched in teams of two, keeping mostly to the tracks near the road, looking for any sign that a bike had been there. It was cool and dark in the wood, the thick cover of the trees maintaining a perpetual greenish twilight. The damp smell of leaf litter mingled with the metallic scent of ferns. Their voices silenced the chatter of the birds.

'Shouldn't we be quiet?' Heather asked Simo.

'No, it's best if we make noise. I like them to know we are here. This is not a good place.'

'Wolves?'

Simo laughed. 'Not wolves. Although this area is known as *Vukojèbina* in Bosnian. It means "place where wolves fuck". In the woods, smugglers sometimes use the old logging cabins as a place to keep the drugs. Is best they know we are here with our sandwiches and radios looking for someone, not interested in their drugs.'

Heather looked at him sharply. 'You're not interested in their drugs, Simo?'

'Not today.'

He saw Heather glance around at the endless trees with considerable nervousness. He guessed she was seeing faces in every swaying branch, hooded figures rushing from behind each silver trunk. Simo chuckled.

'Don't worry.'

'Great.'

'It's almost certainly fine.'

Something about the Ryan Mackinnon story was off. Although he had to admit that it might be nothing more than a man lying to his girlfriend. It was nearly noon and they had been circling deeper and deeper into the woods, further from the road where Ryan had last been sighted, and where Simo had instructed the others to concentrate their search. They could no longer see nor hear the rest of the party. Simo spoke into his radio. It crackled and hissed, spitting out static. He smacked it, trying to reignite it into life. A few broken words came through, then nothing.

'Half the radios are faulty. No money to replace them. Only place more corrupt than Bosnia is Republika Srpska.'

He watched as Heather pulled out her phone. No signal.

Simo waved away her concern. 'It's fine. If we want them, I'll shout very loud. I know these woods well. Besides, you left a trail of breadcrumbs, yes?'

Heather didn't laugh. She looked exhausted.

'I did find one curious thing,' said Simo. 'I wanted to talk to you somewhere private.'

He pointed to a moss-covered log and flicked away a couple of leaves, gesturing for Heather to sit beside him.

'I requested Mr Mackinnon's bank records and credit card details. He's now an official missing person, so I can do this,' he said.

'Okay?'

'And his credit card and his bank account have not been used since the day before yesterday. He paid for the hotel and dinner in Zikoč. Then nothing.'

Heather turned green and looked like she might be sick.

'Deep breath, Miss Bishop. I haven't finished. It's not all bad. A little strange but not bad. Five days ago, he took out three thousand dollars in cash from a bank in Sarajevo. Why?'

She looked at him, her face pale with confusion and shock. 'I have absolutely no idea. He didn't tell me. He's old-fashioned; sometimes he uses cash.'

Simo reached into his pocket and produced a pair of reading glasses and the printout of Ryan's credit card transactions. 'But he paid for dinner and this hotel and this

hotel on a credit card? So, not that old-fashioned. You see?'
he said, pointing.

'I don't need to see. I believe you.'

Simo asked gently, 'Do you know where the cash is?'

She shook her head.

'Then we must presume that Ryan still has it. And this
is why I don't think we'll find him today, or even tomorrow.
Three thousand dollars is a great deal of money in Republika
Sprska. Enough to disappear for a long time. The sort of
thing people do if they are in trouble with bad men.'

They were both silent for a moment, the words heavy
between them. He took his reading glasses off and slipped
them back into his pocket. At last he stood, holding out his
hand to help Heather up. She stood, not taking it.

'Walk a little with me,' he said.

'The search party is that way.' She pointed back in the
direction of the road.

'Humour me.'

He set off at a rapid pace, deeper into the wood. She
followed reluctantly. The path petered out, overgrown by
brambles and matted fern waist high. Something scuffled in
the undergrowth.

'Ryan didn't come here,' she called. 'It's obvious that no
one's been here. Not for ages.'

'I am sorry. Can't hear what you're saying. Keep up!' called
Simo, happily pushing forward. He had produced from his
pocket a sharp knife and was slicing through the thicket with
some skill, clearly prepared for this adventure. Suddenly, the
trees gave way to a small clearing and they stood amongst a
collection of gloomy wooden huts. A shaft of sunlight spun
down, joyless and without warmth by the time it reached the

forest floor. The windows of every hut were smashed, and they gazed out blind and despoiled. The doors were broken, hanging off their hinges. There was something unspeakably wrong about the broken huts and their swinging doors.

Simo gave a shout, and Heather jumped.

'It's fine! See, no one here. Just us.'

'I don't like it. I want to go.'

'In a minute. I promise.'

He took her arm firmly and steered her into the nearest cabin. Heather blinked in the gloom. There were holes all through the walls where glowing circles of greenish sunlight poked through, and black mouldering smears of damp puddled the floor, daubed the walls and spattered the ceiling. It wasn't damp. It was blood. Old, dry blood. The holes were from bullets.

'This is a terrible place,' said Simo in an even tone. 'One drug gang shot up another. Blood and death. I wanted you to see it.'

Spooked by the place, Heather bolted out onto the porch, her feet crunching on old cartridge casings.

Simo followed her out. 'Young Petra is quite sure Ryan ran off with this pretty lady he calls *Dušica*. He took out money and he went off.'

'So why bring me here?'

'You say he was here in nineteen ninety-two, yes? There was no U.N. here in nineteen ninety-two.'

'That's what he told me.'

'Well, there were no Americans here until nineteen ninety-six. I made calls yesterday to check. Either he lied about being here then or he lied about being here with the U.N.'

'I don't know. All I know is that we came to this place to go biking and he disappeared and I'm going crazy with worry, but no one else seems to give a damn.'

The furrow in Simo's brow deepened. 'I'm sorry it seems like that. I give a damn. But I am a police officer and this is *Vukojèbina*. I'm not interested in the drugs today, but tomorrow? I hope your Ryan hasn't got in the middle of something stupid. Because if he has, then this is how it ends. The riders in the Tour de Balkans, they were fined and pleaded ignorance about the cocaine they carried. Maybe they knew nothing about it, maybe they did. In either case, they were lucky. It did not end for them out here in the woods. They'll pay court fines. They'll ride again.'

He watched as Heather willed herself to face the huts, doors agape like broken jaws, walls daubed with violence. A breeze filtered through the trees, fluttering the leaves and carrying the sweetish metallic scent of the ferns, which Simo always thought smelled like blood.

He sat down on a log and pulled out a chocolate bar. He broke it in two and offered her half. She ignored him. The sunlight that penetrated the forest was green, casting his skin with a weird hue. He sighed.

'You see, this is why I think it is better for Ryan if he's gone off with *Dušica*. Not better for you, perhaps, but better for him.'

Methodically, Heather tore up a stem of grass.

'I'm sorry,' said Simo. 'I need you to be scared. I need you to know what this place can be. It is beautiful and terrible and filled with people like Petra who are the kindest and best in all of the world. But if your Ryan has got into trouble, you need to tell me everything. Let me help him.' He looked at her steadily. She stared out at the huts, wide-eyed and uneasy. It was clear to him that she was riled. He also sensed she was lying, but about what?

8

Petra looked at Heather's pale face with concern when they rejoined the group.

'You find something?' she asked.

Heather shook her head briskly, fighting the urge to vomit.

'No, I am pleased to say we found nothing,' declared Simo amiably. 'I'll make enquiries after this *Dušica*. See if I can talk to colleagues in Bosnia, make sure Ryan hasn't gone to Sarajevo. It's very pleasant at this time of year.' He turned to the others, thanking them all for their assistance.

Heather drove back to Zikoč with Petra, politely declining Simo's offer to drop her at her hotel. She fell asleep on the drive, exhausted, and when she woke, she didn't recognise her surroundings.

'Where are we?'

'My house. Come. It's all good. My mother and shit-for-brains step father have gone away for a few days.'

Heather climbed out and followed Petra onto a steep driveway leading up to a small white-painted house, surrounded by orchards and untidy meadows on either side. The gardens and house were pretty, in a dishevelled sort of way. As they got closer, Heather realised the white paint was starting to brown, and the long, uncut grass hid broken garden machinery, old tyres and all kinds of other junk. They entered an old-fashioned kitchen. It was clean but untidy, the peeling counter piled high with unopened mail and tool catalogues. Petra opened a cupboard and grabbed a bottle and two glasses, pouring them quickly and passing one to Heather.

'It's a bit early for me.'

'You look terrible.'

Heather drank.

'Good, yes? Is from our own plums. The mountain summer in bottle.' She pulled out a chair and gestured for Heather to sit. 'You tell me what happened in the wood?'

Heather took the bottle, poured herself another glass and told Petra about the cabins.

'I know it. Everyone from here know it. Is wicked place. But Uncle Simo mess with you. Is not bullets from drug gangs. It's old, from the war. Bosniaks used to hide out there. Serb army hunted them with dogs and rounded them up in the huts, separated out the men and boys and shot them all. That blood is more than twenty years old. I think it should be burned to the ground. But no one go there. Is full of ghosts.'

Heather's head began to swim. She felt nauseous and dizzy. 'Why would he do that? Why would he lie?'

Petra pulled a face. 'I don't know. But Uncle Simo is famous policeman. He used to be high-up officer in Banja Luka. Right at the top. But he make many people angry in war and then afterwards. He has big sympathy towards Bosniak people. He loved my father very much. My father hate guts of most of my mother's family, but not Uncle Simo.

But most Serbs not like him. Call him traitor to his own people. He sent out here as punishment.'

Heather sighed and rubbed her forehead. 'So, he's bored? He's messing with me for fun?'

Petra gave a hard laugh. 'No. I told you. He good policeman. I don't think he trust you.'

'I'm very trustworthy,' objected Heather.

Petra laughed again. 'If you say so. You should ask him about men they find in Drina. They find bodies in river without heads and other bits.'

She took out her phone and showed Heather a headline that for once she was grateful she couldn't read.

'You think there's a killer? And he took Ryan?'

Petra shook her head. 'No. I think he arsehole who left you, but you want to be sure of all possibilities. This is possibility.'

Heather shuddered. She didn't tell Petra about the possibility that Ryan had not been here with the U.N. during the war. Or about the money. She told herself it was because she was tired, and she wasn't sure Petra's English was good enough to understand the nuance. Really, she didn't want Petra to like Ryan even less than she already did.

They went out into the garden and sat on a covered swing with a mouldy cushion, sipping coffee and nibbling baklava. Early bees buzzed amongst the trees in the plum orchard, and Heather inhaled the smell of grass and honey.

'This is *Bosnian* coffee,' said Petra, insistent. 'They not call it that in Višegrad. There you must ask for "Domestic Coffee", but it is Bosnian coffee, whatever stupid name you give it. My father never call it anything else.'

'Okay,' said Heather, not really understanding the

difference. She pointed to the ruins of another building on the slope opposite. 'What's that, a summer house?'

Petra snorted. 'No. That was my uncle's house. They burned him and his wife inside. And the house in those trees belonged to my cousin.' She pointed to where stones poked out amongst a tight knot of ash and hazel. 'We never find his body. He shot and buried in his orchard but he had thousands of trees and we never find him.'

'My god. So no one lives there now?'

'No. People take over the best houses, but not these. Maybe because we still here. Our neighbours are mostly ghosts. But they are family.'

Petra led her to an apple tree. It was in flower, a cascade of scented blossom. Petra jabbed at the trunk with her finger, pointing at a knot or wound a little more than halfway up. In a shaft of sunlight, Heather saw that there was a bullet wedged in the bark of the tree. It had grown to cover it like a callus, but the bullet remained in the centre, a cold metal heart.

'The bullet passed through my father's skull when he killed himself and it stuck in the tree. We couldn't get it out. My mother wouldn't cut it down. It had his blood on, so now the tree has grown with the bullet in it and my father's blood runs in the sap.'

Heather didn't know what to say – words of condolence seemed petty and trite – so she said nothing. Petra gave the tree a good kick and then swore again, recoiling in pain.

'Blood tree. Bullet tree. We never eat the apples. We just let them fall and rot.'

Heather reached for Petra's hand, and she let her take it.

Petra dropped her back at her hotel, and Heather curled up in the single chair. She rang Ryan's colleagues. No one had heard from him. They sounded concerned, but more for her than him. They knew he had form for disappearing. Everyone she spoke to seemed to take a ghoulish delight in regaling her with some account of when he had downed a bottle of vodka in Athens or Chinese whisky in Beijing and done something unrepeatable (although they repeated it, sometimes twice, in case she hadn't quite caught it the first time). Heather found herself growing more and more irritable. Most of these incidents dated back more than a decade. Only his former editor at the *Telegraph* sounded genuinely concerned, until she wondered whether the news desk might be persuaded to write a paragraph.

'"Alcoholic cycling journalist late home,"' he said with a snort. 'Or were you thinking of a different headline?'

'Now you're just being an arse,' said Heather.

'Yes, but you see my point. Before he met you, Heather darling, he wasn't exactly renowned for his fidelity, if you can excuse my frankness. There was a trail of broken hearts around the office. I used to warn the interns and new hires about two things: the faulty coffee machine that sprayed boiling water, and about Ryan. Both equally risky to one's health.'

'Thanks.'

'You're welcome,' replied the editor, without a hint of irony. 'Look, Ryan is still on holiday for another week. If he's still buggered off then, or if the police have something concrete to say, then sure. But Heather, darling, there isn't a story yet. He's basically been gone a day. Let me know if you need anything.'

That's what everyone said: 'If you need anything.' So, she told them what she needed – publicity to help find Ryan – and they declined.

Now that he had gone, these myriad versions of Ryan kept appearing, like distortions in a funhouse mirror. They were like him, but not him. They were a picture puzzle with his features but put back together in the wrong way. Even those who hadn't met him were constructing a version of him out of scraps and fragments. Petra's Ryan: selfish philanderer and alcoholic. Subotić's: a liar hiding three thousand dollars, with possible connections to Serbian drug gangs. The Ryan of his colleagues: a charming raconteur with a penchant for misadventure and interns, liable to fall off the wagon at any moment. Every one of these Ryans was a stranger to her. Heather felt that her Ryan had been dismembered by Simo and then put back together in some horrific Frankenstein's monster version of his worst self.

Where Simo had used the evidence to construct a narrative where Ryan looked guilty of something, Heather attempted to put a positive spin upon the same evidence. All Ryan had done was taken out some money before he vanished (okay, a lot of money, which was a bit odd, but still it was his money). A nagging voice reminded Heather that every time she had suggested they have a joint account, Ryan rejected the idea. It was unnecessary, he'd said. Old-fashioned, he'd said. They shared everything anyway and, he'd complained, it smacked of forcing women into dependence. Heather had recoiled – she didn't want him to think of her as needy. She hadn't mentioned it again, but now wondered whether he had manipulated her. Yet he was generous. And when her sponsorships dried up, unobtrusively he paid more than his share of the bills and costs. But still, she wondered. Was this the first time he had taken out thousands of dollars? She would never know. It would have been difficult for him to do it discreetly, if they'd had a joint account.

Simo had unsettled her, as did this place with its weird beauty; the looming mountains and vast, ever-changing skies, one moment fierce blue, while the next the spring rains hurried in, clouds smudging the sky like a dirty eraser across a clean page. The houses huddled in the shadows of the mountains, orchards of cherry and apple and plum surrounding each dwelling, so every time the winds blew they carried the fragrance. The valleys were marvellous bridal displays of pink and white, frothing with a confetti of blossom that was hurled about in the strong April winds as if by strong, invisible hands. The hands of the ghosts, Heather thought. She imagined them lying beneath the trees, their roots pushing down deep into their bodies, and their dead breath making the cold Balkan wind as they watched the living and their children, knowing what had they done. Simo was right. This place was beautiful and terrible.

Exhausted, she lay down on the bed and drifted off to sleep. She had the dream again. When she used to discuss it with her counsellor, she complained how unfair it was that the dream never started with the morning, the last time she was whole. She couldn't remember that part at all.

Her teammates told her that it had been the same as any other morning: cereal weighed on digital scales and measured out into a bowl with a recorded quantity of low-fat milk, then rice (not pasta, too heavy to digest) and a special energy drink. Then she left to cycle to the velodrome to train. It was perfectly dull, like any other morning, and she remembered those, but she wanted to remember this one, as it was important, the very last time she was herself. 'You are still yourself,' the counsellor would always interject. 'I'm not,' Heather insisted. 'I'm different.' Inferior. Broken. Ordinary.

But even though she willed it, the dream never started any earlier. It only started the moment before impact. She was cycling. The familiar sensation of power and speed, unthinking and effortless. The truck was close but her line was good and it had seen her. It must have seen her. And then, an explosion. She was flying, spinning in pain. A red noise inside her own skull. She was caught beneath the truck's wheel. Her bike was trapped and she was dragged behind, and someone was screaming and there was water everywhere and she was slithering in red water. And as she woke, she was calling out for Ryan, and she was bathed in sweat, and it was then she knew that it had been blood and her own screams.

The voices and the blackouts and the depression had been a legacy of the accident, as much part of her as the steel plate in her skull. Her personality had shifted and been splashed across the road. Was her depression as a result of her damaged brain, or because she was miserable about everything that had been stolen from her? No one could tell her. She supposed it didn't really matter in the end. Determination and brute willpower now sometimes slid into aggression when she was thwarted. That mattered as people's sympathy hardened into dislike or into fear and contempt.

She climbed out of bed and splashed cold water on her face, trying to wash off the bad dreams and self-loathing. She needed to get out of this cheerless room with its fusty smell and stained, rose-patterned counterpane. Tossing her bag over her shoulder, she slammed the door shut and stood in the late afternoon light. Café Bulozi had a few tables outside on the pavement across from the roadside. She hurried over and ordered a coffee, then at the last moment added a plum brandy too. She decided that she rather liked the local brew. The sun was starting to brush the mountaintops, setting them ablaze. Ryan would have liked this. That's what this trip was supposed to have been about: the two of them cycling together, trying to reconnect, enjoying the scenery and one another's company.

She remembered how he'd come to the hospital that second week and somehow charmed his way in. At once he'd got the measure of both the British cycling team and her family – the ineptitude of the weeping Deirdre, the ruthlessness of the squad management. She was conscious and just out of intensive care, and her mother sat in a corner with one of her friends, some crony who kept telling Heather, 'This is very hard on your mother, you know,' as though the accident had been a teenage incident designed to punish her. Meanwhile the Olympic team managers, realising that their star was done for, made sympathetic noises, signed the insurance papers and disappeared into the corridor to whisper their plans for the new line-up, not quite out of earshot. Ryan arrived, made a quick assessment, gave Deirdre and her friend fifty quid, murmuring, 'Yes, it must be very hard, now take her for some lunch far away,' and told the managers to '. . . have your goddamn strategy meeting somewhere else or I'm going to write about what heartless sons of bitches you are in the national press.' Then he set himself to cheering Heather up, mostly by flirting outrageously – despite the leg braces, fractured skull and three smashed vertebrae, brain contusion and broken jaw. Or, as Ryan put it, 'Well, this brings you closer to my league, so I need to make my move while I can.' Despite the fog of morphine and depression, Heather guessed that Ryan had sussed that she had very few real friends. Her training schedule and the pursuit of her Olympic dreams had left little time for relationships of any kind. Her recovery from the accident was slow and tedious. Almost everyone else drifted away. Ryan stayed.

Filled with grief and longing for that Ryan, she started to flick through her phone, looking at old pictures. Her photo library had collated montages of her in the hospital a few weeks after the accident, swollen and drug-addled, with a slightly younger Ryan with a little less grey in his stubble giving a resolute thumbs up. He'd barrel in with anecdotes and daft impressions and flirt with her and use obscene language, and she could tell at once that all the nurses fancied him. Everyone else was so polite and British about what had happened, talking in beige banalities: 'What doesn't kill you . . .' Ryan didn't. 'You probably *do* wish you were dead. I'm real glad you're not. At some point I want to screw you.'

He made friends with everyone, except her mother's cronies. The hangers-on, the misery-hags who sucked on shitty fortune like Marlboro reds in order to tell themselves their own miserable messed-up lives weren't as miserable and messed up as they thought; those gaspers he loathed, and they hated him back. They were friends of Deirdre and they loved to drop her off and 'come and sit a minute' and gaze at Heather and ask to be told the story of the accident and her prognosis again. 'You really won't cycle again, and with the Olympics just around the corner . . . It must be so hard, you poor dear.' Ryan found one of them in Heather's room, with

Heather in tears, and almost physically threw the woman out, calling her a 'misery vampire cunt'.

Of course, Heather fell in love with him. Who wouldn't after that? She'd count down the minutes until he arrived. But she remembered that when he first told her that he loved her, her response hadn't been to tell him that she loved him too, but simply to ask, *Why?* She was nothing. Not anymore. Secretly, she thought the gloom-mongers were right. She couldn't walk more than fifteen steps. She couldn't finish a crossword and fell asleep mid-sentence. He took her hand (bruised from the cannula) and told her quietly that he loved her because she was brave and she had survived and endured, and fought back against fate. She listened and nodded and felt a dizzying numbness creeping into her, because it felt like he was describing his love for a stranger and she felt actually jealous of this woman who was supposedly her. Heather could not recognise herself in his description. She wanted to be that woman because she wanted to be loved by Ryan. She was thirsty for his love. Without him, the horror of it all and her loneliness might swallow her up.

Mostly, Heather was angry and tired. Even through the morphine haze, she recognised that Ryan was in love with a vision he had projected onto the real woman. Heather had tried to become that version. She pretended so hard that, sometimes, she even fooled herself. Occasionally she managed to forget the bitterness at the edges, and to remember she was brave – a real trooper. She walked twenty steps. Fifty. They toasted her triumph with champagne, and she tried not to weep at the smallness of the victory. She stayed overnight in Ryan's flat, and in his bed. Everything had been chaste till then. Stolen kisses, fumbled snogs behind drawn curtains in the ward, and in the canteen smelling of chips, instant hot chocolate and other people's cancer diagnoses. She longed to find their first night together erotic, as he helped her into bed and kissed her scars and told her he didn't see them. He only saw the woman who survived.

She'd moved in with him straight out of hospital. Her old flat in Manchester had belonged to the cycling team and there was now a new girl in her room, in her team spot, living her life.

Yup, here was a picture of the housewarming. Just a few of them. None of the team had come. They were all too busy training for Rio with the new line-up. Jessie as the star, going for the gold medal. Heather had been relieved they hadn't come – she couldn't have faced seeing them. She resented that they didn't keep in touch, but when they tried, it was unbearable. The month of the Olympics was the worst. She'd spent a lot of it on the sofa, drinking wine and yelling at the TV, but Ryan had made it tolerable. He'd helped her turn it into a game. Jesus. He'd even forced her to watch the women's road race. The one she'd spent her entire life dreaming and training for, and for which the team had spent a year practising set-ups to help her win. She'd skulked around for days, and on the morning of the race, Ryan had presented her with a shot of tequila and sat her down and forced her to watch. He had sat with her, yelling at the TV screen all the way through the race. There were great gaping holes all through her memories of that summer but she did remember race day. He was supposed to be in Rio, but he stayed to be with her. He had sacrificed his own career for her. Or so she had thought at the time. Heather still wasn't sure who or what she'd recovered into. She couldn't fully remember who she'd been before. There were these ragged black holes, like her entire personality had been decimated by moths.

Here was another picture of her from that time. God, she looked young and so thin, like she'd snap. And those livid scars all along her hairline. She'd forgotten she'd looked like that. They'd had to shave her head and the hair took ages to grow back. Heather brushed her fingers along her skull and felt a bump – the metal plate – a tiny patch where the hair never grew, soft and smooth.

She flicked through another six months. And then, yes, here was another. She experienced a hot rush of anger. Ryan and her at the Tommy Hilfiger Sports Journalist of the Year Award. It turned out his sacrifice in missing the Olympics hadn't been quite so absolute. They stood on the red carpet, Ryan in his tuxedo, smiling, handsome. His stubble carefully trimmed, eyes movie-star blue, wincing slightly against all the flashes, creases in the corners of his eyes. His arm protectively around her shoulders. Her memory of that time tended to play tricks. It was like watching a TV show, but the scenes were all sliced up and put together in a weird order – some of them missing – and no matter how much she concentrated, she could never quite figure out the right order or find the cut scenes. She still looked too thin, and her hair was short and spiky but at least it was a style. She held a walking stick, but not a crutch. She'd wanted to try and manage that night without one, but Ryan had insisted she take it, and they'd fought.

Heather couldn't remember how she'd felt when she read the article for the first time. Maybe it was one of the blank spaces. Or perhaps simply her later fury had engulfed any earlier, softer feelings like a wildfire swallowing the gentle flames of a campfire. Up until this week, when Ryan disappeared, the ceremony had been one of the worst nights of her life. The accident itself had happened in the morning and she had been in surgery the same night and couldn't remember anything until she was woken from the artificially induced coma five days later. The award ceremony, however, she remembered in wretched detail – everyone coming up to her, telling her how proud she must be of Ryan. It was odd, some things were missing, and yet others she could recall with cinematic clarity.

In her mind, she stood in front of the mirror in the bathroom in their flat in her white dress and tried to put some colour on her cheeks, apply mascara with a hand that shook. Ryan came in and stood behind her.

'You look gorgeous.'

'I don't think I can do this.'

He frowned. 'Sweetheart, they want to see you, not me. My article is all about you.'

Heather whirled round to look at him. 'And did you think how I might feel about that? My lowest moment. The shittiest part of my life.'

Ryan sagged against the shower cubicle. 'The article is about your bravery, about the cruelty of sport. Lost dreams.'

'And yet somehow my lost dream is about to win you yours.'

'I haven't won, Heather.'

'You will.'

As she applied her lipstick, she knew with absolute certainty that he would.

He looked desolate and Heather felt awful, and although

it stuck in her teeth, she apologised. Even so, they were barely speaking when the cab arrived. Ryan helped her in and then put her walking stick in the boot.

'I don't need it. I'll lean on your arm.'

'Take it.'

'Why? Does it look better? The Olympian reduced to hobbling with a stick?'

'No. Because if I have to go and take pictures or talk to someone, I don't want you stranded. What if you need to go to the ladies' room?'

They sat in furious silence in the back of the cab. She didn't apologise again.

'You told me to publish it.'

'I don't remember saying that.'

'The things you don't remember are sometimes pretty fucking convenient, Heather.'

The red carpet was filled with B-list celebrities, and it was co-sponsored by one of Ryan's newspapers; they'd put on a good show in one of the best London hotels. Heather was certain everyone was staring at her. And everyone was telling her how proud she must be and commiserating on her own misfortune. Misfortune. That was a funny word. Miss Fortune. That's what she'd been hit by. Not a bloody articulated lorry that had dragged her a hundred yards and shattered her pelvis and broken three vertebrae and smashed her skull so that her brain had swelled so much they'd had to remove a section of her skull – no, she'd had a tiff with Miss Fortune, the talent show contestant sipping cocktails over there at the open bar.

Heather had realised too late the combination of champagne and painkillers was making her feel peculiar.

Colours whirled and the music was so slow that she was hypnotised by the rests in between the notes. She found she couldn't speak, only nod. I'm truly broken now. Wobbling back through the throng, ignoring Ryan's questioning glance, she sat back at the table ready for the ceremony to begin. There was a tower of lilies in the centrepiece; they smelled so sweet, like air freshener and death. The chandeliers were too bright, kaleidoscopic with vibrating light. Ryan swapped places so that he was sitting next to her. He took her hand. 'Are you all right?' he whispered. She nodded. Couldn't speak. Painkillers.

'Ryan Mackinnon! Ryan. Ryan.'

The room was on its feet.

And Ryan on the podium, dedicating the award to her, and the entire room definitely fucking staring at her now, applauding them both, and flashbulbs going off pop-pop inside her skull, and she worried that a stitch was coming loose on her scalp, only they'd been taken out months ago, but scratching at it as if it was really there. And Ryan pleading with her to stand up and take a bow, but she couldn't, which everyone took as modesty and vulnerability, when actually Heather knew if she stood she'd throw up on the lilies. She wasn't anyone's motherfucking muse. She'd earn her own laurels, or she wouldn't. She longed to give them all the finger. And she longed to put her hands over her ears so she couldn't hear his proud speech. And then everyone was congratulating them both, and at last he took her home.

Later that night, as they stood in the kitchen, he looked at her with such sadness and said, 'Did you have to put your fingers in your ears during my speech? What did you think I was going to say?'

And she realised she'd actually done it, not merely thought about it.

'You achieved the peak of your career tonight.' She paused. 'But I wish it wasn't about the end of mine. I wish I could be a better person, and just be proud and selfless, but I'm not.'

And then, they sat side-by-side on the kitchen floor next to his trophy and cried.

The barman set down her coffee and poured a single shot glass of rakia, but left her with the bottle. She tipped a little into her coffee, enjoying the tingle and burn. Then downed the shot. The buzz was almost immediate and she shuddered. She could bear it better this way. Heather closed her eyes. Where the hell was Ryan? And more than that, who was he? The man who stood by her after her accident? The man who used the end of her career to fast-track his own? The man who withdrew wads of cash and met other women while his girlfriend was sleeping? Women he called 'Sweetheart'. Or was he just the man who loved her?

There was a sudden chill in the air. The sun had slipped behind the mountains and the sky was growing dark. Heather realised she had drunk several more shots of plum brandy. She ought to go back to her room and sleep it off. Grovelling around in her rucksack for some cash, she heard the whirr of a bike and as she glanced up saw a silver bike with a yellow stripe rush past – a Roubaix. Ryan's bike. But it wasn't Ryan riding it.

She stood up, clattering her head on the underside of the metal table and knocking over her chair. Unsteady, she peered down the road after the bike, hurtling past in the gloom. She began to chase after it.

'Hey, you, asshole, get back here! That isn't your bike.'

He sped up. She sprinted after it down the darkening street, but it was useless. The rider hunched over the handlebars, stood up on the pedals and was gone in a moment.

She jogged back past the café. She needed to get her bike and she needed to chase down that rider. A burly man stood in her path.

'You pay for drink,' he said.

'Shit.'

Fumbling for her purse, Heather handed him a note and sprinted back towards the hotel. She unlocked her bike, grabbed her helmet and flicked on her lights in the gathering dark. She knew she ought to put on full reflective gear but couldn't risk wasting more time. There was only one road out of Zikoč. It ran for miles before there were any crossroads. If she went right now, she had a good chance of tracking him. She felt dizzy, a cool fury pooling in her belly. Where had he found Ryan's bike? What the hell had happened to him? Had Ryan sold it for even more cash? She took off out of Zikoč at top speed, narrowly missing a car that hooted, the driver swearing at her. She adjusted her helmet, heart hammering wildly, knowing it was a silly near miss that had been entirely her fault. This was exactly when riders made stupid mistakes and got hurt, when they were frantic and desperate to catch up with the race leader – that's how she needed to think of this. Just another race. Nothing more, nothing less. The road was rough and uneven, the unmarked edge sloping down towards a dirty stream filled with discarded plastic drinks, bottles and old tyres. The incline was steep enough to get the blood going and Heather found a steady, even cadence. She was going to have to hope she'd pass the other rider somewhere along the road, and that there weren't too many turnings. There was little chance he was as fast as her.

It was a spring evening, but the cold air spilled down from the mountains, making the lines of sweat along her back tingle. More sweat trickled down her forehead, stinging her eyes. Her mouth tasted revolting, the brandy sharp and nasty on her tongue. She could already sense the hangover brewing. This was not good form to race. Five kilometres. Seven. Eight. The road levelled off and soon she reached the outskirts of a village, skidding to a stop at a T-junction. No sign of the silver bike.

'Shit.'

She kicked at the dirt in fury. Rage pulsed through her. She'd have to guess which way he had gone. She turned left and, as the road descended sharply, instantly regretted the decision. If it was wrong, she'd have to sweat all the way back up here. She passed a small supermarket and a line of parked cars, and dark stone houses on either side of the street, windows flashing with the lights of TVs inside. In a minute she was out of the village and back on a twisting road that ran through a dark valley. The road curved between boulders and cliffs so that the narrow beam of her headlamp never gave more than a ten- or fifteen-yard view of the road. She gave a cry of frustration. But how could she turn back when he might be hidden just beyond the next bend? She filled her lungs and pressed on.

She sliced through the black valley, the huddling trees looming in the darkness, the wind a roar in her ears. The next corner only another fifty yards. She leant into the bend and pedalled hard on the exit. Her legs were starting to burn. She really ought to stop and drink at one of these little brackish streams. But the next turn was just up ahead. The very last one. And as she swept round it, there he was, four hundred yards in front, bent low over the handlebars, bike rocking from side-to-side with the effort of his pedalling.

'Stop!'

She knew it was useless, but it felt good to shout at him. He cycled faster still, hurtling towards the next bend. Heather swore as he vanished round it. There might be another junction or God knows what. She was not going to let him get away again. Blinking sweat out of her eyes, calm certainty descended. She had the total confidence that occasionally swept over her during a race. She flew at the next corner. She'd gained fifty yards, and a long straight stretch uphill through a tightly wooded road lay before them. She had him. Her legs pulled with an absolute power that in other circumstances she would have taken joy in.

A car passed her, headlights flashing, and she was forced to tuck in, losing her line and some of her momentum. The uphill section peaked, and the road turned sharply downhill, its surface becoming patchy and uneven. Ahead, the rider wobbled, and Heather realised he was feeling the press of her pursuit. Heather knew that on a bike her small stature was irrelevant. Being chased was unnerving, machine and rider hunting you down. Furious, she dug in, upping the pace, forcing him faster still, beyond the limits of his ability.

'*Puši kurac!*' he shouted over his shoulder, sensing Heather closing on his back wheel. He took the next corner too quickly and, trying to correct his steering, lost his balance and ploughed screaming into a tree. There was a crunch of metal and bone and then absolute silence. Heather leapt off her bike and stared at him aghast. He lay sprawled on the ground before the tree, his legs twisted in an unnatural position, bleeding profusely from a cut above his eye. He was early twenties, with a snagged front tooth that, as far as Heather could tell, pre-dated his crash. Ryan's bike rested several feet away, wheels spinning and spinning.

For an awful moment she thought the man was dead. She was filled with instant remorse. She'd wanted him to stop so she could ask him questions.

'Why aren't you wearing a helmet?' she yelled. 'Every dickhead wears a helmet.'

He stirred and opened his eyes. He wasn't dead, but he looked like he wanted to kill her. Heather took a step back towards her own bike. He grabbed uselessly at her and tried to stand, but his body was broken. With a whimper, he slumped back down.

She looked at her phone. No signal. Bloody mountains.

'I'll go back to the little village we passed through and get help. I'll send someone.'

He spat. It was mostly blood, but Heather thought there might be a tooth there amongst the earth and pine needles. She circled back to where Ryan's bike lay, scuffed but unbroken. He swore at her when he saw her stoop to pick it up.

'That's not your bike,' she said evenly, with a calm she did not feel. 'I'm taking it with me.'

'Screw you, bitch,' said the man, with a heavy Serbian accent.

'Before I go, I want to know where you got this bike. I know it's stolen.'

He started to shout and swear in Serbian.

'That's fine. I'll just tell the police that you were riding a stolen bike linked to the disappearance of an American tourist.'

The man looked at her with a mixture of anxiety and hatred.

'It. My. Fucking. Bike. You. Crazy.'

Something in his tone made Heather look down at the bike again. Shit. He was right. With creeping horror she saw that the bike was not Ryan's. It was the same silver, the same racing yellow stripe. But it wasn't a Roubaix. If it hadn't been for the brandy, the darkness and her own desperation, she would never have made such an absurd mistake.

She knelt down, filled with remorse. 'I'm so sorry. I'll pay for the damage.' She reached into her rucksack, fumbling for her purse.

'Get away. You dangerous. You crazy,' he said, spitting more blood on the ground. 'Go!' he screamed at her, the whites of his eyes yellow in the moonlight.

'Why did you try and get away?' she asked.

'Because you crazy! You ride like a crazy witch person. You try to run me off the road.'

She had seriously frightened this man and caused a horrible accident. Heather climbed back on her bike. 'I'll fetch help.' She could try and blame it on all sorts of things, but it had been her fault. He was lying there bleeding beneath the tree in the darkness because of her. All power had gone from her legs. It felt like hours before she reached the last village she'd passed through and alerted them in the shop that there had been an accident on the road. She didn't wait for the ambulance, but rode on to Zikoč. It was late when she arrived back at the hotel, shivering from exhaustion, still no closer to finding Ryan.

9

Simo disconnected the phone in frustration. So far no one in the Organised Crime and Drug Unit in Banja Luka would speak to him about the *Petar Petrović* case. He'd called a dozen times, asking if they knew of any gangs who used decapitation and removal of hands and feet as punishments. No one ever seemed to receive his messages; they were out working a case, or the person he needed to talk to wasn't on duty. Simo decided that he'd give it another day or two and then he'd simply drive up there. He would get answers. He wasn't a fan of the unit; they didn't like working with officers in the districts and rarely shared information, insisting that they would never risk compromising one of their tightly protected sources. To Simo it smacked of bullshit. They had less than forty-eight hours to call him back before he showed up.

He accelerated onto the motorway and headed west towards Sarajevo. He turned up the setting on his windscreen wipers. The rain was turning to hail, and yet a shaft of sun peeked between the clouds and a double rainbow spanned the mountains like a championship banner. Simo sighed. He loved this region. There was nowhere in Europe more magnificent. Sometimes, after a little too much brandy, he wondered whether it was the Balkans' beauty that was her problem; that, like Helen of Troy, she drove her countrymen to madness with the need to possess her, to drive out all rivals to her heart. The hatred was such that sometimes he felt he could see it writhing beneath people's skin. Yet there was also tremendous kindness. The hospitality and kinship here were boundless and soul deep. Despite the bloodshed and the brutish past, there was nowhere like this place. He had travelled to other countries, but he was always desperately homesick, missing the smell of the mountains when snow was coming, and of real, strong coffee, but most of all the people. Their generosity and fierce humour.

He was too riled up to go home, and he had another lead to pursue in the Ryan Mackinnon case. Something wasn't right about Heather Bishop. He'd read up all he could about her, and while he felt sorry about what had happened to her – that accident was a grim end to a career still in its prime – he couldn't shake the feeling that she wasn't quite who she pretended to be.

In another hour, he turned off the motorway and onto a mountain road that snuck between a tightly wooded peak on one side and a steep gorge on the other. High above, a bird of prey circled as if not so much hunting as sightseeing. As he turned a corner, he saw two cyclists pedalling up the road ahead. It was only as he got close and overtook them in his car that Simo realised just how fast they were riding. He pulled over at the top of the rise and climbed out to watch. The first rider rushed the hill, the sound of her wheels a furious hornet buzz, and he realised he was witnessing some kind of race. It seemed impossible that the second rider could catch up to the first, who reached the apex and became a benign dot cruising downhill. The evening sunlight spilled warm yellow light that rolled off her helmet as the second rider came at the hill faster and faster. She reached the top and in a second was past Simo in a spray of pebbles. She hurtled downhill, bent low over the handlebars, and it seemed to Simo as if she must take flight. To his astonishment, she was gaining on the leader.

And then just as quickly, the race was over. Side-by-side the riders cruised to a stop, drinking from their water bottles. Simo climbed back into his car and drove down to meet them. They were sharing an energy bar and laughing companionably.

'Who won?' he asked.

The women shrugged. 'It wasn't a race,' said one. 'Just training.'

He introduced himself. 'Inspektor Simo Subotić. Which of you is Jessie Taylor? We spoke on the phone.'

The second woman, whom Simo had watched chase down the first, stepped forward. She wiped her hands down her bib shorts and held one out.

'You want to talk about Heather Bishop?' she said, in a lilting northern accent.

'I do.'

Jessie frowned, impatient. 'Catch you up in ten, Frankie.'

The other rider climbed back on her bike and started to pedal back up the hill. Simo watched her briefly and then turned back to Jessie.

'Do you usually train straight after a tour? Don't you need to rest?'

Jessie shrugged. 'This tour was cancelled after the drugs raid. But we've a bigger race in Switzerland in less than two weeks. This race was only ever about honing our form – mountains here are good. I don't want the trip to be a total waste of time.'

Simo heard the anger in her voice. 'Did anyone approach your team about carrying drugs?'

Jessie's face hardened. 'No one asked me. If they had, I'd have told them to fuck off. This sport is difficult enough for women without this total bullshit. I'm phoning the team lawyer if you want to talk about drugs. I agreed to talk about Heather Bishop, nothing else.'

Simo held up his hands in apology. 'I was interested in your opinion, that's all. It's not even my case. Truly.'

Jessie's scowl softened slightly.

'You and Heather were friends?' he asked.

'No.'

'Colleagues?'

'I was her domestique. She was the team leader and it was my job to make her ride as well as possible, help her win races. She was entitled and ungrateful. Took it as her right to win. The rest of the team didn't matter to her one bit. We were nothing. Garbage. What happened to her was truly awful. I felt really sorry for her, but . . .'

She fell silent and looked at the floor, kicked at the dirt.

'But what?' prompted Simo.

Jessie looked up. 'It wasn't the tragedy that everyone makes out.'

'Not for you,' said Simo. 'You got her place as leader on the team afterwards. It was you who everyone set up to try and win in Rio. Is that the right terminology?'

'More or less.'

'It was a tragedy for Heather. Her career was ruined. You

didn't win a medal. You weren't as good her. She might have won gold.'

Jessie studied Simo with dislike. He didn't mind.

'She was better than me once. Heather at her best was better than me at mine, that's true. But she was far from her best when the truck took her out. It saved her from humiliation at the Olympics. She would have done far worse than me. Everyone's kidding themselves.'

'You really don't like her.'

'I didn't like her before the accident, and afterwards, well – it was like it gave her the excuse to be the person she really was. Angry, vindictive, violent. Afterwards she didn't hide it. Or couldn't.'

'Violent?' asked Simo.

Jessie met his eye. 'Yes. Violent. Heather fucking Bishop is not who people think she is.'

10

Heather woke early, full of remorse and with a brandy hangover pricking behind her eyes. Deciding to cycle it off, hoping that fresh air would exorcise both guilt and nausea, she headed back along the road where Ryan had vanished and searched again, just in case she'd missed anything before.

It was later than she'd hoped as she reached the series of bends where she and Ryan had raced one another for the last time. She freewheeled slowly down from the mountain peak, the sun warm on her back. Was there something, *anything* she might have missed? Though the pinnacle of the mountain high above the road was still capped with snow like a white paper crown, as she descended it was into lush spring, the grass already metamorphosed from frostbitten brown to dew-damp emerald, the hawthorn and wild cherry and apple trees thick with blossom and the early whirr of the bees. Thousands of polka-dot dandelions had sprung up on a green bank of wild meadow, like a child flicking beads of yellow paint. A cuckoo called, and a cool breeze made the tops of the pines nod like drowsy old men.

The air was filled with a rich herbal scent that she couldn't place. She remembered Ryan telling her that up here in the mountains there could be a sudden shift in the weather and snowfall as late as May. She blinked and the road vanished, hidden in layers of frost, the black pines tinselled in snow, the waterfalls frozen in elaborate chandeliers of ice, the world muffled and deadened. She blinked again and the mirage was gone.

She leant into the corner, and as she flew round the next bend saw three police cars with flashing lights parked at the side of the road. They were half blocking the carriageway, pulled in beside an old rockfall. She slowed down and climbed off her bike.

The policemen looked round at her, at first with bemused irritation, but then one in uniform recognised her and muttered something to a younger and more senior officer in plain clothes. He gave a sharp nod and then came over.

'Miss Bishop? Why are you here?' He didn't give her time to answer before continuing. 'This is a crime scene.'

She swallowed, her throat dry. 'What have you found? Is it Ryan?'

He frowned. 'I am sorry, but I am unable to comment.'

'If you've found Ryan, you have to tell me.'

Heather realised that she was shaking. The police officer either didn't notice or pretended not to.

'I'm Chief Inspektor Josif Borisov. It is good to be meeting you, Miss Bishop.'

The world was beginning to swim and she wondered if she might faint, but she needed to know what they had found down in the gorge. She edged closer to the precipice, but the police cars were blocking it and she couldn't see over. Urgent voices drifted up – they had clearly discovered something.

'Come back, Miss Bishop. It is not safe.'

She felt a hand on her arm and shook it off.

'I'm Ryan's partner. I have a right to know if you've found him.'

Josif stared at her, offering nothing.

'Where is Inspektor Simo Subotić?' she demanded.

'Not here. Will you come to the station with me for the little chat?' he asked, with a smile that was not pleasant.

'And if I say no?'

His smile was unwavering. 'I don't think you should say no.'

It was clear from Josif's questioning that they had found something, but he would not tell Heather what.

'You just show up on this piece of road, at exact spot we search. Is very coincidence. I don't like coincidence.'

Heather gritted her teeth. 'I told you. I was just riding the route where I last saw Ryan and I noticed the police cars. I've been out for hours. I was going to pass them at some point.'

'And can you tell me about yesterday? I have complaint here from man who says that you caused accident. You forced him off the road.'

She paused. 'I was stupid. I made a mistake.'

'You done this before, Heather?'

'No! Of course not.' She looked away, feeling a twinge of guilt, and something in her expression must have made him question her denial.

'So, you have done it before?'

'No. Not like that. I was a professional cyclist. Sometimes there are crashes. Sometimes they might arguably have been my fault.'

'You don't like to take responsibility? Huh?'

'I told you, I made a stupid mistake. I'd had a drink, I saw the bike go past and I thought it was Ryan's, and so I followed him. I just wanted to talk and he wouldn't stop.'

Josif laid it out. 'You got drunk and forced him off the road. He fractured his cheek when he hit that tree. He is grateful he only lost tooth.'

'I'm so sorry. I really didn't mean for it to happen.'

'He could press charges.'

Heather felt sick again. It was no more than she deserved.

'He won't. He is a Serb man. He is embarrassed to press charges against a woman. But you committed a crime – you left the scene of an accident.'

'Only to call the ambulance. I had no signal.'

'Then you must wait for it to arrive, or for the police to come. You didn't wait. Suppose they couldn't find him and he'd lost consciousness again? What if he'd died? I'd be arresting you for manslaughter.'

Heather put her head in her hands. 'I'm sorry. You're right. I stopped in the village. Explained exactly where he was. Showed the woman in the shop on the map. I felt so awful and he wanted me to just go, and the shopkeeper said she'd drive straight there and I didn't think.'

She was babbling and distracted by horrific imaginings of what the police had discovered in the gulley on the roadside.

'I might not charge you with leaving the scene of a crime,' said Josif. 'It is a good deal of paperwork. I'm not a fan of paperwork. But only if you are honest with me now.'

'About what?' asked Heather, alarmed.

'Ryan. Why is he here in Srpska?'

'He was following the race. Then we were taking a few days' holiday.'

'And what else?'

She stared at him, confused. 'Please, what's happened to him? Have you found him? Is he okay?' Her voice shook. 'Is he dead?'

Josif studied her coolly. 'We've found what we believe is his bicycle.'

He slid a picture across the table. The frame was twisted, the paintwork scuffed. It had a distinctive yellow stripe.

Heather nodded slowly. 'Yes. It's Ryan's.'

'One minute.' Josif quit the room.

She sat with her head in her hands in the empty interview room. It stank of damp and cigarettes. She wanted to cry but suspected they were watching. Her mouth was dry and she longed for a drink. The nausea grew and the dizziness whirled around her. She felt like she was on a hurtling carousel, unable to get off. None of this felt real. The only thing familiar was the pain in her neck like sharp probing fingers, worse than usual because of this morning's ride on top of yesterday's. She reached into her bag for her bottle of pills and took one. It was hard to swallow without water.

The door opened and Josif returned. She could smell the sharp tang of his aftershave, but that wasn't what made her stomach roll. He was holding a thin sheaf of papers. His head was buried in their contents. Scanning the information, he continued to ignore her as he sat back down and laid the papers before him. She glimpsed an official-looking letterhead.

'We have carried out a preliminary inspection of Ryan Mackinnon's bicycle.' He flicked at the document. 'The damage suggests he had been forced off the road into the gulley. And there are traces of blood, both in the gulley and on the bicycle.' He looked up. 'Anything you'd like to tell us now?'

She barely heard the question; the world had stopped at the word 'blood'. She could see Josif's lips moving, but his words were distant.

'Anything you tell us yourself is better than if we find out.' The final words resounded through her shock. 'You understand?'

'No.' She roused herself. 'I don't understand.' She was frightened, angry. 'I've been saying for days that something has happened to Ryan and none of you would listen.'

'Why did you come to Srpska, Miss Bishop?'

'To surprise my boyfriend!'

'He certainly got a big surprise.'

Abruptly, he left her alone again. Heather sat in the stillness of the interview room. She closed her eyes. They'd discovered blood, but that was all. If they'd found his body they would've told her, wouldn't they? They had his bike, but not Ryan. At least now they believed that something had happened to him. Now perhaps they would try harder to find him. A few minutes later, the door opened again and this time it was Simo who entered.

Heather discovered she was actually grateful to see him.

'Would you like a coffee? Some tea?'

'What I want is to know what you're going to do to find Ryan?'

Josif appeared in the doorway and Simo spoke quietly to him in Serbian. Josif grunted and turned away again.

'He'll get someone to bring you a hot cup of tea. That's what the English drink, isn't it? Especially after a shock.'

Heather said nothing. She glanced at the opaque glass

window. Josif wasn't making her a cup of bloody tea, he was watching her through the glass. Simo sat on the chair opposite. The two men and whoever else was back there were watching her, scrutinising her for the correct response.

'We have confirmation that the blood belongs to a human male. If it is Ryan's, then we must assume he is hurt and there has been some kind of incident. I am very sorry to tell you this.'

She felt light-headed at the thought of Ryan in pain. Alone on the hillside, perhaps just a few feet from her as she'd cycled passed, yelling for him. She'd called him a dick and all manner of names, wondering at first if he was playing some kind of game, when all the while he was in pain, desperate for her to help him. But she couldn't cry, felt nothing, just numb. She focused on the whirr and tick of the tape recorder on the desk, its blinking red light like a robotic eye. Clung to the possibility that it could all yet be okay. Without a body, Simo could still call her tomorrow or the day after and say that they'd found him, gravely injured at a hospital in Sarajevo or Pale.

'Drink this. It will help,' said Simo not unkindly, pushing a mug towards her.

She hadn't noticed them come back in with the tea. The white mug was chipped, with a caricature of a policeman and a couple of lines in a language she presumed was Serbian. It probably read 'World's Greatest Cop'. She took the mug with shaking hands, and sipped the hot, sweet tea. It tasted revolting but it did make her feel a little better.

'You're supposed to tell me it's not my fault,' she said.

'I'm not your mother. I'm a police officer,' replied Simo.

'First you tell me that it's nothing. That he's left me and

that's all in my head, and now you tell me that I'm guilty of something.'

'No. I've said from the beginning that I think you and Mr Mackinnon are hiding things. You are people with secrets. I'm not interested in secrets. But when crimes are committed in my jurisdiction, then, even though it annoys me, I need to find out what you are hiding.'

'I'm not hiding anything.'

'That's not true, Heather.' He paused. 'Talk to me about Ryan. Tell me about your relationship. People in the café said you were fighting.'

Heather started to object, but Simo held up his hand. 'I know. You say that wasn't true, but I've been talking to people and they say that you've got a temper.'

People? Who had he been talking to? She felt her colour rise at the offence, but bit her tongue in an effort not to prove his point.

'I'm sorry, but I need to ask. Heather, did you ever get angry with Ryan?'

'No. I wouldn't.'

'That's not true. Of course you got angry. He got his career break writing about you. How could you be fine with that?'

She shrugged. 'It was a long time ago.'

'That's not what I asked.'

'I told him it was okay.'

'Again, that was not the question. Did you like him writing publicly about the end of your career? It must have been humiliating for you.'

'What happened to me was an accident. It wasn't humiliating, it was sad.'

'He wrote about coming to see you and your colostomy bag leaking. I think that was pretty humiliating.'

'It was fine,' said Heather, looking at the floor.

'I don't think it's fine. I think it's exploitative. He wrote a regular column about you in a Sunday newspaper, about living with someone recovering from a traumatic brain injury. He built up quite a following. Especially amongst women. I've seen some of the comments on the articles. They weren't exactly sympathetic towards you. They were all about Ryan. Propositions, I'd call them. It must have annoyed you. It would have annoyed me. No, it would have disgusted me.'

'He thought those women were ridiculous. He asked the paper to switch off the comments.'

'So, they did upset you.'

'He was worried that they might. He loves me. I love him.'

'Okay. But sometimes we love people and are also very angry with them. I think you had resentment towards Ryan. From where I'm sitting, it looks like he used you.'

Heather said nothing. Had he used her when he wrote the articles? He swore that he hadn't. It was years ago. Did it even matter now?

'No relationship is perfect, Inspektor. He wrote some things about me, which, yes, perhaps I'd prefer he hadn't. But he did. And I forgave him. He's a good man, not a perfect one. God knows, I'm not perfect either. He forgives me too.'

'How aren't you perfect, Heather? What does he need to forgive you for?'

'It's a figure of speech.'

'You fight a lot, don't you?'

'All couples fight.'

'I don't know. My wife and I fought a lot. And then we divorced.'

Heather stared up at him through red-rimmed lids.

'He meets women when you sleep, but you insist everything is okay. I say that is not okay, Heather. It's not healthy.'

Heather wanted to tell him that he was wrong, that his version of them was skewed and mutated, a ghastly misreading, but when she tried to speak her tongue was a fat piece of Velcro stuck to the roof of her mouth and her thoughts were loose and strange. She was desperate to cling to her vision of them as a couple; she was terrified for Ryan, and the thought of his pain and the blood, so much blood, was a red stain trickling through her vision. And yet, there was a tiny bright seam of anger and uncertainty like a gleam of marble in granite. She needed to keep it together. She met Simo's eye then looked away.

'You are not okay, Heather.'

'It's been a rough few days. I didn't mean for yesterday to happen.'

'Of course not. And is that what happened to Ryan? Something that you didn't mean to happen? You were angry with him. You have a lot to be angry with him about, and so you cycled close to the edge of the road, pushed him, he skidded . . . and you didn't mean for it to happen.'

'No! That's absurd.'

'Is it? It's what happened yesterday. That man is lucky to have got away with a fractured cheekbone. You're a professional racer and you know how to use a bike as a weapon, don't you, Heather?'

'Stop it!' she snapped, and took a breath in an attempt to

muster some composure. 'I told your boss earlier. I'm sorry about yesterday. So sorry. It was stupid. But it doesn't mean that I hurt Ryan.'

Simo looked at her steadily, not giving away whether or not he believed her. 'Tell me about your accident. It was a petrol tanker?'

'I don't like to talk about it.' Heather sat back in the chair and folded her arms. The pain in her neck was throbbing, flaming along the damaged nerves. It was hard to focus her thoughts. She reached for her bag and took out the bottle of pills and started to unfasten it, until she remembered she'd already taken one earlier and began to put it away.

'May I?' said Simo, reaching for the bottle.

Heather handed it to him. 'Painkillers.'

Simo put on his spectacles and read the label. 'And you take these for?'

'Nerve pain,' she answered, defensively and by rote. 'I damaged the nerves in my neck in the accident.'

Simo returned the bottle. 'That sounds awful. I am sorry you suffer so much. But these pills, they are not for nerve pain. They are not painkillers of any kind. They are anti-depressants with an antipsychotic effect.'

'They're not. It's just the pain makes me depressed and anxious.'

'You can lie to whoever else you want, but you and I know better, Heather.'

Simo quietly took out his phone and typed in the drug name, and slid it across the table to Heather, showing her the search results.

Aripiprazole: an antipsychotic drug used in the treatment of resistant depression with schizoid symptoms. Side effects include headaches, shortness of breath, night sweats, nausea, dryness of the mouth . . .

She looked away and shoved the phone back at him.

'I get anxious. That's all.'

'No,' said Simo, quietly. 'Aripiprazole is not for nxiety. This is not a prescription for anti-anxiety medication. You have to stop lying, Heather. I understand that people who have been through trauma do all sorts of things to survive. I am sorry that you had to lie to Ryan about your medication, but you do not need to lie to me.' He paused and forced her to meet his eye. 'You *must not* lie to me.'

She reached for the cup again but fumbled it, sloshing tea over the table. She swore. Met Simo's kind but dogged gaze. 'I'm sorry I lied to you about them. I'm used to lying to Ryan. He worries when I take antidepressants. His fretting makes it worse. He hovers. I feel sometimes like he's there just waiting for me to fuck up again, so it's easier to tell him that they're painkillers.'

Simo studied her. 'But they have an antipsychotic element too.'

She said nothing for a moment, knowing how her next words could seem, but she had already gone too far. She had no choice. 'When the depression gets bad, I can hear voices.'

Simo sat back. A small gesture, but one that signalled to Heather he'd made a breakthrough.

'Do they tell you to do things? To hurt yourself? To hurt others?'

'No! Mostly they just talk about me. It's like overhearing voices on the radio.'

Simo regarded her with great sympathy. 'I very much want to believe you.'

The door reopened and Josif entered and stood silently at the back of the room. She ignored him.

'Can you tell me about the fight with Jessie Taylor?' continued Simo.

What the hell did she have to do with any of this?

Simo slid out a typed document from the file on the table. 'I have some information here, but I would like to hear you tell it.'

Heather stared at him. 'I mean, we bickered, we didn't get on. She was my domestique in the British cycling squad. We barely spoke.'

'You put her in the hospital. The summer after the Rio Olympics,' said Josif from the back of the room.

That was ridiculous. 'I did not.'

Simo turned round the file and showed Heather a typed statement from the Metropolitan Police, complete with her signature. 'This is you?'

Heather read through the statement, which described how she had thrown a bottle at Jessie Taylor in a bar, after she had seen Jessie laughing at her. She gazed down at the document in utter bewilderment and then up at Simo.

'How did you get that?'

'And see here, there are these pictures,' said Josif, stepping forward and producing photographs of Jessie with a nasty black eye and cuts and bruises to her left cheek. He placed them on the table in front of Heather. She stared at them in horror. Josif leant back against the wall, arms folded, and surveyed her with apparent disgust.

'I swear to you I don't remember doing that.'

Heather sat back, bile rising, slick with sweat, unable to look at the photos. 'I was going through a lot of stuff at that time. It was just after my accident. I honestly don't remember. I'm not lying to you. Not now,' she said, a lump rising in her throat and choking her.

Simo nodded, not unkindly. 'That's okay. It's here, in the report. No charges were brought. The police officer who interviewed you says that soon after the incident you had very patchy recollection of the crime. Recent massive head trauma. T.B.I. Traumatic brain injury. No realistic chance of conviction. Jessie Taylor didn't want to press charges. She felt sorry for you.'

Heather put her head in her hands.

'Do you still forget things, Heather? Do you still lie about that?'

'Jesus. I'm not lying! Why would I remember it! I have gaps from the time after the accident. And I have trouble with my short-term memory. Small things. Appointments. Where I put things. Faces.'

'It's more than that. You lied to me about the pills. Lying to the police is an offence. Ryan was here in the nineties, but you can't be certain exactly what he said. Are you sure Ryan never told you about this woman he calls *Dušica*? You committed a serious assault on Jessie Taylor. If she hadn't been so generous and sympathetic, you could have been sent to prison. You repressed the memory. Some things you simply lie about . . .' He paused and then gave a sad shake of his head. 'But I also worry that you have no idea what things you have done and then forgotten.' He pushed the pictures of Jessie's battered face towards her. 'Heather, I cannot be certain that you didn't kill Ryan. Can you?'

She stood rooted in the square, listening to the thrum of traffic. It wasn't true. Couldn't be. And they'd released her – not enough evidence to hold her any longer. Nonetheless, she began to run, desperate to get far from the police station, running until she found herself on the bridge with its curving arches. It was dark and the lights from a dozen lanterns pooled on the bridge, lemony yellow in a glittering arc. It looked so pretty, the foaming water just catching the light as it rushed beneath, the bubbles blinking into stars. Yet Heather could sense the ghosts as they fell, shot from the bridge, their cries mingling with the burbling of the Drina, the blue water turning red then black. Its beauty was an affront. She could ease herself out onto the balustrade and disappear into the surge and all this would be over. The rhythm of the water grinding against the stones was hypnotic. It was only a small jump. She was many things, but a coward was not one of them, and that was a coward's way out. And it galled her to think that if she jumped then they'd all take it as an admission of guilt.

'I did not do this,' she said aloud, hoping as much as believing that it was not true.

Of course you didn't, said a familiar voice in her head. *You'd never do that.*

She closed her eyes and took a deep breath, focusing on the present. She tried to block out the photograph of Jessie with ten crusting stitches along the side of her face. It was true that yesterday – albeit by accident – she had forced a stranger off the road, so that he'd fractured his cheek. The pure fury that had driven her to chase him down had overwhelmed her. Even now the police were considering pressing charges. Calamity stalked her. She had spent days wondering who

Ryan was; the man she'd been living with for years, who'd been keeping secret after secret. But with a jolt of self-doubt she realised, too, that now she needed to ask: who the hell was she?

No. She reprimanded herself. They were playing mind games. She'd raced enough to know that those who won did not succumb to the mind games of lesser riders. And that's what this was: a manoeuvre. She might not understand the motivation, or why the police wanted her in pieces at the kerbside, but she recognised the signs – they were behaving no differently to one of the losing teams pulling desperate and dubious tactics in the last stage of a Grand Tour. She would not let them get inside her head. She must not let them. If she couldn't hold onto her sense of self, then she was lost, and so was Ryan.

A wave of nausea hit her with the force of a punch to the stomach, and she dashed over to a litter bin and vomited. She'd refused Simo's offer to drive her back to Zikoč. She had to get out of this creepy town, with its leering statues and the Disney-esque façade that masked its grotesque past. It was the place that was making her crazy; some inverted netherworld, the beauty of which belied the reality. But she couldn't face the long bike ride back to Zikoč and she couldn't stay here. She pulled out her phone. A few minutes' search on TripAdvisor suggested her best bet was a spa hotel in the hills, a little way out. Shivering with cold and exhaustion, she hurried over to the taxi office in the main street, wondering again at the uncanny emptiness of the town. After a brief wait, a driver was found, willing to take her and her bike the short distance to the hotel.

The journey to the Vilina Vlas Spa was short but it took

her up into the mountain and into the woods. The serpentine road was a paring of bone, white between the black forests on either side. The moon was a blown bubble bobbing above them. They turned off the road and onto a long winding track, leading further into the trees. Where on earth was this hotel? Perhaps she ought to have gone back to bloody Zikoč with Simo. She stared out the window, glimpsing a pair of yellow eyes and a flash of movement in the trees. She gave an involuntary, feral shudder. The track leading to the hotel was surprisingly smooth and well maintained, and the driver pulled up and let her out in front of an ugly modern building with a red roof.

'Hotel,' he said helpfully.

When he made no effort to help her to remove her bike from the car, she did it herself. Heather watched the taxi drive away, fighting an odd urge to wave him back and ask him to take her on to the grotty motel in Zikoč. She listened for the sound of the engine as it grew fainter and fainter, until there was nothing but the stirring of the leaves and the night-time tick and shuffle of the woods. It was very still, but beneath the stillness was a buzz, almost electric. It was the same feeling that Heather had had when she stood on the bridge in Višegrad. She'd come here to get away from that dread, but it had chased her down. Though, after everything that had happened, she had to acknowledge that she was probably carrying it with her. The dread and shock of Ryan's vanishing had seeped into her consciousness, poisoning her thoughts. She chained up her bike in a rack at the side of the hotel, shouldered her saddle-bag and pushed open the door into the lobby.

At first she thought the reception was deserted, and then

a slightly surprised man appeared with a broad smile. He greeted her in Serbian.

'English, I'm afraid,' said Heather.

'Wonderful. So very good,' he said. 'You have very good stay here. We have nice pool. You have massage if you like. You looking tired.'

'I am,' agreed Heather, handing over her credit card and passport with relief.

'You hungry? We have restaurant,' said the man.

Heather shook her head. She craved quiet. A silent room to be alone and think about Ryan. If he was dead, please don't let him have suffered. The man reached for a key and gestured for her to follow. The hotel lobby had been recently re-carpeted and the walls papered in a shiny fleur-de-lis, while banal and soothing prints of waterfalls and lily ponds of the sort beloved of doctor's surgeries adorned the walls. As they went up the stairs, she noticed that the carpets were worn and threadbare and there was the distinctive smell of damp. The walls had been repainted, but the old flowered paper showed through like phantom roses.

'The view is very nice from this floor. Is dark now, but in the morning, you see view of river and woods. Everybody like.'

He unlocked the door and with a proud conjurer's wave gestured Heather into a dank, musty room that did not deserve the build-up. He turned on the light and it flickered orange, a moth thudding dismally against the shade.

'Bath with shower through that door,' he said. 'Towels are included in price.'

Heather realised she hadn't thought to ask the room rate and also that she did not care. She just wanted him to leave.

'Thank you,' she said and closed the door. There were twin beds, and floor-length curtains fluttered before the black windows. She hurried over to close them, noticing that the windows opened onto some sort of balcony. The familiar fingers of pain probed her neck and a wave of anxiety crested and broke in cold ripples down her back. She reached in her bag for the bottle of pills, then with an exclamation of fury grabbed the bottle and hurried into the bathroom. She unscrewed the lid, tipped the contents down the toilet and flushed them away.

She sat back on the cold tiled floor and tried to recall her conversations with the various doctors. She had suffered a brain contusion and had a metal plate in her skull. There had been personality changes. She knew she was more irritable than she used to be, but the assault on Jessie had come relatively soon after the accident and had been a one-off. Hadn't it? It was a terrible thing she'd done and she'd pushed the trauma of it to the deepest recesses of her mind. And yesterday *was* an accident.

Heather knew that most brain injury patients suffered degrees of short-term memory loss. She had all sorts of tricks for coping with hers. The flat had to be tidy, but she could never remember which drawer was forks and which was takeaway menus. Her counsellor had told her that depression was a common symptom after a brain injury, both the trauma and the unwelcome changes to her life and career triggering mood changes. Then there were the voices. The ones telling her she was worthless and useless and good for nothing. But she knew they were in her head. Like she'd told Simo, sometimes she thought she overheard them talking about her on the radio. Occasionally, just to complicate things, the radio really did talk about her. She was a public figure of national pity. She swore aloud, her own voice startling her in the silence. She would not fall apart – she was tougher than they all thought. Part of being an elite athlete was physical fitness, and hell, she was far from her peak – older, with bones that had been broken and imperfectly healed, she would never reach her optimal fitness again – yet she had remarkable stamina. She was relentless: she never, ever gave up. Her former colleagues made snide remarks when they'd thought she couldn't hear – that she was part robot, an automaton – and while an element of that stamina was physical it was also mental tenacity. Heather Bishop was stubborn beyond all reason. However much they tried to persuade her that she was crazy, she would not let them. She would fight back by reminding herself what was real, even as the world unmade itself all around her.

She stripped off her clothes and took a long shower, trying to scrub the horror of the day from her skin with her nails. As the water coursed over her body she thought back to the first evening with Ryan, the look of horror on his face when he'd opened the door to her. She hadn't imagined it. Afterwards they'd been out for dinner and fucked and planned cycle routes and she'd taken it all for granted. And she had not known that he'd been lying to her. About *Dušica*. Nightmares. And who knew what else? She was not good with uncertainty. But there was one thing of which she was sure.

'I did not hurt him.'

She would not live on quicksand. She sank to her knees in the tub and let the hot water cascade over her as she wept, washing away her tears as quickly as they fell. Eventually, trembling with exhaustion, she climbed out of the shower and wrapped herself in one of the hotel's scanty complimentary towels, then collapsed onto the bed and fell asleep.

She woke with someone's hand over her mouth, pinning her to the bed with his legs. She couldn't breathe, and was dimly aware of a frantic hammering, then realised it was her own heart. She thought she was going to die.

'I let go but you don't scream,' said a man's muffled voice. He knelt over her, his face shadowed. 'You scream and I kill you. Okay?'

Heather nodded and he removed his hand, giving her a better look at him. His face was maimed and oddly shaped. Despite her promise, she drew a gulped breath and was about to scream when she felt his hand clamp down over her mouth again.

'No, no. Bad girl,' he said, leaning over her, his face inches away from hers so that she could feel the heat and fetid onion stink of his breath. 'This is bad place for you. You get out here. You need to leave Republika Srpska. You not want to end up like Ryan.'

If the man had hoped to intimidate her, he'd misjudged his victim. At the mention of Ryan, her fear was overwhelmed and she was filled with savage rage. He relaxed for a moment, and in that instant Heather shoved him off her and half leapt, half fell off the bed. He was back on her in a second, but this time her hands were free and she yanked his hair, snatching at his horrible deformed face, realising as she ripped at his skin that he was wearing a rubber mask. She tore it away so that she saw his face in the gloom. Still struggling, her fingernails raked across his face, drawing blood. He cried out in pain and fury, pushed her roughly back down onto the bed, grabbed a pillow and pressed it into her face. She tried to scream, drowning in panic, but she had no air. All she could feel was the burning in her lungs, the fire, the rasping, scolding pain. This is how Ryan died, she thought. I am about to die like him. Even as she fought against it, frantically swimming through nausea and layers of fog, she felt her eyes close and darkness enfold her in a deep embrace.

When she woke again, she was alone in bed, tucked in tenderly, the pillow resting neatly beneath her head. Her attacker had gone. There was no evidence that he had ever been here, other than the dread from last night, which stayed with her, sticky and foul like a stench across her skin. She stared out of the window through open curtains, which she was almost certain she had closed the night before. The door to the balcony was ajar. She *knew* that had been shut. Beyond lay the view of the forest promised by the hotel receptionist last night. Daybreak was bleeding into the edge of the trees. The balcony door knocked against the sill. It gave a steady tap-tap in the rising breeze, which filled the room with the scent of pine and the reedy cry of the forest birds calling out the dawn.

11

Simo decided that Josif must be preoccupied with the election. Flyers had appeared all over the city and lately he'd found the chief pacing his office, practising speeches. But the biggest clue to his political ambitions came when he'd discovered Heather had been released from custody. Josif rounded on Simo, berating him for jeopardising what had the makings of a high-profile conviction, but Simo remained adamant: unless Josif wanted to charge her with the hit-and-run on the Serbian cyclist, they had to let her go. Regarding Ryan Mackinnon: yes, they had his bloodied bike, but beyond that there was no evidence of a crime, let alone Heather's involvement. Until a body showed up, there was little more they could do for now.

Josif had grunted his acceptance of the situation, and Simo had been congratulating himself for playing it straight right up until the moment he'd called Heather's hotel to check that she'd arrived okay, only to discover that she wasn't there. He phoned back several times, but the answer was always the same. He cursed her. He'd explained in the clearest terms that her release was conditional – she had to inform him where she was staying. He'd tried her phone only to find it turned off. No surprise. Now he was angry enough to arrest her, when she did turn up.

Simo's blood pressure was raised thanks to Heather, and the silence from the Organised Crime and Drugs Unit regarding the *Petar Petrović* wasn't helping either. Since, for the moment, he could affect only one of those factors, he decided to speak to them in person.

It was a long drive and he arrived in Banja Luka late and tired, a caffeine headache humming at his temples. In the parking lot, cars twinkled with frost under the street lamps. So much for spring. He hurried into the station, out of the cold, and gave his name to a surprised desk sergeant. The place was quiet at this time – the elite unit didn't deal with the mundane drunks and domestic fights that filled every other station.

The sergeant ambled over. 'Everyone's busy.'

'Everyone?'

'Yeah.'

Simo held up a finger and made a phone call. 'Chief, I'm in Banja Luka. No bastard in the Organised Crime and Drugs squad will talk to me.'

'Give me half an hour,' said Josif. 'Anything else?'

'Yes,' said Simo. He'd had time to reflect on the case during the long drive, mulling over the details. The miles of empty road were conducive to making connections. 'Your interest in the case is bothering me. No offence, chief, but you're never this helpful.'

'A lesser man would take that as an insult,' Josif replied with an amused snort.

'The bodies we pulled from the Drina all have the signature of gang torture. Everyone, including you, believes it's your father's gang.'

'Subotić, is there a point to this, apart from your usual insubordination?'

'I'm getting there, chief,' said Simo, amiably. 'Is it possible that it wasn't Drakulić's crew but a rival gang that dropped the bodies?' There was a confirming silence from Josif's end of the call. Simo took it as an open invitation and pushed his luck. 'Someone else is muscling in on his territory. I think far from believing your father is responsible, the truth is you're frightened for him. That's why you're all over this.'

Josif swore, shouted at him and hung up. But, Simo noted, he didn't deny it.

Simo found a seat, but just as he was contemplating a nap a young officer strolled across. 'Subotić?'

Simo looked up and sighed inwardly. He'd been fobbed off with the youngest, most junior of the unit. However, they were often the ones easiest to persuade to help in the end.

The officer held out his hand. 'Inspektor Dalibor,' he said. 'I'm sorry you came all this way. We do have phones.'

'Yes, but you don't answer them.'

'Come.'

Simo followed him up the stairs to the first floor. The office had the same dreary grey décor and worn lino as every other police station. There was even the identical photograph of the bridge at Višegrad. Dalibor waved him into the smallest cubicle where Simo quickly outlined the *Petar Petrović* killing and the details of the mutilations.

'I'm wondering if it could be tied to the drug gangs. Have you seen this kind of mutilation before?'

Dalibor peered at the photographs. 'I've seen decapitation before but not like your M.O. The killings I saw were clearly linked to gang violence, the bodies left out in the houses of the deceased for show, not disposed of in a river.' He handed the pictures back to Simo and turned to the autopsy report.

'He died just before the raid on the Balkan cycling race,' said Simo. 'I think it's possible his death is connected. Did your team have anything to do with the raid?'

Dalibor continued to scan the report. 'Why the interest, Inspektor?'

'I was there.'

He glanced up, raising an eyebrow. 'Really? I had it on good authority it was nothing to do with you, and I'm not to discuss any details.'

Simo had been hoping to persuade Dalibor to say more than he ought. 'Come on, don't send a tired old man back down that road empty-handed.'

Dalibor sighed and put aside the report. 'We received a tip from an informant that we passed on to local law enforcement. Cocaine worth two million marks was seized at the race. Someone will be very annoyed about their lost business.'

'Dragan Drakulić? That's what Josif Borisov claims to think. But,' – Simo shrugged in frustration – 'I can't pursue any leads properly until I've identified the victim.'

'I didn't think the cycling raid was your case, Subotić. Your chief said on the phone you wanted to talk about bodies in the Drina.'

'The raid isn't, but if they're connected then it becomes my case.'

Dalibor said nothing, apparently unpersuaded.

'Tell me about the tip-off,' pressed Simo. 'Your informant might know my victim.' He tried to read Dalibor's expression. 'Is your informant my victim?'

The young man smiled serenely. 'You know I can't discuss it. We have to protect our sources here.'

'You can't protect him if he's dead. I take it he's not then.'

Dalibor sat still, silent and inscrutable.

Simo swore in exasperation, '*Djubre jedno,* I'm investigating a murder.'

'Yes, but not my drugs case. You have no evidence that they're connected. You just think they might be because the timing *sort of* fits and the signs of torture and mutilation *might possibly* match those used by the gangs.'

Simo felt a mixture of anger and fatigue. He hadn't driven for hours to be patronised by this smug greenhorn. 'I've spent days trawling through the missing person files, trying to identify the victim. But I don't think he's there. No one noticed or cared enough to report my *Petar Petrović* missing. And if I don't identify him, find out who did this to him, then he becomes yet another soul who vanished.'

Dalibor stared at Simo. 'They told us about you in recruit training.' He considered for a long moment. 'Take a drive with me. I need to visit a source in Sarajevo. We're not supposed to operate across the border, but I don't imagine that bothers you?'

Simo tailed Dalibor to the outskirts of Sarajevo, where he pulled into a fuel station car park. In the face of Simo's plea, Dalibor had relented and was taking him to meet an informant that ran with the gang busted in the raid at the women's cycling race. A truck flashed its lights once, and Dalibor exited his car into the pouring rain, dashing across the wet car park and into the cab. Simo stayed put, waiting for the signal. Dalibor was meeting an informant – a class of criminal not known for their eagerness to expose their identity to more cops than strictly necessary. He'd take a measure of persuasion to meet Simo.

The headlights flashed again. Maybe this road trip wasn't going to be a waste of time, after all. Simo left the warmth of the car, dodging puddles as he made his way over to the truck and climbed into the front seat beside the young officer. The cab stank of stale sweat and cigarettes. A man sat in the back seat in the gloom, smoking. Simo knew the drill – no direct eye contact with the informant. He sat and looked forward.

'Erik has agreed to answer your questions.'

'Erik' grunted and rolled another cigarette. The name, Simo figured, no doubt a pseudonym. 'I'm investigating a murder in Srpska,' Simo began. 'Victim was found without head, hands or feet. What do you know about that?'

The informant shrugged. 'Goalkeeper for Partizan FC?'

Erik was a comedian. Great.

'If it was us, I've heard nothing. And I would have, for sure.'

Simo looked at Dalibor, who nodded as if to say, yes, it was likely that Erik would indeed know.

'Anyone missing from your crew? I want to identify the victim. I don't care who he is, or what he's done. Everyone deserves justice.'

Erik rustled his cigarette paper and laughed. 'I'm sure you say that to all the boys. The justice bit. It's nice.' He paused. 'There's no one missing. I'm telling you, he isn't one of ours.'

Simo broke with protocol and turned around to look right at Erik. 'I think you know who my *Petar Petrović* is.'

That was enough for the informant. 'Dalibor, we're done. Get out my truck. I don't know anything.'

Simo tried one last shot. 'It would have been about two weeks before the race. Anything you can tell me? I'll owe you a favour, and I'm a useful man to have in your debt.'

Erik laughed. 'He's a tenacious *puši kurac*.'

'We were all warned about him as recruits,' said Dalibor. 'Pursues the truth regardless of the cost to him or anyone. It's why he's been relegated to *Vukojèbina*.'

Erik howled like a wolf and made an obscene gesture but nonetheless surveyed Simo sharply, apparently weighing up whether he was a friend worth having.

'Okay, Saint Platon,' said Erik, referencing a local saint. 'I'll give you something. Couple of weeks ago, after one of the races near here, I was minding my own business, quietly selling coke and speed to journos, when one of them asked me for something a bit special.'

'Heroin?' Dalibor interjected, and Simo wished he'd keep his mouth shut and let the other man speak.

'A gun.'

Simo sat up sharply. 'Who was the buyer?'

'A girl. And some American.'

'Can you describe them?'

'The girl was some *kurvac*. Seen her around. Red hair. I think he called her Rubi. And the American was tall. Jittery as fuck.'

'What kind of gun did he want?'

'He didn't care, so long as it was something without much recoil. I gave him a Ruger .38.'

'Do you know what he wanted it for?'

Erik shrugged, growing impatient. 'Scared of the bogeyman? All I know is he was willing to pay top dollar.'

Simo considered for a moment. Was this what Ryan had

withdrawn the three thousand dollars for? 'Did you recognise the American? Was he involved with your crew in running the coke in the women's bike race?'

Simo could tell that with this question he'd overstepped. Erik's face showed panic that he'd said more than he ought to and landed himself in shit. He leaned forward past the detective and opened the truck door. 'That shit's above my paygrade. I didn't know him, man. *Jeb'o ti pas mater.* Never seen him before . . . can't remember nothing else. Need to take a leak. Be gone when I'm back.' He slipped out into the rain.

Dalibor walked Simo back to his car. 'He's a *yedno* but he's telling the truth. The body isn't someone in his crew. And, Subotić, the victim is also not my snitch. You'll have to take my word for that. I don't know anything about this woman Rubi. She's new to me.' He looked at Simo through the rain. 'You also looking for an American?'

'You heard if an American's involved in the bike race racket?'

Dalibor shook his head. 'Not a word. But, Subotić, I did hear that the bike racket is not your case.'

Simo drove back to Višegrad, the rain battering the windscreen, the wipers squealing horribly. The American had to be Ryan Mackinnon. He was scared of something, scared enough to buy a gun, and Erik had supplied him with a Ruger .38. It was a revolver, built like a tank, but relatively easy to handle for someone not used to firearms, which cast doubt on another part of Ryan's story. When Heather had said he came out here with the U.S. military as part of the U.N., Simo had harboured doubts. Now he was certain.

Simo considered how Ryan might be involved in the Balkan race scandal. Plenty of people progressed from wartime careers moving drugs and guns to peacetime ones doing the same. The routes even remained the same. During the war, guns had come from Russia and the Middle East and it had been simple – the smugglers kept a third of the weapons as payment, and used them to fight. After the war, they wanted payment in cash instead of guns, but the trade carried on. While Simo knew of countless drug and gun traffickers who had expanded their portfolios to include stolen cars and trafficked women, as well as corrupting politicians and the police who facilitated the deals, he'd not heard rumours of a journalist joining the trade. Cycling journalists moved around a lot, all across Europe. It was perfect cover. However, if Ryan was involved, he was also very naïve, wildly overpaying for a gun when he took fright. Something was off.

12

Simo was woken by the phone ringing. He cursed as he picked up, having managed just a few hours' sleep since yesterday's lengthy round trip. It was Jenny Fraser.

'Come to the Ristić farm at Lake Perućac.'

'Can it wait till morning?'

'It is morning. Just.'

A bleary-eyed Simo arrived in the murk of dawn and drove past a smattering of media stationed outside the gate, mostly local, but he noted one or two from Banja Luka. If the dozen bodies Jenny had found so far turned out to be two dozen or even more, then this lot would be joined by more reporters from all across Serbia and Bosnia. They always seemed to find out about the graves, even before he did. Like teenagers on the scent of a parent-free party, the media and demonstrators turned up the moment the first finger bone was unearthed. The forensics war crimes team were invariably discreet – Jenny Fraser ran a tight ship – although the blue tents did rather give the game away.

A lone cop stood guard on the gate. The solitary sentry looked lax to Simo, almost an afterthought, and he decided that he would arrange for another to join him. The Bosniaks and family members of the missing were understandably appalled that the graves had lain hidden for so long, and, they assumed, common knowledge amongst the local Serbs, whom they viewed in the very least as complicit in the murders. Meanwhile, the Serb majority objected loudly and publicly to what they complained was slander – they knew nothing about the murders. Who was to say that the bodies were Muslim Bosniaks and not, in fact, Serbs buried in the mud? Simo found all the posturing infuriating and insulting. It was extremely unlikely the bodies were Serbs, and almost certainly those of the Bosniaks who'd disappeared twenty-odd years earlier, during the war. Somehow, victory wasn't enough for some; now they wanted to rewrite the history of the dead too, reclaim their bodies, erase the Muslim names from the memorials and carve Serb names there instead. They wanted to be both victors and victims, a stance that frankly baffled Simo. Some fellow Serbs agreed with him, although it was an unpopular and even dangerous public point of view. It made you liable for more than demotion. At the last mass grave he'd attended, Simo recalled the Serbian digger driver helping the task force with the site excavation. The man had pretended to family and neighbours that he was working on a building project forty miles in the opposite direction, and had set off from home and driven fifteen miles the wrong way before surreptitiously turning around and heading to the site.

The yard reeked with a raw animal smell of dung, silage and rotting straw. Drizzle was falling, turning the mud into a runny and glutinous paste that welded itself to Simo's office shoes in clumps, making them heavy. He tried to shake it off but only succeeded in spattering his trousers. Pausing outside the farmhouse, he glanced up to see the pale face of a woman he took to be old Mrs Ristić peering out of an upstairs window. She conveyed a look of withering dislike at the village of tents erected around her farmyard. The task force had offered them a flat in town, but they'd refused to move, declining to speak with the investigators. Mrs Ristić had also declined to let the forensic team use the bathroom, so until the portable toilets arrived they were reduced to peeing in the woods.

Simo walked slowly towards a corrugated barn that stood beside a stagnant green pond. A mortuary had been set up inside, and that's where he'd find Jenny. A guard stationed outside the barn spotted Simo's badge and opened the door for him.

Lights had been strung up from the rafters but Simo didn't turn them on, not yet. The stillness calmed him. There was no smell, only a faint scent of earth and the damp of the barn and the scuffle of the wind against the corrugated roof. Several shapes were laid out on makeshift tables beneath sheets: a femur, a skull. Judging from their current proximity to one another, Simo figured they may or may not end up belonging to the same cadaver. He never forgot that these scattered and mixed bones waiting to be sieved had once been people. They had been loved and were grieved for every day. To be able to identify and reunite these bodies with their sons or daughters or parents was a gift, however sad, for which Simo was grateful. People needed a grave to rest flowers against, otherwise they remained lost too, a part of them forever wandering through the roads and forests, calling out the names of the dead. He listened to the knock-knocking of the wind, which creaked the ironwork of the roof.

'Jenny?' he called, but no one answered. Unnerved amongst the dead, his hand moved automatically to the Glock at his hip. No one answered but the wind and a finger of ivy tap-tapping against the window. He closed his eyes and murmured a prayer from his own Orthodox liturgy and then a prayer from the Koran, and then began a Calvinist hymn that Jenny Fraser had taught him. Her grandmother had taught it to her, and she always recited the hymn in the mortuary at the start of each day. Surrounded by the evidence of man's wickedness and viciousness, she said that she needed to remember the goodness of humanity. Simo only needed to think of Jenny and of how a person would give up time with her own kids to identify the dead, in order to bring peace to some and justice to others. He felt a presence at his shoulder and then Jenny's Scottish voice joined with his own. When they'd finished, she clapped him roughly on the shoulder.

'You do that when I'm not here?' she said, touched.

He shrugged. These souls had lain in the dark long enough. Simo saw spread out on a tray at Jenny's feet the tiny phalanges from several fingers as small and fragile as the bones of a thrush. He made the same promise to the dead in the mortuary that he always made, the one that he and Jenny swore – *We will do all we can to find out who you are and return you to your loved ones.* He glanced at her and saw she was murmuring the same oath aloud. He cleared his throat and stood.

'You told me to meet you,' he said.

'This way.'

They walked past the first excavation site, where the bodies had been found buried beneath the carcass of a horse, poisoning a stream. Then traipsed in the direction of a larger stream, almost a river, one of the many tributaries leading to the Drina. They trudged for twenty minutes across sodden and wind-riven fields. The long grass scuffled and shook with movement, each blade baubled with round drops of dew. The mud sucked at his shoes and Simo wished he'd worn boots.

'This is a long way from the first excavation site,' he remarked over the sound of cattle lowing from the fields, which was startlingly loud.

'This stream had high levels of contaminants too,' Jenny explained. 'We decided to dredge it yesterday. One of the team noticed flint chips in a sample from the bed, but the soil here is mostly clay. When he checked the net again he realised it wasn't flint he'd picked up but teeth.'

'How many?'

'No way to tell yet. We can't be sure how many bodies are jumbled together in the mud. We found five under the horses in the field.' She gestured behind her. 'But here beside the stream there's another grave. More bodies were weighted and simply thrown into the river, where they sank into the mud, covered over by years of silt and sediment. It's going to take time to find them all.'

'Anyone talking about what happened?'

Jenny shook her head. 'No one knows anything, of course.'

Simo wondered about the farmer who owned the land. Old Mr Ristić. The chances were that he knew something about the bodies. Guilt often ate its way upwards, like maggots through a corpse. That was the problem: for all the young ambitious fellows, like Josif Borisov who wanted to live in their clean modern offices and absolve themselves of the past, the land itself belched out these rotten secrets that in the spring refused to stay hidden, rising upwards towards the surface. It was a battle between those in the majority who wanted to forget, and those like Simo, who needed to find the missing pieces – a finger, a shard of hip, a hint of the truth – to put towards the reckoning. A fragmentary payment in flesh towards a debt that could never, ever be repaid.

The early morning light thickened like churned butter, spreading out across the sky. With a squelch, he realised he had trodden neatly into a pile of steaming cow shit. In the distance, just beyond a ragged crop of trees, Simo glimpsed the shores of the lake, the surface shimmering orange and gold. A flock of geese took off with a flurry of honking and white wings, the sun catching them, turning them into flaming arrows. Simo laughed. Always, in the midst of dung and death, beauty caught him off guard and gave him a shove sideways. Jenny caught his expression and smiled, understanding. Then his smile faded. There was an unpleasant feral smell, rotten and foul on the wind.

'I can smell death.'

'One of the bodies might not be old.' Jenny pointed to a mound several metres away, right beside the stream. 'Over here. Come.'

Simo sniffed again and tried not to gag. The smell was stronger here. Something newly rotten.

'This is where we've been digging the first trench. The other bodies almost certainly date back to the war, but this one has been here for – my guess – less than a week.'

Simo stepped over to where a plastic tarp had been pulled across and drew it back to see a half-concealed figure lying on its back, face covered with leaves. He pulled out his phone and took several photographs.

'Drugs execution?' asked Jenny. 'This is border country and they've been pressing the farmer to sell the land.'

'Possibly.'

He crouched down, pulled on a pair of latex gloves that he always kept in his jacket pocket, and with something approaching tenderness brushed aside the leaves and the thin top layer of earth. Even though he had only seen him briefly at a press conference, Simo was certain that this was the face of Ryan Mackinnon. His face was swollen and bruised, whether from injury or from decomposition, he could not yet tell. Simo knelt amongst the leaves and for the second time that morning offered up his ritual prayers for the dead. Whatever Ryan Mackinnon had done, no one deserved to be left here like this: to lie hidden in the woods amongst the birds, decaying leaves and the skitter of insects.

Simo remained while the crime scene was photographed, and the body lifted and wrapped in plastic sheets. He supposed that whoever had buried Ryan's body on top of the old grave site had thought it the perfect hiding place. The ditch was a palimpsest of murders and atrocity. Whoever had killed Ryan knew about the other bodies. Knew that they lay hidden here while their families grieved and mourned without bodies to bury and sanctify. They had remained silent year after year, and whoever had buried Ryan had used their silence to conceal another crime. Briefly, Simo closed his eyes, disgusted at the human race. The mass graves had remained undisturbed, their fetid secret concealed for the best part of a quarter century. There had been no reason for

Ryan's murderer to think that anything would change. Yet as the snow and ice melted from the mountains, bringing sudden and unseasonable floods, the land herself had writhed and twisted, and the groundwater rose and belched out the rotten secrets, poisoning the living with sins of the past. At long last, someone had come looking.

Simo followed closely behind in his own car while Ryan's body was driven slowly away in an ambulance to the hospital mortuary. He felt responsible. He hadn't wanted to leave him alone. Ryan had been alone long enough. Simo did not call Heather Bishop; he wasn't ready for her to formally identify the body, not yet. It needed to be cleaned up, having been left in a shallow grave on the riverbank for days. At least now he could tell her officially she was no longer a suspect. There was no possible way that Heather Bishop would have hidden her boyfriend in a mass grave from the war.

In the cool of the morgue, Simo stood in silence while the body was unwrapped and loaded onto the mortuary table. The pathologist carefully preserved all the debris in the plastic wrappings – mostly leaf mould and the odd stowaway beetle. There was a knock on the door and Jenny stepped inside.

'My friend, Professor Jenny Fraser. Forensic anthropologist from Glasgow,' said Simo. 'Do you mind if she observes?'

The pathologist straightened, like a schoolboy when the headmaster enters the room. 'No. It's an honour. You testified in three war crime trials at The Hague. Isn't that right?'

'Four.'

'And, of course, I've read your book on the Balkans,

Professor. I think it's even here somewhere,' he added, glancing around.

Simo grimaced, hoping that the pathologist wasn't about to ask Jenny for an autograph. If he was, he thought better of it and returned to photographing the body.

'He's not in rigor anymore. He must have been dead for at least three days or more. That's an estimate. I won't know until I've done the full post-mortem,' said the pathologist, finishing his photographs and putting away his camera.

Simo nodded. Ryan had been gone longer than that, so whoever had taken him hadn't killed him straight away. Jenny pointed to Ryan's right hand and Simo noticed that his fingernails were missing. Someone had wanted him to suffer, or had wanted to extract information.

'Cause of death?' he asked.

'We won't know until we open him up. But it looks to me like he's been shot at fairly close range with an automatic weapon.'

Simo said nothing. That was an execution-style hit. It was the mark of the Serbian and Bosnian drug gangs, not the weapon of choice of an avenging lover. What had Ryan Mackinnon got himself caught up in? Whatever he'd done, Simo felt only pity. No one deserved this.

'Here, help me undress him,' said the pathologist.

Simo hesitated. Even though he didn't like to admit it, the fresher bodies brought an involuntary revulsion.

'It's up to you. I share an assistant, and if you're not in a hurry . . . we can wait. I've a heap of paperwork and some lab work I can run.'

Jenny rolled her eyes. 'For goodness' sake, Simo.' She

reached for a set a gloves and overalls. Trying to disguise his reluctance, Simo followed suit.

In silence, the three of them carefully removed the black cycling trousers and the ragged remains of a hooded top and T-shirt from the body, cutting the fabric away when they were unable to peel it back. Simo disliked the task immensely. Sadness and solemnity warred with nausea.

Jenny was looking closely at the corpse's face. 'Ryan Mackinnon? That's who you think it is?' she asked.

'Yes,' answered Simo, surveying her narrowly. Something was clearly bothering Jenny, and he trusted her instincts.

'There's something familiar about him. But his face is pretty swollen. And the name doesn't ring a bell.'

'Ah, a present for you,' said the pathologist, interrupting. He held up a blood-smeared bullet, popping it into a plastic evidence bag. Simo took the bag from him and peered closely at the remains of the bullet.

Once the torso was exposed, the violence inflicted upon the body was revealed. Wounds from several gunshots had torn holes in the body, now a tangle of muscle and exposed organ and bone, fetid and wet. The smell was deeply unpleasant. Simo felt a stirring of rage.

He felt the lightest touch on his arm. As always, Jenny exuded the right blend of professionalism and sympathy. One couldn't empathise too much, or one couldn't function enough to do the job.

'I'll clean him up, so we can get him formally identified,' said the pathologist.

'I can help if you like,' offered Jenny. 'Since you're missing that assistant.'

Simo felt another wave of gratitude toward Jenny. He

knew that she'd make sure nothing was overlooked. He left the room with some relief, stripping off his gloves. It was cold in the morgue but he was perspiring. He glanced at his watch. It was time to let Heather Bishop know.

13

Heather had never been more grateful to see anyone; she was desperate to escape this place. Petra had arrived to pick her up less than an hour after she rang. The hotel in the woods terrified her and she wished she could rid herself of the sense that whoever had been in her room last night was still out there amongst the trees, waiting.

'What the hell did you go there for?' demanded Petra on the drive back down the mountain.

'It was close. The website said it was a spa. I was so tired,' said Heather.

The trees looked almost as dark in the daylight, conspiring together in a thick knot of green, the tops shrouded in a layer of early morning mist as thick as woodsmoke. The road wound and switched between them, while the red-roofed hotel with its empty windows seemed to watch them leave. Heather half expected to find them back there as they turned the next bend and sighed with relief when Petra reached the junction onto the main road.

'Tell me again, what you said on the phone. About man in your room.'

Heather told her.

'Show me your neck,' she said, when Heather had finished.

Heather dutifully turned down the collar on her fleece, saying, 'But I told you, he used a pillow. He didn't try to strangle me with his hands. There isn't a mark.'

Petra shook her head. 'I think it was a bad dream. You under so much stress. Or a ghost. That place is evil and full of spirits.'

'It wasn't a ghost. He had bad breath. Ghosts don't eat onions.'

'It was terrible dream then. What they called? Night terror.'

'I scratched him. Look, blood under my nails.'

She shoved her hand up to Petra's face, close for her inspection.

'Yes. They are dirty. I see.' Petra wrinkled her nose in distaste.

'It's not dirt, Petra. It's blood. It's not mine. You already said, I don't have a mark.'

'Well, what you want to do? Call police?'

'What's the point? You don't believe me, why would they?'

Heather folded her arms and sat back in her seat, frustrated. Petra lit a cigarette. Heather longed to ask her to stop, but it was Petra's car and she'd dropped everything to come and collect her.

'Hotel was used as a rape camp for Muslim women,' said Petra, drawing on the cigarette. 'They were kept as prisoners in the bedrooms, chained up and raped day and night by Serb soldiers. They chained to stop them running away, and from jumping off balconies. More than two hundred women taken there. I only know of three who come back.'

Heather thought of the scratches on the walls, the

unchanged, aging bathroom where she had washed, and felt a wave of sick guilt. Petra and Simo kept quietly reminding her about this country's past, but she remained swaddled in her own misfortunes. She hadn't thought to see what was right in front of her. The room where she had tried to sleep was probably the same room where other women had been tortured and abused. That's what she'd felt – the women's fear and hopelessness had leached into the fabric of the building, reaching down and down into the earth beneath.

'Jesus. If it had been me, I would haunt the place,' she said softly. 'Was anyone arrested?'

'Not for the rapes,' said Petra tightly. She stubbed out her cigarette with more force than necessary and pulled out onto the main road, clearly not wanting to discuss it further.

Heather knew her attacker had been neither a ghost nor a dream, but a man. Whoever wanted her to leave this country knew something about Ryan. Good or bad, she needed to find out what it was.

As soon as they arrived at Petra's, Heather went to the bathroom and washed her face. She studied her tired face in the mirror. There were blue circles daubed beneath her eyes, and the pain in her neck throbbed almost constantly. She had a tic in her left eyelid. It fluttered like a butterfly and she couldn't stop it. She'd been unable to wash her clothes, and she was aware of an unpleasant acid stench of sweat and fear. There was a constant feeling of anxiety in her chest, a burning marble in her stomach that, however much milk or peppermint tea she sipped, wouldn't be soothed. Sometimes, just at the edges of her hearing, she thought she could hear whispered voices. She could not quite hear what they were saying, but knew they were trying to tell her something important, something she already knew that was just beyond reach. She tried to be rational. She was under an inordinate amount of stress. She had suddenly come off strong medication without any supervision, and there were bound to be side effects. Another voice hissed, *What if these aren't side effects? What if this is you?* She closed her eyes and placed a cool palm against the fluttering eyelid. Tried to remember what Ryan used to say, that she was a scrappy fighter, that it was okay to forget your password and shopping list when a piece of your skull was left on the A40. She realised that she was crying. Weeping for him. It felt as if there was a hole in her chest, and a strange noise came out of her, an animal sob of pain. With an effort, she stopped crying and then she heard the doorbell and the sounds of Petra inviting Simo inside.

She padded out of the bathroom and through the hall and stopped as she saw Simo standing in the middle of the living room. She registered the look on his face.

'You've found Ryan. You have. Oh God.'

'I'm so sorry.'

She felt the sound leach from the room.

'Did he suffer? Tell me he didn't suffer?'

Simo said nothing. 'I will not lie to you, Heather. All I can say is that his death was quick.'

Heather focused on the orange-varnished panelling of the wood in the living room, the smoke curling up from the unseasoned ash and pine that stung her eyes. She wanted to cry but found that she could not. She was breathless, cold and her forehead throbbed.

'Please, sit.'

She obeyed unthinkingly, then immediately stood again. 'I should call someone.'

'Can I call them for you?' Simo asked gently.

She shook her head. How do you call a man's mother and tell her that her son is dead? Simo would know. He must have done it before. She couldn't bear it. Not yet. Ryan and his mother didn't speak often. Once a month. Let her have a little more peace before it was all ruined.

'When you are ready, I'll need you to come with me. Do you think you can identify him?'

Heather sent a helpless glance at Petra. She put her arm around Heather, smoothed her hair, pressed a glass of water upon her and moved her closer to the fireplace.

'Sit. Sit here. Look at the flames. You shiver.'

Heather realised that she was shaking from head to toe. She tried to sip the water but spilled it down her front. She looked up at Simo. 'Swear to me you'll catch the people who did it?'

Simo was expecting this question – the families always asked the same thing. 'No police officer can promise that. I can only promise to try.'

He studied her for a moment, unblinking.

'I need to know the truth, whatever that is,' said Heather.

Simo nodded. He recognised that look of desperation; he'd seen it on the faces of so many others. He hoped he could give Heather some answers. Whether or not she would like them, he was less certain.

When they arrived at the morgue, Simo ushered Heather and Petra through a reception area and into a little sitting room. There were a few chairs, a low table with a box of tissues and a banal painting of a waterfall. Heather couldn't stop shaking. She wasn't sure if it was shock, or withdrawal from the pills.

'You wait here. I'll get the pathologist. Do you need anything?' asked Simo.

Heather looked confused. 'Don't I need to come down and see the body?'

'No. We'll bring you a photograph. The pathologist will tell you exactly what to expect. There is no need for you to see the body unless you really want to.' He paused. Ryan's body had been outside for some days and deteriorated markedly. 'My advice is not to see him. Look at this one photograph and then remember him as he was.'

Heather nodded, a lump in her throat, choking her. Petra passed her a tissue, which she screwed up in her hands, tearing it to shreds. They sat in silence. Heather realised how grateful she was for Petra's presence, and how many real friends she lacked at home. Apart from Ryan, she'd allowed herself to become isolated. As a professional athlete, she'd been single-minded and obsessive, without time to cultivate friendships or anything outside training, and then after the accident she'd been so focused on her recovery she'd not even tried. She'd forgotten how. She'd lost all sense of her worth as a person apart from her brilliance as a sportswoman and, when that was stripped away, she couldn't see why anyone would want to know her. It meant that now she was horribly alone. She gazed at the waterfall painting and heard the roar of the current rushing in her ears.

'You need to smoke,' said Petra, lighting up. 'It makes it better. No, it doesn't. But it keeps the hands busy.'

Heather thought about Petra's father and suspected that

Petra had been here before, possibly in this very room, and yet was still willing to accompany a woman she barely knew.

'Thank you for coming with me.'

Petra shrugged and tried and failed to blow a smoke ring. The door opened and Simo returned with the pathologist, who clutched a brown envelope. They all squeezed into the cramped, airless room. Heather found herself mesmerised by the envelope.

'I am very sorry,' said the pathologist, reaching over and shaking her hand. 'When you are ready, I am going to show you one photograph. We believe it is Mr Ryan Mackinnon, but we need you to formally identify. His mother is too old and ill to travel from California.'

Heather looked at Simo in shock. 'You told her?'

Simo sighed. 'It is protocol. You are not married, and she is next of kin.'

'How did she take it?'

Simo shook his head, his air of professionalism compromised by the tired and grey pallor of his skin. Heather couldn't bring herself to burden him with more questions. The pathologist waited patiently and then turned back to her.

'I show you a photograph just of Mr Mackinnon's face. It show his head and shoulders. His eyes are open and they are filmy, and there is bruising on his face and neck – that is natural process of body breaking down, it is not injury. I am telling you all this to prepare you, okay? His face has odd smile or grimace, but again, this does not mean anything, it is just muscle contraction. You say when you are ready.'

She took a deep breath, Petra squeezed her hand, and this time she allowed her to and didn't let go. Simo took the envelope from the pathologist and slid out the picture. He handed it to Heather. She stared at it.

'Can you tell me who the man is in the photograph?' asked Simo, softly.

'Ryan Mackinnon,' answered Heather.

Although it wasn't Ryan anymore. It was the casing of Ryan. His eyes were opened and empty, the laughter vanished. His face was pale and puffy. This was the shell of someone who used to be Ryan. Ryan, her Ryan, whoever he used to be, was dead.

Simo insisted on driving both women back to Petra's house. It was late when they hit the road, and the trees passed in a dark blur and the pale moon bobbed in the dark. Simo's radio crackled, and he apologised and turned it down. Heather remained silent throughout the drive, convinced that they were waiting for her to cry, appalled with herself that she couldn't. There was only a void where there was supposed to be grief, a dislocating numbness. When they reached the house, Petra leaned over and hugged Simo.

'Look after her tonight, okay,' he said in Serbian. 'All the same, I wish you hadn't got involved in this. She's a person, not a stray cat.'

Petra wrinkled her nose. 'I like her. And I prefer dogs anyway.'

'Now hop out and give us a minute,' said Simo, now in English.

Grumbling, Petra did as she was told.

Heather sat back in the car; she felt light-headed, her heart fluttering and fast. He skin was sticky with sweat. 'Petra is kind,' she said.

'She is. Just like her father. Same stupid humour too.'

Simo looked unconscionably sad and, in that moment, Heather didn't feel quite so alone.

'Petra's father was a friend of yours?' she asked.

Simo nodded. 'We were at school together. In those days Serbs and Bosniaks were neighbours and friends. Abdul and I talked about becoming police officers together, but then he fell in love with my cousin, got married and worked on her family farm instead. I thought it was hilarious. Abdul arresting goats and sheep.' Simo appeared lost in thought, and then with some effort brought himself back to the present. 'If you need to speak to a counsellor about Ryan, I can find one.'

'Do they speak English?' said Heather.

'No. Probably not.'

They were both silent for a few moments.

'I don't know who to grieve for,' said Heather at last. 'Who was he? I don't even know that. Am I missing a man who never existed?'

'You mourn for the man you lost. We never know everything about another person – there are always secrets.'

'But Ryan had more than most,' said Heather.

'Perhaps,' conceded Simo.

'What do you think happened to him?'

Simo heard the desperation in her voice. He wondered what he could say that was already out there in the public domain, without giving too much away. 'What did Ryan say to you about the Tour de Balkans drugs bust?'

'Not much. He felt sorry for the riders. He thought they'd been used.'

'That's right. It was clever. They targeted a women's race.

One of the smaller ones where the teams don't have too much money or many sponsors, and they offered them free team cars and hotels.'

He watched Heather closely, but she did not react.

'The cocaine was hidden inside the cars. They weren't checked at customs. Why didn't he write about the scandal?'

Heather just shook her head.

Simo frowned, pressed her. 'It's odd, it was a good story. Even reporters who weren't in the Balkans called us up for quotes.'

Heather was annoyed by the insinuation. 'He said it was too depressing. Sport is supposed to inspire people. The endless corruption does the opposite. Cycling is busy cleaning up its act. This stuff is a distraction.'

Even to herself, Heather decided she sounded prim. But that was what Ryan had said. Was it strange that he had refused to write about a big story when he had been here? After all, the other journos who had been at the race had seized on the opportunity. She was torn between fury at Simo for suggesting something so ludicrous – journalists have nothing to do with arranging the tour logistics, everything about it was absurd – and a niggle of doubt.

Simo walked her up to the house. A sheen of frost glittered across the path, making the old machinery scattered across the orchard gleam.

'Do you think Ryan was involved? Honestly?'

'I don't like to form opinions. I like to follow evidence.'

He waited on the path in the darkness and Heather realised that he wasn't going to leave until he'd seen that she was safely inside the house. She walked slowly up towards the front door and for the first time that night tears rose in her throat, but still Heather wasn't sure whether she had even known the man she was crying for, and her grief was blended with anger and betrayal.

14

Simo stood at the window of his apartment and looked at the rain clouds hurrying across the morning sky, chased by a murmuration of starlings on black wings. Trouble, he feared, was coming. A protest was planned in Višegrad at the end of the week, prompted by the discovery of the war graves at the Ristić farm. At best that meant chaos, at worst a riot. Many Bosniaks were outraged at what they viewed as a conspiracy of silence. Dozens or more dead lying buried on farmland, ignored and disregarded until the land herself belched out her secrets. Those bodies were people who had been loved and lost. They deserved better. Simo thought of Abdul. It so easily could have been him in one of those graves, lost, until his bones were dusted down by Jenny, identified by his teeth. God knew, Simo had other friends still missing.

Yet, many Serbs were furious about the intervention of the International Criminal Court, stirring up old wounds and talking of new prosecutions for war crimes. All Simo knew was that the dead must be properly laid to rest, and the living allowed a grave to visit. He rubbed his eyes. There was a restlessness in the city that he hadn't sensed for some time and it worried him.

He made himself a strong espresso and sat down to read

Ryan's preliminary autopsy findings. The report had arrived in the early hours of the morning. He longed for a quiet summer season with nothing more eventful than a few pickpockets and some disgruntled tourists. Ryan Mackinnon's death had put paid to that. The American had died due to massive organ failure as a result of gunshot wounds, fired at a range of approximately two metres. Ten bullets had been recovered from his chest cavity and five more from his legs and lower torso. Simo checked his email and saw the ballistics report in his inbox. He opened it and scanned the document. The lab tech wasn't absolutely definitive – these were early findings as a favour to Simo – but it certainly looked likely that the bullets found on Ryan Mackinnon were in all likelihood from a Russian-made Saiga semi-automatic shotgun. He read the rest of the autopsy report. Ryan had been held captive for two days before he'd been killed. There was damage to his nail beds and to his teeth. It was grim, but also informative. Whoever had killed Ryan had wanted something from him. That, or they were punishing him. This murder was malevolent, brutal and angry.

Simo checked his watch. It wasn't yet nine. There was another missing connection to Ryan – the woman he had been seen speaking with the night before he disappeared. Who was she, this *Dušica,* and what did she know? He still hadn't managed to track her down. Simo stood up and paced with frustration. Obituaries and reports would start appearing in the press, and he suspected that he would start getting calls from papers in London. A journalist murdered on holiday, even one who wrote about cycling, was still news. He wanted to talk to his colleagues before the soundbites started to appear. He was about to start making calls when

Jenny knocked on his door. He opened it at once, worried. She pushed past him.

'I couldn't sleep. I've been thinking about your other case,' she said, handing him a circled photograph of the *Petar Petrović*. 'Most of the skin on the shoulder had come off in the river, but we've enlarged it here. One of my new chaps is a decent artist and I asked him to have a go at sketching how the tattoo might have looked.'

She pulled out a close-up of the body. Over the photo of the shoulder was a sketch of a double-headed eagle hovering above a pistol.

Simo shrugged. 'Every Serb nationalist has one of those. It doesn't help identify him.'

'No,' said Jenny, 'but this might. We had a closer look, and it was just above.'

Simo examined the second sketch. It was drawn over the photograph of what was left of the neck, and it looked like a crude tattoo of a dog. He took off his glasses and peered at it. No, not a dog.

'It's a wolf. A bloody red wolf.' He thought for a moment. 'All the men in Dragan Drakulić's unit had them. They styled themselves the Wolves of Zikoč. They did the tattoos themselves. Initiation ritual.'

'A good way to get sepsis,' muttered Jenny, unimpressed.

Simo fell silent again. It seemed likely that *Petar Petrović* had been in Drakulić's unit back in the war. Had he been reported missing? That was easy enough to verify. He phoned the station and asked the sergeant on duty to check the missing persons register and cross reference it with any man aged between forty-five and fifty who was also listed as having served in the military, specifically anyone who'd served in the Wolves of Zikoč. They waited.

The phone rang.

'Two dozen former soldiers reported missing of that age range but none of them mentioned as being Wolves, sir.'

Simo disconnected, and gazed at Jenny, disappointed. He was convinced she was right. Their man was a former Wolf; one of the most vicious and brutal of paramilitary units operating during the war, their exploits foul and notorious. Would their families report them to the police as missing? They might view a disappearance as a weakness, even a mark of shame. The former paramilitaries and their families stayed away from the police, reasonably enough since more often than not they found themselves on the other side of the law. Even a prison sentence, whether handed down from Banja Luka or for war crimes from The Hague itself, did little to bring about contrition. The Hague. Something jangled at the back of Simo's mind. He pulled out his phone and tapped in a search. A news story from three weeks ago appeared. He read it out to Jenny.

'"Today Arkan Ćešić was released from prison at The Hague. He was convicted of murder and physical abuse at various camps in Bosnia and sentenced to eighteen years. He was released early after serving ten years."'

'The pathologist estimated our body had been in the river for about a fortnight. Look at the dates. Ćešić was released only days before.' Simo felt the adrenaline tingle of excitement. 'That's our man.' His mind went back to the other *Petar Petrović* from two months before and he began to search through previous news stories. It wasn't long before he had another hit.

'"February 1st. Ivan Fuštar granted early release from

prison. He was sentenced in twenty-ten to twelve years for the persecution, inhumane acts and murder of non-Serb Bosnians."'

'I remember this one,' said Jenny. 'I was a witness at his trial at The Hague. He wasn't a Wolf though. A guard at a camp near Prijedor, I remember. Took sadistic delight in brutalising the prisoners. Twelve years – that sentence was a disgrace. And early release! Jesus Christ. It should have been a life sentence.'

Simo grunted. 'Looks like someone agreed with you. Except they felt only a death sentence was enough.' He looked back at the photos of Arkan and thought of the beatings recorded in the autopsy report. There was a logical conclusion to be drawn from the new evidence, logical but startling.

'Someone is murdering war criminals as they're being released from prison.'

The two of them fell silent, contemplating the revelation that in some ways turned the investigation upside-down. The bodies in the Drina were victims, but also murderers. The worst kind.

Simo broke the silence. 'Whoever is carrying out the killings is making sure that before they die these men suffer for what they've done. And in the same way that they made others suffer all those years ago.'

Jenny shook her head. 'The sentences from The Hague are pathetic, but this isn't justice either. It's murderous retribution.'

There was something else nagging at Simo. He recalled Josif's concern for his criminal father. Another jagged piece fell into place. 'Dragan Drakulić was released about three months ago. There was outrage at his sentence – people marched in the street. If there is someone out there with a list of those who escaped justice, Drakulić is on it.'

'Then why hasn't he turned up in the Drina without his head?' asked Jenny, doubtfully.

'Drakulić is hard to get to. His son is the chief of police and he's still surrounded by supporters. But I think he's worried, Jenny. He knows that Arkan and Ivan disappeared – and those are just the ones we've found. Who knows who else has vanished?'

'Why do you think Drakulić knows about Arkan and Ivan?'

Simo smiled. 'Because Josif has been pestering me about the bodies in the river. He knows someone's out to get his father. And they are, but not for the reason I thought. He isn't worried about a rival drug gang taking out the competition; he's terrified about vigilantes taking revenge on former war criminals. He's petrified that his father will be next.' He paused. 'I reckon Josif Borisov is much closer to his father than he wants any of us to believe.'

Simo scrolled through his phone and tapped a contact.

'Who you calling?' asked Jenny.

'An old friend. She's a probation officer – if I'm right about the bodies, she can confirm it.' The call connected and there was a weary groan from the other end.

'Simo, why can't you call at normal times? Or just take me for a slice of cake?'

'Dora, I need a favour. Can you tell me the last time Arkan Ćešić and Ivan Fuštar checked in with their case officers?'

She grumbled but Simo could hear typing. 'They haven't.

Arkan not for nearly three weeks, and Ivan for three months. Arrest warrants have been issued.'

'Don't bother. They're dead.' Simo sighed, grimly satisfied. He'd identified the victims, he was certain of it. 'Dora, can you send me through a list of any more warrants issued for offenders who haven't checked in? I'm not interested in those out on petty offences, only war crimes.'

She snorted. 'Sure, but I'm not sorting through them. You can go through the list yourself.' She hung up.

Simo turned to look at Jenny. Something gnawed at him.

'I know that look,' she said. 'What is it?'

'How do the murders of Arkan and Ivan connect to Ryan Mackinnon's?'

'Do they have to?'

'I don't believe in coincidences. Arkan was a Wolf. He and Ivan may well have known the location of the mass grave where you found Ryan's body. In all likelihood, just over a quarter of a century ago, Arkan helped put some of the bodies in the ground, under Drakulić's orders.'

'But Arkan was killed before Ryan – makes it kind of hard for him to have hidden Ryan's body in the grave.'

'The crimes are linked,' he insisted. 'I just can't see how. Yet.' He cast his mind over what he knew about the American. 'Heather was adamant that Ryan had been here with the U.N. The date on the photo placing him here was nineteen ninety-two.'

Jenny frowned. 'Ninety-two?'

'Exactly. The U.N. weren't here in nineteen ninety-two.'

'Was he U.S. military, then?'

'A soldier would know how to handle a pistol.'

'So, what was he doing in the Balkans?'

Heather Bishop knew her boyfriend only as a cycling journalist, but had he always been? There was one other reason for Ryan Mackinnon to have been in the country during the war.

15

Simo held the phone to his ear, the handset hot against his skin with the calls he'd made to Ryan's former colleagues, trying to establish the facts of his time in the Balkans. Jenny had left when he started the laborious process, returning to the temporary mortuary to continue her work. It had taken a while, but as soon as Simo started to question Frederick Collins – Freddie – he recognised the signs of obfuscation.

'Tell me about Ryan. When was he here?'

'In the nineties. With the U.N.'

At once he knew that he'd hit paydirt. Freddie knew something.

'You're lying to me, Mr Collins. Lying to the police – even foreign police – is a crime.'

There was silence and then, 'I'm not,' he whined. There was a pause. Then, 'I'm . . . sorry. I just can't believe he's dead.'

'Then help me. Why was he here? Was he a journalist? He wasn't writing about cycling in the Balkans in ninety-two.'

Another long pause, then a breath that sounded a lot like relief. After years of keeping it secret, Freddie unburdened himself. 'No. He was a war reporter.'

'Thank you,' said Simo. It was confirmation of what he'd already guessed. 'Mostly based in Bosnia?'

'I . . . think so . . .'

'Anything else you've missed out, Mr Collins? I can still charge you with lying to police. I haven't checked the terms of the extradition treaty with the U.K., but I can do that right now . . .'

Simo had spooked Freddie. If the man knew anything else, he would spill his guts. 'I'm sorry. I don't know. Let me think. He wrote under Ryan Markovitz. Mackinnon is his mother's maiden name. Changed it after the war.'

'I see. This was when he swapped war for bicycles?' said Simo.

'Yes. New career. New byline. New name.'

'Which paper?'

'*Washington Post.*'

After he ended the call, Simo searched for 'Ryan Markovitz, *Washington Post*' on his laptop. The articles were years old and behind a paywall. He reached for his wallet and a few minutes later he had an unwanted subscription he knew Josif wouldn't reimburse through expenses. More importantly, he was staring at a string of articles by 'Ryan Markovitz'. They were all about the Balkan War in the early to mid nineties. What caught his attention was the photograph above the byline: a black-and-white head shot of a young man. A young Ryan Mackinnon.

Simo began flicking through the articles, but there were too many and it would take him all day. Narrowing the search, he looked for any article mentioning Arkan Ćešić or Ivan Fuštar. Nothing. He searched instead for Dragan

Drakulić. There was a hit. Simo leaned forward and started to read.

The Wolves of Zikoč,
December 3, 1992,
Washington Post magazine,
Ryan Markovitz

Even amongst the atrocities committed in this grubby and desperate war, the violence in this once quiet and pretty little valley has become notorious. The area is known as 'Vukojèbina' in Bosnian, or wolf country, because of its remoteness and the density of its vast primordial forests. It's a different kind of wolf, however, that the local Muslims have learned to fear. Commander Dragan Drakulić and his Serb paramilitary unit, styling themselves 'The Wolves', like to knock on the doors of Muslims just before dawn. That's when they drag out the men, and take them into the square and shoot them. They make the women and children come outside and watch, and afterwards hose away the blood.

We were warned not to come to the hotel to interview the brigade, that it was too dangerous. Those who go to the hotel in the woods do not come back. Rumors abound in Višegrad and Zikoč that Muslim men taken up here are tortured and shot, while the women are taken there to be raped: most of them are not seen again.

It is also the headquarters of the local warlord, Dragan Drakulić, who had invited me to interview him, or as he put it, 'correct various egregious and insulting errors' in my previous articles in this newspaper.

Uncertain and, I'm not going to pretend, extremely anxious, I set off along with photographer Alek. For once, we leave our translator, Marina Tomić, in Sarajevo. Marina is very pretty, and Drakulić likes pretty women. He tends to keep them. Even though Marina is furious, all three of us decide it is too dangerous for her to come. Alek will translate as best he can if it is necessary.

The hotel is in the middle of a pine forest about ten kilometres from Višegrad. It is named after the delicate ferns that grow in the waterfalls nearby, and it might once have been a pleasant spa. It isn't pleasant any more. The red-tiled roof and red painted balconies are at once faded and garish. I notice every curtain is drawn. I both want to know and dread knowing what is behind them. Some of the glass is smashed. I'm not sure what I'm expecting – screams, gunshots. After all, people are supposedly tortured here. But they know we are coming and there is no sound at all. It is very, very quiet. Then Drakulić himself comes to greet us, slapping us on the back like old friends. Clean-shaven and neat, he looks more like a suburban dentist than a warlord, excepting the pistol holstered at his waist. Dragan shakes my hand warmly and gives me a roguish grin, revealing very white, straight teeth, and apologizes in English for the paucity of refreshments. He is charming, polite, and chilling.

'In Serbia, we always like to offer guests something delicious. To share food is to share friendship.'

'But we're not in Serbia,' I remind him, realizing a little too late that this is not the most sensible opening remark to a bloodthirsty and fanatical paramilitary leader. He only looks like a dentist. But he chooses to take it as a joke and I get away with it.

'This man a comedian! Why we put off the interview?' is his reply. He slaps his thigh with enthusiasm, but his eyes don't register a flicker of amusement.

'I love it here. Mountain air. It thickens the soul,' he beams. 'Come. Eat. Drink.'

He calls us over to a terrace covered in vines where, contrary to his apologies, a feast has been laid out. Wine, rakia, roast lamb, figs dipped in honey. Alek doesn't eat. I try. A fig sticks in my throat. Somewhere far away I hear sobbing. It stops, quickly.

'Commander Drakulić, is this hotel used as a prison?'

He laughs. 'What a spot for a prison! So beautiful.'

'A prison is just a place you cannot leave.'

'No. I don't agree. When you are children, you cannot leave your parents' house. It is not safe for you to do so. But it is cozy, and filled with toys and comforts and love. You cannot leave, but it is not a prison.'

I don't want to get into philosophy with Drakulić. It's a rabbit hole, and one I doubt I'll find my way back out of.

'So this hotel is not a prison?' I press. 'There are not women kept here who want to leave?'

He does not answer but signals for coffee. A man in jeans and an apron hurries over. He is very thin and there is a long scratch down one cheek. His jeans are filthy. His hands shake as he pours coffee. I long to ask him questions, but as I watch him, he spills the coffee and looks at the commander with such terror that I know I cannot. It's very frustrating. We're here, so close to it all. I'm being served coffee by a man who is clearly terrified, here against his will, but all I can do is sip coffee and make small talk.

Eventually, I find my nerve. I question Drakulić on his policy of making Muslim women and children watch the executions of their husbands and fathers. He replies with a puzzled frown, his face full of concern. 'I haven't heard this. Have you heard this?' he calls over to his soldiers. They all shake their heads.

He sighs, and states with something that I think is supposed to sound like regret, 'We kill only soldiers who don't surrender. After all, this is a war for the protection and freedom of all our great nation.'

'Freedom of Serbians *and Muslims*?' I ask.

He smiles. 'Sure.'

Then, Drakulić stands, pushes back his chair. 'You want a tour? You want to see the waterfalls?'

No, I tell him. I do not want to see the waterfalls. I want to see the rooms. I want to see if there are women here. I am a journalist. I am not writing a tourist brochure.

He chuckles, apparently amused by my bravado.

But, to my immense surprise, he agrees. He glances towards Alek, a Muslim. 'The Yak can come. He can bring his camera. I don't want lies.'

Yak is a term of racist abuse; it's short for 'Bosniak'. I want to object, but Alek gives a tiny shake of his head. He doesn't want any trouble. He shoulders his camera and follows us into the hotel.

It smells strongly of bleach and cigarettes. Soldiers lounge in what was the reception area. The carpet has mostly been pulled up to reveal the bare concrete floor beneath. I should ask why. I don't. I'm scared and I hate myself for not asking. The soldiers look surprised to see us; they instantly come to attention on seeing Drakulić, immediately tense, jostling for his notice.

He speaks rapidly and quietly to them in Serbian. I think Drakulić is asking which rooms it is safe to show us. He doesn't want us to see rooms where women are inside.

A soldier takes a key hanging above what was once the reception desk and gestures for us to follow. Alek snaps some pictures. The soldiers stiffen, ready to snatch the camera, but Drakulić waves them away. There is nothing incriminating for us to snap. I glance about. It is so quiet, as though just behind the doors, around the corners, everyone is holding their breath, but the guard and Drakulić himself are not going to leave us alone. I'm not sure what I'd hoped to find.

We tread the stairs. There are bullet-holes in the walls. Alek photographs them. Drakulić shrugs, unbothered.

'Is war. Soldiers must let off steam.'

A door is opened for us. We are shown into a room with twin beds, stripped, a pile of sheets on the floor.

'Soldiers sleep here. Nothing more. Is cleaning day.'

I can't help notice some of the sheets are spotted with blood. They look particularly filthy. The headboard is half pulled off the bed. There are scratches on the walls. If this is what they think it's fine for us to see, I can hardly bear to imagine what they're hiding. As we're ushered out, I notice the glint of a pair of steel handcuffs on the floor. I try to draw them to Alek's attention without alerting Drakulić, but to my annoyance, I can't. We don't photograph them.

We follow them along a dismal corridor. We're obedient as school boys, Alek and I. We needed Marina. She wouldn't have done what she was told. She's afraid of no one. There is a window at the end of the corridor, just beyond the stairs. Someone yells, and there is shouting on the floor below. The sound of doors slamming, and suddenly a scream followed by a woman shrieking and sobbing. Drakulić says nothing, but it's clear he is furious. This isn't the pretence he wants us to see, even though we know it's a lie. He knows that we know, but even so he doesn't want us to glimpse behind the bloody curtain. His fingers drum against his leg with suppressed rage. His mouth is a white line.

'Wait here,' he barks at us. 'Don't move an inch. Then we go out and drink rakia together before you drive back.'

He and the guard hurtle down the stairs, two at a time, voices raised.

I can see the window at the end of the corridor. All I can see from here are the vague shapes of the swaying tops of the black pines. I gesture to Alek to follow me. He shakes his head. I won't let it go.

'Come on. We have to look around. Or what the hell are we doing here?'

'Stop it, man,' he says. 'I got kids.'

I almost feel bad. Alek didn't want to come. But we agreed it was too dangerous for Marina, and he wouldn't let me come alone. I should be grateful that he's here. I should listen. He's older, and he knows these people in a way that even after years here and after all I've seen, I don't understand; I can't.

I shrug. I walk to the end of the corridor. It's just a

few steps to the large oval picture window. It's so filthy it's almost opaque. I take my sleeve, wipe it against the glass to clean it, and peer through. Glancing down, I see it has a vantage over the swimming pool, but we are not supposed to see this. The pool is empty of water and filled with bloodied rags. Then, as I look again, I realize that they're not rags but corpses. From up here I can't even tell if they are the bodies of men or women. They are heaped on top of one another with utter disregard. I hear a soft click and nearly jump six feet in the air, until I realize it's the shutter on Alek's camera.

'It's a f*****g war crime,' he says.

'Can you see properly?' I ask.

He stops clicking and hands me the camera, and even though I don't want to, I look. I have to look. I need to witness. I must know what is here. Through the telephoto lens, I can see clearly that there must be at least twenty people lying in the pool. Most of them are men, but there are at least five women. I wish I could say something. Tell these people that Alek and I saw them, and we are filled with rage and sorrow. That we will do everything we can to get them justice. He's tugging on my sleeve. We walk back to the top of the stairs.

Drakulić comes up at the same time. He smiles. I want to punch him. I smile.

'Did you go to the window?' he asks.

'No.'

He looks at us for a moment. My heart doesn't beat.

'Okay then.'

He turns and starts to go down the stairs, and then something makes him stop and turn again. He glances back, and from this angle I realize with horror that the circle where I'd rubbed away the filth is clearly visible on the glass, a tell-tale smeary circle in the center of the pane. He reaches out and grabs my arm, looks at my sleeve. It's black with dirt.

He snatches Alek's camera, breaking the strap, and opens the back and exposes the film. I think with both outrage and relief that's the end of it, but that's because, unlike Alek, despite my months and years here, I still don't know these people like I should.

Without a word, Drakulić pulls out his pistol and shoots Alek in the head. One minute Alek is standing beside me, and the next he's in a pool of blood at my feet. I sink to my knees and I hear screaming, and it takes a moment for me to realize that it's my own voice. The guard grabs me under my arms, and I think I'm about to be shot too. I'm aware of something wet against my leg and I realize I've pissed myself, and I think of Marina and Alek's wife and his gorgeous kids and that I'll never have kids of my own to think of as I die, but he hasn't pulled the trigger yet, and I'm being dragged down the corridor, my feet trailing in Alek's blood, and then I'm being shoved in a room.

'Drakulić don't like it when men scream. Only women,' the guard says, and slams the door.

I'm not dead. My sneakers are covered in Alek's blood; I try to take them off, I don't want them anywhere near me, but I only succeed in smearing his blood all over my hands. I am covered in his blood. I almost wish they would hurry up and kill me. I did this to him. I know even now that it is all my fault. And yet, despite my guilt, my vile self-loathing, my desire for life is animal and strong. I want to die, I deserve to die, and I am terrified that they will kill me and it will hurt, and I am desperate to live even though I don't deserve to.

Hours pass. I sit on the floor. I don't move for several hours. The urine on my trousers dries. I go into shock. I cry a little. I shiver. My muscles start to cramp. I stretch my legs. Alek's blood has dried on my hands. I can feel it cracking on my cheek where I touched my face. It is dark in the room. Night has fallen. I'm in one of the hotel bedrooms. There is a bed. The sheets are dirty. They smell rankly of shit and blood. I don't look too closely. The journalist in me knows I ought to, but the man can't bear any more. There is a bathroom. I pad into it and there is a bath with a shower curtain half ripped off and a cracked sink, a broken mirror. I'm glad the mirror is broken as I don't want to see my face. I wash the blood off my hands and face. I drink water from the tap; I'm greedy with thirst, my lips are parched and cracked.

I go back into the bedroom and I stop dead. My heart lurches. Drakulić is sitting on the bed, knocking back a bottle of whisky.

'Everyone told you not to come here, that it was too dangerous?' he says, softly.

'Yes.'

'And everyone told me it was a stupid idea to let you come. Neither of us listened, and now we are in a big mess.'

He hands me the bottle of whisky and stands, goes

to the French windows and heaves them open, waving me out onto the balcony.

'Come,' he says.

It's December and light snow is starting to fall. I'm not wearing any shoes, but I have the sense not to argue. I walk barefoot out into the snow, realizing that I've not washed Alek's blood off my feet and that I'm leaving bloody footprints. He glances down.

'You've cut yourself.'

I shake my head. I try and say, 'It's Alek's blood,' but my voice catches in my throat and sobs overtake me. I know Drakulić doesn't like it when men scream, but he doesn't seem to mind when men cry. To my horror, he enfolds me in an embrace and pats my shoulder. I can't bear it and shove him off. He lets me. I'm so angry I stop crying.

'He had seen things he shouldn't and taken pictures. There was nothing I could do.'

His voice is sticky with regret, as though he actually believes it was not his fault. He has utterly disassociated from his crime. I feel more guilt than him. I hate him like I have never hated anyone. He studies me with interest.

'Why haven't you killed me too?' I ask.

He sighs and takes a long sip of whisky. 'You are like Schrödinger's cat,' he says. 'You know Schrödinger's cat? It's locked in an airtight box? Until the box is open, the possibility exists that the cat is both dead and alive. Right now, in this room, as far as the world is concerned you are both dead and alive.'

He is slurring as he talks, and I realize that

Commander Drakulić, warlord and philosopher, is drunk.

'I'm going to get my sweater,' I say. 'Even though I'm already dead.'

'And alive,' he adds, with a grin.

I step out onto the balcony with my sweater on and put my sneakers back on. Drakulić passes me the bottle. I sip a very little, pretending to drink much more than I do. There is a noise on the ground and I look down and see that the swimming pool is now empty. It's being hosed down; what must be blood is being washed away. It looks black and tar-like in the darkness. Drakulić looks at the direction of my gaze, and for a moment the mask falls, and he falters.

'You have heard the story of my family and the Ustasha in World War Two?'

'I have.'

'What did you hear?'

'They arrived at your house and asked you who to kill first, your brothers or your sisters, and you chose the girls.'

'They were all already dead. I'd gone for a shit in the woods. But the legend was useful. Fear is better than love for men like me.'

I don't want to discuss Machiavelli.

'How many have you killed?'

He shrugged. 'Me? Myself? That is not my job. I tell the others to do it. One hundred. Maybe more. We have to dig the pits further and further out into the woods. God alone knows. Sometimes the women do it to themselves. They jump from the balconies and they hang themselves in the shower. That is not our fault.'

'Do you believe that?'

'You come from a different place, Ryan. You are not part of this madness. I used to teach philosophy. Now, I do not sleep as well as I used to. My dreams are full of fire.'

'Like the fires in Višegrad? Where you ordered Muslim families to be burnt to death? Mothers, old people, little children?'

He is silent, sipping from the bottle of Scotch, and he seems to have forgotten that I am here. There is the rustle of the pine trees and swoosh of water as the last of the blood is washed from the swimming pool.

'This is a necessary war. But the fires. Those were a pity.'

He gives a sound that is a bit like a snort, and he finishes the bottle. His eyes are unfocused. He is very drunk.

'It is the man who is to be hanged who confesses on the eve before, not the executioner,' he says.

He's telling me that he's going to kill me, that I'm Schrödinger's dead cat, but I suppose that I'm alive now, for what it's worth, so I keep going.

'You're a Christian. It's only natural to want to confess your sins.'

Drakulić gives a humourless laugh. 'I am not a Catholic. I confess only to God, not to a Jew.'

'You're human. We all want absolution.'

He meets my eye with an odd look.

'Will you give it?'

I know what I'm going to say next means he will

probably kill me, but I think of Alek and his wife and daughters, and of the people in the pool, who are even now being hosed away, and the women jumping from the balconies rather than face life after what he and his men have done to them and the nameless others buried in the woods; and even though I know the words he wants me to say and that they might just save me, I can't bring myself to utter them.

'No, Dragan Drakulić. I will not give you absolution. You will never be forgiven.'

He stands up and silently quits the room. I spend the rest of the night writing up my notes. When dawn comes, I expect to die.

Editorial note:
Ryan Markovitz was released five days later. Alekesander Stanišić's body has not been found. He is missing presumed murdered. See obituary on p. 45, News Section. Dragan Drakulić denies all allegations made in this piece.

Simo blinked. Ryan did not die then, not in that room. But twenty-six years later he had been killed and left to moulder in a shallow grave in the woods. There was absolutely a connection between Ryan Mackinnon/Markovitz and Dragan Drakulić. Arkan was Drakulić's man, or had been once upon a time. The fact remained that now Dragan Drakulić was out of jail, suffering and slaughter had started to spread outward once again across Simo's district and beyond, like an infection tracking across a wound. He sat back with his head in his hands, thinking through the new information. Jenny had left hours ago to return to her work at the temporary mortuary, but he needed to check in with her. He called her phone and she answered on the first ring.

He had no time for pleasantries. 'You were a witness at Drakulić's trial at The Hague.'

'Why?'

'Ryan Mackinnon's murder. Think I might have found the motive. He witnessed Drakulić kill a friend of his. Alekesander Stanišić. Photographer. Mackinnon must have been a key witness at the trial. His name wasn't Mackinnon back then. He changed it after the war. Used to be Ryan Markovitz.'

There was a breath of recognition mingled with surprise from Jenny's end of the call.

'You know him?'

'Of him. Never met the man in person. You're right – he was a prosecution witness at the Drakulić trial.'

Simo nodded satisfied. 'So, I do have a motive for the murder. Drakulić is released from prison, wants revenge.'

'No, that's the thing. Ryan Markovitz refused to testify.'

'What?'

'Markovitz was unusual – one of the only people ever to witness Drakulić commit a crime. And live. Drakulić was scrupulous at leaving no witnesses. The women he raped, he had killed. And he never kept records. His men were loyal, through fear or fanaticism – who knows. Drakulić was on the run for ten years before he was finally caught, and even then his soldiers were still too loyal – or frightened – to testify.'

'The prosecution needed Markovitz.'

'They did. Without him, everything was circumstantial. I never saw Markovitz in court – I was called to the stand a few months before he was scheduled to appear. But everyone was talking about what happened. The prosecution was furious; they subpoenaed him, tried to force him to testify. He got a lawyer and appealed. The lawyer argued that as a reporter he had a right not to testify in court. He won.'

Simo shook his head. 'But why not testify? Was he threatened?'

'No idea. Lots of journalists were on his side, insisting that he'd done the right thing. That it was the moral duty of a reporter to stand by his source. Integrity. Objectivity. The sanctity of the source and all that.'

It made no sense to Simo. 'So, Ryan Markovitz refuses to testify. Drakulić is sent to prison despite him, not because of him. And yet, years later, on Dragan Drakulić's release from The Hague, Ryan is found dead.' He mulled it over. With what Ryan had seen he was still a threat to Drakulić, even after twenty-six years. Drakulić hated loose ends. There was another possibility. 'Perhaps something happened to change Ryan Mackinnon's mind and he finally decided to do the right thing. If so, then I believe that one woman knows why.'

'Heather Bishop?'

'No.' Simo was already heading for the door. *Dušica*.

16

Heather gripped the handlebars to stop her hands from trembling. She felt sick to her stomach and a pain throbbed behind her eyes. To her relief it had stopped raining, but the roads were slick and an icy wind shivered the pines, rifling through the needles like the sound of water. The road was black and twisting, a thread unspooling around the steep cliffs. Trees shouldered their way onto the road on either side. The gloom and silence unsettled her. The only sound the whirr and tick of her own tyres and the wind in the leaves. Was this the place from which they had taken Ryan? If someone slid out of the forest and grabbed her, no one would see. She too would simply disappear.

She pedalled faster, heart rattling against her ribs, and leaned into the curve of the next bend. The rushing air was cold against her cheeks and made her eyes water. Then, all at once, there was the neon sign of Café Bulozi, flashing pink and blue, artificially bright. Only a couple of trucks occupied the near-vacant car park. She chained up her bike and hastened inside. To her surprise, Simo was already there, sitting quietly at a booth near the back, nursing a cup of coffee. He looked tired, smudged shadows beneath his eyes. She slipped into the booth opposite him and coughed.

'Thank you for coming,' he said. 'Are you feeling okay?'

'I'm fine. Think maybe I'm coming down with something.' She said nothing about the bottle of pills that she'd flushed down the toilet in the hotel. 'You've found out something about Ryan.' Heather had no interest in small talk.

He was silent for a moment, as though trying to work out what he could say. 'I spoke to some of Ryan's colleagues in London. Before he was a cycling journalist, he was a reporter with the *Washington Post*.'

He reached into his briefcase and pulled out an article he'd printed and pushed it across the table to Heather. She stared at it and then at Simo.

'Look at the photo on the byline.'

She glanced down, put her hand over her mouth. 'Oh my God, it's Ryan. Younger, but it's him.'

'You need to take a look at this article.'

She could feel Simo's eyes on her as she read. She was used to Ryan's cycling columns, as well as his podcasts, but this was different. It was fierce and raw, bristling with outrage and self-loathing. She felt as if it were a piece by another Ryan, one she hadn't known existed, about the bitter heart of the Balkans. A story of war and blood, people who went into the black woods and disappeared.

When she had finished, she took a long breath. No wonder he hadn't wanted to return to the Balkans for years. She felt light-headed. Ryan had been brave and terrified, and she wished, oh God, she wished he had told her what he had seen, so that she might at least have tried to understand. She would have listened. Perhaps then she could have helped him. She realised now that she never really knew him.

She glanced towards the window and watched as the

moon floated upward towards the mountain peak. It looked alien, and she felt very far from home. The unreality of the week's events smashed into her, and for a moment she felt so terrified she couldn't breathe. She tucked her knees underneath her chin on the bench and, hugging herself tightly, bit her lip. For days she'd been unable to cry, but now she wept for herself and both Ryans – the man she thought she knew, and the man that, now, she never would.

To her relief Simo did not insult her with trite words of consolation. He simply sat quietly, letting his presence offer her comfort. And when finally he said, 'I'm sorry,' she could tell that he meant it.

'Why didn't he tell me?'

'Whether you are fighting or observing, war does odd things to a person.' Simo spoke in the frank tones of a person who knew. He signalled to the barman, who brought over a large glass of wine. Heather drank gratefully.

'He was trying to buy a gun. He must have been very frightened about something. Do you know what?'

Heather shook her head. 'Who is Dragan Drakulić? Did he kill Ryan?'

'It is possible. Or had him killed. Drakulić prefers to have others commit crimes on his behalf.' He slid his phone across the table and showed her a picture of an elderly man with silvered hair, thin lips and wide, guileless blue eyes.

'That's him?' He looked like no one at all.

Simo nodded.

A cry of pain escaped from Heather's lips. She wanted Drakulić to pay. She needed justice. 'But why kill him now?'

Simo told her what Jenny had told him about Ryan refusing to testify at Drakulić's trial. Heather shook her head, unwilling to believe it. 'No. That's not Ryan.' He was more of an enigma to her than ever. None of it made sense.

'I believe there is one person who can help us understand. Who might lead us to Drakulić.'

Simo pushed a printout of Ryan's *Washington Post* article across the table towards Heather. She noticed that he'd circled a name.

Additional reporting by Alekesander Stanišić and Marina Tomić.

'We need to find the translator, Marina Tomić. Her name appears with Alekesander's until he dies, and then appears alongside Ryan's until the end of the war.'

'You think she's *Dušica*?' asked Heather at once.

'I think it is possible. I also think it's possible he knew and trusted her well enough to ask her to help him buy a gun.'

'There was a woman with him when he bought the gun?'

'Yes. But the source didn't know, or wouldn't tell me, her name. Marina Tomić is in Višegrad. This is her site.' Simo took out his phone and showed Heather a page from a website.

'It's in Serbian. I can't read it.'

'Actually, the page is in Serbian and Bosnian. It's in both the Cyrillic and Latin alphabets.'

'Is that important?'

He nodded. 'Serbian and Bosnian are basically the same language, like American English and British English. A few words are different. But Serbian uses the Cyrillic alphabet, and Bosnian the Latinate. For her website to use both is a statement. She is not taking sides. Or rather, she works for both sides. She believes in peace. In a future working together.'

'Okay,' said Heather.

'Marina works at a law firm specialising in human rights. She practises alongside her husband; they do work prosecuting war criminals and get compensation for victims. Mostly Bosnian victims, but they have also a few Serbian clients too.'

Heather gripped her glass of wine tightly. Ryan may well have been sleeping with Marina. She recoiled at the thought, but then a stronger compulsion overwhelmed her. She needed to know. 'I want to talk to her.'

'Yes. I think this Marina may well be able to tell us why Ryan would not testify in the trial against Drakulić. And,' Simo paused, 'I believe she also knows why he changed his mind.'

Heather was puzzled. 'Why tell me about Marina? I mean, I appreciate the heads up, but why not go straight to her?'

'This is the thing,' said Simo. 'Marina Tomić works for an organisation called The Silent Women. I admire them. They are highly aggravating and cause me many problems, but they try hard to get justice for women who have suffered terrible things in the Balkans. They, however, are not very keen on the police.'

Heather stared at Simo, realising with some considerable satisfaction that he needed her. 'And you don't think she'll talk to you.'

'Unfortunately not. Or, not without you. You, Heather Bishop, the girlfriend of her murdered old friend. You, I think she will speak to.'

Heather studied him narrowly. 'Is there anything to stop me from going to talk to Marina by myself?'

Simo shook his head, a little weary. 'Only that I would ask you not to. I have an obligation to the dead. I want to find out what happened to Ryan. But I also have a duty to protect the living. Please, I beg you, do not pursue this without me. For better or worse, I am a police officer. This place is dangerous.'

Heather looked at the tired face of the man across the booth. His expression was frank, his brown eyes lined and a little bloodshot, his hair mostly silver but streaked here and there with black, like a badger's. She wanted to believe him. Reaching a decision, she stood up. 'I'm going to Marina's office tomorrow morning. Ten o'clock. You're driving.'

17

They lingered in the street opposite the office building where Marina Tomić worked. A cloud of dizziness and nausea enveloped Heather. Withdrawal from the medication she'd tossed away, she assumed. Spending most of the night reading articles by Ryan Markovitz hadn't helped either.

'You look terrible.' Petra made circles around her own eyes. 'Purple like you been punched.'

When she'd learned of the proposed trip to Višegrad, Petra had announced that she was accompanying Heather and Uncle Simo. Heather was grateful for her continued support, but sure that Simo would object. To her surprise, he had decreed that it was a good idea – the more women the better, apparently.

As she waited, Heather noticed a line of posters plastered to the wall. Half of them had been defaced, but one was still legible. It showed an image of a red lily and a few lines in a language she couldn't read.

'It's for the protest tomorrow,' explained Petra.

'The Silent Women?'

Petra nodded. 'The red lily is their symbol.'

Heather gestured questioningly to the torn posters.

'Not everyone is a fan.' Petra shrugged.

Simo returned from the café next door holding a tray of coffees. He handed the women one each. Heather sipped hers gratefully, feeling the hot drink reviving her.

'This morning,' Simo said to her, 'you must try and think a little bit like a police detective. Okay?'

'But not like Srpska police detective,' Petra teased. 'All useless fuckers.'

Simo shot her a look. He turned again to Heather. 'You must ask the questions we talked about.'

They'd rehearsed what she should say. Simo was very clear about how to conduct the interview. He'd remarked that they'd be lucky if Marina allowed him, a cop, into the office, and even if she did, Heather should be the one to ask the questions. But if Heather pushed too hard, too soon, Marina would shut down and ask them to leave. No pressure.

'You must build up a picture of her relationship with Ryan, gain her trust,' he said, 'before asking the more difficult questions.'

Heather tossed the empty cup into a wastebin and crossed the road to Marina's building, the other two following close behind. She searched the list of names on the door and hit the buzzer.

'*Zdravo?*'

'I'd like to talk to Marina Tomić.'

There was a pause, chatter in Bosnian, and then another voice over the intercom speaking perfect English with the merest hint of an accent. 'No walk-ins. Says it on the sign.'

'I'm Heather Bishop. Ryan Mackinnon's girlfriend. I think you knew him as Ryan Markovitz.'

There was a long silence. Heather and Simo looked at one another.

'It's not going to work,' she said.

'It'll work,' he said.

A minute passed, then another, and then at last there was a buzz and the door opened. They pushed inside to a narrow hall, with empty mailboxes on one side and a staircase in front of them.

'I suppose we go up?' said Petra.

The stairs were dirty and covered with litter and old newspapers. Surprising, Heather thought, for a legal firm. The first floor was registered to a party supplies company. They kept going. As they approached the second storey, Simo fell back, allowing Heather and Petra to go in front. The door to the office was ajar and Marina stood in the doorway, arms folded, surveying them with wary green eyes. She was elfin and slight, with long dark hair spilling out from beneath a cap. Heather reckoned she was about fifty.

'I'm Heather Bishop. And this is my friend Petra Sokolović—'

'Who's the cop?' said Marina, with a flick of her head.

Simo had carefully dressed as casually as he could in jeans and a sweater, but he wore his badge like a facial tattoo.

'Simo Subotić,' he said, moving forward and holding out his hand.

'He's my uncle,' Petra added, much to Marina's bafflement.

She ignored the proffered hand. 'In my experience most cops round here are arseholes.'

Simo smiled amiably.

'Yes,' said Heather. Simo's smile fell. 'I thought he was an arsehole, at first. But he's trying to find out what happened to Ryan.' She paused. 'You know that he's dead?'

'What happened to starting with the easy questions?' Simo muttered.

But the news didn't come as a surprise to Marina. 'I had heard, yes. I am very sorry. More sorry than I can say.'

'I don't want you to be sorry,' Heather said, tightly. 'I want to know who did this to him.'

At this, Marina softened slightly and she seemed to take pity on her. She let them into a small and untidy office crammed with filing cabinets and desks shoved into a corner. Marina gestured to a couple of mismatching and worn sofas jammed in the middle of the office, and the three of them took a seat.

'You're a strange trio,' said Marina, staring between them. She glared at Simo. 'I don't like the police.'

Heather ignored her. 'Are you *Dušica*?'

'Excuse me?' said Marina, puzzled.

'Ryan called you *Dušica*.'

It seemed to Heather that she was about to answer, but before she could speak, a man appeared from a small cubby off the main office and glowered at the three interlopers. He was tall and wiry, dressed in jeans and a sweater that was patched at the elbow, his black hair speckled with white.

'You don't need to talk to them,' he said, voice wary.

'No. But I want to, Nik.' She gave a shrug of both explanation and introduction to the others. 'My husband, Nikola Stanković. Also my lawyer.'

He did not say hello, but instead lurked in the corner, a hostile, nervy presence. Heather tried to ignore him, wondering why Marina would need a lawyer for this conversation.

'Yes,' Marina said.

It took a moment for Heather to realise she was answering her earlier question.

'Sometimes he called me *Dušica*. We are – were – very old friends.'

Simo had briefed her with a set of questions designed to open up the conversation, but sitting here in front of this woman, knowing she was eye-to-eye with *Dušica*, Heather was consumed with another question. 'Were you screwing Ryan?'

She was aware of Simo groaning quietly beside her. He'd been so clear about the line of questioning, and she'd blown it straight away. Their one chance to get Marina on side.

But rather than be offended by the question, Marina's small, rosebud mouth broke wide open into a laugh. Nikola looked entirely unperturbed; he too looked amused.

'Not for a long time,' said Marina. 'Twenty-six years ago. And only once. He wasn't my type.'

Heather released a breath she didn't know that she'd been holding. She believed her. That part of her relationship with Ryan, at least, had held true. With this knowledge she relaxed, and immediately some of the love and grief she'd been holding back out of self-protection seeped through her. She tried to block it out, tried to focus, acutely conscious of Simo's furious glances.

'How did you meet Ryan?' she asked, attempting to guide the conversation back on track.

'In a hotel bar in Dubrovnik back in, let's see, I think at the end of nineteen ninety-one. I was a translator. He was covering the siege for the *Post*. We both got stuck in the middle of it. That brings people together. At that point I was working for Reuters, and we ended up, you know . . .' She gave an unembarrassed shrug. 'Partly because we were drunk and a little frightened, but mostly because we were very bored and there was nothing much else to do.'

And you are extremely pretty, thought Heather. And back then, charming, ruthless, life-of-the-party Ryan must have been hard to resist. Although, to be honest, Marina would have been a bit out of his league.

'We were never really interested in each other in that way,' continued Marina. 'And then later, when he was sent to Bosnia and needed a translator – his Serbo-Croat was not nearly so good back then – he called me up. We worked together for the rest of the war. I think probably the fact that we screwed at the beginning and got it out of the way meant we were perfect colleagues.'

Heather smarted at the other woman's words, realising for the first time that she was envious of Marina. She knew a part of Ryan that she did not, and now would not. 'What was it like working with him?'

'He was so talented, and, Jesus, he was ambitious. We all were. It was his first proper war. He'd been in Iraq during the first Gulf War and complained how dull it was, how nothing happened. Well, the war here was not boring. I hooked him up with Alek, a photographer from the north. We'd do anything for each other. Took crazy risks to get a story. Alek's wife used to plead with me, as the only woman, to try to get the boys to be sensible, but then she discovered that I was as bad as them. In fact, it was Alek who was the most cautious. He was the one with two little girls. He tried to rein in me and Ryan, but we were kids ourselves, and oh my God, the world was on fire and no one gave a shit. Right here in Višegrad they were murdering whole families in their houses, mothers burned to death holding their babies and toddlers. It wasn't fear that kept me awake at night, it was anger.

'And, we thought, if we could just tell the right story, take the right picture, then maybe someone would notice. Someone in London or Paris or Washington might care a little bit. But, really, that was all bullshit. It was all about us. Not with Alek. His parents were dead by this point. His sister had been raped. But me and Ryan? We told ourselves it was about getting the story out there – pursuing it at all cost, risking our lives to save lives – but our ambition was hotter than the sun. We were like Icarus, on our ridiculous paper wings.'

She stopped, reached into her jacket for an e-cigarette and sucked it hungrily. The more animated and stressed she became, the stronger her Bosnian accent.

'We left Sarajevo and got permits to enter the zone around Zikoč where we'd heard rumours of a particularly vicious paramilitary group.'

'The Wolves?'

Marina nodded and poured herself some water and was quiet for a minute. 'We spent months writing about them. We'd stay in and around Zikoč, and then when it got too dangerous, we'd flee back to Sarajevo, then try and get back near Višegrad. By that point Ryan's Serbian was good too. Hardly needed me to translate, but we were a team. And Alek. He was the best.'

'And then Drakulić killed him.'

'You saw Ryan's article?' asked Marina, her face grave. 'It must have been hard for you to read.'

'In the context of this week, not the worst thing.'

Marina gazed at her, dark eyes big with pity, and Heather had to look away. She couldn't bear kindness, not now. If she allowed herself to think about Ryan, let herself feel the full horror of it all, she would be overwhelmed.

Perhaps sensing Heather falter, Petra took over the questioning. 'Drakulić killed Alek that night, why not Ryan?'

Marina started to vape again, her hands trembling.

'It's one thing to kill a Bosnian photographer like Alek. Of course, the *Post* was outraged at his death. They ran a charming obit—'

'Yes, I read it,' said Heather.

'But Ryan's a U.S. citizen, and even Drakulić couldn't really be bothered with the crazy shit-storm he'd face if he killed him. Instead, he negotiated all sorts of foreign aid in exchange for his release.'

'So, you tried to free Ryan,' said Simo, finally joining the conversation.

'And Alek,' said Marina. 'I didn't know he was dead then. They were missing for nearly a week and, when they didn't come back, I phoned our editor at the *Post*. He went crazy. But the *Post* and the U.S. Embassy then put a lot of pressure on the Serbs.'

'And Drakulić let Ryan go. Despite what he'd seen,' said Simo.

Marina gave a wry smile. 'As I said, lots of foreign aid. And none of the bastards were worrying about being prosecuted for war crimes when it was over. They were too busy trying to win. And they were right not to worry.' Her voice rose in anger. 'Nothing happened for years. Even now we're still trying to bring them to justice.'

'It's difficult,' agreed Simo. 'The criminals are now our neighbours and their children go to school with ours.'

Heather watched Marina and Nikola study Simo with considerable interest. In this part of the world, police oficers didn't usually profess such opinions.

'I heard it was you who found Drakulić after the war,' said Simo, looking at Marina.

'I was one of many. We spent a decade tracking him down. At first we thought he was in Argentina, but it turned out he had remained in Serbia, hidden in the mountains. Plenty of people viewed him as a national hero – still do – and it was only when the new government was installed in Serbia that suddenly the money used to hide him dried up, and we found him easier to track.'

'We spent four years preparing the case for trial at The Hague,' said Nikola. 'Drakulić was meticulous at keeping a distance between himself and the genocides.'

'That was why we needed Ryan at the trial,' added Marina. 'The rest of the evidence we had was mostly circumstantial.'

'But he wouldn't testify,' said Heather.

'No. So we did our best with the evidence we had. But in the end, Drakulić, murderer and rapist and perpetrator of genocide, was sentenced to ten years and served just seven in a luxurious prison in The Hague, which I'm told is more like a spa or hotel than a jail,' said Marina, bitterly.

Heather had heard Simo's opinion as to why Ryan had refused to testify, but she wanted to hear Marina's. 'Why wouldn't Ryan help you send Drakulić down for what he did to Alek?' she said, her voice catching.

Marina went over to the window, opening it, as if she was releasing the pressure that had built up in the room from revisiting the horrors of the recent past. She was silent for a long time.

'Ryan was changed by what happened to Alek. He carried on reporting during the war, but he wasn't the same man. He blamed himself for going there at all. It was his fault Alek was dead. He drank constantly. So filled with self-loathing he could only face himself after half a dozen shots of vodka or brandy. Or whatever. He wasn't fussy. After he told me what happened, he refused to speak about it with anyone else. He left me to tell Alek's widow. God. He was even drunk at Alek's memorial.

'Things became very bitter between Ryan and me,' she continued, moving to one of the desks and switching on an old laptop. The drive whirred and the screen bloomed into life. 'We did not talk for many years. It took ten years to find Drakulić. Nearly five to bring him to trial. By then, Ryan was struggling, and mostly failing, to stay sober. His life was in tatters. He wasn't a war reporter anymore. He couldn't bear it. He'd been fired from several newspapers, and he was trying to forge a new career. He couldn't sleep without pills. As far as Ryan was concerned, nothing could bring Alek back. He was a wreck and we were asking him to relive the worst moments and the worst decisions of his life, publicly. He couldn't do it. Here. This is one of the many emails he sent me.'

Marina turned the laptop around to Heather. Ryan's email was displayed on the screen.

Marina,

I'm so sorry. So fucking sorry. I don't expect you to ever understand. I just can't do it. I can't sit across from him in court. I've let Alek down. And you. I'm not even a journalist anymore. The worst bit is the way that others are holding me as some kind of paragon and martyr for the cause, as though my refusal to testify is because I'm a champion for objectivity and the sanctity of the source, when we both know I'm nothing but a coward. Make sure you tell anyone and everyone <u>the truth</u>.

The only comfort I can offer you is that Drakulić will still go to prison without my testimony. I know it won't be for as long. But what would feel like justice, Dušica? What possible sentence could atone for his crimes? Such a man cannot feel guilt. He only feels injury and victimhood that he was caught. He is a monster without remorse or sympathy.

Ryan

Petra leaped to her feet. 'Ryan is right. He is coward,' she spat. 'Drakulić killed my father. My father pulled the trigger, but it was Drakulić who put him in camp and had him tortured.' Her eyes blazed with rage. 'I sorry Ryan died in terrible pain, but he was too chicken shit to send that murdering bastard to prison forever. *Séronja!*'

They all stared at her, no one saying anything. Marina was the first to speak.

'Many felt like you, Petra. I did too, for years.'

'You weren't coward though,' said Petra.

'No,' said Marina simply, not bothering to deny it. 'After the war, while the U.N. sat on their hands, criminals disappeared like smoke. I became one of those who hunted them down. It was my way to try and get justice for Alek. I was working every hour trying to nail criminals. While Ryan was following bike races round the world, getting a suntan.'

Heather thought of Ryan's nightmares, the drinking and the decades of lies, and decided it wasn't quite that simple – although she wasn't ready to forgive him for the years of deception. Not yet. She kept silent.

Marina turned to Heather, taking a more conciliatory tone. 'One of the things he loved about you was that you knew nothing about it. You were too young. You only knew him as the other Ryan, the one he wanted to be. With you, he could be a good man. His best self.'

'Did you forgive him?'

'Not for a long time. We didn't speak for years. But, in time, I think maybe I understood.'

'And why did he ask you to meet him at Café Bulozi?' asked Simo, trying to bring it back to the investigation. 'Did something happen? Did Ryan change his mind?'

Marina closed the lid of the laptop. 'Ryan called and said he was here with his girlfriend. He'd been following some cycling tour. Asked to meet me in Zikoč. When I saw him, he seemed different. Something had definitely shifted.'

'In what way?' asked Simo.

Marina gestured vaguely, struggling to explain. 'So much time had passed. He'd met Heather, said he was tired of pretending to be a good man. He wanted justice. So, I told him that I wanted to bring a new case for the murder of Alek. I asked him to testify.'

'Did he give you an answer?' asked Simo, leaning forward eagerly.

Marina was quiet for a moment. 'He said we'd talk again. We went outside. He kissed me goodbye and said we must speak again. That I was brave and good and that he wished he could be like me.'

'Which you took to mean that he was going to testify?'

'Of course. What else could it mean?'

'You see,' said Heather, turning to Simo, her face flushed. 'He was a good man.'

Simo said nothing for a moment. 'It's possible,' he said at last, his voice heavy with uncertainty. 'Then what did you do?'

'I phoned Nik. I was excited. I thought at last we had a real chance of getting the bastard. Then, a couple of days later, I hear that Ryan's disappeared.'

Heather felt dizzy at the thought of what had happened to Ryan. How he'd suffered.

Marina bowed her head. 'We've been reaching out to witnesses. Very carefully. Drakulić has eyes everywhere. Seems to me that he must have found out Ryan was in the country and decided to take no chances and kill him. Drakulić's running drugs again, so I heard. He doesn't want to go back to prison.'

Heather turned to Simo. 'What now? How will you get Drakulić for this?'

He cleared his throat. 'Evidence. We don't have it yet. We only have a possible motive.'

Heather gazed at him, frustration bubbling in the pit of her stomach. 'Are you frightened, Inspektor?'

'Of Drakulić? Of course,' said Simo evenly. 'Only fools

have no fear. But it won't stop me doing my job. To prosecute Dragan Drakulić for murder here in Višegrad, the case must be very strong. It's not the same as trying a case in The Hague.'

Nikola laughed. 'Drakulić could be holding a bloody knife in one hand and a signed confession in the other and you'd still never get a conviction.'

'I disagree,' said Simo, politely. He got up and began to circle the office.

'Ryan tried to do the right thing in the end, even though it cost him everything.' Heather looked around at the others. 'He deserves justice.'

'The right thing twenty years too late,' said Petra, her voice rank with acrimony.

'No,' said Marina. 'I won't have that. Drakulić has been in prison for many years. And I believe Ryan was trying to make things right.'

'Thank you,' said Heather. The room swam before her eyes; she was so tired. It was an unfamiliar exhaustion that seemed to spread from deep within her, different from the tired muscles after a race.

Marina seemed to notice her flag and asked Nikola to bring in some tea. She turned back to Heather. 'The last few days have been a shock. It's not good for you. You need to be careful.'

Simo had stopped next to a window overlooking the street. Arranged on the wall next to the window was a mixture of newspaper clippings and photographs. One featured a Silent Women march: a group holding placards, prominent amongst them a woman with cropped, dyed-red hair. Simo recalled the informant saying that a red-headed woman had been with Ryan when he had tried to buy a gun.

'Who is this woman?'

Marina hesitated. Simo knew that her natural inclination was to refuse to answer questions from the police. However, she'd already told him plenty. He was betting that one more piece of information wouldn't hurt.

'Her name is Rubi Kurjak.'

The informant who sold Ryan the gun had heard him call the woman accompanying him by that name. Simo needed to speak to her, but he knew too that Marina would never pass on the details of another member of the Silent Women to a cop.

'I'd like to speak to her.'

Marina pulled a face. 'She lives in Sarajevo – out of your jurisdiction, Inspektor.'

It didn't matter. He'd seen the posters in the streets and there was another in the office, publicising tomorrow's protest here in Višegrad. The Silent Women would be there. And so too would Rubi Kurjak.

18

'I'm going to the protest,' said Heather.

The meeting with Marina had ended and Simo was driving her and Petra back to town. He knew she only wanted to go in order to question Rubi Kurjak. But he had a suspicion that Rubi would lead only to more unpleasant truths and, worse, to danger.

'Absolutely not,' he said. The Silent Women's demonstration was intended to be peaceful, but in his experience such gatherings had a habit of turning ugly. Even without the added uncertainty of Rubi's presence, it was no place for a civilian, especially not one like Heather.

'You know what happened to Ryan now,' said Simo. 'He changed his mind about testifying, but Drakulić had him killed before he or Marina could move forward with the case. There is nothing more to know. I think it is time for you to go home.'

He expected her to object – in his experience Heather wasn't good at taking his suggestions, even the well-intentioned ones – but to his surprise she just sat back in her seat and folded her arms in silence. Okay, good, for once she was listening to sense. He had only brought her to Višegrad in order to facilitate the interview with Marina. She'd done her job, and done it well, but now it was time for her to leave the police work to the professionals.

He dropped the two women back at Petra's place. Heather stormed inside, ignoring him, presumably still irritated by his words in the car. He pulled his niece aside.

'Get her on a flight out of here.'

'What if she doesn't want to leave?'

'Use your famous charm.'

Petra wrinkled her nose at the suggestion. She was many things, but no one would call her charming, especially not her family.

Simo shrugged. 'Fake it.'

He got back in the car and sat with the engine off, thinking back over the meeting in Višegrad. He hadn't entirely bought Marina's story. Had Ryan really seen the light after all this time and decided to turn prime witness to bring down Drakulić? Something felt off about that version of events. Something he had a feeling that Rubi Kurjak could throw light on.

Marina had let slip that Rubi lived in Bosnia, and since she was attending the protest tomorrow then she'd most likely be on her way to or in Višegrad already. However, it would be remiss of him not to check. He had good contacts in the Bosnian police force, forged after a number of cross-border cases earlier in his career. He put in a call. *Pleased to assist, Inspektor Subotić.* Yes, they would knock on her door. His name still carried some influence, he thought wryly, even if it wasn't at home. He hung up and began to drive.

The day had brought an ending for Heather, but it hadn't for him. He wanted her and Petra as far away from him as possible, given what he intended to do next. He drove to

David's apartment in Goražde. His friend was waiting on the doorstep when he arrived.

Simo walked straight past him, heading inside. 'I need a favour.'

David gave a weary sigh. 'Why do I get the feeling you're about to do something stupid – and rope me in on it?'

Simo made no answer, knowing that his friend would take that as confirmation of his suspicion. And he'd be correct.

David followed him into the apartment. 'So, first we set terms. What do I get in return?'

'What do you need?'

'A new tourist licence for my helicopter. Last time my application was rejected.'

'No shit. It's not a helicopter, it's a wheelbarrow with a rotor-blade.'

'I take that personally. She's a bird of beauty. I'll give you a ride—'

Simo snorted. 'No thanks.'

During the season David did steady trade, taking tourists on helicopter sunset tours of the beauty spots in Bosnia and Republika Srpska. His 'bird of beauty' was a Russian-made Mi-34 that he'd painted in black and red. It had been built in the nineties and, as far as Simo could tell, was now only held together by sticking plaster and rust. David was typically vague on how it had come into his possession, but Simo suspected from the patched-up bullet-holes on the doors that it had seen action during the war as part of the Bosnian Air Force.

'I don't understand how you have a licence for that thing at all.'

'I have friends in high places,' said David.

'Not me.'

'No,' he agreed. 'Every time I see you, you've sunk a little lower.'

Simo sighed. 'Fine. I'll do what I can from my lowly position.' He pulled out his phone and showed David the photo of Rubi Kurjak. 'I need some background.'

'You have a perfectly good database at the police station.'

'Yes, with perfectly good police operators I can't trust.' Under normal circumstances, Simo would have circulated the photo of Rubi to the squad. Apart from anything else, it would significantly up his chances of tracking her down in the crowd tomorrow. However, he couldn't trust his own people. If, as he suspected, Rubi *was* involved in this business with Drakulić, Simo couldn't risk a cop with sympathies towards the criminal picking her up. He tapped a series of keys and sent the photo to David.

David had resources that would put any police department to shame. Since the war he'd cultivated contacts in all sorts of interesting places, many of them unavailable to law-abiding policemen like Simo. Over the years Simo had learned not to ask too many questions about these denizens of the dark spaces, but he knew that if anyone could dig up information on Rubi, it was David.

'Okay, fine,' he said, studying the photo that had now popped up in his messages. He looked up. 'But you're not here just to find out about this Rubi Kurjak, are you?'

His friend's instincts were spot on. Simo mentally braced himself, knowing how David would react to his next words. 'I'm going to see Drakulić.'

David spread his arms wide and embraced Simo,

pretending to be moved. 'And you'd like me to read your eulogy. I'm touched. Any particular choice for hymns? Funeral flowers, or just donations to your favourite charity, "Pig-headed Policemen with a Death-Wish"?'

'Jeb'o ti pas mater! He's the prime suspect in the murder of Ryan Mackinnon. I need to talk to him face-to-face, see how he reacts.'

'By shooting you in the head. That's how he will react, *idiot*. Or, perhaps, the stomach. He likes to watch people die. Maybe he'll eat popcorn while you bleed out.'

'The Mackinnon case is connected to the Drina killings. I'm certain of it. And until Rubi Kurjak shows up, Drakulić is my best shot at working out how.' His plan wasn't as risky as David painted it. 'There's a vigilante killer taking out war criminals and Drakulić is shitting himself that he's next on the list. He's desperate for me to break the case. I'm his best chance of survival. He's not to going to harm me – he needs me.'

'Mm-hmm,' David mused, doubtfully. 'And you're so confident he's not going to try anything that you don't want me to come along for the ride and hide out nearby with a Remington 7600? Just in case.'

Simo grinned. 'Well, you don't get out much. So, it's really charity, having you come along. But if you're busy . . .'

David slapped him on the back with an enormous hand. *'Govno jedno.* Like I'd let you go without back-up.'

The meeting with Marina and her revelation about Ryan's past had taken more out of Heather than she'd anticipated, and soon after she stumbled through Petra's front door, she'd flopped out on the couch and fallen asleep.

A sense of heaviness remained with her on waking, coating her in a shroud of dust. She had pursued Ryan through her dreams, chasing him bloodied and barefoot through the woods in the snow, following the red footprints as she called for him, but he was always just out of sight, hidden beyond the huddle of blackened trees. She shouted for him in rage and grief. Yet he seemed oblivious to her torment. He was there, could see her but wouldn't turn around, would not comfort her. When she woke, it was with relief and a fresh sense of resolve.

Ryan might not have cheated on her with Marina, but he had betrayed her. He had lied to her every day that they had been together. During their entire relationship, Heather had felt inferior. Before him she had been an athlete, a freak of nature, a mortal god, able to endure and achieve, but with him she was no one, a prematurely aged twenty-something stumbling with a walking frame, falling asleep halfway through a newspaper. Slowly she had put herself back together, piece by piece, and he had helped where he could, but how much easier it would have been if he could have confided his own frailty. The hurt hit Heather like a physical pain and she doubled over, a fierce ache deep in her belly. But in the twisting pain she understood, at last, that she had recovered in order to deserve him, this imperfect, flawed man who lied and lied and whom she loved. She would have loved him all the same. She still did.

'There's a flight leaving for Heathrow tomorrow, two p.m.' Petra stood over her, finger poised over the airline booking website on her phone.

Heather ignored her. 'The Silent Women protest tomorrow – is it a march? What happens?'

Petra lowered the phone. 'They're going to throw flowers off the bridge in Višegrad – red lilies – remembering all who were murdered.'

'On the orders of Drakulić,' said Heather, quietly.

'Some of them. Yes.'

'I want to throw a lily, for Ryan.'

Petra put a hand on her hip and cocked her head on one side, studying Heather critically. 'No, you don't. You want to find Rubi Kurjak and question her until she tells everything she knows about lying boyfriend.'

A familiar well of nausea rose from Heather's belly to her throat and she raced to the toilet and vomited. Afterwards she sat in her underwear on the tile floor and splashed cold water from the bath over her face. She was never usually sick. Occasionally, during training or a race when she'd eaten too close to the start and pushed herself beyond endurance, or when she had a fever. Yet it occurred to her that during the last week or so she had frequently felt dizzy and nauseous. She'd assumed it was due to the absurd amount of stress and anxiety loaded upon her, so much that sometimes she felt she couldn't even breathe. It had been stupid to come off her medication quite so suddenly. There was nothing she could do now; she'd flushed it all away. She felt sweaty with anxiety. Colours swirled. Automatically, her hands fluttered to her throat, and as they did so brushed her breasts, which she realised were incredibly sore. Heather sat upright on the bathroom floor, touched her breasts again and winced. That was not a side effect of withdrawal.

'Think useless lying boyfriend has knocked you up.'

Petra stood watching her from the bathroom doorway. Stunned, Heather said nothing. Pregnant – was it possible?

She tried to remember when her last period had been and found she could not. They had stopped altogether when she was competing, and even afterwards, when her cycle returned, they had been irregular. A nagging voice told her that her erratic menstrual cycle meant that she was sometimes lackadaisical with contraception.

Dizziness gripped her again. Petra stepped into the bathroom and caught her under the neck, gently laying her down on the floor. Heather felt the relief of the cold tile against her cheek; she had no idea whether she wanted to be pregnant or not. 'Test,' she managed to stutter. 'I need a pregnancy test.'

'No shit,' said Petra, helping her to her feet.

Leaning on Petra for support, Heather walked to the living room and resumed her spot on the couch.

'Store in Zikoč will be open,' said Petra. 'I be back soon. You be okay for ten minutes?'

She didn't wait for an answer. Heather heard her in another part of the house swearing as she searched for her 'fucking car keys'.

As much as she appreciated the other woman's concern, Heather's impulse was to act for herself. Taking several long, deep breaths she raised herself onto her feet and slipped out of the house before Petra noticed. She pushed her bike onto the road. Ice gleamed on tarmac and bangles of hoar frost tinselled the pine trees on the banks. As she pushed off, her breath hung in the air like fog. There was a definite shift in the weather and she shivered despite her fleece. It took less than fifteen minutes to reach the scattering of shops at the centre of Zikoč. The small grocery store was open and she chained the bike outside and hurried in. Amongst shower caps, condoms and foot cream was a stack of pregnancy tests. Heather picked one up and took it to the counter, grabbing a few biscuit bars and packets of sweets and raisins as both snacks and camouflage, and handed her cash to a disinterested girl behind the counter who was preoccupied blowing flaccid blue bubbles with a mournful pop. Heather shoved the test into her pocket and retreated into the empty street.

She needed to pee on the stick but for that she required a toilet, and first, a coffee. The grimy café opposite was open. The last time she'd been there was with Simo, right before they'd searched the woods for Ryan. She shuddered as she recalled the bullet-strewn huts lurking amongst the trees. She bought herself an Americano and wondered vaguely if she was supposed to drink coffee if she was indeed pregnant. With a sudden pang of guilt, she remembered the number of brandies and large glasses of wines that she had consumed over the last few days. Shaking off her misgivings, she downed the coffee – she was getting ahead of herself.

She started to ride back towards Petra's. The sky was bleached white, the sun a small tangerine bobbing above the black trees. Heather's hands ached with cold. She rued not wearing her gloves. There was no noise but the whirr of her tyres and the ribald chatter of the birds in the pines. She braked, sending up a flurry of pebbles, suddenly gripped with the urgent need to pee. She set her bike down on a bed of moss, deciding that she would prefer to perform the test right here amongst the trees and the insects and birds. She'd last seen Ryan not so far from here, on a morning rather like this one. It made her feel a little less alone.

She scrambled off the road, down a muddy bank into a

thicket of trees. Wood anemones like white stars spangled the ground, petals dusted with frost. She took the box from her pocket and scanned the instructions. Pretty straightforward. Holding out the plastic stick, she pulled down her trousers and knickers and squatted amongst the dead leaves and urinated on the stick, cursing as she managed to pee a little on her hand. Standing, she hitched up her trousers and replaced the cap on the stick. She needed to wait a few minutes. Setting a timer on her phone, she leant against a tree and listened to the noisy chirrup of the birds. What would she do if she was pregnant? She could barely take care of herself, let alone someone else. And now she was by herself. Dear God. Let it be negative. Heather knew absolutely that there was no possible way she could cope. Her mother would be no use and she had few friends back in England. The timer on her phone beeped. Heather opened the cap on the test.

Positive.

She crumpled, hugged her knees and wept. Wept because she was alone and suddenly not alone. Because Ryan was dead and she loved him, and now she had a piece of him. Here was unexpected joy – and to Heather's immense surprise, she realised it was joy – in the midst of confounding sadness. She had something to focus upon, something tiny and good. She had a purpose. She thought back to the ride up to the Olympic rings with Ryan. He'd been so certain that she'd come up with a plan of what to do next. It never would have occurred to him that it was this – motherhood. Was she already pregnant back then? She realised that of course she must have been. At once, her grief was thrown into relief. Ryan would never know. Not only had he been taken from her, but so had their future, their family's future.

The size of her loss continued to grow, a wound whose stitches kept being ripped and reopened so it gaped. Heather mashed her fingers into damp and partially frozen ground, grinding her nails into the dirt. It wasn't fair. She wanted justice. She screamed and screamed into the woods, trying to empty the rage from the pit of her. The scream tore through her, echoing amongst the trees until her throat hurt and the muscles of her stomach ached. The forest was silent, listening. It made no reply.

They took David's truck instead of Simo's police car – no point in advertising his credentials. The valley was steep, and David drove his truck like he flew his damn helicopter, at high speed, seemingly barely in control. They hurtled around bends, the truck slithering along the mountain road, at one point hitting a patch of black ice. Simo cursed as he sloshed coffee all over his trousers. Beside him, David chuckled.

'If we weren't off the books, I'd give you a ticket,' muttered Simo. He lowered his window and inhaled the chilled air. Cool light spilled across the European Black and Scots pines along the side of the gorge. At the base of the road the river was a slick dark ribbon, but later in the afternoon it would change to unearthly blue. They swerved around a pothole and Simo ended up wearing the rest of his coffee.

'Son of a bitch.' He dabbed at the spreading stain on his sweater.

'I hate that sweater. You never wear anything else, Simo. Buy another.'

'My wife gave it to me. It's sentimental.'

'She divorced you and is giving sweaters and blowjobs to another man.'

Simo winced. It was possible that David had a point. He stared out of the car window again. Here and there the leaf litter was tinged with white, the startled spring flowers sugar-coated with frost. The cold snap had been sudden and harsh. Almost every year winter played this trick, sneaking back up on you just as you relaxed and thought that it must finally be over, the first cuckoo had sung, the apple blossom was humming with bees. The Balkan winter was cruel and liked to catch you when you weren't looking.

'This time of year always makes me think of Abdul,' said Simo. 'It's been nearly seven years. Every time I look at Petra, I think how I failed her father.'

'Bullshit,' said David. 'You did everything you could to get him out of that camp. Used up every favour any lowlife ever owed you. Or me.'

'And we still couldn't save him.'

'Not true,' said David. 'You bought him many years. He saw his daughter grow from a child into a woman. Petra got to know her father. If you'd left him there to die, she wouldn't even have had a grave to visit. He would have been one of the numberless dead in a mass grave.'

Simo shook his head. 'I took too long. By the time we got him out, he was broken. His soul was in pieces. He wasn't Abdul anymore.'

'I miss him too. Every day I think of him. But we tried. And Simo, my friend, you can't save everyone.'

'Most of the time, it seems I can't save anyone. And I do the same job for them all – Serb, Muslim, even American journalists. Blood is the same red for everyone.'

Simo felt David's concerned gaze on him. 'Does Josif know you're off to speak to his father?'

He shrugged, affecting a nonchalance he didn't feel. 'He looked busy.'

David chuckled. 'Soon you'll be sweeping floors in that station.'

'Not allowed. Janitors have a different union.'

David braked sharply, parking up as they reached a curve in the river where it shallowed into an oxbow lake, dark pine forests lining the steep valleys behind them on every side. Simo climbed stiffly out of the car, grateful to be released from the bone-jarring ride. The woods were so dense they appeared black, the mountains shadowing them from the sun. He scanned about him, aware that eyes may already be watching.

'We should walk the rest of the way. We'll seem less threatening on foot,' said David. 'If we're very lucky, they won't see us coming.' He picked up his rifle and several magazines of ammo. They walked the two miles without speaking, watching for tell-tale signs of lookouts on the route, aware that they, too, were in all likelihood being stalked. After half an hour they spotted a wisp of smoke rising above the treetops, and soon after they paused at the edge of a clearing where a lone cabin stood, smoke puffing from its chimney. Several burned-out cars blocked the rough road leading to it and three men with guns lazed on the porch.

'I want them to know you're in the woods,' said Simo. 'It's best they know I'm not alone.'

David agreed and, rifle in hand, retreated noiselessly into the treeline. Simo unholstered his Glock and tucked it in an inside pocket in order to seem as unthreatening as possible, but then changed his mind and re-holstered it. They were bound to search him anyway, and a concealed weapon would only cause trouble. He wondered if David was right and it was a mistake to come here. It was too late now.

He gave his friend a few minutes to disappear amongst the trees and then strolled towards the front door, arms raised high above his head. In three-and-a-half seconds, he was on his front in the dirt with a boot on his back and a gun in his face. The door to the cabin opened and a man with perfectly brushed silver hair appeared on the threshold in leather slippers.

'Coffee, Subotić?' Drakulić glanced into the trees. 'Is your friend coming in? Or is he going to lurk in the bushes?'

'David?' Simo called from his position in the dirt.

There was no sound.

'The bushes, I think,' said Simo. 'But I take milk and sugar.'

Drakulić retreated into the cabin, mouthing a command to the guards. The guards gave Simo a good kick in the ribs, which he knew he was going to feel later, before allowing him to stand. One of the guards patted him down, removing his Glock. Unarmed, he brushed himself off and went inside.

'Wipe your feet,' called Drakulić. 'There's no need to tramp in half the forest.'

Simo tried to gauge the other man's expression to see if he was kidding. Hard to tell. He supposed one could be a fastidious psychopath. The cabin was clean, if sparse. Simo observed bars on the windows – whether to keep people in or out, wasn't clear. The guard who'd claimed his pistol followed him in and presented the weapon to Drakulić.

'You understand,' said Drakulić, civilly. 'You may have it back when you leave.'

He moved to the sink and filled the kettle. 'Wait outside,'

he said to the guard. 'The Inspektor won't be any trouble.' It was both an instruction and a warning.

Drakulić motioned to a small kitchen table, improbably covered in a cheerful red gingham oilcloth. He sat at one of the carved wooden chairs and gestured to the other. There were faded checked curtains and a calendar with icons of the saints, and a collection of china dogs, some of which had been unceremoniously shoved to the side to make way for a CCTV screen, which displayed the track leading up to the cabin and the layby where David and Simo's truck was parked. So much for discretion. Another screen showed different angles of the cabin and various spots in the woods. The kettle began to sing. Immediately Drakulić stood.

'Coffee.'

This was not how Simo had expected the meeting to go, and he found himself knocked off course, watching as Drakulić stirred in milk and sugar. The smell of wood smoke drifted through from the small living room beyond.

'My grandmother's place,' said Drakulić conversationally, as if they were two old pals making small talk. 'Cold in the winter, but very pleasant in the spring.'

'Remote, and with one road in and out that's easily watched,' said Simo, indicating the CCTV.

'Too many potholes for the postman. He won't drive up the track,' said Drakulić, benignly.

He watched Simo from behind horned spectacles, with eyes as clear and blue as the Drina. Simo knew he was in his early sixties, but when it suited him Drakulić liked to play up his age, to feign frailty and pretend he was much older. Simo took in the leather slippers and the knotted cashmere scarf, as though he felt the cold. His hand even trembled as he stirred and carefully set a flowered coffee mug on the table. It was all a careful lie, designed to imply impotence and infirmity. Beneath the slouch and too large woollen sweater, Simo could see the muscular bulk of the man, honed from prison. The silver hair had barely thinned and, when he spoke, his teeth were white and strong. This was the Wolf, pretending to be grandpapa. Simo didn't believe a bit of it.

'I want to talk to you about Ryan Mackinnon.'

'Who?'

'American journalist murdered here. Used to go by Ryan Markovitz.'

Drakulić shook his head. 'My memory . . . not what it used to be . . .'

'I think you remember just fine.'

As Simo watched, Drakulić seemed to straighten and grow, shrugging off the old man act like it was a cape falling to the floor.

'Haven't seen him since the war.'

'Really? Because I have witnesses who say Ryan was about to testify against you in a new trial.'

Drakulić shrugged.

'You don't seem concerned?'

Drakulić took off the thick glasses and banged his fist on the table. Simo's untouched coffee jumped.

'Why would I kill some reporter, Subotić? That's what you're asking, right? I don't care about a witness in a trial; I'd be safer in prison.'

'Why's that?'

For the first time Drakulić looked unsettled. He shook his head and rubbed heavily pouched eyes. 'Someone's coming for me. You know that.'

Now they were getting to the meat of it. 'Who's coming?'

Drakulić boomed a great laugh. 'If I knew that I sure as hell wouldn't be up here in old *baka*'s cabin.'

Simo snorted with disbelief. 'You want me to believe that you're quite happy to go back to prison.'

Drakulić shot him a sly smile. 'Happy to be in protective custody awaiting trial, at the taxpayer's expense. Who says anything about being sent down? They'll spend four years arguing and waiting for a trial date. I'll split another million dollars in trial fees, all paid for by the ICC, with my lawyer. No problem.'

Simo watched him. It was bravado for sure but smacked at least partly of the truth. He didn't seem concerned about a possible trial. He seemed worried about a vigilante killer. Simo wondered if part of the old-man get-up was actually some sort of bizarre disguise.

'If you're so concerned, why not go to the police?'

'I did. I told my son. He told me to stay out of it and gave the case to you. Told me you were *Djubre jedno* but a great fucking cop. I'm not so sure. Took you long enough to identify the bodies.'

So, he admitted he knew who they were. That was worth something. 'How did you know Arkan Ćešić and Ivan Fuštar were dead?'

'They missed fucking bingo night,' he snarled, with a look of derision.

'Are there others?'

'You're the detective. Shouldn't you know?'

Simo was convinced that for all his bluster, Drakulić was scared. Restless fingers tapped on his bouncing leg and his eyes continually strayed to the CCTV screens. When he moved, Simo noticed that the sweater tightened over the impression of a gun holster. Simo placed his hands carefully on the table, suddenly hyper aware that he was sitting in the kitchen with an edgy, armed psychopath who was seeing killers stalking him in every shadow.

'Usually, in a situation like this, I would ask if you know of anyone with a grudge. Anyone who might want to harm you. But in your case, I know that will get me a very long list.'

Drakulić laughed. 'I couldn't begin to tell you the names on it.' He leaned back in his chair. 'Anyone whose family passed through Vilina or believes there were concentration camps near Zikoč. The men who went through the prison camps tend to exaggerate their experience to make themselves sound macho. You know how it was, Inspektor.'

'I do know. I lived through the war.' It wasn't part of the scope of his current investigation, but Simo couldn't resist taking this opportunity to bring up something that had tormented him for years. 'Of course you won't remember Abdul Sokolović.'

Drakulić shrugged, his face blank.

'He was a friend of mine, husband of my cousin. You had him tortured.'

'It was a war.' Drakulić formed his lips into a moue of disinterest. 'You didn't say he was killed. Was this Abdul released? Perhaps he is the one who is now killing off his former enemies. I hope your fondness for him doesn't mean you haven't checked him out.'

'He's dead.'

'Okay, so not Abdul,' agreed Drakulić, evenly.

Simo struggled to stay as calm as the man sitting

opposite, knowing he mustn't lose control. 'You sent men to my parents' house when I wouldn't join your army.' His voice rose in anger, despite himself.

Drakulić grinned, delighted that he'd got to him. 'Yes, didn't you pussy your way out of it by becoming a translator for the Americans?'

'If that's what you heard, it must be true.' Simo mustn't let him in his head.

Drakulić went back to staring at the CCTV screen, searching for shadows stealing through the woods to kill him. 'This is how they fight the war now, Subotić. These coward vigilantes. They come after war heroes one at a time in the dark. They are too scared to fight like proper men. *Jeb'o ti pas mater!*'

Simo longed to tell him that's what he deserved for ordering the torture and death and brutalisation of hundreds of people – to spend the rest of his life looking over his shoulder. Hate and fear had stalked him to this miserable cabin in the dark woods. But despite Drakulić's serene smile, Simo didn't rise to the provocation. That wasn't how this encounter was going to play out. Simo realised he'd been right about Drakulić needing him to solve the case. Beneath the calm veneer and polite offers of coffee was a worried and frightened man. Dragan Drakulić was losing it. Cold dread gripped Simo at the realisation. There was one thing worse than a psychopath in control, and that was one out of control.

19

Petra drove them to the city in silence. Heather was grateful. She couldn't face small talk and once she'd informed her about the pregnancy test result, Petra hadn't asked any more questions. She hadn't even offered her congratulations. Then again, Petra didn't seem like the kind of person who threw baby showers. There was a long traffic jam leading into Višegrad. Petra broke her silence with a stream of swearwords and a blast on the car horn.

'I hadn't realised the Silent Women had this much support,' said Heather.

'They don't.' Petra frowned at the gathering throng. 'Counter-protestors.' Spinning the steering wheel, she scooted down an alley, weaving through several side streets before parking the car opposite the same office building they had visited the day before. She left the engine running. 'I can still take you to airport in time for flight.'

Heather had made up her mind. Rubi Kurjak was the final piece of the puzzle about Ryan; she had to talk to her. Having made her decision, she'd called Marina last night, asking her to put her in touch with Rubi. When Marina was sufficiently reassured that Heather was acting for herself and not on Simo's behalf, she told her to come to the office in the morning. She'd see what she could do.

The office was full – mostly women, although there were several men – ferrying boxes of crimson lilies downstairs. She watched as a stream of people left the office, hurrying past her on their way to the protest. More boxes of lilies were piled high across the floor. The mood was an odd mix of grim and carnival. Marina greeted Heather and Petra, kissing them on both cheeks.

'Is she here?' asked Heather, searching the room, but not seeing a woman with red hair.

'We are all gathering at the bridge in half an hour,' said Marina, hefting a couple of boxes into her own arms. She gestured with a nod. 'Take one and come.'

Heather grabbed a box and Petra followed suit. The sounds of the crowd drifted up from the street to the office window, an unsettling cacophony of shouts and chants, curling and uncurling with the threat of sudden violence.

'Are you ready?' Petra asked.

No, thought Heather. How could anyone be ready for this?

Simo marched reluctantly into the chief's office. He'd come in early only so that he could leave for the protest in time, but Josif had learned about his unscheduled visit to Drakulić's lair the day before and hauled him in for what promised to be a dressing down.

The chief looked frazzled. He ran a hand through thinning hair. 'Never go and see my father without clearing it with me first. What the hell's wrong with you?'

'The usual insubordination.'

'Don't be a smartass. You want to speak to him, let me set it up. Don't go around me ever again.'

Simo was tired of this. 'Why? You told me to investigate. So, I investigated.'

Josif couldn't have it both ways, Simo thought to himself, believing that he could be a decent police officer while at the same time protecting his father; deluding himself that he could keep Drakulić like a big croc on a chain. At some point the strain would become too much and the chain would snap. Before then Josif would have to choose a side. Simo could see that the younger man was struggling with the dilemma, even as he denied it to himself. He decided that one day he would tell the chief to his face, but not today. Today he needed to get out of here, and soon.

Josif seemed to lose heart for the fight with Simo. He reached into the back of the filing cabinet for a bottle of whisky and a single glass and poured himself a drink. 'You could've ended up dead.' Josif swallowed the measure. 'Now get the hell out of my office.'

Heading out of the station and climbing into his car, Simo felt oddly gratified – Josif's concern for his health had seemed genuine. Surprising, but welcome. He set off for Višegrad and the protest. As he reached the outskirts of the town, his phone buzzed. It was David.

'Rubi Kurjak – Rubija Bekić as she was before she married – was one of the few survivors at Vilina Vlas Spa during the war. Fourteen years old when she was taken there for the first time. Drakulić had seen her on the school bus and ordered her off. Took her to the hotel and raped her. He allowed her to go back home. Her mother and grandmother nursed her, but he kept coming back for her. Six months this carried on.'

'*Govno*,' Simo swore softly. He had listened to these stories so many times before, but it never grew any easier to hear.

'Her grandmother and mother wanted to hide her in the woods, but she refused.'

Rubi knew what would happen to them, thought Simo. If Drakulić learned they had deprived him of a favourite girl, they would have suffered a brutal fate.

'Eventually, she was so weak that she couldn't resist them. They told Drakulić she had committed suicide. Lots of the girls did – he had no reason to doubt them. Later, they managed to get her out of the country.'

'And after the war?'

'She went to England as a refugee. Was in a psychiatric hospital in London for a long time. Post-traumatic stress. Then, about fifteen years ago, she moved to Sarajevo.'

Simo pondered. 'With Drakulić out of prison, she has a motive for either wanting him back in jail, or dead. And I'm guessing there's a good chance that while she was in London she found time to meet Ryan Mackinnon.'

She was without a doubt the missing link between the cases.

'One more thing,' said David. 'She's a collector.'

'Of what?'

'Unpaid parking fines. My friend at parking enforcement tells me she acquired a new one this morning. The address is in Višegrad – I'm sending it now.'

'Don't suppose you've got her mobile number too?'

'What do you take me for – some kind of rank amateur? It's with the address.'

Simo never ceased to marvel at David's list of shady

contacts. It struck Simo that since he had agreed to acquire a new tourist licence for his friend, with dubious justification, that made him part of the same list. He hung up and made his way slowly into the city. The protest wasn't due to start for another hour but already the streets were swamped with people. It was barely eleven o'clock, and already they were drinking and hurling bottles. The air was chilled and full of menace. The police presence was significant, but he wondered whether they ought to have called in reinforcements from Goražde or Banja Luka. Having Jenny and the ICC in the area was a problem. Their work was vital for the victims and their families, but wounds that had never really healed were suddenly open, seeping sores. Simo was concerned that this demonstration posed a real risk to public safety. He adored Jenny but he would be glad when her work was complete.

Simo listened to his radio as officers across the city radioed in reports of petty unrest and scuffles. Still more people flooded into the streets. Simo scanned the faces passing by: people shouting, men drinking and cheering, women holding one another's hands, women clutching placards. It was going to be a long day.

Fifteen minutes later, guided by the address David had forwarded, he located Rubi's car, an ancient Opel with Bosnian plates and a fresh parking ticket tucked under one wiper. The street was close to the bridge where the protest was due to take place, and, judging from the full-throated roar, it had begun early. He called the number David had supplied. A woman's voice answered, immediately wary.

'Who is this?'

She was clearly struggling to hear him over the noise of the crowd.

'Ms Kurjak? Rubi Kurjak? Are you the owner of a white Opel, licence . . .' He glanced at the plate affixed to the front of the car and reeled off the registration number. It was obviously her car. Simo explained that he was from the towing company and was about to remove her vehicle, but he noticed the Bosnian plates and, being a fellow Bosniak – he lied – decided to give her a chance to make good. The implication being: a bribe for your ride.

Simo was counting on the fact that the inconvenience of having her car towed wasn't worth missing half an hour of the protest. He was right. It wasn't long before he spotted a woman with vivid red hair turning into the end of the street. As she approached, she grew more suspicious.

'Rubi Kurjak?'

'Where's your tow-truck?' she asked, peering at him.

He pulled out his official ID. 'Inspektor Simo Subotić.'

Instantly, she turned on her heel and was about to make a run for it when he grabbed her arm. At first she looked so shocked to be grabbed by a police officer that she stopped dead. The scene attracted the attention of a crowd of people making their way to the protest. Simo flashed his ID at them, warding them off. Indignant, Rubi tried to yank her arm away. Simo didn't let go. For a moment he thought she would spit in his face.

'I need to talk to you about Ryan Mackinnon,' he said, drawing her gently away from the crowd.

'I don't know any Ryan Mackinnon.'

'Don't lie to me. I just want to talk.'

With Rubi's protests drowned out by the noise of the protesters, he steered her firmly away from the street into an alley. It stank of refuse and stale urine. The strains of nationalistic songs and furious counter songs echoed around them. Someone began to bang dustbin lids. Simo hoped it was just a dustbin lid. Yet the bustle and din offered them an odd sort of privacy.

'You can't stop me exercising my right to protest,' Rubi snarled.

She had no reason to talk to him and her dislike of the police was palpable. But he had to persuade her, and quickly. He couldn't detain her for long. So, even though it disgusted him to pretend, knowing the horror of what she'd been through as a young girl, he decided that he would be the cop she assumed him to be.

'Give me one good reason why I shouldn't take you down to the station and tell Josif Borisov you're our lead suspect in the targeted assassination of his father. How do you think that interview will go, hmm? Yes, you'll walk out of the police station. But for how long?'

She stared at him aghast, her face drained of all colour.

'Five minutes,' said Simo, dropping his grip on her. This time, she didn't try to run. 'Marina Tomić is pushing for a new trial for Drakulić? Do you think that's the right way to go?'

'I'm here, aren't I?'

'It's a protest. Not a trial.' Simo had to raise his voice as the crowd's voice suddenly swelled. 'Did you ask Ryan Mackinnon to testify?'

Rubi swore. *Jebi si.* Screw The Hague. Do you know how much money Drakulić made out of his last trial?'

'A million dollars.'

'Who told you that?' asked Rubi, surprised.

'Drakulić himself.'

She spat another oath. 'You see? He doesn't even have to hide it. He was paid by the International Court of Justice to spend on his defence, and he split it with his lawyer. He came out of prison a rich man. A rich rapist and mass murderer! Why would I want to conspire to put him on trial again, so that he can earn more money?'

As she spoke, spittle formed at the sides of her mouth. Simo watched her, calmly and with sympathy. He did not like to wonder what they had done to her to make her so angry and intent on revenge. She kicked at a beer can.

'Did Ryan want to testify?' he asked.

'He was thinking about it,' said Rubi. 'Until I talked him out of it. I didn't mean to. I just told him about the money. The futility of it all.'

'And that put him off?'

She nodded and glanced down at her stubby, filthy nails. 'Then, after he died, I felt like shit. I suppose it was my fault. If I'd let him go along with Marina's stupid plan and he'd agreed to testify, he wouldn't have . . .' She looked down at her hands again, her eyes filling with tears.

'Wouldn't have what?' pressed Simo.

For the first time Rubi looked alarmed.

'Ms Kurjak?' He tried to shut out the caterwauling all around them.

She looked up at him with round, wide eyes. 'Nothing. It wasn't me. It was all Ryan.'

'What was? As well as Ryan's body in the Višegrad morgue, I also have the bodies of Arkan Ćešić and Ivan Fuštar. And, at the moment, my best lead is you. Josif Borisov is convinced his father is next.'

'So, if it was all Ryan,' asked Simo slowly, 'then tell me what did he do?'

'He took a hit out on Dragan Drakulić.'

Simo sighed; she was still lying to him. It wasn't so easy to hire a professional killer, not even in Srpska. He'd have needed help. 'Ryan hadn't been in the country for years, and he didn't have those kind of contacts. But I think perhaps you know the right kind of people.'

'I don't know anything about that,' said Rubi.

Simo realised she wasn't going to incriminate herself, not if she could help it. 'Okay. Let's pretend I believe you. How did Ryan end up dead?'

She looked stricken. 'No one can get close to Drakulić. He's so careful. Doesn't go anywhere without guards. Never leaves that cabin. His shitbag chief of police son watches him all the time, lets him do whatever the fuck he wants but keeps the police looking out for him like his own personal bodyguard service.'

Now this Simo believed. He scrutinised Rubi and she met his eye.

'Ryan came out here as bait.'

Jesus Christ. Of all the terrible, desperate plans. *Bait.* And yet, it made a kind of twisted sense. Drakulić was notoriously cautious, emerging into daylight less often than a vampire. But someone who knew as much as Ryan Mackinnon *could* have drawn him out. Unfortunately for Ryan – and Rubi – their bait had been swallowed whole, but with no catch to show for the loss. An image of the distraught face of Heather Bishop flashed across Simo's mind and he felt his temper flare. It must have shown on his features, because Rubi took a step back.

'Knowing what this place is, what Drakulić is,' he railed, 'you suggested to Ryan that he come out here and offer himself up. I take it all back – I should arrest you. You knew that Drakulić would try to kill him.'

'It wasn't like that!' Rubi wailed. 'Ryan *wanted* to help. He offered. We had people here who were protecting him.' Her voice tailed off as she realised how hollow that must sound now.

Simo made a derisive grunt.

'Ryan and Drakulić had history,' Rubi continued. 'He was sure that if he was here, in Srpska, and asked Drakulić to meet and talk, he could get close. Lure him out.'

'Is that why Ryan bought a gun? If the plan had worked, he was going to kill Drakulić himself?'

To his surprise, Rubi gave a short laugh. 'Ryan didn't know one end of a gun from the other. He was no killer. And neither am I,' she added, defensively. 'But I told you, I don't know the details. I don't know who he hired. Ryan didn't tell me. I would have tried to talk him out of it.'

Despite the half-truths Rubi had strewn in his path, Simo was confident that at last he had reached the truth. Ryan Mackinnon had come to Srpska to tempt Drakulić out of hiding, but the bait had ended up as prey, tortured, murdered and dumped in a war grave. 'Did Marina Tomić know about the plan?'

'Marina?' said Rubi, voice dripping with contempt. 'No way. Justice is the only thing that gets her off. Fucking girl scout.' She sniffed. 'Now, may I go, *Inspektor*?'

He didn't reply, which Rubi took as permission to leave. She slouched off along the alley.

'Don't forget to pay your parking ticket,' he called after her.

Without looking back, she hoisted a hand and gave him the middle finger.

Simo headed back to his car and watched the ill-tempered crowd with lazy interest. He didn't believe for a second that Ryan alone had ordered the hit. Rubi had performed contortions trying not to incriminate herself – much safer to blame it all on a dead man. Ryan was involved in the scheme to kill Drakulić but Simo doubted he was so intimately involved in the killings of Arkan Ćešić or Ivan Fuštar. He certainly hadn't been in the country at the time of their deaths. And Simo had believed Rubi when she said that Marina knew nothing about the assassinations. But what of the other Silent Women? Not so silent, after all. What had become evident was that Drakulić clearly did not know that the women's group was involved in the move against him, for the simple reason that Rubi Kurjak was still alive. Ryan must not have broken, even under torture. He knew the blood and wrath and misery that Drakulić would have wrought upon the members of the group and their families and everyone they'd ever loved. It was the bravest thing Ryan had ever done.

Simo realised with a sting of self-awareness that it had taken him so long to discover the identities of Rubi and the Silent Women vigilantes because he had been looking for men. But it was the women. So angry at the lack of justice, they'd taken matters into their own hands. He experienced a prickle of discomfort at the thought that he and Drakulić had something in common. The Wolf was still hunkered down in his cabin, still looking out for men.

The radio in his car crackled with urgent communications between the officer co-ordinating the police response and his deputies. Simo listened in to their increasingly anxious exchange. One of the deputies was reporting that his line was breaking under the push and pull of the crowd. The protest was descending into chaos. The deputy's strained voice came again from the radio, calling for urgent assistance. Simo headed to the bridge.

20

Outside the office, pavement drizzle pockmarked the asphalt. The last of the boxes of lilies had been loaded onto the van, and slowly it began to make its way through the crush of people who had spilled off the pavements onto the road. Heather drew her jacket around her, deciding that it was at least ten degrees colder than the previous week. She joined Petra and Marina, and the three of them walked behind the van for the main protest. The closer they came to the centre of town, and the nearer to the bridge, the denser and angrier the crowd became. Windows that Heather had only ever seen tightly shut were now thrown open, and furious yells rained down upon them, along with the odd tomato and rotten egg. One landed with a mucous splat on her head and trickled into her eye. Revolted, she wiped it away.

'I thought this was a peaceful protest?'

'It is by us. Not necessarily by them,' muttered Marina.

It was with some relief that Heather saw the stern-faced police in their blue uniforms and matching baseball caps. It was with less relief that she noticed they carried guns and riot shields. Heather found herself jostled and shoved in each direction. Marina slid her arm through hers, and Heather linked her other arm with Petra. She counted about fifty women and twenty-five men walking with the van; many of them held signs.

'What do they say?' she asked Petra.

'*No more mass graves. No more lies. Justice for Victims. Justice for Rape Victims.*' Petra hesitated, and pointed to a banner carried between two women. '*Dragan Drakulić is a murderer and a rapist and deserves to burn in hell.*'

'I want to hold that banner.'

'Okay,' said Marina.

The three of them shouldered their way through the crowd over to the women and picked up the slack in the middle of the banner. The women looked surprised for a moment and then smiled, gratified that Heather and her friends wanted to join them. It was the first time Heather had ever joined a protest, or marched united behind a cause, and she felt gratitude and relief towards these women – they knew the horror that was Drakulić, the man who had tortured and murdered Ryan. Left her unborn child without a father. It was not a comfort exactly – she would have preferred that no one else had suffered – but for the first time she realised she was part of a sisterhood, whether she wished for it, or not.

Heather quickly regretted her impulse to pick up this specific banner. It was a target of particular outrage. Missiles and cries were hurled at them, and soon the banner itself was spattered with paint and, to Heather's disgust, the dripping viscera from the rotting carcass of a chicken. The throng grew denser still, a steadily moving mass of people, a hum of anger just beneath the surface. They found themselves borne along towards Sokolović Bridge, where she could see the van parked, already swarmed by people. It was being rocked with such vigour it looked like it might tip over.

'Are you all right?' yelled Petra.

Heather opened her mouth to reply, and found it filled with rotting salad leaves, mouldy and revolting, hurled by another objector. She let go of Marina's hand to smear the filth from her face. It left a trail of slime across her mouth and nose like snot, and she spat in disgust. A moment later, she felt the banner being torn from her hand, and shouts of fury from the other women as it was trampled underfoot. While cleaning her face, Heather had inadvertently fallen behind, and now, as she tried to catch up, she discovered that there was nothing she could do to reach them, such was the press of bodies. Marina yelled to her, but her shout was a call across the ocean, distant and useless. Heather let her go.

She could sense the suppressed violence prickling like electricity and wondered at the wisdom of coming here today. She wanted to meet Rubi Kurjak, ask her about Ryan, desperate for any more she could learn about the man she thought she knew. Instead she found herself surrounded by a hostile mob, many of whom still idolised Drakulić as a war hero and refused to accept his guilt. The thoughts of a few minutes ago – of sisterhood and mutual suffering – were lost in fear. She was carried along on the wave of the protesters, no longer an individual but absorbed into the marchers and swept up and onto the bridge. The police were trying to keep the protesters and counter-protestors apart, but it was impossible. She felt an arm sneak around hers and with relief saw that it was Petra, who had somehow manoeuvred back to her again. The Silent Women had mostly found their way to the balustrades on the south side of the bridge. She and Petra were shunted towards them and then, with a rush of terror, she felt someone trying to tie something around her mouth and throat. She struggled and then heard Petra hissing at her to calm down and saw that all the women were tying white bandages around their mouths as part of the protest. A young girl held out the bandage to Heather, mouthing an apology. Heather nodded and tied it loosely herself. She had to admit that as a symbol it was effective – chilling and striking.

All of the women stood along the same side of the bridge, mouths gagged in white gauze, clutching thousands and thousands of red lilies, one for each of the souls murdered in Višegrad. The roar of noise from the mob was a wall of sound coming at them, creating a competing mix of wrath and cheers of sisterhood, of grief and rage, admiration and hate. The police closed ranks, attempting to keep the two factions apart and also prevent anyone else coming onto the bridge.

Heather was jostled against a stone balustrade so that it dug sharply into her hipbone and briefly she was looking down. The water tore beneath the bridge, green and wild. It was impossible not to think of the thousands who had been pushed off each dusk during the war, some shot first, some stabbed, others falling as they tried to clutch their children to them, the gunshots coming later as they drowned.

A handful of lilies was thrust into her hands and she stared at them for a moment, forgetting what she was supposed to do with them. Looking along the line, she saw more than a hundred other women casting them into the water below. She did the same, watching her blooms fall through the air before disappearing into the river. The waters of the Drina were awash with blood-red lilies for the dead. At once, a furious buzzing of outboard engines started up and the waters were churning with half a dozen speedboats. The boats hurtled amongst the flowers, propellers slicing them to pieces, crimson petals eviscerated so that it looked as if the water was once again full of blood. Men stood up in the boats, clapping and laughing in vicious delight that they had spoilt the protest. A violent wake rocked the boats, and one man swayed, tumbling overboard. His friends reached down, grabbing his shoulders to haul him back in. He sat down hard, bellowing with fierce laughter, spitting out water as he cracked open a beer. The boat thundered away, passengers clinging to the side.

A few seconds later, another sound cut through the bellowing of the crowd and the thunder of the engines – a static crackle of music over amplified speakers, thumping out a song Heather didn't recognise. At once a furious cry of outrage went up amongst the Silent Women and their supporters, while rival hoots of delighted laughter rose from the others as they started to echo the song, in hollers and roars.

'What are they singing?' yelled Heather.

'Drina, Bloody Drina,' shouted back Petra. 'Is Serbian Nationalist song. They don't like it when we remember Bosniak dead.' Even she looked pale and anxious.

Heather felt an elbow in her ribs and winced. She was pinned against the edge of Sokolović Bridge, unable to move, unsure if she was going to be pushed over the side or crushed. Frantic, she scanned the crowd and noticed Marina, her white gag removed, her mouth contorted wide open. It took her a second before Heather realised that she was screaming, her voice silenced by the baying of the crowd. It was hard to say for sure in the mêlée, but it appeared to Heather as if someone was holding her. For a moment, she wondered if Marina was hurt and the hands were carrying her to safety, but then the crowd thinned momentarily, and she glimpsed the other woman fighting and kicking out with everything she had. Marina had removed her gag, but now hands fastened it tightly around her mouth. Heather filled her lungs and yelled, trying to draw attention to Marina's predicament, but no one could hear her thin voice over the frenzy of the crowd. It was out of control, shoving and pushing in every direction, anger reaching a crescendo with each verse of the Bloody Drina song. Heather looked round for Petra, but she too had gone, carried away by the surge. Marina was sobbing now, kicking as she was dragged off, but no one else seemed to notice. There were police everywhere – didn't they see? She yelled in vain, and then she saw him.

Simo.

There he stood, alongside the line of police officers attempting to control the protesters. He couldn't hear her, so she decided to go to him. But crushed against the bridge, Heather tried in vain to move through the press of bodies – it was like pushing against concrete. She waved her arms in an attempt to attract his attention. And then, unbelievably, he saw her. Recognition slid across his face and he dived into the crowd, shouldering his way through the hordes towards her. He was coming. But just as she allowed herself a moment of hope, he went down. One second he was there, the next he was gone, submerged beneath the mass of bodies. She felt arms grab her waist and lift her bodily. A man's tattooed arms wrapped around her. She kicked and writhed, but his grip was like steel. He half-carried her off, forcing the crowd aside as he ploughed through them. So much noise. Everyone shouting. Blows rained down, fights and scuffles amongst the crowd. No one was interested in a woman yelling in a foreign language words they could hardly hear. She was angry. They were all angry. She screamed for Simo. She screamed and screamed, and then she felt a searing pain in the back of her head and then there was nothing but darkness.

At the north end of the bridge, Simo held his radio close to his lips and barked commands, ordering officers into new positions, moving them around strategically in an attempt to prevent any more people from joining the other protesters on the bridge. It was dangerously close to overcrowding. Sweat dripped behind his visor. Arriving at the chaotic scene, he had taken control from the junior officer in charge, who was clearly overwhelmed by the task. Simo had been reorganising the men when he spotted Heather gesturing to him from amongst the Silent Women protesters. What the hell was she doing here? She was supposed to be on a plane. She was gesturing across the bridge. He tracked the direction of her signal and saw two men holding a woman. For a moment he assumed it was a clash of protesters, but then he saw the woman. Even with the white gag covering her mouth he recognised Marina Tomić. The men were hauling her off and there was no doubt in Simo's mind who they were acting for Drakulić. He tried to find Heather again in the seething crowd. With growing horror, he watched a man ploughing towards her, like a shark finning through the water. Heather hadn't seen him. Calling to several officers to back him up, Simo plunged onto the bridge. The crowd was twenty deep in every direction and he was quickly separated from the other policemen. Music pulsed and fireworks hissed through the sky. The acrid tang of gunpowder mingled with the stink of diesel, and the air hummed with the sound of boat engines.

He watched them take her, impotent rage burning his chest. He waded on, so focused on Heather he couldn't understand why his legs suddenly wouldn't move. He sank to the ground, woozy with pain. Boots and shoes clattered past him, some stepped over him, others didn't bother. Reaching around he felt a wetness in his lower back and knew in that moment he had been stabbed. The knife had missed his ribs, protected by his Kevlar vest, but there was an unprotected spot just above his kidneys where they'd known to aim. He needed to get up or be trampled to death. He needed to get back to the other officers, or he'd be in no position to help Heather. He stumbled to his feet, aware of sweat coating every inch of his skin and understood that his damaged body was going into shock. He heard a voice calmly issuing commands.

'Officer down. Shut down the protest. Now. I'm authorising necessary force. Start making arrests. Over.' There was a hiss of static.

'Understood. Who's been hurt, boss? Over.'

'Me,' answered Simo. He closed his eyes and fell.

When he came to, the streets were much emptier, occupied only by discarded beer cans and a few stragglers. Sirens wailed. It was horribly still. Panic engulfed him. How much time had passed? Heather. *Puši kurac* – the pain in his back. He was so cold. He started to shake. His mouth was dry and two cops were kneeling beside him, faces tight with anxiety. One of them had a nasty red scratch down his face. He started to reach up but it hurt too much to raise his arm. A medic was injecting something into his other arm while another applied pressure to the wound in his back. Simo tried to get up but they gently held him down.

'Stay there, boss. You're hurt. Do you know what day it is? Do you know where you are?'

Višegrad. If Simo wanted to help Heather and Marina, he needed to be careful. Not knowing who was loyal to Drakulić. He couldn't trust his own department. He wanted to be sick. The paramedics began to lift him onto a gurney next to a waiting ambulance. That wasn't going to work. As soon as they took him, he was out of action. He needed to regain some semblance of control. He shoved them away with surprising force.

'Hey, hey. It's okay. Can you tell me your name?' said the younger paramedic, a pup of a boy with a downy moustache on his upper lip.

'Inspektor Simo Subotić of the Višegrad police department. Today is April 9th. I feel like shit. Two thugs stabbed me between ribs eleven and twelve, but despite the blood loss I'm almost certain that they missed my kidney.'

He finally shook them off, giving the stretcher a filthy glare. 'I'll sit in the back of the ambulance while you stitch me up, but that's it.'

The paramedics muttered, irritated, half under their breath.

'Give me codeine. And I'll take an IV to go. I've lost a lot of blood.'

The two cops sniggered. This was the Inspektor Simo Subotić that they were used to.

Simo was relieved to see them. They weren't efficient or smart, but he was almost certain that they were honest, and that they were his men and no one else's. If only he could be sure. It simply wasn't worth the risk.

The older paramedic folded his arms, incensed. 'We'll take you to the hospital in Goražde. This is not a dispensary.'

'Then not to worry,' said Simo, lurching to his feet. 'I'm sure I've some tape at home. I'll stick it as best I can.'

The cops caught him before he fell. 'What happened to your face?' he asked the officer, wincing now he could see the wound close up.

'Bramble,' said the policeman.

'Funny,' said Simo. 'It looks like someone scratched you. Didn't arrest him?'

'Can't arrest a weed, sir.'

'No,' said Simo, eyeing him closely. He felt that he was being lied to but couldn't understand why. He was instantly less certain that these were his men and not Josif's. Now he thought about it, they were close by when he came to and close by when he went down. He hoped to hell that this wasn't an inside job.

Between them, the paramedics shuffled Simo to the ambulance and removed his protective vest and the blood-soaked clothing covering his chest and back. The blood, which had started to congeal, began running again as they tugged the T-shirt free. The senior paramedic probed the edges of the wound with a gloved finger.

'It looks clean enough, but you need to go to hospital. They'll want to see how deep it is. There might be internal bleeding. I can't be sure whether they nicked your kidney.'

'Well, if you had to guess?' asked Simo.

The paramedic shrugged. 'I'm a medic, not a psychic. I can stitch it. But it's a stupid idea. You're at risk of infection.'

Simo suppressed another wave of dizziness. 'I'm fine.'

The older paramedic threw up his arms, giving up in the face of Simo's relentless objection. 'If the bleeding starts again, you need to go immediately to hospital. And see your own doctor this afternoon. Tomorrow at the latest.'

'Sure,' lied Simo, reaching into his pocket for his phone. He dialled David, who to his relief picked up on the first ring.

'Have you got my licence yet?'

Simo ignored the question, wincing as he switched the phone from one hand to the other. 'I need you to make a house call.'

21

Heather woke to find herself in the back of a van, her hands cinched at the wrists with a plastic tie, legs bound together at the ankles. The windows in the back doors were covered with roughly cut cardboard squares taped to the frames, but judging from the motion of the van and the strained note of its engine they were speeding along a fast road, maybe a motorway. Marina lay motionless beside her. Her skin displayed a ghastly waxy pallor and she was bleeding from a snaking wound on her head. Heather studied her closely and, with relief, registered the slight rise and fall of her chest – she was alive. Heather's leg throbbed with cramp, stiff from lying in the same position. She wiggled her toes and fingers to keep the blood moving. It was then she noticed her sleeve had been rolled up past her upper arm, revealing a pinprick of blood and a blossoming bruise. They had injected her with something. The notion of someone shooting her up with an unknown substance filled her with a cold rage. God knows how it might harm the baby. She took a deep breath. They mustn't find out she was pregnant. She couldn't protect it if she panicked. Her thoughts turned to escape.

She tried to feel if her phone was still in her coat pocket, but no, they'd taken it. The rear doors were chained shut and a solid metal partition divided the driver and passenger from the load-space in the rear. The partition vibrated to the pounding of loud music, presumably to cover any cries of help the two women might make. Heather wriggled herself upright. The situation could hardly be worse, but she experienced an odd sense of calm. This is what the other riders used to snipe about behind her back, that she was never rattled even under the most stressful circumstances. She willed herself to pretend that this was just another seasonal disaster: mislaid bikes before a key race, or when the driver got lost on the way to the start line in Switzerland and she'd had to navigate through the mountain roads in the Alps so that the entire team didn't face disqualification. At the time, those things had seemed like life and death. Now, she needed to pretend that this wasn't, to lower the stakes in her mind.

The vibration of the van had loosened a corner of the tape holding the cardboard screen over one of the rear windows. It flapped as the van hurtled along the road, letting in daylight, enough for her to see that it was now late afternoon. That meant they'd been on the road for at least three hours. With a sinking feeling, she realised that they could have travelled quite a way from Višegrad in that time.

They slowed right down and started to climb. They were heading into the hills. The van swerved around a bend and Heather was thrown against the side, her face smacking against hard metal, slicing her cheek open. She ignored the pain and nudged Marina with her foot, trying to wake her.

'Marina. *Marina.*'

Marina groaned, her eyes fluttered and then opened to

slits. One looked swollen and the white was crimson, the pupil of the other appeared to be dilated. Heather feared that they'd hit her hard enough to give her a concussion. She needed to see a doctor.

'Hey, Marina, sweetheart. It's Heather.'

Marina muttered in Bosnian, her speech slurred. Heather sat close to her, hoping that the warmth of her body would provide some comfort. The pounding music ensured that their kidnappers couldn't overhear.

'It's okay. We're going to be okay. They didn't kill us straight away, so they want something.' She paused. 'And Simo is looking for us.' At least, she hoped he was. Last time she'd seen him he was being trampled underfoot by the protesters. 'He'll find us – we just need to give him time. We just need to be smart.' Heather hoped that despite her injuries Marina would understand.

She struggled upright and shambled to the front section of the van and banged hard on the partition. At first all she could hear was the thud-thud of the music. Awkwardly, she tried again. Suddenly the music was switched off. Her heart pounded. There were loud and angry voices in Serbian.

'My friend is ill!' she yelled. 'She needs to see a doctor, right away.'

'Is she dead?' asked one of the voices, switching to English. Far from concern, his question evinced casual amusement.

'She doesn't look good.'

'She going to look worse soon. You too.'

The music went back on, louder than before, and the van hit rougher ground. She jammed herself against Marina, trying to protect them both from being tossed about in the back of the van as they ascended higher and higher. This wasn't a hill, but a mountain road. The switchbacks grew closer and closer together, and Heather's ears popped. The gravel road gave way to unpaved track. They drove on for what seemed like hours, the temperature in the unheated cargo section plummeting. Heather pressed as close as she could to Marina, attempting to keep them both warm. And then, finally, the van stopped, the door opened, and Heather blinked in the sudden daylight.

Two men, stinking of sweat and beer, dragged her out, towards a wooden avalanche hut tucked into the mountainside. They trailed her along the ground between them, not caring as she caught her ankles on rocks and uneven ground. Desperately, she looked around, trying to get her bearings. The sun was sliding down the mountains like a weeping sore. The peaks still glistened with snow and the air felt oddly heavy. The cold stung her teeth. Spring had not touched this place. Heather closed her eyes, trying to visualise the maps she had studied with Ryan. Something familiar about the ridgeline told her they were on the border with Bosnia and Herzegovina; the very edge of the Srpska district.

She cried out as a slap landed on her face, opening up the wound on her cheek that had just started to congeal. Her vision swam and when it settled again she was looking at an old man in the entrance to a dilapidated wooden hut, his hands thrust deep in his pockets.

'Hello, Heather,' he said, politely.

Dread like ice water pooled in her stomach as she realised she must be standing before Drakulić.

22

Simo sat in his car, exhausted and in pain. His bravado in front of the paramedics had carried him this far, but he needed to rest up. Shame there wasn't time. He'd dispatched David on a task and was waiting to hear back from him. In the meantime he owed Petra a call. There were a bunch of missed calls from her on his phone and one panicked answerphone message. She'd been there on the bridge when Heather and Marina were taken.

'Uncle Simo!' Her voice burst from the other end of the line.

'I know. I'm on it.'

'They were Drakulić's men. Had to be. You need to organise a search. Right now.'

'I can't do that, Petra. I can't trust anyone in the department. I'm not entirely sure it wasn't one of Josif's officers who stabbed me.'

'*Stabbed*?'

Ah. He'd forgotten that she didn't know that part. 'I'm fine. Just a flesh wound,' he lied, and winced as he shifted uncomfortably in his seat. The phone beeped with a call waiting. It was David.

'I have to take this. Go home. Lock the door. I'll be in

touch.' Without waiting for a reply, he switched to the other line.

'I've got him,' said David.

'Put him on.'

There was a pause as Marina's husband, Nikola, took the phone.

'Have you heard from her?' asked Simo.

'No.'

Unsurprisingly, he sounded agitated. Simo asked another question. 'Have you called the police?'

'I don't trust the police.'

'Good.'

'It's Drakulić, isn't it?' Nikola's voice faltered.

Simo paused. 'We're going to get them back.'

'No one comes back,' said Nikola. 'You know that.'

'Two people did,' said Simo. 'Rubi Kurjak and Ryan Mackinnon. Long time ago. And then they decided to take revenge.'

Simo swiftly explained how Rubi and Ryan and other members of the Silent Women had organised the assassinations of former war criminals, Ryan coming back to Srpska as bait in order to lure Drakulić out of hiding.

'Give my friend the phone, please.'

Nikola did as instructed. Simo checked with David. 'So, how did he react when I told him? Did he already know?'

'Either he's a very good actor or he was hearing it all for the first time.'

'I swear I knew nothing.' Nikola's voice cut in. 'Neither did Marina. We would have tried to talk Ryan out of it. Crazy idea. It must have come from Rubi. She wanted nothing to do with bringing new charges against Drakulić.

She and Marina had a big falling out over it. So did other members of the group. Half the committee resigned.'

'At some point, I'm going to need a list of those members,' said Simo. 'But not now.'

David's voice interrupted again. 'So, are you just wasting time filling him in, or do you have an actual plan?'

'I have a plan,' said Simo. 'Admittedly, it's a terrible plan. Put Nikola back on.'

David gave a bitter laugh. 'I would've expected no less from you, my friend. Here, talk to the man.'

'Nikola,' said Simo, 'the bodies had their heads and limbs removed. I find it hard to believe that Rubi did that herself. She doesn't have the strength, or likely the stomach. Ryan wasn't in the country during the first killings. So who would Rubi have contracted to carry out the executions on her behalf?'

There was a long pause as Nikola considered the question. 'Her former boyfriend was in the Kajinksy Brigade during the war. If he wasn't involved himself, he knows people.'

'I need his name and any contact details you can remember. Give them to David. He's excellent at finding people who don't want to be found.'

'And while I'm performing this miracle?' grumbled David.

'I'm going to see an old friend,' said Simo.

23

Don't open your eyes. Then they can't get you. Like a child in the dark, if she only kept her eyes shut then the shadows couldn't get her. She wouldn't open them. Then none of it was real. She would stop being afraid. She could smell the acid stink of her own terror. They stopped hitting her. The scrape of a chair. Its metal legs rung oddly, like bells in her ears; her hearing distorted and strange. There was a sudden tension in the room and she sensed the men stiffen.

'Won't you open your eyes, my dear?'

She complied with the polite request, the first gentleness she'd experienced in a while. Heather couldn't say how long they'd been hurting her. Not Drakulić himself. He had left that to the other men.

It was as if the Devil himself had strolled in from the mountainside. Through one swollen eye, she saw him sit before her, smiling. She gave an involuntary moan of fear. His hair was a beautiful clean white, without a hint of yellow, his skin strangely unlined except for creases around his eyes. He wore a pressed shirt and a knitted navy sweater that brought out the blue darkness of his irises. He looked like a facsimile of everyone's favourite grandfather. On the pristine shirt collar Heather noticed a tiny bead of blood, bright and scarlet, as though a ladybird had just alighted on him and he hadn't the heart to brush it away.

He sighed, as though this whole business was a great sorrow to him.

Heather watched the ladybird of blood. It seemed to flutter at his throat. It took her a moment to realise that for the first time in a while no one was hurting her. Even so, the pain didn't stop. She focused on every training technique she'd ever learned, trying to separate herself from sensation. This wasn't her body. It was happening to someone else. Dimly, she heard whimpering in another room. A nasty wet sound. They seemed to like hurting Marina more.

The hut was some kind of enlarged avalanche shelter divided, as far as she could tell, into two sections. The floor was concrete, covered with torn and rotting lino; the walls were wooden, the roof wooden too, and here and there falling away and badly patched. There were panes in some of the windows, the rest broken and the shutters fastened shut. It was bitterly cold. A wood-burning stove and paraffin heater squatted in the corner, and after a while Drakulić ordered them lit, clearly unwilling to endure discomfort himself. Heather tried to listen for Marina's voice, but all she could hear was screaming.

Heather noticed Drakulić's tie. It was askew. The only thing out of line in his spick and span appearance. He leaned into her, offering a bottle of water, unscrewing it so that she could drink. A part of her longed to spit it in his face, but she knew that she needed to show that she was damaged, her resistance all but broken. She gulped. It tasted faintly of blood.

Drakulić straightened his tie, once more immaculate.

'Hit her again,' he said, his voice brimming with regret.

The blow landed across her face. She felt a hot bloom of pain and then a trickle of blood as her eardrum burst. She thought of the metal plate in her skull. Her head was more fragile than most; if they carried on like this, she was going to die. Her vision swirled with lights and colours, like she was swimming through a kaleidoscope.

'Who's coming?' asked Drakulić, almost bored.

Heather's eyes were watering, and her jaw was stiff and tender from the beating. 'I don't know who's coming. I keep telling you. I have no idea what you're talking about.'

'It doesn't matter.' He stroked her hair. 'Marina will tell us. Though I think she'll have to write it down,' he said, his breath on her cheek, as though they were two children sharing secrets. He smelled of aftershave and soap, but his breath was sour.

She conducted a survey of her own body. She was almost certain that they had fractured her collarbone and, based on how it hurt to breathe, at least two of her ribs were cracked. She'd endured worse in collisions – and gone on to finish the race. She was used to suffering. Pain was an old companion. Pain she could tolerate, but real animal fear was new. It struck her that she was worried less for her own life, more for the tiny life inside her; her body important only for its continuing ability to take care of someone else. They must not find out. *Must not.* Through her own agonies, Heather felt a well of pity for Marina. But even as her thoughts flitted to the other woman, she was aware that Marina had stopped screaming.

The storm lanterns in the hut flickered and pooled strangely, forming glaring puddles of light. Her thoughts were not as clear as before. She stared at Drakulić. His eye had the frantic gleam of the zealot.

'I'm not like those idiots.' He waved dismissively at the two hulking men the corner. 'I want to make this place better. Sometimes unfortunate things have to happen to bring about great changes.' He paused, seeing the disgusted look on Heather's face. 'You are a tourist. You know nothing.' He slapped his leg with his palm for emphasis. 'This country needs to build a future. We've had enough of raking over death. Time has passed. All of you outsiders, you are always wanting us to go back into our history. And when should we start, Heather Bishop? With the Ottomans? I tell you, sometimes a little blood is spilled or there can't be a brighter future.'

What, did he want a fucking debate about the future of the country? At this moment, she didn't give a shit about any of them. The wind battered against the wooden roof tiles and hissed through the holes in the rotting walls.

Drakulić fell quiet, apparently lost in thought. He stretched and she noted the thick muscles of his torso and coiled strength in his arms. He dressed like an old man, but he had the physique of one much younger. It was disconcerting. He yawned and then his focus flicked back to her like a searchlight beam.

'I liked Ryan Markovitz very much. And Ryan Mackinnon. I read all his articles too, even listened to his cycling podcasts. You know, I was one of his first subscribers?' He chuckled. 'Sometimes I left questions in the comments sections – not under my real name of course – and he always replied. Very good manners, Ryan. Not everyone does that. But your Ryan – so courteous.'

She hated it most when he spoke about Ryan. This was the part of the torture that she found hardest to endure, and Drakulić recognised it and derived great satisfaction from goading her.

'Ryan always gave one his full attention. I liked that. Now, Heather, can you give me your full attention? Because I am feeling that you are not, and I don't like it.'

Beneath the grandfatherly façade there was a new, harsher note in his voice. He smiled at her and patted her hand, all benevolence once again. His hands were cold and dry.

She glowered at him, brimming with loathing and terror, and he beamed back, returning her hate with a face full of apparent goodwill.

'Good girl. You're doing so well. I really am feeling very sad about Ryan. He had a gift. His articles had a – how do you say? A bounce. A spring in them. Whether he wrote about war or cycling, that man could make anything interesting.' He raised his eyebrows. 'Do you know, it gives me an idea. My son, Josif, he is not pleased with me. He doesn't like mess. He is a policeman who likes everything to be tidy. This isn't tidy. American and British tourists disappearing.' He shook his head sadly. 'So much paperwork and questions. He will be very cross, so I need to make it up to him. He has big ambitions, my smart son. He wants to be a politician. A real good boy.' He leaned back, spitting a little in his excitement. 'I think what I'll do is sponsor a bike race. Right here in Republika Srpska.' He gave a contemptuous wave. 'I hear that the Balkans Tour has a problem with drugs, yes? Your Ryan was involved. Very sad.'

Heather longed to scream and yell and call him a liar.

They both knew it was nonsense, and they both knew that she did not dare to deny it.

'Yes,' said Drakulić, warming to his theme. 'A new race. A clean one. With, how do you say, a good purse? But men, not women. Real riders. Hmm, what do you think? Will top cyclists come for a competition?'

Heather exerted every ounce of self-control to quell her outrage.

'Excuse me, I asked you a question.'

'Yes,' she snapped. 'If it's a good purse and an interesting route, you'll attract top teams.'

'See? We can be friends. It is a shame about your career. You were once very good. The best, in fact. British Champion. World *Ladies* Champion. You won Olympic medal – silver, I think? Everyone hoped you win gold medal next, but . . .' He made a gesture with his hand like sand pouring through his fingers. 'And now what?'

'I don't know,' she said, voice shaking.

'Good girl. We are remembering to answer. Good manners hurt no one, my grandmother always said.' He reached into his pocket and removed a toothpick, then, taking her hand and tracing the veins on the back, flipped it over and stared at her palm. She suppressed a shudder as the sharp edge of the wooden pick nipped against the underside of her nail, and steeled herself for the coming agony. He dropped her hand.

'Excuse me. I know it's not polite but I have something caught.' He opened his mouth wide, unembarrassed, maintaining eye contact as he reached deep into the recess of his pink worm-like gums and rooted around amongst gold and black fillings. 'There. Better,' he said at last, satisfied.

He toyed with the pick between his fingers. 'Now you are getting very good at answering questions. We've not needed any consequences. My good girl.' He patted her hand and smiled as though she was his adored niece. 'Who's coming?' he asked again, this time in a voice so soft that with her damaged eardrum Heather only just heard him.

She shook her head. 'I don't know.'

For the first time, Drakulić displayed genuine annoyance. 'You see, I don't want to die yet, Heather Bishop. I just got out of prison. I like it here. I like the smell of mountain air.' He massaged the joints in his fingers. 'Who's coming?'

'I don't know.'

Drakulić clicked his tongue with displeasure. At a signal, one of the men passed him a supermarket carrier bag. Heather gagged. It stank of something foul and rotting. Drakulić pulled on thick black rubber gloves, reached in and withdrew an object wrapped in several layers of plastic. Now the stench was unspeakable. Bile rose in Heather's throat.

'You see, I received these "gifts" a while back,' said Drakulić conversationally, steadily unpeeling the reeking layers. He finished unwrapping and placed two putrid, severed heads tenderly on the table in front of Heather. One was severely decomposed, the skull peeping through wizened hair. The other was putrefying and wet. Heather vomited on the floor.

Drakulić picked up the first skull and held it in his hands, surveying it quizzically. 'Alas, poor Arkan! I knew him, Heather, a fellow of infinite jest.' He glared at the mouldering head. 'Actually, the son-of-a-bitch was a humourless prick.'

Heather wiped her mouth with the back of her hand and stared at Drakulić, aghast.

'Whoever sent me these charmless gifts wanted me to

know I was next on their list. Your Ryan wasn't surprised to see my friends when I showed him. I know he was involved,' he said, his voice betraying his fury.

'Ryan wouldn't. He's a good man,' said Heather, outrage making her brave.

'Liar! He blamed me for what happened to his unfortunate friend. He wanted revenge.'

Heather stared with horror and fascination at the heads on the table.

'Ryan must have told you about the assassinations. He must.' He wiped a large hand across his mouth. 'Heather, who is coming for me?'

She closed her eyes so as not to see the viscera in front of her. Unfortunately, she couldn't block out the stench. She resolved to tell him something. She needed to play for time.

'Who's coming?' he repeated, overtly angry now.

Heather sighed. 'Simo Subotić.'

To her surprise, Drakulić laughed with what seemed like genuine amusement. 'Well, of course he's coming. Not yet, I'm afraid.' He shook his head, sat back in his chair and picked up a flask from the floor and poured himself a cup of coffee. 'I hoped you would know. You or your friend Marina. I thought Ryan must have told one of you. He either loved you too much or not enough.' He sipped the coffee. 'Now we will never know.'

She tried to concentrate through the crimson fumes of pain. Her mind felt sharper. She needed to use her hatred and anger to block out the fear and focus. This wasn't just about her. She needed to survive this for the tiny flicker of life inside her. She would find a way.

24

Josif was waiting for Simo in a café on Omladinska Street, a block back from the river, hunched over a coffee. The chief looked up as Simo shuffled to the table.

'Your officers didn't manage to kill me.'

Josif stirred sugar into his coffee. 'I told them to miss anything vital.'

From anyone else, Simo would've taken this as grave-black humour, but Josif wasn't given to making jokes.

'For the record, all of me is vital,' said Simo, levering himself painfully into a chair opposite.

Josif took a sip of coffee and lowered the cup. 'Be grateful it was me. If it had been one of my father's men . . .' He shrugged, letting Simo fill in the rest himself. Then added in an indignant tone, 'I'm trying to protect you.'

Simo stared at him. 'Are you waiting for my thanks? Do you really believe I should be grateful to you for arranging for your man to stab me in the back?'

Josif gazed back at Simo. With a father like Drakulić, was it any wonder Josif had a warped sense of morality? The chief's eyes were ringed purple and he looked tired, older. Simo almost pitied him. Almost. 'You had me bring Heather in and question her on bullshit charges. You were angry when I let her go because you were trying to keep her safe in jail. I'm right, aren't I?'

Josif nodded miserably. 'I kept trying to protect her. I had her followed. And sent someone to her hotel room and told her to get out of Srpska. I tried to scare her away. Why didn't she go? I did everything to hold my father off. He's convinced Ryan told her who's coming for him. But you were too slow at solving this, Subotić. He got crazy and desperate.'

Simo shifted painfully in his chair. 'Who is running the district – you or him?'

'Don't push it. Remember who you're speaking to. What do you want, Subotić?' said Josif, his voice hardening.

Simo glanced to the café entrance, where David had arrived and was scanning the tables. On seeing Simo, he held up a document and gave a nod. The plan was in motion. Simo turned back to Josif.

'It's time. You need to pick a side.'

Josif turned his coffee cup around and around, avoiding Simo's gaze.

'Talk to your father, tell him I know who's coming for him and I'm ready to make a trade. The information for the women. Jesus, man, they don't know a goddamn thing.'

'I believe that,' said Josif. 'But I'm not sure my father does.' His face was tense with conflict.

Simo picked up Josif's phone from the table and handed it to him. 'The women for the name – call your father. Make the offer.'

Josif hesitated, and then took the handset. Sliding out of the booth, he went to another part of the café to make the call in relative privacy.

Simo gestured to David, who took a seat next to him and pushed across the sheet of paper. It was a handwritten list of names and addresses. Three were ringed.

'You think these are the most likely?' asked Simo.

David went down the list. 'Rubi's ex was in the U.S. at the same time as one of our murders, so he's unlikely to be our hitman. But these guys served in his unit – and they were all here at the right times. All have criminal records. Two were captured during the war and Marinko Hubjer here was even in Ivan Fuštar's prison camp. I'd start by interviewing him first.'

'There isn't time,' said Simo. 'And I can't give Drakulić three possible names and say we're not quite sure. We know they might have been working together but I don't want to present him with that narrative. We need to choose one.'

'You're not going to feed one of these guys to Drakulić?' said David.

'Of course not,' said Simo. 'I'm going to send this list to my colleagues in Bosnia and Herzegovina, where the suspects are residents, and ask them nicely to bring all three men in for questioning. By the time Drakulić has the name, they should all be safely in custody.'

'*Should* be,' said David, dryly. 'I've been party to worse plans of yours.'

They waited for Josif to finish his call and return.

'I've spoken to my father,' he said, coming back to the table. He made no remark that David had now joined Simo. 'Text him the identity of the man who's coming. Then he'll release the women.'

Simo laughed. 'What, and then he'll put them on the bus home? That's bullshit and you know it. I'll tell you how this goes. He'll meet me on the steps of the justice building in Banja Luka. With the women. Unharmed.'

Now it was Josif's turn to be amused. 'Forget it. They'll arrest my father on sight.'

Simo winced as he clasped his hands on the table. 'I've been stabbed and I'm not feeling my best, but I'm not an idiot. Once he's got what he wants, he has no need for me – or them. Here's my final offer. Neutral ground – Bosnia, not Srpska. Somewhere outside your jurisdiction, Josif.'

The strain of suddenly being made a go-between showed on Josif's face. He walked back to the empty section of the café and made a second call. Simo studied him as he pleaded with his father.

'What do you think?' asked David.

'Fifty-fifty.'

Josif ended the call and came back over.

'Okay. Bosnia. Bjelašnica, where the old cable-car station is. He'll you meet there with the women. Dawn. Just the two of you. Two old friends, he says.'

Simo and David left the café together. They walked down the street, which a few hours ago had been thronging with protesters but was now empty but for a solitary street-cleaner tidying up the detritus left behind by the march.

'Bjelašnica?' said David. 'The moon would be less remote. And you're in no state.'

Simo knew why Drakulić had chosen Bjelašnica. Technically it was in Bosnia and thus out of Josif's jurisdiction, but the place was so inaccessible that the Bosnian police would struggle to assist. Not to mention that the mountain range had been on the front line during the war and the area was still peppered with landmines.

'What do you think?' said David.

Simo shrugged. 'This all started because twenty-six years ago Drakulić let Ryan walk away knowing too much. Well, I know plenty – and so do Heather and Marina. Drakulić isn't going to make the same mistake again. As soon as I've given him the name, he's going to kill us all.'

They reached David's car and he opened the boot. The lid sprang up, revealing a cache of weapons and ammunition.

Simo raised his eyebrows at his friend. 'Planning on arming a division?'

'No, just you and me.' He smiled. 'We'll all play along.'

David was inviting himself on the trip. Simo didn't argue. Despite Drakulić's line about just 'two old friends' meeting, Simo knew he would be there with back-up, and the mountainside would be crawling with his men. He and David would be significantly outnumbered, although judging by the display in the boot, what they lacked in manpower they might make up for in firepower.

'You should replace that pea-shooter of yours,' he said.

Simo patted the Glock holstered at his hip. 'No thanks. Not the time to start with something new.'

The journey to Bjelašnica would take hours on the road. They'd have to leave in the small hours in order to make the meeting and to give David enough time to find a hidden vantage-place from which to cover the handover.

'I'll drive,' said Simo. 'We'll leave at two-thirty a.m.'

'It's hours by car,' said David. 'And on those roads, in your state? Forget it.' He grinned. 'We'll have to take the 'copter.'

Simo groaned. He'd thought being stabbed would be the worst thing to happen to him that day.

25

They'd loosened Heather's bonds and left her in a corner with a blanket and bucket, before tossing her some bread, water and a piece of dried meat, which she dunked in the water to soften as she couldn't chew with her bruised jaw. She still had a couple of snack bars and some sweets and raisins in her pockets from yesterday – those they had not taken from her. It was possible her jaw was fractured rather than merely bruised, and it was likely that she had a concussion. Her head ached fiercely and she was seeing weird pulsing lights. Touching her left eye, it felt puffy and sore. Her swollen collarbone hurt the most. She padded under her shirt with the softest strands of straw she could find to cushion it as best she could. Still, it wasn't dangerous, and it wasn't the first time she'd broken it. There had been the crash in the Giro d'Italia, and then she'd fallen off halfway up Alpe d'Huez during the Tour de France the following year and fractured it in the same place. Still, she longed for a soft feather mattress rather than a bare floor, and a couple of codeine.

As she tried and failed to find a comfortable position, the brief feeling of hope that she still had a tiny piece of Ryan all but vanished. She could see no way out. No one was coming to save her. Ryan was dead; Heather and his tiny, never-to-be-born child would join him soon. At least she didn't need to worry about the fact she'd been drinking alcohol, had been on antidepressants and had confused a hangover and withdrawal from her medication with morning sickness.

She and Ryan had only ever discussed children in the vaguest, most noncommittal way – Ryan wasn't keen, and Heather was ambivalent, too uncertain of her own mental stability after the accident to press the issue. And yet she had a grim sense that if she permitted the joy tapping at the edges of her consciousness to wash in, it would overwhelm her and defeat her. She had too much to lose. The pregnancy was about to be taken from her, along with everything else. She must remain firm and resolute. Her thoughts kept drifting back to Marina, the screams and the silence.

She wondered vaguely why she wasn't already dead. *Who is coming?* The same question, over and over. She had no idea. Drakulić must believe that now.

An explosion of shouting and cursing came from another part of the hut. There were three guards as well as Drakulić, and one of them was yelling Marina's name, his voice wild with trepidation. A few seconds later came the clatter of doors and running footsteps, then Drakulić bellowing. She glimpsed him hurrying past, white shirt with sleeves rolled up, streaked crimson with blood, carrying a medical kit and syringe.

The noise and panic continued for a while and then stopped, replaced by an empty silence. The guards walked back, heads low, Drakulić haranguing them in Serbian, his curses humming in the air around them like flies.

'What's happened,' said Heather, her voice cracking. 'Is Marina okay?'

Drakulić ignored her, instead barking a command at one of his men. A bony man with a straggly beard, he'd been in the room earlier where they'd tortured her. He hadn't taken part, only watched. He peeled off from the group and remained behind to stand guard over Heather. Rifle slung across his chest, he leaned against the wall, barely paying her attention.

She repeated her question. 'Marina. Is she okay?'

'She dead,' he said. 'Heart stopped. It was accident. Boss not happy.'

She sank back into the straw but didn't cry. Refused to cry. It might not be true. Fear prickled across her skin like gooseflesh. This could easily be another grotesque trick they were playing on her. Even now they were probably playing the same one on Marina. A traitorous thought wriggled into her head: she hadn't heard a sound from Marina for hours. She quelled the thought, pushing it to the back of her mind. 'Marina!' she called out, hoping for an answering shout.

'She dead!' snarled the guard. 'I tell you already. *Dupa Kurva.*'

Heather lay back down on the straw and tried to focus on something else. Anything. But she was so tired, and she hurt so much, and to sleep for just a minute, a brief moment of respite from it all . . . then she'd have more fight in her. She knew she mustn't close her eyes. She must not sleep – with a head injury it was dangerous – but it was too hard to stay awake. She pictured the map. The mountains. The peaks covered in snow. The snow was falling. It was sliding down, down the slopes and into the black sea.

Heather woke to more shouting. Her swollen eye didn't open right away, sealed shut with crusty sleep. She couldn't understand the words, but something had clearly rattled the guards. Only Drakulić was calm, but beneath the placid exterior she could hear his rage bubbling. The morning was still, dark and ice cold. A bitter wind sang through the holes in the walls. The stove had gone out long ago and her breath was like smoke. The cold tortured her broken shoulder. But then, through the fog and haze of hurt, she heard the name 'Simo'. It was a light in the dark. She swam towards it.

'Simo Subotić.'

They hissed the name like a curse. But not to her. Every time they uttered it, it worked like an incantation, summoning her back to life, telling her to reassert her will. Simo must be somewhere, trying to help. She marshalled her thoughts, preparing herself mentally as best she could to seize any opportunity to escape, however fleeting.

A few minutes passed. There was the sound of a car engine starting outside. Heather strained to hear over the ringing in her left eardrum. There was more yelling. She peered into the gloom, but all the commotion was in the other room. The door swung open and searing cold air blew inside, along with a few feathering flakes of snow. Her guard came into the room, shouting at her in Serbian, forgetting for a moment that she could not understand. He switched to his halting English.

'You. Outside. Walk.'

She shuffled as best she could. The bonds were at least loose enough now for her to stagger along. She expected they were going to kill her, but a tiny voice asked, *If so, why not inside the hut?* It was still dark out and snowing gently, a layer many inches thick blanketed the ground, and where it had been blown to the edges of the road it was drifting. She shook violently with cold and fear, sticky tears streamed down her cheek. The van they'd brought her and Marina to the mountains in was parked beside a small Renault. The third guard, bald and heavily tattooed, knelt beside the back wheel, wrestling with snow chains, swearing loudly. The fat one whose trousers always slouched low, revealing a hairy outcrop of belly, stood watching and offering advice.

The snowfall had smothered the landscape with powder, transforming the rocky peaks into Alpine white, and a cathedral hush had descended. Even the hut, the scene of her suffering, was transformed, its roof heavy with snow, the lintels above the windows like sleepy lids.

Drakulić waited beside the car, flakes of snow landing on his hair and eyelashes. Heather stopped dead. She wanted to back away, turn around and run back into the hut. He stepped forward and took her hand in his dry one, rubbing it. His skin felt like parchment.

'We go in the car to your friend. Simo Subotić. It's good, yes?'

Heather blinked, bewildered. That's what the urgent mention of his name was about. They were heading for a rendezvous with Simo. It was the first sliver of hope she'd felt since being taken. 'It's good.'

To her horror, Drakulić leant forward and kissed her on the forehead. She felt his saliva on her skin and longed to scrub it away.

'It is very sad about our friend Ryan.'

Heather said nothing, but her head felt very clear. This man had murdered Ryan and yet here he stood offering condolences. Fear and revulsion knotted in her belly. How dare he, when they both knew he was going to murder her, along with the new life inside of her? She felt the round spit mark on her forehead dry in the wind and it burned like a cattle brand. She stared at him with a blend of hatred and hopelessness. Despair seeped into her, colder than the mountain air.

'Get in the trunk,' said Drakulić.

She hesitated. The trunk of the Renault was tiny.

Drakulić snapped, 'I said, get in the goddamn trunk. You know I do not like to repeat myself, Heather.'

With her feet tied together, she shuffled towards the back of the Renault, perched on the edge and stopped. Marina lay inside, crumpled into an unnatural position, eyes open and unseeing.

'Oh my God, oh my God.'

'Horrible accident,' said Drakulić, shaking his head with affected sadness. 'You must tell that to the Inspektor. Now, you get in.'

She looked round at him, incredulous. He couldn't be serious. Impatient, he shoved her over and she toppled onto Marina's cold body.

'No, no, no.' Frantic, she tried to sit up, unable to bear being trapped like this.

'Lie down!' Drakulić commanded.

Whimpering, Heather tried to obey, but the boot was small and Marina occupied most of it and Heather had a fleeting thought that she didn't want to hurt her, but then of course that wasn't possible, not anymore. She was close to panic. Drakulić grew more and more infuriated.

'I tell you to lie down.'

'I can't! It's impossible to move with my feet tied.'

Fuming, he saw that she was telling the truth. Producing a knife, he sliced through her ties. That was better but even then one hip stuck out proud. Drakulić didn't wait for her to adjust herself again and slammed the lid. She yelled in pain as it cracked off the bone.

'You stopping it on purpose,' he said accusingly.

Under different circumstances, Heather could see that the situation was macabrely amusing; the kidnapper blaming the hostage because his car boot was too small for his crime.

He slammed the lid on her hip again, but then gave up. Evidently accepting that no matter how many times he slammed the boot-lid, she wasn't going to fit inside. He dragged her out and called over the fat guard. Heather recognised him as the particularly vicious one, who seemed to take visceral delight in hurting her. He had sweaty hands, and every time he hit her, her skin was sloppy with his perspiration. After Drakulić, she hated him most. The two men conducted a rapid conversation in Serbian, then the guard hit her again. This time she saw it coming and moved aside so that he only just caught the edge of her cheek, but she sprawled backwards in the snow and lay there, unmoving. She wanted them to believe he'd hurt her more than he actually had. She forced herself to be calm. Taking quiet, steady breaths, she methodically lowered her heart rate.

'Get up,' snapped the guard.

She whimpered as though dazed, until he hauled her by the arm and pulled her to the passenger compartment of the car, shoving her into the back seat before sliding in beside her. She slumped across him. Muttering, he propped her back up, strapping her in with the seatbelt to keep her from falling again, and then grabbed her neck to feel her pulse. Drakulić climbed into the driver's seat. The guard swore and said something to Drakulić, who cursed. Heather was gratified. She knew her pulse would be very low, barely over fifty b.p.m. It would help persuade them that she was badly hurt. Her resting heart rate was always low. It had been even lower still when she was riding professionally, but even now she was extremely fit. It always confused the nurse's blood pressure monitors when she went for routine check-ups.

Drakulić started to drive away from the mountain hut, following a set of vehicle tracks that were partly covered by the recent snowfall but still mostly visible in the glare of the headlights. He cranked the heat right up and the soon the rattling heater was pumping out hot air. Heather lolled in her seat, eyes half closed, trying to appear as if she was drifting in and out of consciousness, secretly enjoying the welcome relief of feeling warm for the first time in ages.

She'd avoided being locked in the boot, even if that was more by accident than design. Now if she could just capitalise on that. She assessed the situation, probing for any detail she could turn to her advantage. Drakulić and the guard were both armed, both wearing holsters at their hips. The guard's was closer, but she'd never handled a gun in her life. The idea that she might succeed in taking it out of its holster, let alone manage to get off a shot, was pure fantasy. Physically, too, she was outmatched. The guard probably had a hundred pounds on her and, unlike her, neither he nor Drakulić was beaten and bruised. In fact, Drakulić looked pretty fit to her. She had no chance of taking on the two men.

She kept looking, hoping for some crack of daylight. What else? Come on, Heather. Two of Drakulić's guards were headed down the mountain in the van, but that still left one unaccounted for. Where was he? She thought for a moment and concluded in dismay that it was his vehicle's tracks they were following . . . Which meant he'd gone ahead – almost certainly to lie in wait for Simo. There was no way to warn the policeman.

The car rode over a bump and there was a hollow thud from the boot. Heather's focus was interrupted by a vision of Marina, lips blue, mouth agape. Dead. A vision of Ryan's decomposing body replaced Marina's. No. She shook herself out of her reverie – this was no time for grief. She'd mourn later. If she gave into her feelings, she'd be joining them.

Her head ached and her jaw pulsed with a pain worse than any cavity drilled by the dentist. She let out a groan, playing it up as much as she dared. Drakulić snapped at her to shut up. Snow continued to fall slowly, like down from a slit pillow, settling on the road. The forested patches of mountainside she'd seen earlier had thinned out, though there were still clumps of trees scattered around, which meant they weren't yet high enough to be above the treeline. The air felt thin; it was mountain air, but the snow would increase the oxygen content – helpful if she got the opportunity to make a run for it. She wished she knew how far they were driving and where they were headed. It was even harder to make a plan when travelling blind.

There was only one route, but it was uneven and cratered with potholes and large stones half hidden by the snow. That and the darkness made progress slow and treacherous. The snow chains rattled as Drakulić diligently traced the tyre tracks in front. After about twenty minutes they reached a crossroads. The driver of the earlier vehicle must have been confused about which route to take, as his tracks led both ways. Heather concluded that he must have chosen one, then changed his mind and turned around and headed in the opposite direction. The snow was churned up and it was impossible to see from inside the car in which direction the earlier vehicle had finally gone. Drakulić stopped dead and swore loudly, slapping his hand on the steering wheel. He picked up his phone, saw that there was no signal and tossed it down in disgust. There was no signpost, and low banks of stone covered in snow led in several directions. The only way to tell which way the first car had gone would be to climb out and follow one of the tracks and see if they continued. Drakulić had clearly come to the same conclusion. He turned around and issued an order to the fat guard. As cowed as Drakulić's men were by him, the prospect of leaving the warmth of the car for the blizzard conditions outside provoked an objection from the guard. Grumbling, he obeyed, and a minute later his podgy figure had disappeared into the snow and darkness. Drakulić drummed his fingers on the steering wheel, impatient for the guard's return, but when after five minutes he hadn't come back, he made a decision. He killed the engine, removed the ignition key, and exited the car. He flung open the back door and levelled his gun at Heather.

'You. Out.'

After the soporific warmth of the car interior, the blast of cold came as an unwelcome shock. Drakulić picked the same track that the guard had opted for and, with a wave of his gun, he forced Heather to march. There was no sign of the missing guard, but soon they could see from the tracks in the snow that the vehicle they were following had performed a U-turn and gone back in the other direction. Drakulić shoved her again with the gun and grunted at her to turn around.

The light was changing, the sky no longer black but bleeding to grey at the horizon. They half-slid across the snow as the track turned down, and suddenly Drakulić lost his footing. The end of the gun barrel slewed away from her as he fought to stay on his feet. With an electric-like jolt, Heather realised this was her chance. She turned and fled, her unsuitable shoes scrabbling for grip, her legs heavy and slow. Not caring where she was going; anything would be better than remaining in his hands. And, she reminded herself, somewhere out here Simo was waiting. Maybe just around the next bend. But even if not, a slow, cold death on the mountain was preferable to the alternative. She ventured a glance over her shoulder. Drakulić was fast, displaying a sure-footedness that belied his age. She remembered that he had fought in these conditions, knew this ground. Had killed here again and again. The pursuit was over before it had even begun. He caught up, grabbed her from behind and threw her to the ground. Panting over her, he extended his gun-arm, taking aim at her head.

'Do not make me chase you again.'

He motioned with the weapon. Up. Her chance had gone. They trudged back to the car, to find the fat guard already in the back seat, puzzled at the absence of his boss and the hostage. Drakulić rounded on him, berating him loudly. It was clear to Heather what must have happened. After finding the end of the track, the guard had circled back but they'd missed him in the murk and ever-falling snow.

Drakulić shoved Heather back into the car and resumed

his place in the driver's seat. He stamped on the accelerator and they set off again with a jolt. Breathing deep and slow, Heather allowed the warmth of the car to seep into her limbs, oxygenating her muscles, while allowing the men to think she'd fallen asleep. She'd failed this time, but she swore to herself that the next time would be different.

26

Simo surveyed the helicopter in dismay; it looked even more dilapidated than he'd remembered. David was already in the pilot's seat. He'd tossed a bag with his hunting rifle and ammunition into the cockpit and started the engines. The rotor blades spun up. He beckoned to Simo to get on board. With a grimace, Simo realised that David was enjoying this part. He'd been trying for years to get him up in this death-trap. Now was the time. The downdraught forcing him low, Simo clambered in beside David, sliding a headset over his ears so they could talk. David was dressed all in white, in the winter camouflage fatigues of a soldier, his insulated coat topped with a hood and a white fur collar.

'You look like a fucking yeti,' Simo remarked.

'Laugh it up, asshole.' David cast a judgmental glance up and down Simo's civilian gear. 'At least I won't be freezing my balls off on the mountain.'

Simo settled into his seat, strapping himself securely into the harness. Beside him at knee level were several poorly patched bullet-holes in the door.

'What do the tourists make of those?' he asked.

'Local colour.' David flicked some switches and feathered

the controls. 'It's going to be a bit bumpy. What about your Bosnian friends?'

He meant the police back-up. Earlier, Simo had spoken to them and filled them in on the exchange.

'Are they coming?' asked David.

'Waiting for a break in the weather. Apparently, it's too dangerous to fly.'

David grinned again, flicked a handful of overhead switches and eased the stick controls. They rose swiftly and Simo felt he'd left his stomach back on the rain-soaked field in Goražde. Airborne, the helicopter lurched from side to side; even a sizeable aircraft like this one was buffeted by the strong winds. David hummed loudly in his headset and Simo fumbled with the volume of his own, in an attempt to block him.

'You can't. It's broken.'

Simo suspected that he was lying but was taking perverse pleasure in annoying him. It was how David operated. When they had achieved something approaching level flight, he reached down for a bag of potato crisps. He opened the bag and the powerful smell of onion filled the small cabin. The smell made Simo's stomach roll.

'I'm distracting you from the task ahead, and the significant risk of death.' He crunched loudly in his ears. 'Is it helping?'

It would take more than a foul smell to lift Simo's anxiety about what they were flying into. David and he both knew that Drakulić would send at least one armed man ahead to intercept Simo. That's why David was here. He would provide cover for Simo while he made the rendezvous with Drakulić and carried out the exchange picking up the two women. They flew on into the early morning gloom. After a while, Simo found to his surprise that the buffeting ride ceased to worry him. But only because much bigger things weighed on him. So much could go wrong. Not to mention that Simo had hid from his friend just how much pain he was in. He wasn't sure how well he could handle a gun right now.

'We're approaching,' said David.

A splinter of dawn fractured the darkness, giving Simo his best sight of their surroundings since they'd taken off. But if they were on final approach then where were the mountains? Where they should be was only a bank of fog. A second later, he could see absolutely nothing. It was like flying through a steam-filled sauna.

'Can you see?' he said into his headset, frantic.

'Not a thing,' said David.

Fuck, thought Simo. His friend clearly hadn't read the chapter in the pilot's manual about reassuring nervous passengers.

'Freezing fog,' David went on. 'Hold on. This could get a bit dicey.'

Simo gripped the handle affixed to the bulkhead beside his head and clung on. If David was admitting to it being dicey, the reality was many times worse. Simo was not a religious man, but at that moment he prayed to the Father, Son, Holy Spirit and any other deity that might be listening – to please get them down safely. The helicopter bobbed in the turbulent air, tossed around like a cat toying with a mouse. Simo swore if he survived this, he was never, ever going up in this thing again.

'Humid air is less dense,' said David, delivering the least

appropriately timed chemistry lesson Simo could imagine. 'As long as we don't have ice forming inside, we'll be okay.'

'Right,' said Simo, dubious.

As David spoke, a plume of freezing crystals formed along the windscreen in front of them. 'Grab the can at your feet and spray the windshield,' he said, his voice calm. 'Just try not to drip onto the controls. They don't like it.'

Simo groped at his feet and found the can. It was regular antifreeze – he was sure he had the same one in his car. He sprayed liberally where David directed. It made no difference.

'We'll just have to hope the instruments work,' said David, resolutely upbeat.

'Do they usually?' asked Simo.

'More than half the time.'

That was too much for Simo. 'Get this piece of junk on the ground or I'll see you never get another fucking licence, so long as I live.' Given the terminal consequences of David failing to land safely, Simo knew that this was an empty threat. The wind howled through the patched bullet-holes and the helicopter was abruptly swept across the sky. Just as Simo was sure he was going to throw up, the clouds parted and a narrow passage appeared, revealing the mountains and the smudged bronze circles of the linked Olympic rings.

'There's Bjelašnica,' yelled David.

A jagged mountain reared up, smothered in snow, clouds eddying around its peak. Somehow, amongst the swirling chaos, David found a section clear from falling snow and pointed the nose of the craft towards it.

'Here we go.'

To Simo the approach felt less like descending and more like plummeting.

'When we come into land, we can't hover,' added David, as if things couldn't get worse. 'If we do, the downdraft will disturb the snow and it will blind us.'

'*Jebi se*,' Simo swore. He wondered how he'd let himself be persuaded that the helicopter was a good idea.

'So, we have to land fast. Really fast.'

'Or we crash.'

'You got it.'

The engine note increased with their velocity, and the bulbous nose of the aircraft pitched down violently.

'It would be better if we had a proper look at the touchdown area before we land. Have to cross our fingers that there aren't too many rocks under the snow.' David craned his neck to spy the precise landing point. 'Snowfield there, beside the building. Should do the job. Hold on!'

Simo again clutched the handle above his head, which was still slick from where he'd been gripping it. The helicopter dropped, the winds catching the small craft again, tossing it from side to side. The wind shrieked past them but somehow the rotor-blades continued to turn. The needles on the instruments spun; Simo couldn't tell if they were doing so because they weren't working or, equally alarmingly, because they were. His ears rang and painful pressure was building between his eyes and in his sinuses.

The helicopter dived for the ground and the mountain rose up outside his window. Suddenly, Simo could see the concrete building of the abandoned cable car station. He squeezed his eyes tight shut, but that only made the nausea worse, so he opened them again, which was no improvement. The landing zone was coming at them rapidly and at an unnatural angle. How the hell was David going to steady the machine and slow it enough before they hit the ground? It seemed an impossibility. As if to underline his dire prediction, an alarm in the cabin sounded, high-pitched and insistent. Beads of sweat trickled down David's usually calm brow. The ground was white, the sky was white and perspective impossible. Simo gave up on God and muttered various apologies to his ex-wife, his daughters and his mother. And then, with a wrenching thud, they hit the ground. But they weren't down yet. The helicopter bounced and there was a grisly squeal of metal, a scrape and a violent crunch. Sparks flew, fiery orange against the white. Simo was hurled forward and then back, the harness at least keeping him in his seat. They juddered to a halt, the noise and fury of the landing drifting away on the winds, silence settling along with the snowfall. Cautiously, he opened one eye and then the other. He coughed. The cabin was filling with smoke and David was slumped forward, slack in his harness. Blood poured into his right eye from a nasty cut where he'd smacked his brow against the hard switch or button on one of the controls. Simo quickly unfastened both of them, but with his injuries he knew he was too weak to drag a fully grown man away from the burning helicopter.

'David! David!'

David gave a snore and a gurgle, and then a mutter: 'Fuel shut-off valve.'

Through the thickening smoke, Simo scoured the controls for the switch that would stop fuel pumping to the engine and turning them into an inferno. The dials and switches were a mystery to him, not helped by the fact that the labels in the Russian-build helicopter were all in Cyrillic. He swore loudly. David's eyes flickered, and he extended a hand and swatted a red selector.

'Fuel shut-off,' he mumbled again.

At least that reduced their chances of going up in flames. With David conscious and able to move, albeit gingerly, Simo helped him from the smoky cockpit. Simo groaned as his stitches split from the effort of supporting his friend. Blood began to seep through his jacket. Ignoring the pain, he kept on going until they'd put some distance between them and the downed helicopter. They collapsed on the snow, panting with the effort.

David wiped a hand across the open cut on his brow and then tried raising his head. He winced, clutching his neck.

'Don't move,' said Simo, checking him over. 'It's probably whiplash. For future reference, you need to work on your landings.'

David gestured to the stricken helicopter. Black smoke clung in the air around it, mingling with the fog and falling snow. 'Locker behind the seats. There's a first aid kit. Should be some Vicodin in there.'

Simo nodded and began to get up. He felt like an old man creaking slowly up from his armchair. And then it crossed his mind that if the day continued like this, he almost certainly wouldn't ever get to sit in that armchair.

'And my rifle and backpack,' added David.

Simo returned a few minutes later with the items. David swallowed the pills and Simo handed him the hunting rifle, which sported white camouflage like the rest of David's kit. David went to take the weapon by the stock but dropped it with a cry of pain. Simo studied his friend – the crash-landing had left him in worse shape than he'd initially assumed. David was in no condition for a mission like this. Far from being Heather and Marina's best hope, the two of them were a couple of broken men. But they were the only hope.

To make matters worse, if that was still possible, the cut on David's brow had swollen, pushing down on the eyelid, severely compromising his vision. Unfortunately, Simo knew that it was the eye he sighted his rifle through. Hardly auspicious. 'If we find you a vantage-point where we can dig you in, can you still cover me?'

David grunted. 'Sure. Never felt better,' he said, adding with a shrug, 'So long as I don't have to move.'

What a shitshow. There was nothing more to add, so Simo turned his attention to the tree-less landscape. 'If they didn't hear us come down, then they'll see the smoke from the wreckage. Either way, we're sitting ducks here – let's get going.'

They stumbled through the drifting snow, hearing voices in every snap of the wind, seeing shadows in the whorl of flakes. Simo supported David, who groaned with every step and leaned heavily on his friend. Suddenly, through the snow, the giant Olympic rings rose into view, looming over the shell of the abandoned cable car station. The two men dropped to the ground. David pulled a pair of binoculars from his backpack and hesitated, before passing them to Simo.

'Probably best if you look,' he said, his other hand going to his tender and now completely swollen eyelid.

Simo pointed them at the cable car station less than a hundred metres away. It was a high, bluff building, braced against the vicissitudes of mountain weather, the neglected exterior flayed by the winds. There was a line of broken windows about halfway up the building, but no signs of activity that would indicate Drakulić's presence. So where was he? Drakulić was well resourced, but as far as Simo knew he didn't have access to a helicopter. Which meant he would be driving here with Heather and Marina. Simo turned the binoculars to point back down the mountain to a road – a track, really – that only a properly equipped vehicle could hope to traverse. The road terminated a couple of hundred metres from the station, meaning the final approach had to be navigated on foot. The roofline of a solitary car poked up. Judging by the thin layer of snow that coated it, the car hadn't been there for long. Simo briefly adjusted his position to focus the binoculars on the rest of the vehicle. There was no one inside, unless they were crouched down beneath window level.

'Drakulić?' said David.

'Possibly. But if I were him, I'd send an advance party, wouldn't you?'

David nodded, forgetting for a moment about his neck. He let out a wince of pain.

'If you were a sniper covering the approach, where would you position yourself?' Simo asked.

'Any-fucking-where I like,' said David, gesturing to Simo to hand him the binoculars. He swept them across the snowy vastness. 'It's wide open. A killing ground.' He stopped. 'Hello.'

'What is it?'

'He's in the cable car station.' David indicated the line of windows Simo had already checked. Even with two fully functioning eyes, he had missed the man's presence.

'Didn't fancy waiting in a freezing hole in the ground, I guess,' he said, with a degree of sympathy.

A further sweep revealed no one else in the immediate vicinity, unless they were well dug-in, of course. The consequence of which was the first positive thing that had happened since they'd survived the crash-landing. 'Drakulić's not here yet,' said Simo. They'd beaten him to the rendezvous; the only benefit, as far as he could tell, of taking that damn helicopter. Now they had a chance to prepare.

A glint of light flashed from the sniper's position at the cable car window. 'Scope reflection,' said David, dismissively. 'Amateur.'

Despite David's opinion of the man's skills, Simo knew that the sniper's presence meant that Drakulić was planning to finish things here. As soon as Simo gave him the name of the assassin, that would be the signal to kill everyone, either with a long shot or, knowing the man, something much more close-up and personal.

'Change of plan,' said Simo. 'How's that Vicodin working for you?' David gave a non-committal mutter and Simo went on. 'I need you to take care of our friend in the cable car station.'

The task required crossing the snowy plateau and getting into position without the sniper noticing the advancing figure. A difficult enough proposition for a soldier at the top of his game, let alone one in David's condition.

David raised his binoculars again. 'There's a building to the side of the station. Some kind of storage shed, I guess. If I can get to it, I'll have an angle on him and some cover of my own. Assuming he doesn't have a friend.' He passed the binoculars back to Simo, took a couple of short-range walkie-talkies from the backpack and handed Simo one of them. Then he slipped on the backpack, shouldered his rifle and turned to Simo. 'Don't do anything brave.'

'Goes against my nature.' Simo clapped a hand to his friend's back. 'See you later.'

'Count on it. You owe me a new helicopter – and I plan to collect.'

With that, he began to make his way up the mountainside and in a few strides his camouflaged figure had vanished into the snow. Despite David's bravado, Simo knew it may very well be the last sight he ever had of his friend.

An uneasy stillness hung over the mountain, nothing but the falling snow and the faint sound of the wind in the empty cable car building, wheezing through the broken windows. The sky was fully light now, increasing the visibility. Simo trained the binoculars down towards the single track that twisted up towards Bjelašnica. It was empty, no sign of an approaching car. Drakulić had said dawn. He glanced at his watch. It was after six, so where the hell was he? Something wasn't right.

27

The falling snow caught in the rosy dawn light, turning pink like cherry blossom. As pretty as it was, Heather felt only dread for the arrival of the new day. The track was hard to see from the back of the car, and it appeared as if Drakulić in the driver's seat was having just as much difficulty making out the treacherous route. He wasn't helped by the fact that the road wound up and up in a series of ever-tightening hairpin bends. Although the car was hot, the pudgy guard next to her was alert, wincing at every unplanned motion of the car.

Out of nowhere a rabbit bounded across the track, and at the appearance of an obstacle the nervous guard cried out. Instinctively, Drakulić braked. There was a rattle as one of the snow-chains came loose from its tyre, like a spooked horse throwing a shoe. They lost grip and slewed across the road. As the car skidded, the guard was thrown against Heather and she noted that he wasn't wearing a seatbelt. Drakulić corrected the skid and brought them to a stop, turning around to issue a snarling rebuke. Heather saw that his face was coated with sweat – the strain of the drive was taking its toll. They abandoned the broken chain and set off again, only for the track to vanish in the latest snow flurry. Drakulić drove blindly, peering into the blankness, the wipers flailing uselessly, until suddenly the way ahead appeared again. On the right-hand side was a rock wall covered with snow, and on the other a steep slope where tall strands of spiked mountain grass still poked through the layers of powder like spiny fingers. The slope was a sheer drop, and in the poor visibility Drakulić crawled forward, mindful that one misjudged corner would likely be fatal. Heather realised there was a chance they might not even make the intended rendezvous. Not because she might escape, but because they'd all die here on this god-forsaken road.

Drakulić fell silent with concentration as he positioned the car for another sharp turn. After the bend the road straightened and Drakulić accelerated. Beside Heather, she saw the guard open-mouthed with nervous anticipation, warily scanning the road for another obstacle. Neither man was paying her any attention.

Heather studied the speedometer. Fifteen miles an hour. Sixteen. Eighteen. Twenty. Twenty-two.

As the needle hit twenty-five, she leant forward through the gap between the seats and lunged for the steering wheel. She missed. Jolted into action, the guard tried frantically to yank her back, pulling at her hair, her waist. Drakulić was yelling at him in Serbian, presumably to deal with her. Fumbling for his gun, the guard couldn't shoot her without risking hitting Drakulić too. She elbowed him hard in the crotch and he doubled up.

She reached forward again and wrenched on the handbrake. As she planned, instead of slowing the car, it locked the back wheels and sent them into a skid. At once, the car started to turn away from the rock wall and veer towards the snow bank on the other side. But as they collided with the bank, it gave way.

Too late Heather saw that it hid a drop. At first the car slid down the steep slope, but the angle was too acute and it quickly flipped over, bouncing and crashing, careering down and down. Drakulić smashed against Heather and then was thrown against the roof, cracking his head against it. The guard screamed and then was silent. Everything was moving too fast. Heather was briefly aware of snow and rocks rearing up through the broken windshield as they tumbled end over end. She screamed with pain as her shoulder and broken collarbone were hammered again and again, and then with a boom and heavy jolt, they came to a stop.

The car was on its crumpled roof, Heather wedged tightly against it, the pressure on her fractured collarbone almost unbearable. Blood pounded in her head. The guard was no longer in the car. She recalled his scream, but nothing else. In the tumbling chaos it seemed he had been flung out through the windshield.

Drakulić lay sprawled beside her, a gash seeping on his forehead, his leg twisted at an odd angle. She couldn't tell if the crash had killed him, but if it hadn't there was one way to put an end to this now. She reached for his gun. As she did, Drakulić's eyes flicked opened. He stared at her, confused and unfocused. Then he saw her hand down at his hip, poised over his holster. He swiped it away and then made another swipe for her.

Heather leapt back. Thoughts of turning his gun on him gone, she groped for the door, slicing her hand open on a jagged piece of the chassis. Adrenaline stifled the pain. The door was wedged shut with snow and she'd have to force it.

Gritting her teeth, she heaved against the frame with her damaged shoulder. She daren't look round, but behind her she could sense Drakulić stirring like some ancient monster awakened from its slumber. With a final desperate push, the door sprang open, her momentum carrying her tumbling out into the snow. She lay there, face-to-face with the pudgy guard. Scrabbling away from him on her knees, she saw with relief that he wasn't moving, and his body looked crooked and wrong. She was almost certain he was dead. But Drakulić was very much alive. He slithered out of the car behind her.

She pulled herself to her feet, looking around frantically to get her bearings. Her only hope was to follow the vehicle tracks. They would lead her to Simo – she must get to him first. It was a race. And one that she had to win.

Heather heard the crack of a gunshot, the sound reverberating around the mountains. Drakulić knelt on the snow, pistol extended in his hand. Still shaky from the aftermath of the crash, his aim was wild. Heather couldn't help but recall that it had only been an hour since the last time she'd made a break for it, and then he had swiftly chased her down. But the car crash had levelled the competition – now they were both injured. She began to scramble up the slope to where they had first veered off the road. She must reach the track.

The gun went off again. She ignored it and continued her climb, scrabbling for handholds among the rocks and snow. Drakulić stopped firing. Heather presumed that he was saving his bullets for when he was closer with a better chance of hitting his target. She risked a glance over her shoulder. Years of competitive cycling ensured that she could judge distances with the accuracy of a laser. He was three hundred metres behind her. She must not let him close that gap. Was he limping? God, she hoped so.

The snow had drifted unevenly on the slope, leaving some of it patched and thin, exposing bare rocks, while other sections were thick and padded with heavy snow. Every time she landed in deep snow, it slowed her to a crawl. The mountains glowed with a weird backlight, casting the world with the unearthly light of a dream. The cold and pain reminded her that it was anything but. She took another step and, with a yell, sank up to her waist, caught as if in quicksand. Easy pickings for Drakulić if she couldn't get out quickly. A glance back confirmed that he'd made up ground; now the gap was two hundred metres. Frantically she tried to claw her way out, but she could only use one arm; her broken collarbone meant her right side was useless. She hoisted one leg free, used it to lever herself out. A hundred metres. She started to scramble again. The boulders and rocks made it hard to find a route through the snow, hidden obstacles under the layers of powder lying in wait to trip her up, but Drakulić was struggling too, stumbling and falling. As she watched, he too fell into a drift.

Heather noticed a dark shape ahead of her in the snow. As she drew closer, she saw that it was Marina's body. The car boot must have burst open during the descent, throwing her out and now she lay half buried on the cold mountainside. Heather glanced back to Drakulić, still caught in the drift, digging furiously. That gave her just enough time to pause and whisper a hurried goodbye, before setting off again. Her legs were cold and stiff, and starting with a cruel uphill was not ideal, but at least when they'd hurt her yesterday they'd left her legs alone. The only sore spots were on her ankles where the bonds had rubbed them raw, but they were superficial wounds, the sort that Heather was accomplished at ignoring.

She reached the edge of the road where the car had come off and hoisted herself back up onto the level. With the ground flatter and more predictable, compacted in places by the passing of the earlier vehicle, she was able to break into a run. But how fast? That was the difficult part. She was in a running race, but with no idea how long there was to go to the finish line she couldn't judge what kind of pace to set. Too slow would risk being caught by Drakulić; too fast risked exhausting herself if it turned out she was in an endurance race. Without knowing which race she was running, she decided her tactic would be to watch her opponent, respond to him, fending off every attack and ensuring she kept up a pace that maintained the distance between them. If he caught her, then she was dead. Of that she was certain. Whatever his earlier plan had been – to pretend to hand her over to Simo before killing them both, most likely – her escape had changed everything. Now he just wanted to kill her. As if to underline her point, another gunshot rang out. It impacted off to her right, spitting up rock and scree, the shot wide, but not as wide as his earlier attempts. Drakulić had reached the path.

What Drakulić didn't know was that she had stamina. Once upon a time, Olympic fucking stamina. She might be broken and bruised but she was in the goddamn lead, and when Heather Bishop had the lead, she defended it. It was up to Drakulić to attack, and she would respond. This was a game of tactics; she would race with her head. While adrenaline and fear were telling her to hurry, to get away from Drakulić, a dark and malevolent presence behind her, it took all her willpower to disobey every instinct and to pace herself.

She heard him shouting but she did not turn around. *Just keep running.* He was yelling at her to stop, in Serbian and then in English. But she would not stop; she would never stop. Not till the finish line. The adrenaline masked the pain. And the pain had a rightness to it now. She was supposed to hurt. She'd raced with a broken collarbone before. Crashed on Alpe d'Huez and broken it, then climbed on a fresh bike and finished the stage only ninety seconds down. That's what separated long-distance riders from other athletes: we can endure it all, thought Heather. Drakulić was still shouting and Heather smiled grimly. He was wasting breath. He seemed to realise it and stopped, saving his energy for the race. The mountain was silent except for the steady huff of her breathing, the thud-thud of her trainers on the compacted snow. She was grateful that she was wearing comfortable shoes and decent leggings. She hadn't packed much else for cycling with Ryan. Her T-shirt and fleece were a bit thin, but the sheer exertion was warming her. Her left eye was cut and swollen and watering badly, and as she ran Heather noticed that her balance was off; she stumbled more than usual. Her shoulder was throwing her. It ought to be in a sling, but she needed the right rhythm and weight to run. She had to be careful of her footing. Her ear was trickling blood again and the bitter cold made it very uncomfortable – a sharp pain that pierced through the endorphins. She glanced back. Drakulić ran steadily behind her, about a hundred metres between them. He wasn't trying to close the gap, but neither was he giving up. He might have been hurt in the crash, but even with a slight limp he was otherwise in good shape. And motivated. If he didn't catch her, he risked losing everything. Those opponents, Heather knew, the ones with everything at stake, were the most dangerous.

The snow began to fall more heavily, and the light turned a weird unearthly grey. The tracks in front of Heather were soon feathered with a fresh layer of snow. She could see them for now, but she guessed that in an hour or so they would be hidden and if she hadn't reached Simo by then, she'd be lost out here on the mountainside with no one but Drakulić and his gun.

Another glance back told her that Drakulić was attacking, rushing forward, closing the gap between them. Only eighty metres separated them. Heather surged forward, urging her legs on. There was the crack of the gun again. This time it came too close, dimpling the snow beside her. She began to run in zigzags so that it was harder for him to get a bead on her position, but it also meant it was much harder to sustain the pace. She had to run twice as fast to keep up the space between them. She breathed steadily and deeply, filling her lungs. The cold air burnt her chest as she inhaled it and her legs ached, while each thudding footstep against the iron-hard ground sent shockwaves up and into her collarbone, ripples of furious pain. She must not stop. Must not slow. Come on, legs. She felt a trickle of sweat tickle the length of her spine. She dared to glance back. Drakulić had slowed and the distance opened up again. He wasn't firing, saving his last bullets until he was certain of a clear shot. She'd seen off the attack. She carried on at the same speed, no longer zig-zagging. It was a good tactic, taught to her by her first ever *director sportif* – show them when they're hurting that you're not. Even if it's a lie, pretend you're not suffering. Heather was in agony and the throbbing of her sternum was making her vision play odd tricks – she could see shadows at the edges and her ear jabbed with pain – but she kept up the same pace for another fifteen minutes, purely to torment Drakulić, to show him how strong she was, that she felt nothing. At last, she slowed, but as she looked back in expected triumph, instead she saw to her horror that the gap was only a hundred and fifty metres. That massive effort at great physical cost had barely gained her fifty metres. He probably hadn't even noticed that she hadn't slowed, her acceleration had been so small. She cursed herself. She bent down and scooped up a handful of snow, sucking it to keep hydrated. She stuffed a hand in her pocket, glad of the biscuits she'd secreted there yesterday. She'd bought them at the same time as the pregnancy test, along with some sweets and raisins. The last thing she needed was her muscles to go into shock for lack of energy. The dreaded *fringale*. She'd suffered it in many a race, and while out training when she hadn't taken on enough calories. Black vision. The shakes. Confusion. She took a bite, then another and felt in her pocket and discovered the raisins. It wasn't enough, but it would have to do. She saved the sweets for later.

The road was still going up and up, disappearing in stretches of fog and falling snow, the visibility growing worse. As Heather ascended a hairpin bend, she could look down to see Drakulić. Unlike her earlier snatched glances, from here she was able to get a good, long look at him. He was still dressed in his blue jumper and court shoes, his coat discarded, hot from the exertion, but what frightened her was his expression. He exuded primeval anger and he was pushing all that fury into his legs, gun clasped in his fist. He took aim, and a metre away from Heather a rock split, pebbling the snow with shrapnel. She ran faster. As she gained height, spools of fog began to tangle around her body, so that she had to concentrate to see the way, but she felt only relief – Drakulić wouldn't be able to see her to shoot at.

The road began to dip again, going lower and then sharply lower again. Heather saw trees in the distance – a dark forest of pines, lavishly coated with snow. Somewhere a woodpecker rattled, reminding her that it was still supposed to be spring. This winter was a mirage, a sudden barrage that would bloom and then vanish. Her thoughts were drifting, slow and unclear; like she was reaching for them through water. A sign of exhaustion. The black pinpricks reappeared in her vision. She was at high risk of the *fringale*. She felt drunk. She was dizzy and her thoughts were becoming thicker and unfocused. There was no way of knowing whether it was exhaustion and the effects of torture and her injuries or, the lingering withdrawal from the drugs. She fumbled in her pocket for one of the sweets. It didn't help. Her muscles were trembling and her own voice was one of many chattering in her head. She mustn't lose it. Not now. Keep it together, Heather. You can do it. Some of the voices urged her on, but others hissed their doubts. Then, another voice, sharper than the others, hissing at her that Drakulić was attacking again. Sure enough, he'd picked up the pace. Oh God, she wasn't sure if she had anything left in her. She hiccupped and vomited the sweet she'd just eaten along with the snow. She couldn't stop. She wanted to cry, but she forced herself to steady her breathing. The gap between them was narrowing like the disappearing crack in a slamming door.

He must not win the race. She wouldn't let him get the leader's yellow jersey. She'd endured so much. It was hers. She had suffered. It wasn't fair, she complained. Where was the peloton? Why was she alone? Where were all the other riders? Heather looked around for them. There was no one. No team cars. No other riders. Only the snow and fog and the thud-thud of her own feet, the whirr and click of her own bike. She and Drakulić were in a breakaway, way out in front. But it was a bitter, cruel rivalry, a race with only one winner, and they would not work together and help each other. She was alone on this mountain, pursued by a demon rider. No, she whispered to herself, I'm pursued only by a man. All riders are human. All have frailties. If she was suffering, then so was he.

And she could suffer longest.

She must. Only if she reached Simo first would she live. Yes, she was in worse physical condition than Drakulić, but she had more stamina. Remarkable, superhuman stamina. She needed a hill. A steep, horrible hill, the kind that terrified other riders. Drakulić would see it and give in, but not her. Give me a damn hill, and I'll win.

It was so hard to keep going in a straight line; she knew she was weaving all over the road. She reached into her pocket and pulled out the last of her sweets before it was too late and exhaustion overtook her. Then she scooped up handfuls of snow to suck, but that wouldn't quench her terrible thirst. The falling snow was slowing and the fog was starting to clear, but the endless flurries had completely covered the route and, for the first time, Heather realised she couldn't see the vehicle tracks. Without them to guide her, she was blind. She couldn't stop to find them again. A feeling in her legs. More pain. Its significance lifting her spirits. The ground rose steeply in front of her. A hill. A nasty, steep hill. Two hundred metres to the top. If she could just get there, perhaps she would see the way again.

Sweat stung her eyes, mingling with tears as she pushed with everything she had. The noises coming out of her were animal. The incline was sharp. Nothing that would usually get her, but then again she wouldn't usually race in this physical condition. She daren't look back. Daren't see how close Drakulić was. Just keep going. Fifty metres. She felt a buzzing in her ears. Voices. Tried to block them out. The voices hadn't been doing her any favours. They'd been nothing but trouble after the accident. All she wanted was silence. For her mind to be her own again. She was all alone on this hill. She was a real long-distance rider. A champion. Drakulić was not. Twenty metres. He's an ordinary rider. Her legs burned. Fifteen. Ten. Nearly there. Five. You can lose him. Her lungs screamed.

She reached the top and saw, high above her in the distance, beyond the last of the trees, was the wedge-shaped outline of a building, and over it the glittering circles of the Olympic rings. She gave a little cry of desperation. The *fringale* had caught her. Her eyes were playing tricks, fooling her with an illusion conjured from old desires, summoned from the recesses of her unconscious. And then she remembered: Ryan had wanted to bring her here. He'd wanted to show her the site of the abandoned Winter Olympics and to cycle here together – before the snow had come, before they'd taken him. The fear dissolved and, for the first time, she allowed herself to think of Ryan. Ryan, who she would never get to tell that she was pregnant. Never speak to again. Never hear his laugh again. Even if she won this race and lived, she would never hold him again, or feel the scratch of his stubble against her cheek.

The rings. Aim for the Olympic rings. Don't stop. Keep going. You can do it. You can fight it.

The voice in her head was Ryan's. This was a macabre joke, but it might just save her. As long as she could see the gold of the rings, she had something to aim for. The Olympics had been over for her long ago, and yet this race, the one for her life, was going to finish there, after all. The tarnished rings were as broken and forgotten as she, and even through the pain and the uneasy fogginess of her thoughts, Heather sensed that it was fitting. For the first time since she'd climbed into the car beside Drakulić, she knew where it would all end, one way or another.

Go, Heather, go! He's coming for you.

'Will you stay with me, Ryan?' she asked.

Until the end. But you need to go now. He's coming.

As she started to race again, she reached down and brushed her stomach. The baby inside her was minute, no bigger than a grain of rice, but it was part her and part Ryan. As long as she lived, so did Ryan. She must live. She must. She took a gasping breath and accelerated down the descent, faster and faster. She heard Drakulić's footsteps padding behind, deadened by the snow.

28

Simo's walkie-talkie squawked and he told David to go ahead.

'Am outside the cable car, in position. No sight of the shooter. Over.'

Simo replied. 'Copy that. Possible he exited the building? Over.'

'Oh, he's in there, all right. Just hunkered down.'

This wasn't good news. If they were going to have any chance of getting through the rest of the day alive, they had to neutralise the threat of the shooter before Drakulić arrived for the exchange.

'I would go in after him,' David continued, 'but, y'know, I'd rather not get shot in the face. Over.'

Simo had an idea. It was a terrible idea, but there didn't seem to be another option. He keyed the talk button. 'I think I know how to flush him out. Over.'

'You're going to walk straight up to the front door, aren't you? Over.'

Hearing it spoken aloud made his plan sound even worse. Simo pressed on regardless. 'He's expecting to see me here. Drakulić needs me alive; his guy won't shoot me. Over.'

'Sure about that?' asked David doubtfully. 'These are

Drakulić's men we're talking about. Fucking morons. He'll probably shoot you by accident. Great plan. Okay, let's do it. Over and out.'

Simo surveyed the terrain. His current position, the distance from the cable car and the conditions meant that even if the shooter decided to target Simo, he had little chance of making a kill shot. But as Simo trudged uphill, he reminded himself that every step closer increased his percentages of winding up dead in the snow with a bullet through his chest. The sleet was dimpling the snow, creating puddles of slush. Simo's foot slid from under him. He managed to stay upright, but in doing so wrenched his back, which was already hurting. The stitches had snagged and the pain was making him woozy. He should have taken one of the Vicodin himself. As he drew closer to the building, he raised his arms, hoping that the shooter recognised him. His Glock semi-automatic was tucked out of sight in a deep pocket of his coat, though if he needed it, by the time he got to it he'd be dead.

Out of the corner of his eye, shielded by the maintenance shed and his winter camouflage, he saw David with his rifle trained on the row of broken windows. David was sighting through his one good eye. Jesus Christ, what a nightmare.

There was a crack and a moment later the snow exploded ten metres in front of Simo. The shooter had fired a warning shot, which had landed far enough away from him that Simo knew it was meant as a message: I see you. Come no further.

But in taking aim, he had exposed himself at the window. There was an answering crack from David's hunting rifle. Simo didn't wait to find out if the shot had hit its target. He half-ran, half-limped for cover. As he dashed across the snow, sleet stinging his face, he was aware of several more shots as the two gunmen exchanged fire. There was a loud report from David's position in the snowfield and then, this time, no return fire from the cable car building. Simo made it to the shed, panting with the effort of the short run. He put his hands on his knees and caught his breath, but as he looked down he saw David lay sprawled in a drift, bleeding from his left side.

He looked up at Simo with a beatific smile. 'Got the bastard.'

'Looks like it was mutual.'

David was indignant. 'I'm still alive.'

Yes, thought Simo, but for how long was another matter. He knelt down beside him. There were medical supplies in the backpack. Without hurting his friend by moving him, he unzipped the pack and tentatively removed them. But bandages wouldn't be enough. Simo had to get him off this mountain, and soon, or he'd die from blood loss, shock, exposure or a combination of all three. He patched him up as best he could with the limited supplies, propped him in the lee of the shed and walked to the end of the building.

The Americans had a term for missions like this, where everything that could go wrong, does go wrong. Clusterfuck.

Where the hell was Drakulić? There was a new urgency to resolving this damn business. The sooner they got the exchange over with, the sooner they could all get off this damn mountain. Simo raised his binoculars and turned them to scan the track leading up to the mountaintop. The sleet had subsided, and thin sunshine was attempting to make its way through a break in the clouds. There was still no sign of a car and he was about to lower the binoculars when on the path below, at the limit of the scope, he spotted a small figure, running. Just behind came another, moving faster and gaining on the first. And as it did, catching in the sunlight Simo saw a metal glint of what he had no doubt was a gun. He didn't have to wait for them to come closer in order to identify the figures. He knew in his bones.

'It's Drakulić,' he said. 'And Heather Bishop.' There was no sign of Marina Tomić. Even without confirmation, he understood what that signified. But Heather was alive and she needed his help. However, that would mean leaving behind his mortally injured friend.

David seemed to sense his dilemma. 'Go,' he mumbled.

'I'll be back as soon as I can. Try not to die on me.'

'I'll do my best.'

Simo began to run.

They had regained the treeline. Trees loomed, sunlight flashing through the gaps in the canopies. The silence that Heather had been racing with for hours was now punctured by the chatter of birdsong. She pretended that it was the roar of crowds lining the route along the Alpine stages of the Tour, where the cheers willed you on when you thought you were done in, ready to surrender to the mountain. Her face was sloppy with tears and sweat and blood. She had exhausted the last of her meagre supply of sweets and raisins some time ago, but there was still snow to slake her raging thirst and keep her hydrated. She bent to scoop up a handful, but in her exhaustion tripped and fell and found herself lying dazed on the ground staring up at the sky. She pulled herself up into a sitting position, every part of her aching. She saw Drakulić sprinting through the trees, bearing down towards her, teeth bared. The Wolf incarnate. She scrambled to her feet and ran, but he was closer to her than at any time since they had fought over the steering wheel in the car.

'You look terrible, Heather,' he called.

She rubbed her tailbone. She'd bruised it when she fell, and she'd dropped the snow. All she was left with was a handful of wet dirt. Furiously thirsty, she licked it all the same. She tried to play the usual mind games to cope with the pain: reciting the speeches of her old coaches; song lyrics; visualising the moment of crossing the finish-line, a winner. But she couldn't see it. Nothing worked. She was used to discomfort. Suffering. Anxiety. But this raw, feral fear was sharp and pierced through everything. The adrenaline had made her muscles work for a time, but now it was fading and her body had worked beyond even its great capacity, and she was approaching the very limits of what she could physically endure. At some point soon – and she sensed it would be very soon – her mind and her body would shut down. There would be no more sugar in her blood to supply her muscles, and without more adrenaline to take its place, she would go into shock. The uncontrolled trembling would start. Confusion and dizziness would follow. Then more vomiting. Although, with Drakulić behind her, she doubted she'd get to that point. It would all be over long before then.

She felt a wetness along her inner thigh. Vaguely, she realised that she must have peed herself. She'd been unable to stop to relieve herself, and now she was losing bladder control. Through the wooziness of her thoughts, she felt a stab of indignation. The race leader was supposed to be able to stop for a call of nature and the other riders would not attack. Those were the unwritten rules. But Drakulić didn't play by her rules.

She touched the smooth cotton of her leggings and her fingers came away daubed with red. It wasn't urine, but blood. *No.* Rage ignited through her veins like electricity. She wouldn't die and she wouldn't let them take away her last piece of Ryan. They had stolen him; they wouldn't steal his baby too. She swallowed back tears, not out of pride but necessity. She couldn't cry and breathe, and she needed every gasp. The altitude was making her suffer more than usual. She felt another rush of wetness between her legs and tightened the muscles in her pelvic floor as though she could hold it in, could tighten her womb around the foetus, cradle it safely. It wasn't fair. Her anger powered her on.

The sun was out now and the snow glinted fiercely, beginning to melt in patches, and sliding off the trees. The ground was slippery, and she skidded, catching herself.

'Give up, Heather!' shouted Drakulić. 'You die anyway! This way, I make it fast.'

She didn't answer. She called on all her resources, even though she knew there was little to nothing left, and tried to accelerate away from him. When that didn't work, she attempted to conjure Ryan's voice to call her onward, but he was silent. She had nothing. She was spent, scraped out. The distance between her and Drakulić shrank – she could feel it melting away like the snow. Soon he would be on her. There was another gunshot. By the time she heard it, it was too late to duck, but she did so automatically. The shot went wide in any case. Dimly, she wondered how many bullets he had left.

The road turned sharply upward – a final brutal ascent towards the rings perched on the hill. A hundred-metre near vertical climb. Heather's shoulders shook with the effort. She grunted and cried out, giving a final silent agonising wail. She was desperate. He was just behind her. She could sense him without looking. Out of the corner of her eye she saw blood dripping into the snow through her leggings. Along with it, cool despair trickled through her, slowing her almost to a stop. A wave of despair engulfed her. What was the point? Perhaps it was better just to end it here, to submit and give in. To sink into the soft ground and rest. She was moments away from giving up. At this point, most people would have succumbed. But this feeling wasn't new to Heather Bishop. It was an old friend. She'd trained for it – over and over again. She'd never abandoned a race unless she'd had an injury so brutal she'd been directed to quit. And today was not the day to start. She put one foot in front of the other and carried on. She had to reach the rings. She had to reach Simo.

Another gunshot, this one so close to her head she felt the whistle of splitting air. He was just behind her. Ten metres. She braced herself for the inevitable next bullet. It didn't come. Why wasn't he shooting? Vaguely, she supposed he must be out of ammunition. It wouldn't stop him from killing her. Five metres. She could hear the gasp and huff of Drakulić's laboured breathing. He was suffering too. Good. But she had done all she could. She had kept her promise to herself. And really, what was left to live for? Dying couldn't feel much worse than this. It was nearly over. Black specks appeared at the edges of her vision and she stumbled. She was struggling to see. Simo emerged out of the snow, a final self-delusion. He couldn't be here. She hadn't reached the Olympic rings. She blinked to rid herself of the figment. Both the black specks and Simo remained. Her swollen eye seeped tears and her ear was buzzing, her hearing distorted. Someone was yelling.

And it wasn't Drakulić.

Simo shouted at Heather to get down. Drakulić was behind her, his gun up high in his hand, ready to bring it crashing down on her skull. Blood trailed in the snow behind the two runners; both were in a bad way. He longed to take a shot, but the distance was too great to hope for any accuracy with a handgun, not to mention that with Heather in front of Drakulić it wasn't a clear shot and, anyway, he wasn't as good a marksman as David.

'Heather!' he shouted again. 'Get down!'

She could hear him, of that he was sure, but she stared through him, as if she didn't really see him. Drakulić, however, did see him and, recognising the danger, accelerated in a desperate burst, clearly eager to finish this. Simo watched in horror as Drakulić's fingers reached out, snatched at Heather, gun raised. He brought it down, but he was as exhausted as she was and his aim was off. He missed her head but connected hard with her shoulder. She let out a cry of agony that reached to the sky, and went down. In a heartbeat Drakulić was on top of her.

Slipping and sliding in the melting snow, Simo ran towards them as fast as his injured body could carry him. Every painful step a sharp reminder to him of his own mortality. He could see them sprawled in a tangle of limbs, Drakulić's arm rising and falling, punching her over and over, but with no real force or strength behind the blows. In the frenzy of his attack he had spilled his gun, which lay to one side of the path, half buried in a pile of snow.

Simo continued limping towards them. He was close enough now to risk a shot, but Heather was in the way. She lay prone on the path as the near-shattered Drakulić rained blows down on her.

'Heather, get up!' Simo yelled, but without any expectation that she could. So, it was to his amazement that, weeping and bleeding, summoning the last dregs of determination from God-knew-where, she pulled herself into a crawling posture and began to drag herself out of Drakulić's reach, leaving him to grab uselessly for her ankles. He attempted to get to his feet, but he was worn out. Scrabbling at the ground, he could only rear up like some demented half-dead creature and howl at the escaping woman. Heather crawled one metre away. Two.

It was enough.

Simo skidded to a halt, steadied himself and levelled his gun. 'That's enough. On the ground, face down.' Drakulić stubbornly ignored the instruction and Simo watched as he glanced to the edge of the path, towards the worn grip of his pistol poking from the snow. Surely he wasn't stupid enough to make a grab for it? And anyway, he was out of ammo, *wasn't he*? Why else try to club Heather with the gun? Simo resolved that if it came to it, he wasn't going to take the chance.

There was a rumble in the sky and, for a moment, Simo thought it might be an approaching thunderstorm, but then he spied the insect shapes of two helicopters skimming the tops of the trees, the percussive beat of their rotor-blades filling the air. His Bosnian police counterparts; with the weather lifting they'd got here at last. They were heading for a landing at the cable car station. Drakulić had seen them too. Simo motioned with his gun again.

'Dragan Drakulić, I'm arresting you for the murder of Ryan Mackinnon.'

Drakulić didn't hesitate. His hand twitched as he made a lunge for the pistol.

Simo raised his Glock and fired twice. He would never get used to the noise. But here, amongst the trees, the dense forest smothered the report. Drakulić slumped to the ground, blood seeping from the fresh holes in his abdomen.

Knees pulled up to her chest, Heather stared at the dying man and then at Simo, her expression a question. Is it over?

Drakulić closed his eyes and for a moment Simo thought it was, but then he opened them again.

'I lied,' he said, struggling for breath. 'I do remember your friend Abdul. You did everything to get him back. There was no point.' His chest rattled and Simo wasn't sure if it was with his death throes or with laughter. 'There wasn't much of him left.'

Simo clenched his fists, resisting the urge to shoot him again. 'Do you regret it? Any of it? Abdul, Ryan?'

But the question would never be answered. He was talking to a dead man.

Heather blinked up at Simo, her face slick with tears and sweat. He holstered his gun and enfolded her in his arms. She sunk against him.

'Can I stop running now? Is this the finish line?'

Simo held her tightly. 'Yes. This is the end.'

He looked past her, to where Drakulić lay in the snow. *Who's coming?* That's what Drakulić had asked, over and over again. And now the detective had the answer.

I am.

He had become the Silent Women's assassin. But this was not what he wanted. He believed in justice through the courts – for Ryan, Abdul and the countless dead. Justice, not vengeance. Yet, deep within him, he felt an animal flicker of satisfaction. He tucked it away and knew he would tell no one, not even David.

Heather started to sob in fury and relief.

'Where is Marina?' Simo asked softly, releasing her.

'Dead,' she whispered, confirming what he had suspected when he hadn't spied her on the road. 'Everyone is dead.'

'You're not,' said Simo. 'You lived. You won.'

Heather began to shake uncontrollably, finally overcome with exhaustion. Simo hugged her to him again, cradling her tightly, soothing her.

The sun shone brightly and obscenely; the snow dripped and glittered. The three figures remained quietly on the mountainside. One dead and bloody in the snow; the other two clinging to each other as they listened to the drip-drip of the meltwater and the cheerful note of the cuckoo from his perch on a nearby pine tree, insistent and indifferent as it called out the green notes of spring.

29

Simo sat outside the hospital in Sarajevo where the Bosnian police helicopters had flown Heather and David. He'd been waiting inside for hours while his friend underwent surgery, only leaving his post when the surgeon emerged from theatre to reassure him that David would certainly live. Although he would be walking with a stick for a while. Simo winced at the thought of how David would take this news. With David out of danger he'd tried to check in on Heather, only to be informed by an officious nurse that she was resting and to come back later. Having had enough of hospital corridors, for the time being, he went outside and found a bench that caught the late afternoon light. A police car with Višegrad plates was parked illegally – and provocatively – in an ambulance bay. Simo had little doubt who it belonged to.

'Subotić,' called a familiar voice from the hospital entranceway.

Simo turned to see Josif marching towards him, whey-faced and thin-lipped with a mixture of shock and anger. He'd clearly been searching for Simo inside. Having found him at last, he looked him up and down with barely concealed disgust and fury. Drakulić had been a psychopath and a monster, but he had also been Josif Borisov's father.

'Did you have to kill him?' he spat.

'Yes.'

'Did he suffer?'

Simo met his eye, unflinching. 'Not as much as his victims.'

Josif closed his eyes and was silent for a minute, trying to marshal his self-control. When he spoke at last, his voice quavered. 'Maybe you really do believe that you did what you had to. And, as your police chief, I accept your course of action, but as his son, I can't forgive you.'

Simo made no reply. Only yesterday he had told Josif that he needed to choose between being a son or the Chief of Police, but in the end, Simo had made the choice for him, and Josif Borisov despised him for it. Simo would have to accept the consequences.

Josif left without another word, heading back inside the building, his face contorted with loathing and grief. Yet, he hadn't driven all the way to the hospital purely in order to berate Simo – that was just a bonus. He was here for a much more sombre reason. After ferrying the injured and the living off the mountain, the Bosnians had gone back for the dead. The bodies of the shooter and Drakulić were currently in the morgue here. Simo watched Josif's figure disappear along the corridor, knowing that he was going to officially identify his father. Despite the firm line Josif had taken with him about Drakulić, he knew that his own actions on the mountain would weigh on his conscience for a long time.

Josif had said nothing about Rubi Kurjak or the Silent Women. Simo hadn't presented any evidence of their involvement yet. While he was furious with Rubi for encouraging Ryan to come out here and get involved, Ryan Mackinnon was a grown man capable of making his own decisions. He thought back to everything David had told him about Rubi and how she had suffered at Drakulić's hands during the war. No wonder she had broken. He'd get David to send her a message – he wouldn't pursue her this time. But if she got so much as another parking ticket, he would track her to the ends of the earth. The news of Marina's death would be punishment enough for Rubi. She would have to live with the guilt of that for the rest of her life – it was her actions that had put Marina in the Wolf's jaws.

Simo sighed and shook his head. He wondered how Nikola was coping with the news of his wife's murder. He resolved to visit him at the earliest opportunity – he owed him that much at least. He could only hope that Drakulić's death would provide Nikola with some solace, but he doubted it.

Simo's phone buzzed with an alert. A message from his Bosnian counterpart, a young detective from Sarajevo. He was new and Simo hadn't shared any history with him, so he should have expected what happened during the helicopter flight off the mountain. The detective had informed him that acting on Simo's information he'd brought in the three men implicated in the Drina murders of Arkan Ćešić and Ivan Fuštar for questioning. Infuriated, Simo had nonetheless bitten his tongue. It was a violation of professional courtesy and the implication was clear – this was their case now. For Simo, it was over. Fuck it. He wondered if the case would ever reach court. Any court. The defendants would almost certainly receive a more sympathetic trial here, where Drakulić was considered a war criminal rather than a hero.

Stiffening with the pain from his back, Simo got up from the bench and attempted a gentle stretch. When he'd first arrived at the hospital an ER doctor had insisted on taking a look at his knife wound – along with all of his other recent injuries – and concluded that given the damage, it was remarkable he was still walking, especially for a man of his age. Impertinent son of a bitch.

As he stretched, he saw a familiar figure running towards him. He winced as Petra flew at him, flinging her arms around his neck.

'Uncle Simo, you crazy stupid bastard. You're far too old for this shit. You cut it out, I tell you. I thought you were dead for sure.'

Simo put his arm around her shoulder, 'Come. Let's go inside and see Heather.'

Heather lay in her bed hooked up to a drip feeding her antibiotics and fluids. She was in considerable pain but had refused anything stronger than paracetamol. She didn't want morphine or anything that would make her feel that the world was weirder or darker than it already was. Someone from the British Consulate had brought her a phone, but she wasn't ready to start calling people. Instead, she found herself looking for Ryan's old articles. Not Ryan Markovtiz, but her Ryan, and the pieces he'd written about her.

It's a terrible confession, but I didn't call Heather Bishop after the first time we kissed. I didn't call, because although she was hot – and believe me she was gorgeous – she was boring, in that self-involved, obsessional way brilliant world-class athletes are. It's a necessary narcissism. They need to be like that in order to win. The truth is, back then when she was an Olympian I wasn't that into her. I like her way better now. I know she worries about it sometimes, because she asks me and then forgets she's asked me, and asks again. And, no, I'm not a sicko who likes wounded women. I like fierce women. Now, after all she's endured, she's the fiercest woman I've ever met. She never ever f**king gives up. She's fierce, angry and kind. The woman you want on your side.

As she'd re-read the article laying in her hospital bed, Heather felt a curious sense of relief mixed with her sadness and loss. Ryan might have lied to her about many things, but he had loved her. Their relationship wasn't perfect, and perhaps he did include too many personal details about her struggles, but they were written with such compassion and tenderness – and love. She would make sure that she passed on that love to his child.

There was a knock on the door and Petra and Simo entered the room. Petra let out a cry when she saw her battered face.

'You should see the other guy,' said Heather, struggling to sit up. 'It's okay. I'm okay.' She gestured to her bedside table, at a print-out of a scan. 'Have a look.'

Petra took it and examined the sonogram. 'Looks like tiny gremlin.'

Heather laughed and then gasped in pain. 'Don't make me laugh.' She took the scan from her and stared at it. 'I heard a heartbeat.'

Petra squeezed Heather's hand, the only part of her that seemed not to be bruised or pierced with a cannula. 'I'm so happy. Seriously. No joke.'

Simo stood and opened the window to a distant view of the green mountains. Fresh air blew into the room. He recalled that when the Bosnian police arrived on the mountain, Heather had told them about a third accomplice, a guard, now also dead. The third man's body had yet to be recovered from the ravine where it had been discovered along with an upturned car. Heather hadn't been able to talk much, so severe was her exhaustion, but from what she had said it was clear that she'd got the better of Drakulić and his men. Remarkable.

'I know you want to go home,' he said. 'But the police here will need you to make a statement about what happened in the cabin. When you're ready. We want to send Marina's killers to prison.'

'The doctors want me to stay for at least a week.' She hesitated. 'When Ryan's body is released, I want him cremated and I'd like to scatter his ashes here.' She swallowed. 'Somewhere near Jahorina peak. The stretch where I last saw him. I didn't know it at the time, but there were three of us then, too.'

'If you'll allow us,' said Simo, 'Petra and I will come with you.'

'Thank you. For everything.'

Simo waved away her gratitude. 'You thanked me enough already.'

'Did I?'

She lay back pale-faced. Simo could see that the exertion of even this brief conversation was too much for her right now. He adjusted her pillow and she closed her eyes. He stroked her forehead. Soon, he thought, Ryan would join the thousands lost across the Balkans. His ashes would drift on the breeze across the pines and rivers. Perhaps he'd find his friend, Alek. Ryan would be here in the Balkans amongst all the other missing.

A note on the author

N. E. Solomons is a screenwriter and novelist. She lives in the countryside with her husband, also a writer. She is the internationally best-selling author of six previous novels. Her work has been translated into seventeen languages. This is her first thriller.